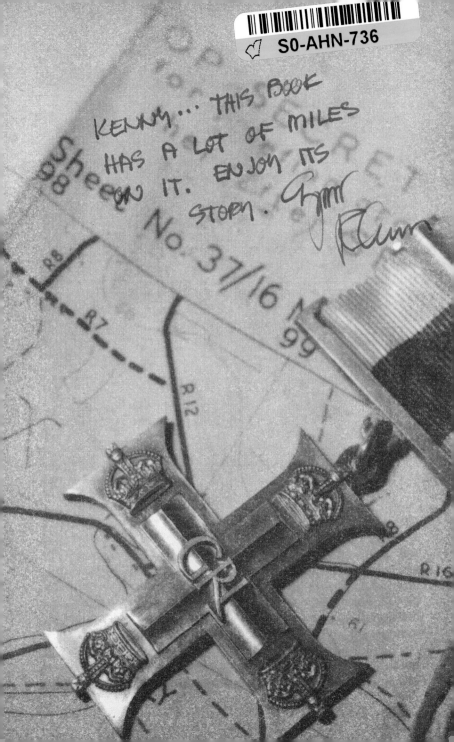

KENNY... THIS BOOK
HAS A LOT OF MILES
ON IT. ENJOY ITS
STORY.

CONSEQUENCES OF THE HEART

"Cunningham has created a masterful, funny and moving story steeped in Irish and European history. He has remarkable powers of description, and his landscapes are breathtakingly visual, but he can also turn his hand to smaller, domestic detail, and there is a wonderful twitch of dry humour in his prose"

STEPHANIE MERRITT, *Observer*

"Cunningham is uncompromising in his commitment to the plain storytelling of old-fashioned romance and the effect is something like that of an old-fashioned movie that is apparently uncomplicated but yet becomes a classic"   JOHN KENNY, *Irish Times*

"A brilliant portrayal of rivalry and passion"   *Belfast Telegraph*

"The intense passion of this book, like the nature of love it attempts to portray, is seductive, courageous and spellbinding"

JIM CLARKE, *Sunday Independent, Dublin*

PETER CUNNINGHAM was born in 1947 and spent his first 20 years in Waterford. He originally trained as an accountant and it was not until 1979, when he wrote a short story that was published by The Irish Press in *New Irish Writing*, that he considered writing for a living. He wrote a number of fine and successful thrillers before his first literary novel, *Tapes of the River Delta*, was published to critical acclaim.

Also by Peter Cunningham

TAPES OF THE RIVER DELTA

WHO TRESPASS AGAINST US

Peter Cunningham

CONSEQUENCES OF THE HEART

THE HARVILL PRESS
LONDON

First published by The Harvill Press, 1998

This paperback edition first published in 1999 by
The Harvill Press,
2 Aztec Row, Berners Road,
London N1 0PW

www.harvill-press.com

1 3 5 7 9 8 6 4 2

Copyright © Peter Cunningham, 1998

Peter Cunningham asserts the moral right to be identified as the author of this work

A CIP catalogue record for this book is available from the British Library

ISBN 1 86046 619 2

Printed and bound in Great Britain by Mackays of Chatham

Half title: photograph by courtesy of the author

CONDITIONS OF SALE

All rights reserved. No part of this publication may be reproduced, stored in a retrieval system, or
transmitted in any form or by any means, electronic, mechanical, photocopying, recording or otherwise,
without the prior permission of the publisher

This book is sold subject to the condition that it shall not, by way of trade or otherwise, be lent, re-sold,
hired out or otherwise circulated without the publisher's prior consent in any form of binding or cover
other than that in which it is published and without a similar condition including this condition being
imposed on the subsequent purchaser

Ralph Counahan

We have built a house that is not for Time's throwing.
  We have gained a peace unshaken by pain for ever.
War knows no power. Safe shall be my going,
  Secretly armed against all death's endeavour;
Safe though all safety's lost; safe where men fall;
And if these poor limbs die, safest of all.

Rupert Brooke (1887–1915)

Summer's last days have come like the sweetest kiss. Mellow light lacquers the houses from Long Quay to Balaklava. This evening will be balmy out in Main, and if you looked back here as dusk falls you would see the mouth of the river glowing like a rose.

I have not been well. Recently I spent three weeks in hospital. I must, it seems, get used each time my watch chimes to spraying nitroglycerine down my throat.

I take down a ring-binder, one of a row, all fat with glued transcripts and letters. Each day I try to advance a little further, culling the hearts from the computer-produced sheets, gluing them to blank pages and filing them in here. On the days I fail, and today I will fail, I always at least take down a binder and open it. Funny that, how a life can sit on six feet of shelf. I'll miss it when it's finished. The culling, I mean.

I lie on my bed, a piece of furniture dear to me for the last five decades. My flat has four rooms and a small kitchen. The upstairs flat is larger. I have not hung onto many possessions: paintings with special meaning, a child's wicker chair that plays Strauss when you sit in it, a set of frosted glasses and a jug that once were used to serve lemonade in the garden. A row of old photographs. My bed. I lie, listening. For movement upstairs. I wonder where she is now.

Mine is a tale of great love. How could it be otherwise, given my origins? Mine is the story, too, of a proud family, and of a brave woman whose memory has always been my salvation.

Don't judge too harshly, my friend. Long ago, before you were born, there happened something that changed our lives for ever. I took the blame alone. Yet – and why this is, I have no answer – in that lay the source of all my happiness.

So this is very much the end at what is, in fact, the beginning. Look, it happened, sixty years ago, and the papers here tell the story of how it happened and what were the consequences.

RING-BINDERS
1-2

One

M Y GRANDFATHER WAS THE county doctor. He was a mighty handsome man if my old photographs tell the truth. He went out in his trap in all weathers to Baiscne and to Deilt, to Irrus and Eillne, even to Sibrille by the sea. I've met old people who told me that Dr Church delivered them, and threw open the windows of their cottages to the long ostracised air, and closed the tired old eyes of their parents and grandparents when they could go no further. They told me these things about Dr Church with a wistful expression on their faces as if they wished he were still available for their dispatch as he had been for their arrival.

Descended from a somewhat misty line – some say, Celtic-Scots, some English-Norman, you can never really tell in Monument – my grandfather grew up in a world where loyalty to the crown was taken as read. Embodying virtues of uprightness, probity and an utter inability to dissemble except to the terminally ill, the most his detractors could ever point to was his predictability.

It was not until the late 1960s, by the dying bed of the beautiful woman who is about to enter our story, that I learned the details of a famous week that had occurred during the final, exciting decade of the nineteenth century and whose effects were still being felt when I was in late middle age.

It was June. Dr Church was summoned urgently to the Small Quay, where a great yacht had put in from harsh, summer weather. The property of an earl whose ensign proclaimed him to be aboard, the yacht was a floating mansion of mahogany and rigging that drew crowds from twenty miles away and needed the constant presence of constabulary to restrain the curious. Amid much whispering my grandfather was brought on. He found no less a person than the lord-lieutenant of Ireland ill. Happily, no more than gripe accentuated by port had felled the potentate, but Dr Church counselled a thorough enema and three days at the quayside as the best answer to the case.

My grandfather, now indispensable, each evening came on board to dine. He encountered ladies of delicious scent and bearing around the companionways, below and between decks, and in the bunkers, galleys, holds and fo'c'sles. The earl, drunk in a moment, kept wanting to put to sea and needed the constant attentions of my grandfather and the ladies to distract him from delusions of mutiny.

One lady in particular seemed to occupy a position of authority. Her foxy hair brushed up and clipped, she was introduced as Miss Mabel. Tall, much taller than the earl, Miss Mabel's height was accentuated by the S-shape of her figure, which carried her proud bosom ahead of her tiny waist. Her bare shoulders and the long sweep of her neck presented themselves with a perfection that far exceeded the doctor's experience of anatomy. When the doctor was encouraged to describe for the amusement of the party the habits of his more eccentric patients, Miss Mabel's luminous, green eyes exerted a power on his attention that made his anecdotes disjointed and presented the young man of science as a mediocre raconteur. When the captain, a man in dread of his employer, was in discussion with the earl, Miss Mabel would conjure inlets of intimacy for the doctor and herself wherein she could establish the substance and circumstances of this earnest young man. When the earl would bark, "Isn't that so, Miss Mabel?", or "Miss Mabel knows her Hebrides, sir!", Miss Mabel would rejoin the upstream conversation, flattering the earl or gently abrading the captain as was called for, and then a minute later tack back to young Dr Church.

My grandfather was invited by the earl to country houses in England and to moorings in Cowes. In his honourable mind, for him to have reciprocated Miss Mabel's attentions would have amounted to an abuse of hospitality. He bestowed imaginary complaints such as asthma upon her wonderful chest. No use. At home, as my grandfather lay awake, he resorted to fantasies of professional misconduct.

Although she was but twenty-one, Miss Mabel's working life had begun eight years earlier in Portsmouth, and so, although she had reached the top of her vocation, implicit in such a station was the prospect of redundancy. She saw her position changing from that of tantaliser of men to one of mere companion; and whilst the earl valued Miss Mabel's presence at his table, when it came to choices late at night Miss Mabel found herself more and more alone in her cabin, the insidious laughter of some sixteen-year-old hussy seeping through the teak hull.

By Saturday evening, the lord-lieutenant was able to walk, if shakily. Corseted, uniformed, bedecked and trimmed, he appeared topside for a few minutes to acknowledge the constant little crowd who had taken up position on the shore. The earl bid the captain sail on the next daylight tide and sailors swarmed over the rigging.

As a rule Dr Church went to ten o'clock mass in the cathedral. That Sunday as he knelt in a prominent pew for the *Confiteor,* my grandfather

6

became aware that the mood of the congregation had ebbed from one of whole-hearted contrition. He turned. In cascading black silk with dramatic insertions of white valenciennes, her face obscured yet recognisable through a black lace mantilla, Miss Mabel was gliding up the nave.

It was never established whether my grandmother had been born a Catholic but seven decades later she died one and was interred beside her first husband in the grounds of the cathedral at whose Sunday morning mass she had once played her hand with such success. My grandfather never wondered at the happy confluence that brought Miss Mabel's trunks to his residence at Six Half Loaf even as her yacht was disappearing around the first bend of the Lyle. He was a simple man who had discovered the only woman he would ever love. For her part my grandmother loved him unstintingly and exclusively for the rest of his life. She gave him fourteen children, including identical boy twins, the pride of his life, who in 1914 both went to war on the same boat from Long Quay and never came home. Dr Church would die suddenly in 1920 at the age of fifty-five, one moment sitting at dinner, smiling; the next, dead. A kind man and a healer, by everyone he was sadly missed.

Monument is a town on the underside of Ireland, an ancient and proud settlement built entirely on one side of a great river, the Lyle. The beauty of the river Lyle, rising in the Deilt mountains and by degrees widening into a regal flow of water, is said to have captivated St Melb sixteen hundred years ago. The saint, a close associate of St Patrick, was traversing Ireland with the great man to install a bishop in Connacht when word came of a woman needing the last rites. Patrick sent Melb. With a small handful of men he rode south three days on mules into ever wilder territory. On the morning of the fourth day, lost, Melb began mass in the pre-dawn to a chorus of wolves, and asked God in his mercy to allow him to rejoin Patrick. As if in answer, the sun rose to illuminate a range of mountains. In the days that followed Melb would discover the source of the Lyle and would follow it until the point six miles seaward, where, between handsome banks, it became a river. Here he founded a community, built a church, wrote his famous letters to St Patrick, died and allegedly was buried at the spot on which the altar of Monument's cathedral now stands. Centuries later when a settlement had grown and ships began to use the Lyle for trade, a great monument to the saint was built beside the river. Ships sailed for the monument. People kept referring to it, even when a spring tide had swept St Melb's monument clean away.

* * *

Number Six Half Loaf was inadequate for sixteen people and therefore my grandfather built a house on The Knock which he called St Melb's. A hill overlooking the Monument river, The Knock, had been acquired to graze my grandfather's mare. When she had a foal he also bought the adjoining thirty acres of marshland running down to and along the bank of the river Lyle.

Three months after Dr Church's death, one morning grave men in high collars and bowler hats came to St Melb's. Taking whiskey in glass thimbles, they eulogised my grandfather framed above them in sepia. Deeds of sale already completed, which needed only my grandmother's signature to transform landlocked fields prone to flooding into cash in the bank, were produced. The more my grandfather's solicitor, Beagle by name, purred and pressed, advised, cautioned and, finally, remonstrated, the more Mabel Church demurred. Long practised in reading the minds of men from their faces, behind Beagle's simpering performance she could see ever clearer his cupidity.

"Maybe another day, darling," she said, getting to her feet, putting an end to the meeting and, in the process, becoming the wealthiest woman in Monument.

Mabel Church built first one warehouse, then another. Trade flourished. Into Church's sheds went bales of jute and sacks of oats and chests of Mazawattee tea. Paint and paper, salt and sugar, baccy, towelling, fruits in tins, steel cutlery from Sheffield, flooring brads by the hundredweight; they came in on ships to Monument and in rolls, batches, bundles and bindles were taken into Church's stores. With an inherent understanding of business formed in her early years, my grandmother kept in her head all the many details of the, first modest, then thriving facilities along the busy river. This was no standard widow. Look at her photographs from that time and tell me if beauty does not beckon you back over the decades. The translucency of her eyes outshines black and white. Thirteen confinements and her neck is still smooth and graceful, her face unlined, her figure such as to make men take deep, consoling breaths. Within her family her hegemony was total. She ordered not only their lives but their attitudes, ensuring that the Church admiration for Union and Empire was carried on intact even when Ireland was no longer a part of either. She became an institution. And to everyone, family, employees and most of Monument, she was known as Ma Church.

Hilda was the oldest but one of Ma Church's children. Although blessed with her mother's fine, tall body and proud bosom, her russet hair, her pale, unblemished skin and her green eyes, which glowed in darkness, Hilda

Church was deaf or, at best, heedless. Deafness was attested by the way Hilda spoke, her words soft, almost stillborn enunciations. Questions to Hilda mostly went unanswered, that is if her glorious smile did not count as a response, which even if it did was taxing of patience in the case of simple requests for the salt or the time of day. Ma Church, wedged in the cleft of an unbudging prejudice that refused to admit the possibility of a handicap in any daughter of hers, waged a fruitless battle to get Hilda to enunciate.

"Speak *up*, 'ilda!" Ma Church would snap, but so often it became a reflex, used even on those rare occasions when Hilda could be properly understood.

Although she smiled radiantly at them all, men avoided Hilda because: A, they were uneasy with women reputed to be strange, a description that covered everything from Hilda's sunny vagueness to outright lunacy and was compounded by ancient fears of imperfect issue; B, in Hilda's smile some saw blatant importunity and thus assumed they would not be the first and that Hilda came with the risk of scandal attached; C, those, if any, left, for whom neither scandal nor the madness of future generations was a concern, even the Cs balked when faced with the prospect of having Ma Church as an enemy, and joined the As and the Bs of Monument in their distant admiration of Hilda Church's curious beauty.

On the north side of MacCartie Square was situated the drapery establishment of the Misses Flynn. Ma Church had dealt so long with the Misses Flynn, her requirements were so axiomatically catered for, her regular presence in the comforting, musty shop so taken for granted and her business so valued, that in many people's minds, including, some said, those of the Misses Flynn, my grandmother seemed, if not the proprietor of the shop, at least the proprietor *manqué*. When the older Miss Flynn died – choking after Sunday mass on a chicken bone eaten in the larder; she was eighty – Ma Church, as part of the general role she assumed with the younger Miss Flynn, installed Hilda in the place of the deceased, that is, behind the left-hand counter as one entered the shop.

The drapery was the perfect place for Hilda. It was dark and still. Noise may not have been a distraction for Hilda, but in any case there was none. Two counters faced one another inside the doors, whose blue blinds were always fastened because daylight is harmful to fabric. Behind the right-hand counter worked the younger, now the only, Miss Flynn. Behind Miss Flynn lay boxes on shelves and within the boxes, in tissue paper, the items of lingerie, in a range of sizes, that are best traded in the atmosphere of a long-standing relationship.

Hilda lived and worked in her own world of private sounds and wavebands, fetching down bolts of cloth to order, measuring them off on the rule incorporated into the counter and cutting the piece with gigantic scissors. Many believed that Hilda had always been there behind the left-hand counter in the Flynn establishment, as indeed she was one February morning in 1922.

Miss Flynn was at the bank. The bells overhanging the shop door chimed. A young man entered and paused in a bewildered way to take stock of his surroundings. He saw Hilda. Hilda smiled. He removed his seaman's cap and bowed; Hilda laughed. The sailor shrugged. Hilda smiled her most dazzling smile. The stranger raised his hands and turning slowly, murmured little gusts of delight for the pretty young woman, the quaint shop, even for the doorbells, which now chimed once again.

"Hilda! Go to the loft and fetch me six boxes of foundations!" cried the returned Miss Flynn, sizing up the situation from a lifetime's embattled maidenhood.

The sailor had time to glimpse Hilda's pleasing outline on the ladder before the outside of the shop door was closed to his face and its blinds, which had snapped up, were snapped down.

At ten past six that evening Hilda made her way home by way of an alley known as Conduit. Who knows what she was thinking then, or ever? Who can tell her exact state of readiness for what was about to take place? From under a gaslight, cap in hand, stepped the sailor. He smiled and bowed, repeating the ritual that had earlier been so well received. Hilda smiled like the sun on the August Bank Holiday. In what would be the most mute of relationships, the lovers (for surely they had been lovers from first sight!) hurried across Monument to a low inn on Dudley's Hill called the Sailors' Rest.

Ma Church's writ ran to most places in Monument, but when it came to the Sailors' Rest, property of a cat-like woman named Cissy the Lick, her suzerainty dissolved. Perhaps it was a case of professional recognition. Ma Church who could, one hip cocked, subdue a rebellious band of steve-dores, was strangely reluctant to storm the Sailors' Rest. Instead she turned to the superintendent of the guards, a family man who tried to bustle his way past the door, but Cissy, with a few quiet remarks delivered out of everyone else's earshot, disarmed him. A Garda sergeant was finally allowed up to ascertain whether or not Hilda was being held against her will. He came back down, bemused of expression and mute.

Ma Church now cornered the district justice and put it to him that Hilda, though in years an adult, was still a child by disposition. The judge, I almost said fatally, demurred. He wanted to hear a medical depo-sition. As Ma Church laid siege to the judge, and as the judge barricaded himself into his chambers and drank whiskey, at the other side of town the lovers were on the move. Together with Cissy the Lick and a party of well-wishers from the Sailors' Rest, they went aboard the sailor's ship and one hour later, amid much good-natured carousing, returned to shore.

It must have been with the foretaste of victory that Ma Church, court order in hand, marched the guards back across town. The judge, like all men, had capitulated in the end and made Hilda Church a ward of the court. The sergeant (the superintendent had had to go to Deilt) presented the order to Cissy the Lick as Ma Church sat across the road in her Studebaker. After a delay of minutes a certificate of marriage, completed by the ship's captain and duly notarised came downstairs. Hilda Church no longer existed. The eager bride in the upstairs room was named Mrs Paolo Conduit.

A photograph exists, taken as the handsome newly-weds stepped from the ship. There's no doubt that Hilda was an attractive woman, and the way she looks at Stickyback, Monument's snapshot artist, the way she *pouts* at him, for no other description will do, is nothing less than erotic. Paolo Whoever-he-was came from Naples and is a fine, broad-chested young fellow with black ringlets tumbling down over a wide forehead.

On and off down the years, like shapes forming slowly out of a river mist, or from my blood, the manner of those days in the Sailors' Rest has come to me. Infused with the pollen of physical love, Hilda bursts to life. From her marvellous body suddenly tumbles forth everything she ever has or will want to say. As if she knows that the brief season for her flowering, and deflowering, is upon her and that these few days will be all she will have to draw on in the times ahead, Hilda sucks from her week the very marrow of time with sweet desperation.

Paolo kisses Hilda, holding her face between the palms of his big hands so as to press their mouths together urgently, so as to hold steady her head and give his questing mouth more purchase. When Paolo so kisses her Hilda can feel his length lying on her thigh, and she shifts so that this exotic visitor can press inquiringly at the very doors of her sex, its probing head soft like the muzzle of a horse. And although Hilda now wants this caller in the very heart of her welcoming kingdom, Paolo insists on its continued deference, as if its audience has not yet been earned, and whispers into Hilda's irresolute ears, *"Pianissimo, pianissimo."* In the intervals when Paolo is half asleep (Hilda never sleeps; she has the years ahead for sleep), since conversation is limited not only by lack of a common language but in Hilda's case by unfamiliarity with the basics of discourse, time is passed in more primal pursuits, such as tender grooming, or the wondrous exploration and endless acquainting that follows infatuation. As Paolo lies, eyes half lidded and watching her, Hilda blows to make his long lashes quiver, and his chest hairs, and his stomach's, and the rugged line that plunges like a black rope to the bell of his reclining penis. Hilda whispers across the small, shining globes of Paolo's scrotum, down the tiny, dense creepers along the insides of his thighs, that skip his knees like islands, that continue down and out like new shoots across the bridge of each foot to his toes. The return journey is of a closer order. Hilda can take half an hour to work her tongue from her lover's feet to his lips, pausing at certain points along the way when new tastes disturb the previous, sweet uniformity of her saliva, injecting fresh measures of excitement, first to her tongue, then into her blood, so that by the time she reaches his mouth her curiosity for his body, far from being satisfied has, in fact, only been re-initiated.

As Hilda lies, Paolo makes his sorties. His hands are big and chapped from ropes and salt, the skin on them is hard and the nails imbedded like shells in sand, but nevertheless this roughness works its own magic since the intent behind it is soft. He leaves Hilda's mid-section to last. His thumbs polish the whorls of hair at the base of her neck, his fingers skim out on the bones of her milky shoulders, and down her fleshy, upper arms. Inwards he scoops her firm breasts, making them firmer still, before gently lowering his head to each one, circling unhurriedly the dark stars with his tongue, drawing with his lips each proud, rubbery teat. Hilda lies in suspended time. Paolo draws rounds on her belly, and then goes off south, to the bed end, where with great skill and patience he finds tiny zones not even known to Hilda, postage stamps of pleasure that lie hidden in her feet. Hilda's own hands find Paolo's head during his re-ascent when he lingers on her smooth thighs with his ticklish face, caressing the insides of her rippling limbs with his chin. Paolo comes to her womanhood. With big thumb and forefinger he opens the lips, like the soft beak of a hatched chick, and then resumes his probing kisses as Hilda clings onto their ever-increasing beat.

Paolo took his ship, his ship caught the tide. Hilda absolved him from even the need to pretend he might return. Their life together had been spent in one, small room. Hilda walked down Long Quay her head proud and went straight back to the Misses Flynn's as if nothing had happened.

She fainted at work after Easter and Dr Armstrong diagnosed a pregnancy of twenty weeks. My grandmother, who saw the outcome as a penance for all the sins of the past, set about planning the reception of the unwanted child, assuming that Hilda was incapable of being put in charge of anything.

A son was born on November 4th, 1922. The mother's name was registered as Hilda Conduit and the child christened Charles Paolo, first after St Charles Boromeo, whose feast day it was, and then its father. At two weeks the infant was brought by its grandmother Church to Six Half Loaf, now the home of her eldest son, Percy Church, and received by his wife, Opalene, whose only child, a son, had recently died, and given into the care of the housemaid, Tassy.

My memory of Hilda in the street is of a shy woman who never looked at anyone. She had chosen to use in a single week the supply of colour we are given for a lifetime, and to live the rest in monochrome. At fifty she caught pneumonia but declined all medicine. Four days later she died, leaving behind the only person who was living testament to the fact that she had ever existed. Me.

Two

"YOUR NAME IS CHARLES Conduit. Say, Charles Conduit."

I am sitting by the kitchen range, gazing into Tassy's ardent face.
"Say, Charles Conduit."

"Ah . . ."

"Charles Conduit! Say it!"

"Ch . . ."

"Go on!"

". . . ch . . . ch . . . chu . . . chud . . ."

You entered Six Half Loaf by a side door into a small hall, off which were
found a morning room and, down two steps, a freezing toilet. Little light.
The dining-room table, waxed and brightly buffed, reflected Parnell
brooding from the overmantel. In the bathroom, sponges wherein dwelt
the essences of Uncle Percy and Aunt Opalene. Outside, a coach house and
sheds for anthracite, in which Tassy smoked the cigarettes that Aunt
Opalene absolutely forbade.

Uncle Percy and Aunt Opalene had waited a long time for little John.
Uncle Percy, with a sense of boundless horizon, had had constructed a
nursery the size of a small ballroom; alas, the rocking horse and building
bricks and toy soldiers in a castle and colourful murals of romping
dwarves all waited in vain, making the nursery a place cold, sad and
doomed to be forever associated with its dead pretender.

Uncle Percy wore high collars and Homburg hats, supplied by firms in
London. On Sundays as I slobbered through my meal, he sat unspeaking,
and once the door of the dining room caught his fingers four-square in the
jamb, but Uncle Percy closed his eyes and bit the trembling lip beneath his
moustache and uttered not a word. At night, the deep drone of Uncle
Percy's voice. No words I could make out, just the one, sawing pitch, and
when it stopped, Aunt Opalene's sobs, rising and falling into the great,
painful void of the night.

Each morning she went to the morning room and its upright piano.
Never played. If I looked in she would clutch a handkerchief to her
mouth. The more I tried, the more Aunt Opalene shook. I wore hats of
little John's in her presence. She shook and wept. I made posies which
I left on the keys. She wept and shook. I gave up. In the end it seemed best

14

we avoid one other, and so we did as the only means by which our lives could advance without daily displays of desolation.

Scents from that last summer: oily lavender-blue curling from the outward-facing timbers of little John's summerhouse; fleece oil and dung from a flock being hunted up Half Loaf to the abattoirs of Balaklava. Fucshia. The sweet, released treasures of grass, surging and stopping with the lawnmower that trimmed the lazy edges of the afternoon.

Tassy had come to Ma Church aged twelve and upon Uncle Percy's marriage, like his house, had been given to him. From an area in the Deilt mountains where all the people had crow-black hair and yellow eyes, Tassy's demeanour was of a night creature. She took me to the top of Buttermilk, the highest point in Monument, and called out the names of the peaks of her distant mountains: Dollan, Dirma, Ferta, Laeg and Caba, she called out their names like a she-wolf keening.

In the seven and a half months during which Aunt Opalene had stayed in bed in order to have little John, Tassy had assumed control of the household. Now an inversion of the normal authority existed, with Aunt Opalene moving uneasily ahead of Tassy's established routine and the mood of the day determined by where it fell in relation to Tassy's monthly cycle.

I am balanced on the steps of a forgotten ladder in the nursery, as if on an atoll, examining the pictures in books. On the back of the nursery door hangs a board with pegs and rubber rings, new and unused. Inwards bursts the door. Rings fall and wobble in circles. Seething and hissing, Tassy drives Aunt Opalene inwards. Aunt Opalene secures a handhold on Tassy's face and pushes back her head. Tassy grabs and rips Aunt Opalene's dress. Unmindful of me, the two women stand, taking their breaths in little cries. Tassy lunges with her teeth. Aunt Opalene screams.

Aunt Opalene had found Tassy smoking in the house, a violation that drove her over the precipice. But for Aunt Opalene to demand her servant's removal would have been an assault not just on Tassy but on Ma Church herself, from whom Tassy's power derived.

Commotion late one night. An ambulance reverses up the gravel drive. From my room I see Aunt Opalene's face, pale and anxious, looking from its stretcher to Uncle Percy, his expression unyielding as ever. The lights and noise that attend these events. The voices of strangers. All next day people come and go. My aunts ferry plates and teapots and trays, discussing me.

"He's Hilda's child."

"Mother of God, where did he get the head of tar?"

"Ma thought he'd cheer poor Opalene up."

Tassy butters bread with furious rhythm, and keeps a kettle on the boil. Men wander in and begin opening the doors to presses.

"Any tonic, Tassy?"

Outside I climb the ash tree beside the side door, from whose branches a view down through the topmost, unfrosted part of the toilet window is possible. As each aunt or uncle comes to relieve themselves I put names on them by reference to the only part of them that's visible. Thus the fingers that first unbutton, then coax the flesh of a long, hooded sausage belong to my uncle, Mr Gus, a frequent visitor. A slow swelling towards the head of the sausage, like the digestive process of a snake. A rod of water. When it slacks, then ends, the fleshy hood is peeled back and the red tip shaken with vigour. Parnell placing his bearded chin with great care on the crest of the bowl, as if on the guillotine, is Aunt Margaret. Aunt Justina hovers, arms braced to the walls, and when finished, shakes herself like a horse. No mistaking Tassy. A cigarette in her mouth, she hikes up her dress, places her heels on the top step, lies back legs wide apart and pisses for joy into the air.

The months that followed were heavy with fermenting sorrow. Uncle Percy, more a shadow than a man, looked through me as if I were invisible. At night his voice still sighed like a wind that gets up only on midnight and has long attended at the same, lonely spot. He spent more time in St Melb's than he did in Six Half Loaf, as if the place he had endowed with such hope had done no more than act as a setting for premature death.

For Tassy, however, the circumstances seemed a setting for opportunity. She arranged that I eat with her in the kitchen, thus allowing her my uncle to herself in the dining room, where she served him up eggs, back rashers and kidneys, and plates of toasted spotted dog. She now smoked about the house and took to wearing lipstick. But Tassy's plans were short-lived. Instead of going to his office one morning Uncle Percy went straight on, walking down a boat slip and into the Monument river, his face no doubt unflinching, the lip beneath his moustache no doubt the only part of him to betray a little twitch as his footing was lost. Small children found his swollen body tangled in the sluice gates where the Monument river is grafted from the Lyle. On view for almost an hour so that even the photographer from the *Monument Gazette* had time to be dug from a public house to record the scene – "Prominent Monument Figure in Unfortunate Fatal Accident" – Uncle Percy was at last removed by engineers and placed on the quayside on a white sheet, where the water ran from him as from one of his bathroom sponges.

A month later Tassy and I, like the surviving members of a regiment otherwise wiped out, came to St Melb's. Although it had a fine drive up to it and views, albeit of stenching coal barges on the Monument river, the house itself had the darkly appointed rooms and telltale, dim corridors that I was used to. Tassy and I dug in and with the instincts of mice made ourselves inconspicuous. Soon no-one could say for certain how long we had been there nor imagine us elsewhere, and so St Melb's became our home.

Three

TODAY A GERMAN INDUSTRIALIST lives in St Melb's. I have never met him and I doubt if the sight of an old man peering over his hedge would mean anything to him. Yet a deep curiosity draws me. I know this businessman's house with intimacy. Without ever crossing the threshold I can wander around inside and descend to its foundations.

Although I was Hilda's child, the fact that I was attached, as it were, to Tassy allowed the venomous discussions about my family that took place in St Melb's kitchen to continue at will.

"That Justina complained one of her breakfast eggs was broken," said Olive, a little redhead who carried trays and dusted.

"Cow," said Mrs Finnerty, seething. The cook was a woman of great size and strength with generous sprouts of hair from face warts. "What did the ol' wan say?"

"Nattin'," replied Olive, putting down her tray and unloading the frosted, wafer-thin glasses with red hoops in which lemonade was served on the lawn during the summers, when my grandmother entertained. "Uncle Mary cleaned his plate anyway, poor blind creature."

My late grandfather's younger brother lived alone in Cuconaught Street, but ate in St Melb's. I called him Uncle Mary, and my twin aunts Miss and my grandmother Ma'm, just as Tassy did. My Uncle Augustine I called Mr Gus. Gus Church was known as a man who never spoke unless addressed and whose face forever conveyed the impression that he had just heard or seen something that had amused him.

"The most decent man in the world and she killed him," said Mrs Finnerty grimly, her demented pride in the matter of eggs ranging for a victim. "Look at that Margaret upstairs, Mother of Divine, terrified of her own shadow." Mrs Finnerty shook herself. "As for Faithful Tadpole."

"Told me Christmas I'd make no cakes till May," Olive said. "By February every egg in the waterglass was bad."

Faithful Tadpole could tell the future. She had been found, four months premature, floating in a pond of blood as my grandmother thrashed in fever. My tiny aunt never grew higher than thirty-six inches. Like the sweetest hamster you ever saw, she remained all her life within the confines of St Melb's, painting bright but appealing pictures of places she had never seen.

"Mr Percy was a lovely man," ventured Tassy.

"A block of wood," Mrs Finnerty said. "Didn't he do away with himself?"

"Loved lamb's liver, just turned on the pan."

"I saw him and the dirty water running out of him. Twice his normal size."

"A fresh egg."

"She never cried one tear."

"He never got over the child."

"Tears, I've always said, come not from the eyes but from the heart."

"And spotted dog."

"Hilda Conduit, sweet heavens tonight," said Mrs Finnerty, blessing herself at sprinting pace, then glancing at me.

"We must have Bensey the bookie for luncheon today," said Olive. "'Olive, not one speck o' dust in the front room, mind.'"

"I cleaned all this silver last week," Tassy said.

"And you'll clean it twice more if Bensey's calling, have no fear," said Mrs Finnerty and lugged a quite massive pot from one place on her range to the other. "And the daughter. Butter wouldn't melt."

"Lovely skin," said Olive, whose own skin was always blotchy.

Lying upstairs on the landing when the Benseys came, I could gaze down at the fat, black plait that nosed between the bare blades of Rosa Bensey's caramel shoulders. Those nights I dreamed of snakes.

"Eyetie!" cried Mrs Finnerty.

"What?" Tassy asked.

"Eyetie," said Mrs Finnerty. "Eyetie. Can't you see it in Bensey, Mother o' Jesus, if he put a hand on me I'd die o' shame, the eye of the old bastard."

Olive giggled.

"They keep their women in barrels out there!" Mrs Finnerty cried. "What decent woman would have anything to do with the like?" Mrs Finnerty rolled to her sink. "Of course, it takes one to know one."

"That's shameful, missus," said Tassy, responding to the well-aired jibe at Ma Church's origins.

"Indeed it is," Mrs Finnerty sniffed, "but as my husband used to say, money will kneel at any altar."

A sudden silence gripped the assembly. The door to the passage had clicked to.

"I 'ear there's not 'alf the talk in the 'ouses of Parliament," said Ma

Church, sweeping into the centre of the flag-stoned kitchen. "Shall we be lucky enough to taste your parsley sauce today, Mrs Finnerty?"

"We have acres of parsley this year," muttered Mrs Finnerty.

"And stewed apples for pud," said Ma Church, turning to Tassy. "Be sure you core 'em proper, mind."

"Ma'm," said Tassy.

Ma Church's eye swept the kitchen, taking in blotchy Olive assembling crockery and glassware on her tray, Mrs Finnerty's steaming and gurgling pots, and, finally, me. Her inspections of me were always followed by a despondent sigh, as if it was only when I came into view that I came to mind.

"We shall 'ave to find a school," she said, making for the door. To Olive: "The lace tablecloth the doctor brought 'ome from Rome. And Mr Bensey's madeira. Shine the decanter, there's a girl."

Tassy went that morning to the apple house, climbed to the top shelf and fell. From that day on her ankle was swollen and she could get no more than a few steps at a time without sitting down. Life was like that: one day someone walked straight and sound, the next they were lame and in pain. No-one could do anything about it.

Binn's Street School was run by men banded together as Brothers in the name of Christ. This Christ must have been a monster. Information such as twelve times tables or the forty-nine states of America was beaten into our brains via our hands by leather straps and failure to parrot information on demand meant being caught up and swung by the lugs. During breaktime my dark curls, sparkling teeth and sallow skin gave rise to unquenchable appetites in my older peers. Behind the lavs they demonstrated their strength by stretching out my foreskin as if it were a rubber band, then inviting me to do the same to them.

I began to absent myself. Letters purporting to be from Ma Church were penned by Olive in an unexpectedly neat hand and had me prey to all the diseases reported from post-mortems by the *Monument Gazette*. Since no sensible body of people wished to be exposed to contagion on the scale I represented, my absence from school was accepted with relief. So I roved Monument, meeting the knowing glances of the old stagers, who in good weather came out and sat on the sunny corners, clattering their pipe stems around their mouths. The steep hills of Monument rubbered my knees. Up the back of the cathedral and into Candle Lane, shebeens with their ale smells. Pig and Litter, a row of terraced houses built under the bluff of Balaklava. Mulberry was the name given to the street that led gently downwards to Half Loaf, where Uncle Percy's old house with its stillborn nursery and ghosts stood empty for want of a buyer. Sometimes I would spot one of the Brothers nipping from Binn's Street through the side door of a pub in Skin Alley; and when once we came face to face – his face crimson and radiant – he patted my head in passing, undeterred by the fact that I was at that moment meant to be consumptive.

Although Six Half Loaf had not been sold, its coach house, now a garage, had been rented by Ma Church to a family recently arrived in Monument. Called the Bellis, they lived in the space where Dr Church had once stabled his mare, and their father ran a business repairing punctures, whilst Bruno, the eldest son, sold matches door to door. It was said they had worked in a circus in Italy. Bruno took me up Mulberry on the pretext of teaching me how to ride a bicycle.

"Pedal!"

I swayed forward with dreadful uncertainty and threw myself sideways. Bruno helped restore me to the horizontal.

"You didna pedal."

Crashing again to the earth as if I were a magnet to all its mighty metals, I threw the bicycle aside.

"I can't do it."

"Stoopat lil' cun'," Bruno remarked.

He leapt on the bike – "The Famous Rudge, Made in Sheffield" – and with hands folded on chest, rode in a tight circle. Heels up on the handle-bars, Bruno rode without once unfolding his arms or wavering in his circuit. Hefty, sallow skinned like me, strong limbed, four years my senior (he was twelve), Bruno was fascinated by my smallness. He liked to undress completely and have me lie lengthways upon him under the cover of bushes. He liked to beat me with his hard, bare hand, one resounding slap at a time until I cried out for pity. And then, beginning to grasp the manner in which life's favours are traded, as Bruno lay across my diminutive knees I flogged him with the belt from his redundant trousers.

Bruno upended the Rudge onto its hind wheel, jumped onto its pedals and caressed the leather saddle. Graceful as a girl, the triangle of English steel glided in Bruno's arms, its front wheel nestling by his face.

"*Mi ama, sì, sì, mi ama* . . ."

In one hop he ended with his right knee on the saddle. With fingertips he turned the front wheel at right angles to the frame so that the Rudge seemed to be looking to me for approval. Bruno's left leg began to reach out in the air over the rear wheel, its many muscles rigid, its toes forming a delicate point.

"Oopla!"

With smile fixed, Bruno turned his head left and right.

"Alley-oop!"

His foot replaced his knee. With graceful strength Bruno released the handlebars and unfolded like a flower, till he stood tiptoe aloft, his free leg at exact right angles to his body, his hands steepled atop his head, the Rudge beneath him solid as a mountain.

"Signore e signori!" cried Bruno in triumph. *"Il Grande Tintini!"*

When I came again to pump the pedals, I did so with renewed zeal. Dragged down but held halfway between ground and sky, I grasped momentum. Ah, Bruno. Throughout life, at the unfolding of events that have become unstoppable, when a certain point is reached that means the flowering of new and independent forces, I think of you.

Years before my grandfather's demise, when the telephone was a bizarre and novel invention, there had come at two, one freezing morning, a call to the postmaster in Monument from the estate of General Santry at Main. The doctor should come at once, the message was. No further details were given. The postmaster hurried up to St Melb's and roused my grandfather, saying that for the general himself to have called, he must be at death's door. Dr Church hitched up his mare and set off on the five-mile trip into the frosty foothills of the Deilt mountains.

The first Santry at Main had done his duty for Cromwell in establishing an administrative bulkhead. Successive Santry heirs had always performed the twin duties of marrying a well-bred Englishwoman and then, their succession safe, fighting for, and, as a rule, dying for the crown. Perhaps it was fearing an upset in ancient customs that my grandfather, a sucker for tradition, set out.

The wheel rims of my grandfather's trap crunched through the crusted frost on Main's mile-long drive. He arrived at the massive house to find it in darkness. He pulled the bell for fifteen minutes, and a servant was at last aroused, but advised from behind the bolted door that no doctor was needed. My grandfather came home so famished that it took my grandmother until dawn to thaw him out.

Given Dr Church's high regard for the likes of the Santrys, he would probably have preferred to overlook the incident, explaining away the sick call as a manifestation of Anglo-Irish whimsy. But Ma Church would have none of it. She oversaw the sending to General Santry of a bill for two guineas, a stiff fee then, and when the usual time for payment had passed and the account remained unpaid, she sued.

The case became something of a cause. The general, who denied using the telephone that night, or ever, was represented by one of the most eminent benchers in London, who arrived in Monument in his own railway carriage. My grandmother clung to the fatal assertion that General Santry himself had made the call, even when it was proven beyond doubt that the general had not been in Main that night but in London. The postmaster was an unreliable witness, agreeing with any suggestion put to him, and admitting to a hitherto unsuspected weakness for drink. Although the judge made a point of emphasising Dr Church's good faith in making his fruitless journey, the whole business was put down to the well-known uncertainty surrounding telephones and the court found for the defendant.

Decades later, when all the participants were dead and the hullabaloo long forgotten, I would learn of an English house guest in Main that night, come from Albemarle Street to shoot snipe with the general and arrived from London a day before his host. This man's custom in London after several decanters of port was to lift the telephone and call anyone who came to mind, including his physician, to join him as he faced into the wee hours. His seat in the House of Lords derived from great antiquity and his grace and favour were much sought, despite his eccentricities.

Of course Ma Church knew none of this. The general suspected what had really happened but hid his friend behind an unbreakable alibi. Although the Church enthusiasm for the Empire and the Union remained undiminished, the Santry name was evermore held by Ma Church in contempt. Her attitude encompassed not just the Santrys and their descendants, but also their estate at Main, their servants, the produce of their farms and the society they kept. No softening of this stance occurred, even with the ending of the Great War and the death of the most offended party, my grandfather. To speak the name Santry, even in my day, was worse than to utter the most foul oath.

Four

I AM SORRY IF this recounting does not peel off each year and neatly present its contents, if my cutting and pasting jumps, as it now does, from a truant urchin, the object of a one-time circus performer's lewd fascination, to a still short but now blocky, downy-lipped, Woodbine-smoking adolescent of fourteen spending more of his time in Paddy Bensey's betting shop than in Binn's Street School. Truth is, there's much I just don't remember. Of course with time now so precious, it dismays me that entire years seem to have dissolved like gossamer to my touch, that I leapt great chasms without even bothering to explore their treasures.

Tassy died.

It had become hard to reconcile the slow, painful creature of white hair with the wiry vixen who had so vanquished Opalene Church. Tassy receded. Her energy drained away through her useless, angry leg and what pain had begun immobility finished. Tassy saw the County Home looming and, in truth, the day she entered it she looked happier than at any time I could remember since Six Half Loaf.

There were dozens of Tassys in there, wizened, abandoned little women, the unwanted runts from poor, country families, and those like Tassy without families at all, whose lives had been spent in the service of others. This was death's nursery in Monument, the great leveller, where great and humble were all reduced to the confines of standard beds and a bleak regime, where the county and the city met, where everyone was called by their first name, pretensions and formality swept aside by the singular realisation that this was the Last Stop. It never occurred to Tassy, nor to anyone, that there might be a remedy for her inward-turned and always throbbing leg. Tassy had always been like that was the general view, she bore her cross well, God showed his love in the strangest of ways and the time would not be long in coming when Tassy skipped through the gates of heaven like a filly foal.

On a January day of plunging mercury, I came into the kitchen and found Mrs Finnerty, Olive and Olive's sister all crying. My first thought was invasion. Invasion was on everyone's lips.

"Poor Tassy," said Olive looking up at me, her face red and sore. She collected me to her, as if claiming a piece of untitled property. "Poor Tassy, Chud."

Olive's sister, Cherry, who had taken over some of Tassy's jobs, said I should drink hot milk.

"She loved you like you was hers and hers only," wept Mrs Finnerty, reaching. "Her little cratur she called you. Look at the size of you now."

"Poor Tassy," said Olive with consistency.

"She's better off," said Mrs Finnerty.

"How old was she?" asked Cherry, from the range, heating milk.

"Forty-eight," said Mrs Finnerty.

"Seven," hacked Olive. "The missus said forty-seven."

"Forty-seven?" frowned Mrs Finnerty. "She was twenty-eight when Mr Percy married, she told me once. When did Mr Percy marry? He married in eighteen. What's this? Thirty-seven. Thirty-seven take away eighteen? Olive?"

"Nineteen," Olive sobbed.

"Nineteen, add twenty-eight?" asked Mrs Finnerty.

"Forty-seven," said Cherry, setting down my milk.

"We'll say a decade of the rosary," said Mrs Finnerty, fumbling in her apron for her beads and sliding in one heavy movement from chair to knees. "Our Father Who Art in Heaven hal'ed be Thy Name . . ."

Although Tassy had not been in St Melb's for nearly two years, I felt empty that night. We had been the nearest thing to flesh and blood and many ways exist in which to call someone your own. There had been times when I could have visited Tassy but did not. It was not, after all, as if time for me was other than something to be used up nefariously; there had been time, but I had squandered it. The once only I had gone to the County Home, I had had to ask which was Tassy, and all along I had been standing at the foot of the bed in which she lay asleep.

Part of the Franciscan cemetery on Plunkett Hill was set aside for those of no kin. Sepulchral gas lights flickered. I crossed the nave and eased my way towards the yellow light of the mortuary, a constituent of shadow, spectral. Either side of Tassy's coffin stood deep-yellow lighted candles whose petals of flame quivered in the polished struts of the coffin's brass crucifix. The tangy dimness of the room contained within it the sap of the cheap, pinewood coffin, the fug of burning tallow and whatever varnish had been applied that day to the mortuary's appointments. Eight wing nuts, I counted as I spun them. One was stubborn, frozen perhaps. The candlestick had a heavy base and the last nut gave easily to it. Sniffing – a new smell, as when Mrs Finnerty was off and Olive had forgotten to throw out unsafe giblets – I worked the lid till it went askew on its box. I saw nothing. Then a head. I pulled the lid back further because Tassy, if this really was Tassy, lay some way down like an infant put into a cot too big.

White hair, slicked back like a man's, much whiter than I remembered, just as the skin was much more yellow. Eyelids like tiny cakes that hadn't risen. Nothing remained of her expressions, yet it was Tassy all right, by her nose and her high cheekbones and by the shoots of raven hair from her nostrils and ears that reminded me of Half Loaf and Aunt Opalene. Yet the difference between the person of my memory and this corpse was dramatic, and if Tassy had strolled in at that moment, a cigarette dangling from her mouth, and told me that I was looking at someone else, I should not have been surprised. Pinching a strand of waxy nostril hair, I slid down it. Yes, she was dead, there was none of Tassy left – and yet what was lying there was none other than Tassy, or what piquantly was termed, her remains.

The Churches seldom used the Friary and so at next morning's funeral mass the guardian himself presided, his unctuous voice gliding between the portentous marble pillars. So full of comfort, the foreign words, the clink of thuribles and clouds of incense. Even the weeping of Mrs Finnerty and Olive consoled me. The priest came forward to shake Ma Church's hand and, as we left, I overheard him commend her generosity.

Outside my grandmother steered me to where her car lay steaming on Military Parade.

"Shall we?" she said.

I sat in, overwhelmed by the smell and the substance of leather.

"I shall 'ave to make somethin' of you myself," she said and allowed me the full of her startling, green eyes.

Instead of going home to St Melb's, we were passing the Esplanade and then traversing the snow-crusted streets of Balaklava that led to outskirts of the town known as White City. The car checked as the driver changed gears, then churned uphill.

"If you're addressed, just say, so very kind of you to ask me, Mr Bensey," my grandmother said.

I squirmed. Although Bensey the bookie had long eschewed all the common practices whereby he had prospered, relying now on minions to stand up and bawl the odds, and to take in the cash, and to make veiled threats to the overdue accounts, I still had caught his baleful eye over his shop counter more than once and now feared that he might reveal my habits to my grandmother. We bumped in the short drive of a big, square house, its parapet of unadorned concrete jutting against the sky, a blunt testament to new and dodgy money.

"Ah, Mabel, good, this must be Chud," said Bensey with a little wink to me over my grandmother's shoulder. "D'you see these two hands?"

Dwarfed by the pillars of his hall, in a three-piece check suit and spotted dickie-bow, the bookie stood, his two fists thrust in front of him.

"Yes, sir."

"Would you believe me if I told you there was a half-dollar growing in one of them?"

He always came to St Melb's packaged in seamless *bonhomie*, but the quickness of his mind settling dockets in his shop, or the coldness, as now, in his eyes recalled his disreputable fundamentals that Ma Church must have recognised with old excitement.

"Yes, sir."

"Oh, this young man'll go far, Mabel! Right. Pick the hand and the half-dollar is yours."

I went for the fist on which the knuckles were not white.

"Huh," Bensey grunted and a brief shadow of anger crossed his face. He held out the coin by its rim like a dispensing priest. Then he flipped it high into the air. "Heads or tails?" he cried, although a further wager had not been mentioned.

"Tails."

The coin landed on its edge, rolled for the stairs and tumbled flat just short of them.

"By golly, tails," exclaimed the bookie, swallowing his irritation. "Well, well, well. This is your lucky day." He left me groping for the coin and turned away, shepherding my grandmother before him. "You must be exhausted, Mabel. That's a terrible place that Franciscan's, I wouldn't bury a dog in it."

We trooped into the dining room, all polish and silver. Rosa Bensey stood at the fireplace, hands behind her back.

"Rosa, sweetie."

"Mrs Church."

Their cheeks dipped to one another's. She was older and taller than me, by a year and three inches.

"What a beauty you are, Rosa!" cried my grandmother.

"Her poor mother'll never be dead," said Bensey, helping Ma Church from her coat.

"Chud's come too," said Ma Church. Then, sideways, "'E was 'ers, you know?"

Rosa said, "Stand here near the fire, Mrs Church."

"Oh, this is lovely, all the trouble you've gone to, Paddy," said my grandmother, making her way to the flames. To me: "Don't take all the fire, Chud."

"Let the creature warm himself," said Bensey.

To one side I could dwell at leisure on Rosa's slim legs.

"What a winter!" shivered Ma Church. "Shall we ever see the back of it?"

27

"From the windows of the Poor House," said Bensey, rasping his round hands together and shivering in a caricature of penury. "Eight weeks since a race meeting. Nothing freezes quicker than money."

"I know, I know. Three of our ships due this month are still frozen in Liverpool," said my grandmother, joining Bensey in a show of concern over money particular to people with an abundance of it.

"Ah, well, you can't eat it," said Bensey. "Come along now, Mabel, food waits for no-one. You sit here, Rosa my pet."

Rosa and Ma Church were put facing, either side of the bookie, then me one down beside Ma Church. Paddy Bensey tipped sherry into Ma Church's glass.

"We need to warm our blood, Mabel, on a day like this," he beamed.

Their two amber glasses sparkled as they raised and touched them with a clink. Ma Church sipped and as she did I observed the bookie lingering on the smooth planes of her neck.

"Met the general in Main the other day," Bensey remarked, smacking his lips. "Says a war is odds on."

"Oh, yes?" responded my grandmother with sudden if reliable coolness.

"He has two years' tea put down," said Bensey, wiping balls of broth from his moustache.

"Tea is surprisin', from what one 'ears," said Ma Church.

"These people are in the know, mark my words, Mabel."

"I choose not to listen to wind bein' broken," said my grandmother.

"You're too hard on the Santrys, Mabel," breezed Bensey. "What have they only harmless traditions? Even young Jack will follow his father into a regiment – which one is it, Rosa, my pet?"

"Royal Engineers, Daddy."

"– *Royal* Engineers. There's courage. They're bred to it, of course. The general still has German metal in him, you know. German metal from a shell, a shell. Hah-hah, they'll stand up to that fellow Hitler and let us get on with our lives."

"Talk is cheap to them without responsibility," said my grandmother.

"They have their own rules, the Santrys, it's all England this and that, isn't it? Dear me, I sometimes think they think they live in England," Bensey sighed.

"Too much to hope, that would be!" my grandmother snapped.

I saw Rosa turn her face away so that Ma Church might not catch her amusement. Bensey decided to treat the whole thing as a joke and threw his head back, braying, using the opportunity to catch Ma Church's arm as if steadying was needed. Corned beef arrived and was put in front of him for carving, which he did in a way I knew would not have been tolerated in St Melb's, hacking thick skelps from the red, gleaming round. The kitchen women served mashed potatoes and cabbage from bowls and parsley sauce from a milk jug.

"Maybe this chap'll fight a war, eh?" Bensey surveyed me as he chewed. He winked to Rosa. "They could use him like a ferret. Put him down a German foxhole."

"What regiment is for ferrets?" asked Rosa, causing Bensey's lips to spray forth atoms of sherry.

"What a card you are!" Ma Church said. The many gold hoops on her arm fell to her wrist as she reached to Bensey. "Rosa's got your wit, Paddy."

Bensey was flapping his hands at the maid to bring him water.

"An army officer," sighed Ma Church, but now behind her affected mirth I detected a new thoughtfulness. "Poor Dr Church had friends in the army, Chud, but they're all dead now, I fancy. Still, maybe we could find someone."

I said, "I'd like to be a soldier."

Bensey gulped water. "It's not like getting on the bus to the Curragh races, you know," he gasped and this set him off again.

Ma Church giggled like a girl. "You're the limit today, Paddy."

"Oh dear oh dear oh dear," sighed Bensey the bookie. "It's not often we get a chance of a good laugh up here, is it, Rosa, my pet? I'm so happy, Mabel, that you didn't let that bloody funeral upset you."

Trifle in a glass bowl was spooned out for us, despite my grandmother's vigorous assertions that she had nowhere left to put it. I became aware of the bookie's eyes dipping my way, as if the substance of what had been aired so far had not evolved to his liking. I was also conscious, in those moments when she thought I had my eye on her father or Ma Church, of Rosa's deep, dark gaze.

"So, tell us this and tell us no more," said Paddy Bensey, as if he could no longer contain himself, "what are they teaching you at all in Binn's Street?" and winked at me with transparent magnanimity.

I said, "Lessons."

"My goodness, you don't 'alf mutter, Chud," said Ma Church. "Speak up when Mr Bensey asks you somethin'."

"Lessons, lessons," chortled benevolent Bensey and winked his little eye again like a toad. "But what lessons, ay? What lessons?"

"Tell Mr Bensey what lessons, Chud."

"I learn tables."

"*Tables,*" said Bensey with great significance. "Well, well. Is it kitchen tables or dining-room tables?"

Rosa giggled.

"So, tell us this, what *else* do they teach you in Binn's Street?" inquired the bookie, leaning back so that tea could be poured.

I cast wildly in my mind. "Geography."

"Gee-ography!" boomed winking Bensey. "Where to find a hap'orth a baccy on the mitch, is it?" His own repartee convulsed him. "Tell us now, what geography?"

"The forty-nine states of America."

"The forty-nine states of America, bedad! Did you hear that, Mabel?"

"Indeed I did."

"He learns the forty-nine states, he says, by golly. But do you know them?" asked the bookie, smiling left and right like a matinée vaudeville.

"Yes, I do."

"Well, well." Bensey's little eyes were clever now and I understood anew that by winning from him earlier I had also sinned. "Do you still have that half-dollar you took off me?" the bookie asked, although where he thought I might have spent it was beyond me.

"Yes."

"Would you like to bet double or nothing?"

Rosa was taking everything in.

"Even money your half-dollar that you can't name all forty-nine states," Bensey said, smacking down another coin and smirking around the table.

"But even *we* don't know 'em!" cried Ma Church, ever ready to defend family assets. "So 'ow will we know if 'e's right?"

"Rosa knows them," said the bookie smugly, "don't you, my pet?"

"Yes, Daddy."

"You see, Mabel?" said Bensey, tapping his bulging crown. "She takes after the sire in the upstairs department."

"Course he doesn't know 'em," Ma Church hurried. "Oh, you young people, such a tonic. Your tea is gettin' cold, Paddy."

"I do know them."

My grandmother blinked. Bensey hit the edge of his table a bang. "I know a gambler from a mile, bedad! Right. Put up your money."

He could not bear to lose even sight of the coin. His eyes were burning as I placed it in front of me.

"Mind now, Rosa, that he doesn't miss a one!"

I drew my breath. "Alaska Washington Oregon Nevada California Idaho Utah Arizona Montana . . ."

Bensey's smile froze.

". . . Wyoming Colorado New Mexico North Dakota South Dakota

Nebraska Kansas Oklahoma Texas Minnesota Iowa Missouri Arkansas Mississippi Louisiana Wisconsin Illinois Michigan Indiana Kentucky Tennessee . . ."

I saw Rosa look sideways at Ma Church in a way that made me rush on with excitement.

". . . Alabama Ohio West Virginia Virginia North Carolina South Carolina . . ."

Bensey's open mouth was like a lump of coal.

". . . Georgia Florida Maine Vermont New Hampshire Rhode Island Massachusetts Connecticut Maryland Pennsylvania New Jersey and New York."

"By Jove," Bensey exclaimed, leaning back. "By Jove and by golly."

Rosa's face shone. Ma Church, the businesswoman, was saying, "Pay your debts, Paddy. Never let it be said."

"Were they right, Rosa?" scowled Bensey.

Rosa looked at me and bit her lower lip mischievously. "Yes, Daddy."

Bensey frowned, "Are you sure?"

"I counted forty-nine, Daddy."

My grandmother was beaming at the bookie. Planting a square thumbnail under his second coin he flicked it at me. Then he refilled his water glass and drank its fill. He had seen his strategy work against him and like many ambitious men he wore his failures without grace.

We are all out in the hall again, when I recall that day, Bensey to one side, loading Ma Church into her coat and stole, Rosa on the other, with me.

"You only gave forty-eight."

She is looking ahead, all innocence. I put my hand into my pocket and grasp my coins. I know.

"Are you all right, Rosa my pet?"

"What a lovely luncheon, Paddy."

Paddy Bensey is glaring at me across the hall, my proximity to his daughter unacceptable.

"Are you going to tell him?"

More than sixty years on I can still recapture the exact texture of that moment. Rosa is on the brink of a conspiracy against her father and is fired by it, by its blasphemy, just as she will be fired in the long years ahead by the many other standards we will desecrate together. She turns to me, her face vital with excitement. I have introduced her to risk and she likes it.

"Is there anything the matter, Rosa?"

"Tell me the one you left out and I won't tell him."

"What do you have to say to Mr Bensey, Chud?"

"Delaware," I whisper. "So very kind of you to ask me, Mr Bensey."

"Was that fella saying something to you?" I hear Bensey ask, before the doors of our car are closed.

Rosa says, "No, Daddy, he never said a word."

Five

THE BEST DAYS AROUND Monument were the soft ones when sun picked out parts of the Deilt mountains, browns and deep greens, ever changing, like caring eyes, when the pure bell-tones of the Friary swam into every corner of the town, telling their old story of an ancient crusader fleeing for his life and seeking sanctuary here among gentle people. I set off down the back of the cathedral, out onto Small Quay and past Samuel Love's, where tea chests were being offloaded from a small freighter into the pungent, quayside premises. An inspiring day. Swallows had appeared and the spices of the countries they had relinquished flew with them. I breasted the foothills with ease, sailing through rich stands of beech, catching a glimpse of Dollan's peak before plunging once more, my thumb clicking through the gears.

Since the winter before, when her father had identified me as a threat, I had become more and more fascinated by Rosa Bensey. She enthralled me. I learned she was being driven out, almost every day, to Main, and the thought of her with Jack Santry made me lustful in the extreme. I had seen him in Monument, trailing behind his father, a huge man, as they made their way in search of hardware, or English newspapers. Now I tried to compare myself with what I knew of Jack and to speculate on how Rosa might judge one of us against the other. His skin and hair were pale and blond, whereas mine were those of my dark, Mediterranean father. Blue eyes versus deep brown. Height from cavalry officers going back generations and sustained by wealth and scarce calories, compared to my tidiness.

Although visible from many places in the mountains, Main's front gate was reached by a route that took in the boundary of the new golf course, (on land given by the Santrys), and a bridge over a tributary to the Lyle known as the Thom. Outside the gates stood the chapel wherein the spiritual needs of the Santrys were ministered to, and beside it the rectory of the clergyman and his wife. Granite piers, each as tall as a house and surmounted by bronze eagles cast in their moment of strike, stood at the threshold of this kingdom. Changing gears, I passed the gate and rode uphill along the boundary of the estate for fifteen minutes.

I had twice before come out here, and on the last occasion, from shrubbery within the estate, spied Rosa being driven in a horse-trap by

Jack Santry towards the foothills of the mountains. A pool lay up here and lovers in Olive's magazines were always drawn to such locations.

I write this down and paste it in and the moment loses all its years. I freewheel through pine smell and scent of gorse as the trees of Main sink beneath the mountain. Pebbles skittering, I slew a-halt by a big rock, then on foot descend further, face itched by the soft teeth of ferns. What appears as a gleaming coin lies beneath me, perfectly round, then, with each step, it grows into a pool clasped around by smooth, pearl-like boulders. Water pours from somewhere under me in an arc and where it meets the pool forges glitterings.

I hear the beat of hooves, and all my fantasies wither into a small, hard nut of apprehension. Below me, around the corner of the bluff, steps a pony with trap. The pony is a grey, the wheels of the trap the colour of wine. Jack Santry's knowing hand gathers the reins and at his side is Rosa. I sink down in a last attempt to defy my fate. Rosa is now standing, her neck to me, its lustrous hair combed upward revealing the nape, begging to be kissed, and the uppermost point of the valley to her back, edged by the ruff of her blouse and contained within the supple wings of her shoulder blades. Hot sunshine breaks over. Rosa turns and stares straight up at me.

"Chud Conduit!" she laughs. "Jack, this is the boy I've been telling you about!"

"My parents are off, one never knows where exactly, least of all them. I mean, about each other. They don't frat, you see. My father married for money. They keep their own quarters. And servants. I think the general has his bit of fluff in London."

Jack Santry clicked his tongue and the mare lengthened her stride, her ears pricked with well-bred determination. Jack's hair, licking out from beneath a straw boater, was blonder than I had imagined, and his eyes, when he turned them in my direction, more blue.

"So you don't have to stew about being found here or anything."

Rosa sat between us as we spun past immense trees and shrubberies, cutting through rich smells with the even steps of the mare, as the path joined another and, like tributaries flowing into a river, became an avenue. Jack brought us in under a stone arch, putting up dust, and a boy dashed forward to grasp the head of the grey. I gaped upwards.

"Big place, eh? One chap does nothing else but clean the windows."

A dark room, zesty with tack, led to a walled enclosure of sagging apple, plum and cherry trees, abuzz with enthusiastic insects. On brick walls pear trees were wired and fixed by their limbs like martyrs.

"D'you like plums?"

I didn't know but took one anyway, sinking in my teeth with caution. Jack spat his stone on the path, then resumed through to a courtyard with peacocks. Into the sunlight a wolfhound meandered and sank in a dull collapse of bones. We entered through a side door as Rosa took out cigarettes and matches – the rush of her sulphur! – and Jack lit a pipe, leaving clouds of St Bruno in successive halls and corridors and eventually in a place domed and hung with portraits.

"I'll be up there one day. Looking slightly happier than some of them, here's hoping."

Santry men all had blue eyes like Jack and, unlike Jack, grim mouths. As if the imminent deaths in uniform of their husbands had preoccupied them, Santry women looked either sad or resigned.

"A horror, isn't she?" said Jack, grinning at one old hag. "Once lived in St Petersburg and played cricket with the tsarina. What the hell are you gaping at, Fleming?"

On the stairs, lips drawn back to reveal sharp side teeth, lurked a man in a dust coat, one arm withered, a dusting chamois gripped in his blighted hand.

"This is the Earl of Monument," Jack said. "Say, 'Good morning, me lord.'"

Quicksands of doubt bubbled in the servant's face.

"'Morning, me lord."

Rosa giggled.

"This way, Monument," Jack winked, leaping upstairs past the wide-eyed retainer. He turned, one hand on the banister. "House is like a bloody tenement, Fleming. General won't be one bit pleased."

As many stairs as windows.

"A complete fool, Fleming," Jack said. "Believes anything."

Bright sunshine daubed the head of a narrow stairway. Never doubted from the ground, the size of the house from up here was gigantic. Over endless ridges, skylights, parapets and pediments, the distant town of Monument seemed insignificant. Rosa pulled her dress off over her head and in a silk slip wriggled into the clenching warmth of a lead roof gully. Jack had somehow acquired a shotgun.

"Take this and throw it hard as you can in the air," he said, handing me an empty wine bottle from a chest.

I pitched in an arc away from the house. Jack fired. The noise rolled on. I looked at Jack.

"Another!"

I pitched the whole box. There were fifty bottles and he hit three. When we had finished the air was sweet with cordite and the roof at our feet an inch deep in empty cartridge cases.

Nestled down beside Rosa, Jack opened the buttons of his shirt and took out his pipe.

"This is the life, ay? A bit like another country in here, you know. Not that it came about by chance, far from it. The old forebears knew what they were doing."

"You're being pompous," Rosa said.

"Sorry if that's the case, wasn't meant to be." Jack squinted for me with one eye. "I just like it up here is all I was driving at, which may be obvious, but nonetheless. I shall miss it, I suppose is what I mean."

I asked, "When you go back to school?"

"Not school. After. There's a price to pay for all this, you see, you just can't lounge around like this for ever, you have to *do* something, which in our case means fight. Each generation makes its own war, the general says. It may be the only thing he's ever been right about."

I was staring. Two butterflies, one scarlet, one the colour of fresh butter had come to bask on Rosa's close-eyed face.

Jack frowned from the gully. "You see, a Santry can't drift off into old age like your ordinary chap. General's an exception, but perhaps not. He's dead upstairs." Jack looked out over the parapet. "D'you know what the Santrys despise most in people? Yellow. You can be a gambler, a drunk, an idiot with money or a fornicator, none of them matter. As long as you can climb out of a trench or onto a horse and ride straight out into a field of enemy fire and die with your face fixed on your executioner, any other fault will be overlooked." Jack stretched his bony white chest and yawned as, beside him on the lead roof, his pipe lay, smoking like a bomb. "I know what'll happen, of course. When my turn comes I'll be one of the first killed, not doing anything brave, bloody hell no! I'll probably be hiding behind a tank and catch a sniper's bullet."

I was seized by pity for Jack but also by a base elation that the one impediment to my life with Rosa seemed to regard his own early death as a foregone conclusion.

"You're not going to get killed, Jack," said Rosa. She sat up as a car's engine could be heard somewhere below us. "Damn, he must be early."

She put on the dress and we made our way downstairs again where, as I remained hidden, Jack saw her out to her father's car. Then he had the mare tacked up and spun me back down to the pool, swans now pinned on it like brooches.

"Any time you like, dear boy," Jack said. "Place is empty. Cheer us up."

"My grandmother would kill me."

"A tart with horns, the general says. Being squired around nowadays by Bensey the bookie, dreadful man, although he's Rosa's father."

"He hates me."

Jack's face skewed. "Sod him. Who's to know what we do out here? I'll have the kitchen make up a picnic." His blue eyes idled over my features. "We need a code, you know the sort of thing, a word conveyed to everyone. 'Waterloo', perhaps, although that's also a railway station."

I said, "Delaware."

Jack frowned. "Isn't that a place?"

"It's a state in America."

"Very well. Delaware," Jack smiled. "Delaware. Bloody lovely. Absolute cracker."

I fell in love with Rosa that day, and I believe that was the day on which she fell in love with me. I began to write her letters which I dared not post but passed to her when she left school on Dudley's Hill as Bensey's Rolls approached along the Esplanade. These notes led to stolen minutes on a street corner when she or I were meant to be elsewhere, and during which a day and a time for Delaware could be transmitted. I slipped her trinkets of Ma Church's, knowing that Ma Church would not have minded over-much since her regard for Rosa was so high; and once I walked all the way out to White City to receive a coded message and stood alone in the roadway outside the house, waiting for her, as prearranged, to appear at an upstairs window; which she could not since her father at the last moment had removed her with him to a race meeting at Baiscne. I contrived for our contingent to be early to Sunday mass so that if Rosa and her father were already installed we could easily sit near them and be told the plans for Delaware, but it never worked because Paddy Bensey took to varying the times at which he chose to worship. I suggested to Rosa she acquire a bicycle, which she did at once; but Bensey saw the ruse and imposed strict conditions on where she could cycle and for how long. One morning I heard the sweet ripple of women's voices – of Olive laughing and of another voice I knew from my dreams – and then the deep tone of a car's horn. Bensey's Rolls was at our gate, its chauffeur peering in; and Rosa was standing in the porch, attended by Olive. She had dropped by to whisper 'Delaware' and 'Tuesday' in the one breath, which she accomplished as Olive swam in and out of the shadows of the hall pretending to dust but, in fact, consumed by curiosity and jealousy. Then Rosa laughed and turned for the car, the cream hem of her linen kissing her bare calf and making of the slim muscle there a statement of perfection that went to my quick. She skipped once on her way down the path, then waved from the gate. No doubt she had a light word for the impatient driver and no doubt his impatience leached when it met her smile, for the Rolls pulled away from St Melb's with unhurried dignity. But Bensey found out. He warned Rosa that if he ever again found her consorting with me or in the vicinity of St Melb's he would send her to the nuns in Leire, and Rosa knew he meant it.

Bensey's loathing of me deepened. In front of Ma Church I was tolerated, but once her back was turned he was ruthless, beading me with his eye in his shop, and making my every attempt at contact with Rosa a contest.

To do one's duty was not only the Santry philosophy but also its motto: "Which We Ought". This was emblazoned on a shield over the door of Main. Santrys had, over centuries, died in their duty and were remembered on tablets on the walls of Main's little church. To a brave and compassionate colleague who did his duty. Erected by his fellow officers. In the stillness of the chapel, garnished by the flags of regiments, the words of these marble inscriptions fell around us in whispers.

"Not a bad place to be remembered, eh?"

Other accumulated Santry duties, Jack explained, included living in the same house and place, and with unchanged traditions, thus preserving the memory of those whose sense of duty had assured the posterity one was now enjoying. Every first-born Santry son was called Jack and went, as Jack now did, to Eton. Duty at Main, enshrined in architecture, looked down from every wall in oils, the women who had come to live in this place and the men who had gone from it to die, all in the name of duty.

"'Which We bloody Ought!'" as Jack put it.

If any creed stood out from others in this canon of obligations it was the duty of the male Santry heir to import a wife. An absolute duty, Jack revealed; more, far more than ought. It was not enough to seek her elsewhere in the county, or in Ireland, even from families whose sense of duty was no less than that observed at Main. Bred deep into the bones of every colonist was the fear of reprisal from an ancient act and the need to buttress at every opportunity. To marry locally was a failure to expand the pool, but I could see that even as he allowed himself to slowly drown in the calm of Rosa's beauty, Jack was having second thoughts about the traditional arrangements.

"My mother came from Chicago. Of course, her father owned a railway."

Rosa leaned over and kissed him, then stood up and dived out, clean as a trout.

"Go on, Chud!"

"I can't swim!"

"D'you hear that, Rosa? Chud can't swim!"

Delaware is still there, but I've only been back once. I prefer to remember it as we found it and for it to live in my mind in its untrammelled images: me waiting for them to arrive, then bursting down upon them, leaping up on one shaft, the pony dancing in fright; Jack laughing and holding Rosa around with one arm to keep her steady; me plumping myself down on her other side on the narrow seat and kissing her cheek. My swimming lessons, gliding with hands on Rosa's shoulders, Jack's arms at my waist. Or lying back in Jack's arms with Rosa at my feet. Or being tugged along, one of them either side, our chins breaking the silky water, three prows. Then, when I could struggle on my own, Jack splashing us with kicking feet is what comes to mind. Or our jumping in, all as one. Or Rosa swimming like an otter, me pulling her back up on the warm rock, spreading out the only towel, using our clothes as pillows. Or Rosa wearing her straw hat. And Jack surging out, clad in glistening water. Me jumping up and, using the towel, flicking at him. Jack fighting his way up, laughing. Rushing. Me tottering backwards over Rosa. Her shrieking. Us all falling in a heap. Jack lying, pinning us down with outstretched arms. Him kissing Rosa. Me.

Six

THE WINTER OF 1937–8 arrived with exceptional severity and intent. It rained until the river burst its banks and even the high ground of Balaklava was flooded. Wind blew in tempests and lifted roofs from houses as if they were paper hats and bowled unlucky heifers before it the length of Long Quay. Then came snow. A novelty in our near-maritime clime, it fell in flakes the size of sycamore leaves. For eighteen days it fell. All work, even by Monument's inexacting standards, ceased. Schools closed. Roads and railway were blocked, the Lyle was closed by ice to ships, old people froze to their beds and a famine hit the town.

It was not the same since Jack had gone. Although we had promised otherwise, Rosa and I each harboured our excuses for not seeing the other, in Rosa's case the taking of lessons at piano, or in riding, or accompanying her father to race meetings, or any of a thousand other such projects which, if Jack were at home would never have arisen; in my case, an apprenticeship to a draughtsman which my grandmother pressed on me, the other option being enrolment in a Dublin reformatory school (true), illness (the old Binn's Street strategy), and simple lies, such as pretending to have waited for Rosa in such and such a place and then having gone home when she failed to turn up. It was not the same. Not that Rosa's beauty did not outrank any other in my short experience, but with Jack gone the dangerous nature of our relationship was missing. Main, apart from the embellishment of Jack being there, embodied risk on a grand scale and one to which we had become addicted. For Rosa and I to meet at the back of the cathedral, for example, seemed humdrum after what we had been through, or so I must assume, since all that famous winter went by without us seeing, and I daresay, thinking of one another. But at the back of these evasions lay the understanding that there would come another summer and with it Delaware and that only the pages of the calendar lay between us and the sight again of one another.

"Germany today announced the immediate re-introduction of conscription and the formation of an army of thirty-six divisions. 'Germany's Air Force today,' said Mr Winston Churchill in a speech to the Commons, 'is probably larger than that of Great Britain.'"

The kitchen's main concern was bombs dropped from German aeroplanes. Mrs Finnerty, who had an opinion on everything, stated that St Melb's would be one of the first targets, since the devotion of the Church family to the Empire was known everywhere, including in Berlin. It did not seem impossible. She began to mumble about going home to Sibrille, but Ma Church talked her out of it.

St Melb's went on a war footing. Uncle Mary, a most unlikely guardian of the coast, began going out to Sibrille and to Leire with binoculars. Since he needed the full-time services of a hackney to perform these duties, he was redeployed by Ma Church to parcelling chores (see below) and thereafter did coastguard duty only on Sunday afternoons. Mr Gus became acquainted with air raid precautions and began lining the cellar of St Melb's with sandbags. Like everything else he attempted in life, the project foundered: half-filled sacks lay in everyone's way all summer and in the yard a cartload of abandoned sand attracted the attention of cats from as far away as Buttermilk.

Knitting overran St Melb's. You stood in the hall after supper as in some tropical twilight, listening to the chattering of knitting needles transforming balls of wool into men's combinations. In the drawing room, Margaret and Justina and Faithful Tadpole, down the long hall to the kitchen, Mrs Finnerty and Olive (who now had a little baby called Buddy) and Olive's sister, Cherry, who, obviously desperate for a cause, came up every night and joined the action on a voluntary basis. Between the two groups roved Ma Church. With a natural instinct for line production she assigned legs up to the waist to the kitchen and waist up to the arms to the drawing room. Cherry sat at a foot-pedal sewing machine and joined kitchen and drawing room. Sections of knitted wool went into Cherry's basket and a minute later, out from her machine shot combinations like decapitated and deformed soldiers. Ma Church, helped by me or anyone at hand, folded and parcelled them in bundles and laced them closed with waxed twine. Every other morning Ma Church was driven down to the post office, where the output of St Melb's was dispatched to the Red Cross in England for onward transmission to field hospitals where, no doubt, men whom battle would leave with uneven arms and legs or reduced torsos would find some transitory comfort in the snug fit of our woollens.

In the midst of this activity appeared Uncle Giles. Ma Church's eldest living son, he had once been apprenticed in the merchant navy, and now arrived with a youth in tow, a shifty item of no more than twenty with the eyes of a stunned gazelle – an Italian prince, Giles informed Ma Church. Foreign nobility were dirt to Ma Church and she put the pair of them in a boxroom in the attic, adding further excitement to a house

41

already atwitter under the strain of the anticipated emergency. Giles, spade-bearded, rudderless, unpredictable in the matter of emotions and wearing the tunic of a sea captain, paced the hall of St Melb's humming "Happy Moments" from *Maritana*. His fascination with Faithful Tadpole was reciprocated because she listened spellbound to his stories about the Yellow River and the Nile and indeed it was this impetus that set her off painting her seafarers. He also had an eye for me, God bless Uncle Giles. On excursions to MacCartie Square he bought me cigarettes and put them down to his mother. He had Stickyback, Monument's snapshot artist, snap me against the background of the Lyle and when two copies were delivered Ma Church was obliged to pay for them. (Uncle Giles took away his photo, but I still have mine. I came across it recently and wondered what connection there could be between the beguiling, nearly-sixteen-year-old youth of soot black curls and deep eyes and the effigy that looks out at me every morning from my bathroom mirror.) The prince, who smoked a hokum pipe and appeared for meals in a caftan, greatly affected Mr Gus, who took to following him around the house and up to the attic, and, on one occasion, to sitting beside him on the landing and taking alternate puffs from his pipe stem of mottled ivory.

On Sunday when Ma Church had gone to a race meeting for the day with Bensey, Uncle Giles loaded all of us into a hackney car and took us down to the Commercial Hotel. There, on Ma Church's slate, he entertained us to cigarettes and the champagne stock of the hotel's cellar. At five o'clock we returned to St Melb's like a team of horses suddenly turned loose. My aunts Justina and Margaret romped at the old piano whilst Uncle Giles and the prince danced a waltz. Old Uncle Mary, my grandfather's brother, walked three times into doors before being sat down by Olive, whereupon he fell asleep. Mr Gus chased the prince round and round the kitchen table before Mrs Finnerty intervened. Thereafter he wandered in and out, the top buttons of his trousers undone, until at half-past six everyone sat down in the kitchen and was tucking into gammon when Ma Church walked in.

Giles Church would never again set foot in Monument, but neither would he forget me in the course of a long and profitable life during which Church Chandlers of Portsmouth would become the biggest in its field. One evening after their departure I was on my way to bed when I came upon Faithful Tadpole sitting like a doll in the wicker musical armchair I had years before brought with me from Six Half Loaf. To bars of Strauss, arms clasped around a drawing pad, she was looking at me.

"Tadpole?"

"You've been in my dreams, Chud."

Her face, much nearer in age to Ma Church's than to my own, was bisected by a line of smoke from her ever-present cigarette. Sometimes before washing was put out Faithful Tadpole was asked by Olive whether or not it would rain, and often, an hour after a wet forecast had been given into a clear sky, Olive and Mrs Finnerty could be heard shrieking as they ran from the kitchen to the clothes line in a downpour.

"You're with a girl and you're both crying."

"But it's only a dream."

"My dreams are not only dreams, Chud, they are a place I go."

"What does she look like?"

"Dark and beautiful."

"Why is she crying?"

"I'm not sure. You and she are together. It's sunny. Something big and ugly comes from the sky and blots out the sun. When the sun comes out again you're both crying."

I laughed. "From the sky?"

She nodded.

"A German bomb, maybe?"

"It doesn't really matter what it is, does it?" asked Faithful Tadpole and resumed her sketching of the Nile as revealed to her by Uncle Giles.

Heat took hold of Monument. Canny old people who had survived the dire winter shrivelled in the boiling days of June. The Lyle, parched at her source, dropped to permanent ebb tide, revealing ugly mudbanks, scarred and hardened like tuberculosis. Cattle, maddened with thirst, died for want of fodder. Roads melted. Whereas bad frost had made only the top foot or so of the graveyard iron, now drought baked the earth to its core and led to despair in those who had been grave-diggers all their lives. Heat did away with the waking days between death and burial on which many of the living depended for their recreation; for in the new climate of swift putrefaction a man dying in Friday's small hours, who might have expected to be laid out in his own front room till Sunday, now found himself, by that same evening's dusk, interred under upwards of a ton of flinty earth.

As if merely days and not a year had passed for our threesome, Jack brought picnics to Delaware, pressed tongues on wafers of homemade bread, chicken breasts in aspic wrapped in cooling lettuce, salmon smoked and packed in lime-flavoured crushed ice and bedded in flasks of silver. Drought had made clean water scarce, so Fleming brought wine to Delaware on the stroke of three; but Rosa told Jack he had been foolish to disclose our secret to Fleming and that she did not like the knowing, almost insolent way the butler looked at her, so the practice was not repeated. A sense of timelessness took over my mind, and I assumed, those of Jack and Rosa too. Not just timelessness in the sense that no end to our pleasure seemed possible, but that life had always so been, that our circumstances were inherent to our lives, and thus beyond the right of anyone to alter, ourselves included. So passed the dizzy days of June. To meet Rosa on Long Quay and whisper "Delaware" was not just to share a secret but to pronounce something that meant happiness. To me, even after all this time, it still does.

The main rooms of St Melb's overlooked the Monument river. A glass-panelled door marked the end of the hall and the beginning of the passage, a frontier further differentiated by the sudden onset or easing of strong food and body smells, depending on which direction you were travelling in. By lifting a trapdoor in the larder and reversing down a steep ladder, a low-roofed, seldom-used cellar was reached. With a lamp you could see the curving, pink brick substructure of the house rising from the sandy clay of The Knock. I smoked down here, sitting directly below the sitting room, where every time Ma Church shifted in her armchair overhead I could hear her do so. One boiling day, when nothing had been set for Delaware and the cellar of St Melb's, next to the crypt of the cathedral, was the coolest place in Monument, I became aware that above me Ma Church had a visitor.

"What a nice surprise," she was saying, "an' me just about to ring for tea."

The cue for a distant bell and Olive's flat heels a-scamper.

"I hear Half Loaf has a new owner."

Bensey.

"Yes, at last. Can't say I'm sorry to see the back of it."

"Word is you sold it to young Little, could that be right?"

Ma Church chuckled. "Not much escapes you, Paddy."

"I'm told at nights he puts some concoction into bottles and sells it to hucksters for a fortune."

"I met Rosa yesterday in a very pretty dress, a real eye-catcher she is," said my grandmother, changing the subject before Bensey could ask the price for which she'd sold the house. "Our Chud's agog everytime he sees her."

"She likes the countryside."

I could tell at once by the deliberate way he laid down the word "countryside", that Bensey had not come to St Melb's to dispense blessings.

"Oh, yes?" said Ma Church.

"Yes. She likes me to bring her out to Main," said Bensey, this time emphasising "Main". "Young Jack Santry brings her driving in his trap. She likes that, Rosa. She likes young Jack Santry."

"I . . . see," answered Ma Church, her long-standing revulsion for the Santrys momentarily overtaken by her respect for any stratagem of the bookie's.

"Ah, the young, they know their own minds nowadays," Bensey sighed, as if he had little option but to accept the position. "And who can blame them, the different world we all live in?"

"Main *is* a different world, no doubt," said Ma Church. "And not one I'd care to 'ave been born into, ta very much."

"Times change, Mabel."

"But not people!"

"More's the pity, Mabel, don't you think?"

From the unwavering tone of the bookie's voice came the steel of his intent for his daughter, which Ma Church must have recognised; for then she said, "They lead another life to ours, Paddy, is all I meant."

"And one which I think Rosa will like," said Bensey.

"Poor Augustine," said Ma Church, going on a change of tack. "Too nice for business. Lets the shippin' types walk 'im right into the ground. Chud on the other 'and 'as spirit. I 'ave plans for Chud. The army first. Discipline. I think every boy needs discipline in 'is life."

"The *army*?"

"The British army."

"That old joke?"

"It's no joke, Paddy. We still 'ave connections. The boy is wild, I can't think of anythin' better. Then 'e can come 'ere and take the weight off my poor shoulders."

Ma Church was, I was sure, smiling at Bensey as she signalled this devolving of her empire. I heard the clink of a cup set down on its saucer.

"I would not normally have brought up this subject," said the bookie, "and it embarrasses me beyond words to have to do so, but Rosa says he has her persecuted."

"Chud?"

"I'm afraid so."

"You're 'avin me on."

"On Dudley's Hill, Mabel, whenever she goes into town, up and down the Long Quay. I didn't want to upset you . . ."

"Oh, God."

"I'm sorry, too, Mabel, but Rosa's nature is just like her poor mother's, God be merciful to her; she wouldn't hurt a fly. It just isn't in Rosa to tell this young fella to leave her alone, but I'm her father and I suppose that's what fathers are for in the heel of the hunt."

"Poor Chud."

"Poor? Hmph. A bit too rich in the blood, I'd say, from what Rosa tells me, if you take my meaning, Mabel, no offence, I hasten to assure. But I understand young Jack Santry is of the same opinion."

"Then I shall speak to 'im in no uncertain terms," said my grandmother.

"This mustn't come between us, Mabel," said Bensey. "Rosa's heart is set on young Jack Santry, but mine has been spoken for since the day I first set eyes on you."

I crept from the cellar to my bedroom and drew the curtains against the light and curled like a dog awaiting death. Ma Church somehow knew. She came up and sat beside me, never uttered. She, too, had been wounded. She now knew that she would always be second to Rosa in Paddy Bensey's affections and for a woman used to primacy wherever a man was concerned, this realisation was hard.

Although we might have been silent allies in distress, Ma Church still had her life to be getting on with whereas I saw mine as at an end. Mine was, it must be said, a unique perception of the near hereafter, for it embodied almost continual visions of Rosa as if we had both been thrown into an emotional desert in which only acts of aggravated sex had any meaning. In the confines of my undisturbed room I sought a poor man's comfort in the free rein of my fantasies, so that even nature, a profligate provider, must have felt the strain of my output. To think that previously I had not even considered that deep within me might reside this extra resource that smelled of cornflower, this chugging, creamy addition to blood, piss and phlegm whose nightly (and daily and sometimes twice-daily and thrice-nightly) letting so preoccupied me. Other young women worthy of inclusion in my illusions lived in Monument – some of them exotic as jungles in their semi-origins, others pure Monument with milk-white skin and green eyes – and might easily have earned their place as the cause of great tossings off, but it was no use. Rosa alone knew the track to my bursting mind. She was the scorning queen of carnal desire from whom the best of all things flowed, as it did from the Queen of Heaven. Some days she would come to me demurely dressed, others in rags, others in the outfit of a Turkish concubine. Her look was one moment wanton, the next shifty. I forced myself stickily between her and Jack at Delaware, whereupon she turned her face to me with an imperiousness I had not captured before, so that for several nights I had fresh matter to work and warp to my designs. I can only speculate on the death this association would have suffered in the end, because not even I, I don't think, despite my quite ravenous approach to sex, or perhaps because of it, could have managed to squeeze much more out of this very one-dimensional affair. In the end I recognised the ultimate poverty of my approach and considered, briefly, becoming a Franciscan.

Starvation at last drove me from the forge of my room, self-ravaged, empty and set. Having gorged in the larder on cold lamb to the point of gagging, I then walked beneath a blanket of unabated Bengal heat to the Monument river and sat dully as a barge laden with coal nosed for the Indigent Home. It was a filthy enterprise, the vessel, its cargo, and the three, black-faced members of its crew. I remembered hearing Ma Church once say, "There's money in dirt." Beneath its curd-like skin the water trembled in the barge's wake.

I was well rid of her, of them both. And yet, in an atmosphere cleared of sexual torment, the extent of the injustice to me now pierced even deeper, its barbs bit without the balm – I laugh! – of lust and the indignity of my treatment began, drip at a time, to demand reprisal. I could justify anything in the light of the duplicity of which I had been the victim. Not alone had my own unsuspecting nature been abused, but those of my family, not least my father, a stranger in every sense bar the one in which I knew him to be a man of honour.

For two days I tramped Monument, hoping, I suppose, to see Rosa and to let her know, if only by the hardness in my face, what I thought of her attitude. She was never in White City, nor in the places where we had once gone just to breathe the same air, nor did I see her along Long Quay, nor even at a race meeting held near Baiscne where her father sat in the back of his car with my grandmother, drinking champagne and eating hard-boiled eggs. Then, freewheeling home one day, I saw Bensey's Rolls returning from Main, the driver with his cap off and the top button of his shirt undone.

Wind from the south eased me up through the foothills and past the stone bridge near Main. If I listened I could hear an occasional gong of iron caused by an unloading ship on Long Quay and borne on the warm breeze, but otherwise only the droning made by communions of insects attended me. It's not as if I had evolved a plan of any kind; rather, I wanted them to see the change in me, believing in it myself as I did and never imagining that jealousy was even more destructive than lust. Cattle sighed and swished in deep parkland. Main itself was beset by inactivity, the staff either lying restoratively in their quarters, or deserted to cool, primal streams. As I stepped over the wolfhound it did no more than roll its eyes in my direction, but even that effort seemed a trial and it slipped back into its torpor. The stable yard was no better. Where you might have expected a lad or two to be prodding at a mound of dung or shining up a harness, all I could find was an irritated bantam cock. But Jack's grey mare was gone, as was the trap.

Buzzing in my ears, through green clouds of dragonflies I flew by mottled paths, by trunks of trees cast in leering faces. Where the path forked I veered left-handed for the upper way, which rose above the pool and which was the conclusion to the route I took as a rule when I came out from Monument. The day once more: endless, pre-Eden blue, peaceful as laudanum.

I knew where they were, and now prurience, a most underrated vice, overhauled my indignation. I halted by the big, overhanging, horse-sized rock, jumped down and lifted my bike after me, parting the ferns that would close over again, every movement a re-enactment of another, every second another milestone in an odyssey of subterfuge. As if bitten, I recoiled. Another bike winked out at me from where it had been placed, spanking new in the sunlight. Tumbling, ferns at my cheeks, I rolled in a new, branching, left-hand way across the mountain. Even then, at that giddy, penultimate moment, I was conscious of my separation from myself, aware that I somehow now lay between the ticks of time. Insects caught and held the sun in their translucent, emerald bodies. I crawled out. Delaware quivered like an eye of mercury. Down on the hot, white rock lay Rosa and Jack, brown and white, naked as creation. And on the ledge below me, staring down at them, lay Bruno Belli.

I went home. All I could think of, and this is being honest, was how most to hurt Rosa and Jack for their belittling of me. Bruno existed only as the instrument for my hurting. At no stage did I dislike him. We each had changed. Bruno, now nineteen or more, looked stunted and wizened where once he had appeared powerful. Around the town he was prey to pranksters and once up in Balaklava when he had been caught groping a boy, he had been so beaten that his nose would now always be crooked. I suppose what wakes me up in the dead of night in sweat is the thought that, what happened next was – God! – *accepted*, that we three somehow mattered more than Bruno. And for that, for each of the many days that we outlived him, there is a debt.

Cigarettes alight, on chairs of India cane in Main's propylaeum from where, through spilling palm fronds and potted bamboo a vista of park-land entailed for twelve generations was visible, I told Jack. At once, my craving to wound transformed into deep remorse and all I wanted was to recapture my syllables, still almost organic in the smoky air, to reswallow them whole. Yet I had to bluster on, for watching Jack's face a-crumble I knew that what I had set in motion was beyond stopping and that revenge is always two-edged. I remembered, too, Faithful Tadpole and wondered wildly if her alchemy could be somehow employed to reverse time. Highly agitated, Jack was striding up and down, running his hands through his hair.

"The one I've seen selling matches? God!"

"He's harmless."

"God Almighty! This is a disaster! Why have you waited till now to tell me this? He'll tell the whole town!"

"He won't. Even if he does, no-one will believe him."

Jack smacked the heel of his hand against his broad forehead. He rang for tea, then when the girl came, cancelled it, lighted one cigarette whilst another lay untouched in an ashtray and stamped his foot down hard. He turned to me, pained and confused.

"What were *you* doing there anyway?"

Good question.

"Just coming out to swim."

"We've been expecting you every day. What's happening?"

"You should ask Rosa that."

"Rosa?"

"She complained me to her father."

"Rosa? She's damned by the man. He thinks if she looks sideways at anyone but me she's going to marry him. Ghastly little scalper, of course she didn't." Jack shook himself. "She can't understand why you've stopped coming, that's all. She thought it was all rather fun. So did I, as a matter of fact. Now this. I want to be sick."

A plan for killing Paddy Bensey by setting his shop afire sprang into my mind, complete in every detail.

"We'll have to tell Rosa," Jack was stating. "She has to protect herself."

"Don't. I'm telling you, Bruno won't say anything."

"How can you be sure? Can you guarantee that? Of course you can't. Christ, imagine what bloody Bensey will think!"

"He won't know."

"It's not you he saw, Chud! It's me. And Rosa. I'd like to see you if the shoe were on the other foot."

"Don't tell Rosa, Jack."

"Let her walk into a field of enemy fire, is that the plan? I thought you liked her, Chud. I'm damned if I'll let her do that! Damned!"

I tried to explain that Bruno, if I knew anything of him, would not utter, but Jack, over the course of that long and fateful afternoon when we should have been wallowing in nature, instead was like a bee in a bottle. Patience had never been a trait of the Santrys, who saw hesitation of any sort as cowardice. The fortunes of the adjacent men in oils had been founded on courage, on grasping the moment and moving forward, on never shirking the enemy, which in this case was the truth. Rosa must be told, Jack insisted. She has the right to know. The more I told Jack not to, the more Jack felt the need to purge the atmosphere of deceit and, if necessary, attack. Read your military history, Jack told me. Read the duke's campaigns.

A last word, Bruno, before our lives go on, before this century, damn it, ends and all its events that you could never know of are finally forgotten: you didn't deserve what happened. But if living after death is done only in the minds and memories of others, then Bruno, you live on in mine. I remember you, not just for the great injustice done to you, but for one day long ago in Mulberry when you showed me by the graceful tricks from your proud past how in the hands of the gifted even a bicycle can be made to bloom.

We sat in our clothes on the rock, Rosa looking from me to Jack.

"Jack, you look as if you've swallowed a frog!"

I had never loved her more. Love punished me for my lack of trust and made me even more miserable than I had been when hating her.

"Jack?"

He told her, then, in the offhand way of the Anglo-Irish whose need to trivialise is a metaphor for their own relevance. Rosa heard him out, her face bled of colour.

"He's never mentioned it since," Jack went on. "You don't think there were other times, do you, Chud? I doubt it. So you see, Rosa, it's not such a fuss, but at the same time you had to be told, don't you agree?"

Rosa screamed. She fractured the universe. An awful, lost howl of anguish that went on, and when I attempted, laying my hand on her arm, to calm her she flew around in consternation, screaming louder, then jumped up, and, although I believed it to occur only in books, began wrenching at her lovely hair. All three of us were on our feet, Jack and me helpless and wondering, frankly, if countryfolk might not come running, for her screams must surely be heard in Deilt. Rosa seemed enlarged in every way by the extent of her indignity, at once terrifying and irresistible. Part of the wonder was, from where exactly her torment came, from what inner pocket it sprang.

"Chud! Quick!"

She was dashing for the most sheer side of the rock. We grabbed her. At close quarters her scream was deafening. Down we went – a grim caricature of former times! – as she battled and kicked. Then Jack tried to gag her and she bit him.

"For God's sake . . ."

Now, as Jack tended himself and Rosa tried to lurch up, I lay on her, stifling her cries by squeezing her throat until the scream became a gasp and all at once she went limp and the sun came out and bathed her distracted, beautiful face in forgiving light.

At first, I think, I suspected a trick, for I held on in the position which had disabled her, aware of her breath beneath me coming in erratic jumps.

"Get off her, for Christ's sake, Chud! She's passed out."

So she had. Jack went for water and I took off my shirt and put it beneath her head. Jack forced water into her mouth, which at first dribbled out making her appear dead, but then her eyes opened and she sat up, spilling the water from his hands, and fell forward on hands and knees and vomited.

"It's all right, Rosa, really," Jack kept saying.

We took her, shaking, feeble, to a clean part of the rock and held her between us as her words came.

"I hate you." She sobbed as a great tide of fatality swept her away. "I hate both of you."

"It's not as bad as you imagine . . ." Jack ventured.

"Oh my God . . ."

"He's a bit of a fool, Rosa . . ."

"It couldn't be worse!"

"I'm sure he won't say anything . . ."

"The thought of his eyes! Oh, God! Have you ever seen the way he looks at you? My father . . . Oh, Jesus, what's my father going to say when he hears?"

"Rosa . . ."

"Jesus Christ, I want to be dead! Dead!"

I could feel the softness and warmth of her in the crook of my shoulder and at the same time the wiry sinews of Jack's forearm, where he also clutched her, pressing into my chest.

"Rosa, nothing will happen," Jack said.

"Dirt, that's what I am now. Dirt."

"We won't let him," Jack said.

"I can never go home again."

"We'll see to it," Jack said.

Rosa checked.

"I swear we will," Jack said.

"Do you?" Rosa whispered.

I said nothing, too preoccupied lest I might upset the sudden prospect of her rekindling happiness.

"Of course," Jack nodded, "we'll sort him out. Isn't that right, Chud?"

"That's right," I swallowed, without warning feeling more powerful than I ever had before. "We will."

"You both swear?"

We nodded.

"Oh, please," she said and closed her eyes, "please don't let my father hear. I'd rather die than that. I would really."

I looked at Jack. "We promise." Never had I loved her more.

Can you understand me when I tell you, this is still too raw for me to paste up in detail? I can't do it. Maybe I will, someday, but not yet. I'm not ready yet.

I used to dream of that youth, Chud Conduit, on that terrifying day a week later, what would be his last Sunday for nearly five years in the town he so loved. Wind has been getting up since dawn and driving strange clouds into the sky. Rain, which was prayed for at all the masses, is suddenly a possibility. This is the day of change.

Noon has come and gone. Beside Delaware, Chud, Rosa and Jack clutch one another in a circle, crying like puppies. Behind them, as if the sky is raining not flecks of water but symbols, their pool has been taken up by an immense, dark shape. Their faces are rubber masks of terror as they realise what we all do eventually, if we live long enough, that the broad highway of life is of all our illusions the cheapest by far.

"Oh no oh no oh no."

Chud has to drink. He drags himself free and reels towards the water. Collapsing he scoops double-handed. He gulps. He gasps. His lips and hands brim of blood.

"Oh no oh no oh no oh no oh no."

Chud begins to climb. He sees the other two's faces writhe in renewed consternation as they see him leaving them, but he knows he must. Whereas up to this sabbath morning many aspects of his life have been informed by base motives, from this moment on all his actions will be inspired by a particular valour. This is the way of it. Just as death and life replace each other as if by whimsy, so we change utterly in a second, in less than a second, shedding one skin and flying free in a way which, a blink ago, was unthinkable.

Chud fastens his hands to his ears to cut off the cries below him. He has to clean his mouth, but cannot spit enough and thinks the blood on his hands is coming from his ears. Gaining the high track, cut and scraped, wide-eyed, he falls on dock leaves, which he chews in frantic clumps until he retches. Spent, he lies back watching the new clouds. Each one of them has a canine mouth and double-breasted lapels.

When time goes by and he rises, Chud finds he cannot breathe. So he screams, in fright. A name. Screaming this name he runs and runs, smothering, he thinks, sensing on his hot-cold neck the hand of death, but not his own. Would it were his own! For the thought of what lies ahead is nothing to his own death, he will laugh at that one day in fact, but now he wishes it in place of what he has to face. So when he reaches Small Quay, where enough water lies between the river banks to drown himself, there is a moment when all the future lies in the balance. But as he looks down he thinks of salvation, not of his own soul, but of Rosa's and Jack's. He will take the blame for them, he then knows. He will suffer so that they can go free. And, knowing this, he smiles. Cherished moments these, whenever they come, even in the midst of dark despair.

Chud turns from the river and runs by the cathedral, where lie buried his mother and his grandfather, the kind doctor, and on up Dudley's Hill, where, shivering and faint, he cowers under a column of the Esplanade, wondering if he'll ever hear again. Deaf, he looks across the road and sees a family pushing a barrow down Dudley's Hill. Their cow has died, he knows, the town knows, the family lived on the sale of its milk, and now they are pushing before them all they own on a borrowed cart down Dudley's Hill to catch the train to England.

"Chud!"

One of the children waves. The woman, blank-faced, turns in Chud's direction, then smiles. She too waves. Chud cannot wave back. He wants to, but he cannot. He wants to go with them. The destitute family continue down the hill. What would they think if they knew that in their darkest hour they were the object of someone's envy?

Chud's legs are heavy. He is walking now, with great effort, dragging himself by the old ice rink, over Pollack Street. It helps to hurt himself, he finds, to crash into walls with his knuckles. It somehow clears his ears.

"*Stop!*"

The nose of a big car has appeared behind him, guards hanging precariously between its roof and its running boards.

"You!"

Chud begins running again, into curving Moneysack, an alley shaped like a weal, whose cobblestones make running difficult. He runs through the belch of lucky, teeming life in fetid Moneysack. Even in that bad, bad moment he knows that he has discovered something of rare value, that bad and all as what has taken place, that something good, too, has happened. Not that it should have, but then nothing should have. Children are batting spokeless rims down Plunkett Hill. They stop, staring at him. The understanding that he lacks a destination breaks over him, yet his new, discovered treasure burns like gold in his chest. Out across the top of the road stroll two giants in uniform.

"STOP!"

A set of doors stands open. Chud runs headlong. So cool. He runs up the centre nave and jumps the altar rail. Evening light streams downwards. He shouts. Ahead, the sacristy breathes its own air, its vestments harbour the essences of dead men. An old friar looks up in gentle confusion.

"Sanctuary!" Chud yells. "Sanctuary!"

Running into the bell tower he leaps on a chair and drags the thicker of two ropes from its keeper.

"Sanctuary!"

How many beats, he has no idea. Far above his head the bell doles out its sane, level beat.

"Sanctuary!"

Swinging, Chud can see straight out through the robing quarters, across the altar and into the body of the church in the fading light. It is empty. He finds a rhythm.

RING-BINDERS
3 - 4

Seven

ANOTHER GAP IN MY ring-binders, I'm afraid. They now leap from a scene of youthful grief in 1938 to my graduation from Father Tell's reformatory school two and a half years later. Why this gap? Is it because I wanted to forget? Perhaps. But bear with me, if you will, while I attempt to fill in some of the blanks.

There was no Father Tell, that I do remember. He had long died off having devoted his life to the erection of this barracks somewhere in County Dublin, where I don't know since we were never allowed to leave it, a late Victorian structure which gazed over treeless, damp, flat countryside. We were fifty boys in the care of Father Tell's ragtag order of priests and brothers, fifteen in all, most of whom had grown up themselves in Father Tell's. In theory, the institution owed its existence to its stated principle: A New Beginning, but in practice, despite how it may have set out in Gladstonian days, by the time I arrived it was little more than a self-perpetuating safe haven for men whose general dissolution had been nurtured in the only world they knew, and which they now clung to.

Father Tell had decreed that everyone in his house should live together like one big family and so we all came together each evening, but separately, the priests in a room with a reasonable library, the brothers and ourselves in a small, cramped room with only two armchairs, long bespoke. When we gathered as one in church, albeit in different parts of the church, we spoke to God not with one voice, but divided, the priests reciting their divine office, the unlettered brothers leading us in the rosary. And since nothing speaks more of the level of men's humility than the company in which they choose to eat, the priests did so at the high table of the refectory, why so called I am unsure as there was only one, whilst the brothers and ourselves ate in a tiny room beside the kitchen. Some of these brothers masticated like big, vacant herbivores, the juice of their cud streaming down their chin, and some ate the very bones of chops, cracking them to splinters between their teeth.

I now become stuck, patient reader. It is as if in 1938 Chud Conduit went into hibernation in County Dublin and in early 1941 emerged, changed in only three respects that I can think of.

I learned at last to be a draughtsman. In a clammy shed adjacent to the piggery, Brother Mel – his name comes springing from my tongue – a middle-aged, good man, worked with the T-squares, pencils, straight edges, triangles and other tools of the drawing trade. (I at first thought his name was Brother Melb and was drawn moth-like to such auspiciousness.) Brother Mel he was, however, and he taught me scale. He showed me how to present the different elevations of a building, and the plans of each of its floors, and even its roof as seen from the sky, a wonderful revelation, where by dint of measurements reduced to scale and a good pencil, what could never be seen by the eye could nevertheless be set down on paper.

Why Brother Mel worked in this vocation remains a mystery. The board on which he drafted was supported by ancient volumes containing the drawings of Italian palaces and churches. He had extrapolated the heights of bell towers and the length of colonnades overlooking sunny piazzas and then assigned himself exercises of setting down these buildings in scaled plans, then judging his efforts by removing the book from its pile and turning back its pages. Thus I am still familiar with the ethereal proportions of the main courtyard of the Palazzo Ducale in Urbino, the extraordinary complexities of Palladio's Teatro Olimpico in Vicenza and the unique integrity of the church at Todi called after Santa Maria della Conciliazione.

Mysterious Mel, my tutoring draftsman. Kind soul, he never laid a hand on me.

The most marked difference between my new life and my old was the absence of women. Women had been at the heart of St Melb's. Nothing similar existed in Father Tell's, apart of course from God, who was ever promoted as the universal remedy for everything including loneliness; but God, in the end, lacks the tangible warmth of a woman.

I thought often of Delaware in the first months. I realised what it had been, which caused me pain. I thought too of Faithful Tadpole's forecast, which if I had heeded it would have meant avoiding the disaster, but this only made the pain worse. Letters were forbidden. It was better to let go, to ease the pain.

After that I thought little of Rosa and never of Jack. You would imagine that characters of such significance in my life would have continued to cast their shadows through it, but they did not, as if the blade that had sliced through our trio had done so on the point of noon. Neither did I grieve for my loss, nor even contemplate the extent to which I might be diminished by it, so far as I was aware. The past, like a delicate fabric, faded with each new airing until all that remained for me were symbols. A freshwater pool, a straw hat. Contrasting shades of skin. Sunshine. The past itself became a myth, its people mythical, myself included. All that was left in the end was the tiny, lingering glow of comfort that I awoke to, and then that too died.

Summer came round again. Bog irises bloomed in the arid, snipe-grass plain in whose centre sat our house. The kitchen, wherein I took my turn early in my tenure, was staffed by brothers, some of them quite old, who shuffled between tables and sinks, their thin hands seizing like claws upon pots and colanders.

Sherry was served to the priests at one on Sundays before dinner. Some, for whom age had not yet brought a respite from sexual torture, saw the kitchen as an opportunity to gaze on the bare arms and necks of the boys, and at times, above all at steamy times, to touch us. Into the shouting and clatter of the kitchen came Father French, a big man with swooping eyebrows, still handsome in his mid-sixties, and now, following his quota of sherry, a satyr.

"Ahhhh! I'd eat a child! Ahhhhh, the smelly, bellyful! Conduit, isn't it?"

"Yes, Father."

"What are you cun-cock-ting, Conduit? Reply!"

"Parsley sauce, Father."

"Parsley sauce, parsley sauce. It melts like nothing else, Conduit, on a sweet little knob of pink bacon fat!"

In one step he had me, his left arm like a steep hoop around my waist, his right hand travelling with great determination between my legs and up my short trousers.

"It's all right, it's all right, Conduit," whispered Father French.

Elsewhere in the kitchen brothers looked away and continued their tasks as if Father French had not come in.

"It's all right."

He had reached my flaccid member, his big hand cajoling it. I struggled, but in doing so launched us backwards towards the steps of the larder. Father French lifted me into the air and sprang the two steps upwards, crashing the larder door in before him then kicking it closed.

"Be still or I'll brain you!"

He was now pressed into me from behind, his pleasuring hand attempting affection, his tongue licking my neck. Through the fine wire mesh of the door panels I could see a brother looking up at us. He was in his forties, timid, the butt of jokes. I am sure from the look on his face that he knew all about Sundays in the larder with Father French.

"Ah!" gasped Father French. "Ah, sweet mother!"

His hand came out. Moments followed during which he attended to his new discomfitures.

"I'm hearing confessions at six," he then said, and marched out.

The system whereby all sin could be dissolved by those involved in its committing was a particular wonder of our little institution and was on a par with the practice that allows governments to remain wealthy by printing the money which they spend. For his part, Father French confessed to Father Cal, a man of fifty best known for his halitosis. Both Fathers French and Cal had over long years enjoyed an intense relationship that necessitated at its peak daily sessions of joint confession. In my last year their transgressions were uncovered and excommunication avoided only by confessions of the most awesome magnitude by each to the bishop.

But I have promised to say in what other respects Father Tell's changed me, or in what aspects I changed whilst in Father Tell's. I grew. Grew and became strong. So that one December evening in transit down a long, dark passage, when I was jumped upon by Father French I hit him so hard that he lay gasping for thirty minutes on the cold, stone floor and thereafter never touched me again.

In one final respect I emerged altered from Father Tell's to take up my first job as an assistant to a clerk of works in Omagh, a position arranged through my grandmother's connections.

Ma Church was no tuppence-ha'penny operator. In her eyes, it was not a family but a dynasty over which she presided and since I was the one chosen to succeed her – oh! – she was determined that her plans would not be spiked.

On the very night of Delaware, Jack had been transported to England and by the Wednesday evening Rosa was in the convent in Leire. I remained. I told them I had acted alone in Delaware; no-one came forward to suggest otherwise. The state solicitor, Beagle, although by that time married to the plain woman who had been his secretary, had continued to admire Ma Church. Perhaps her fecundity attracted Beagle, for in this respect his own wife had failed him. She was a most attractive woman, my grandmother. So yes, as we used to say as children, she *let him in*. As Monument whirled, dizzy, as the entire structure of our town cracked and people rushed madly to cement it back together, Ma Church allowed Beagle his way with her. Just once. In exchange for his agreement not to prosecute me. I *know* it happened. I saw it in later years in the self-satisfied look on Beagle's face whenever he looked at my grandmother and the professional way in which she ignored him. This wonderful dame traded her body for my freedom, or at least, for my incarceration in a halfway house. Beagle was Ma Church's last trick.

She never flinched from what she saw as her duty. She identified a cousin of her late husband's whose job in the British army in Belfast was to hire civilian labour and persecuted him into employing me. To forestall lengthy and potentially hazardous explanations about my whereabouts since 1938, she cajoled the county engineer in Monument into a reference for my mythical years served in his office. Her money, her influence and her body had all been expended on my behalf. What else could she give? Just one thing: in case any attempt was made to verify my new credentials, she gave me her name, and so on February 1st, 1941 I left Father Tell's Chud Conduit and arrived in Omagh as Chud Church.

It is not easy for me to recall Omagh. I don't mean I can't recall its steep streets and its barracks along the Strule, or how its citizens wore an air of begrudgery, or how this market town's unadorning countryside of wet hills and close horizons hung threadbare. No, it hurts me to recall Omagh is what I mean. Time leaps forward for me to a weekend after the war when I found myself back in the army barracks which occupied the site of the old gaol. War had given me a sense of invulnerability. I had come over for rugby at Raven Hill and when afterwards it was suggested that sport might be had in Omagh, I never considered that for me to return there would entail, at least, irony.

The next morning I went to mass in uniform. At first I did not recognise the woman. Then, with a shock, when I did, my first thoughts were, my, how she has aged. Aged and wasted. She looked at me along the pew. Her eyes blinked pain. She left the pew. Alone, she walked in echo down the church to another. One by one so did all the others on that pew. Then those from the pew in front and from that behind. They left their places until I only remained, alone in a pool of hostile prayer.

"Mr Church, isn't it? How are these blighters behaving?"

The officer was small and genial with a winged moustache. I knew him as Major Elmes, a headquarters man from Belfast.

"No trouble to you, are they?" he asked, cocking an eyebrow at thirty men toiling to clear a shivering, elevated site.

"Not much, sir," I replied, pleased that the officer had singled me out.

"Ah, that's good, you must be keeping them on their toes," said Major Elmes.

"Thank you, sir."

"This is for their own good, y'know," said Major Elmes. "Gerry comes and bombs this godforsaken spot they'll have some place to hide – that's if they don't throw in their lot with him."

"Gerry'll hardly come this far, sir," I said, a touch of cheek.

"I wouldn't bet on it," said the major sternly. "Any part of the Empire is fair game to Gerry, y'know."

I envied this officer and his disarming, leisured way.

"Still, I know what you mean. Bloody place," said Major Elmes, wheeling around and then including me in his measured pace across the straggling works. "Not a lot for a young chap like you to do here, I imagine."

"It's a morgue, sir."

"A morgue?" Major Elmes threw his head back and guffawed. "I must remember that one. What do you get up to, then?"

"Nothing, sir. Play cards, sir."

"Nothing like it," said Major Elmes.

"Sir . . ."

"Yes, Mr Church?"

"I very much . . . I want, sir, in fact . . . Can you get me into the army?"

The major, dancing the tips of leather-gloved fingers along the rim of his briefcase, was observing me from eyes that were small, curious and pink.

"Let me think about it, Mr Church."

"You'll . . . think about it, sir?"

"Yes, that's what I've just said. Now, you're doing good work here, Mr Church, so keep it up."

"Yes, sir!" I snapped.

The British army was taking great pains in 1941 to protect territories from aerial bombardment. The war would overspill any day, we were told, Panzer divisions would race across the green, Irish countryside and German gun- and U-boats would nose their way up Irish estuaries, discharging Boche troopers led by officers with monocles. I suggested to Ma Church that I might come home, but she wrote back, pressing me to inquire about a commission in the army proper. She said I must think of a career. Get into the army, Chud, she said, and then come home.

"You 'av about as much chance, mate, as my movver 'as of 'avin' triplets," an English NCO told me when I inquired, "an' she turned sixty last munf."

So much for you, I thought, and watched Major Elmes picking his way out through snaking foundations and freshly made concrete blocks.

Arrayed under Omagh's garrison engineer, a man possessed of the murkiest credentials, were me and my likes: clerks of works and their assistants. We maintained the records relating to men and materials and were the engineer's eyes and ears, liaison officers I liked to think, except we were not part of the army structure in any sense other than as civilian employees. Every night I crawled between clammy sheets in a galvanised lean-to at the edge of town. In the other bed slept a dipsomaniacal Scotsman, an engineer by profession, reduced by drink at the age of fifty to attending the garrison engineer in a menial capacity. One night, stating that he had pissed in his own bed he begged to be taken into mine.

Above us were engineers and below us foremen and labourers. My foreman, McDevitt, black-bearded and enormous, communicated with me and the men under him by grunts and barks that fell short of speech. With his twin brother, also massive and hirsute, he sometimes came to the barracks canteen for poker and one Saturday when this arrangement was cancelled because of manoeuvres, the school re-formed two hundred yards away, in the front room of McDevitt's house in Castle Street. Next morning as everyone stood for the priest, Mrs McDevitt, that is, the stout woman of forty married to the foreman, looked to the aisle and recognising me, shuffled sideways in the pew to make room, although I took up little, and after mass asked me home for the dinner.

The McDevitt twins had over the years been so pumped with her food that Mrs McDevitt was quite unable, even by tiny fractions, to increase their measures. Lacking children to fatten, she alighted on me with delight. And upon learning of the regime in my lodgings, she had her husband put another bed in the back, upstairs room so that that very evening I moved in, all found at five and six a week.

"Been to Belfast, Mr Church?"

"Not really, sir."

"Not the worst little city in the world. More people than here, that's for sure. Wouldn't be hard, would it?"

I put the major's friendliness down to a natural affinity; my grandfather, whom I had never met but with whose attitudes I was so familiar, would also have found a spontaneous *rapport* with Major Elmes, I knew.

"Sometimes it's a bore my having to come down here for these reports, you know," said the major, holding up the sheaf of quantities, materials stock records and other oddments that I was obliged to prepare.

"I can post them," I suggested.

"And have them floating around?" said the major. "For some Boche-fancying Paddy to get his hands on?" He cocked a grin in case he had gone too far.

"End up in Berlin," I smirked.

"I'd like you to deliver them now and then," said the major. "Expenses paid, you understand. Think you could manage?"

"Very good, sir."

"That's the spirit, Mr Church."

The taciturn McDevitt twins always left together after tea for undisclosed destinations. Some evenings, beyond the kitchen in a small bathroom whose hot tap spat scalding water, I bathed my shanks, but mainly I sat at the kitchen range with Mrs McDevitt, who had taken to me greatly, listening to reports from the BBC. At two one moonless morning, hearing a bump outside my bedroom window I drew the curtain back. The bluff-like contours of the twins were bobbing about as they hefted long boxes up a ladder and onto the flat roof of the bathroom. One brought up a tarpaulin, the other spread it over the boxes giving them the suggestion of coffins.

"Mr Church," said Major Elmes, "let me introduce Sergeant Oates. Mr Church, Sergeant, our assistant clerk of works, has come up today from Omagh."

"Sir!" cried big Sergeant Oates, a man whose fair moustache had yet to achieve the distinction of the major's.

Out of the window I could see a great crane that dominated the horizon, men in their thousands on bicycles, air raid wardens readying night lamps.

"The sergeant here is a stickler for neatness," said Major Elmes. "A box for everything, eh, Oates?"

"The better to find it, sir!" snapped Oates, his blue eyes on some distant object.

"Oates will fodder you and bed you down," the major said, scrutinising his watch. "We'll rendezvous at, what, o-eight-hundred hours? Show Mr Church some entertainment, Oates, introduce him around. Life isn't just about balancing some ruddy ledger or other."

"Sir!"

Sergeant Oates marched ahead of me and my small, leather suitcase. In a jeep we drove out of the barracks and two streets distant to my digs.

"Leave your bag, pal," said Oates, more matey since we had left the major.

The next stop was a house with a large, marble-floored hall, fluted cornicing – my clerk-of-works-eye now saw such details – and heavy oak panelling.

"Fancy a wet?"

I asked for bitter, and so did Oates, except that Oates accompanied his with a large sherry which he poured into the beer, swallowing the concoction in one and then closing his eyes as a shudder briefly took him.

"Same again," Oates belched to the white-coated bar steward.

This time I, too, included sherry. I drank the mixture in three and felt purpose stirring in my chest like a lion.

"Don't get many Catholic gentlemen like yourself on the staff," Oates remarked.

It did not occur to me to ask him how he knew.

"Major likes you. You've a friend there, if I may say so."

"He's a good sort, the major," I remarked as fresh bitters and sherries made their appearance. "My sort."

"Glad to 'ear it," Oates grinned and he downed in the standard manner.

"'Allo, 'allo. Brought new blood in, 'ave you, Sarge?"

A soldier in mess tunic with beer in hand stood sizing me up.

"Hello, Bates," said Sergeant Oates. "Bates, this is Mr Church. Mr Church this is Corporal Bates. Corporal Bates 'ad neither mother nor father, 'e was found in a pool of toss-off on Shaftsbury Avenue, isn't that so, Bates?"

"That is absolutely correct, Sergeant Oates," responded Corporal Bates. "And where does Mr Church 'ere 'ail from?"

"From Omagh," Sergeant Oates said. "Our clerk of works."

I wanted to correct Oates, to say that although I had come from Omagh I hailed from Monument, which was really Corporal Bates's question, but I let it go.

"Oh, a figures man," said Corporal Bates. "Think he'd be able for our little school, then, Sergeant?"

"Oh, I don't know, Bates. There's laws against taking money off the likes of wot can't defend themselves proper."

"Mr Church wouldn't take my money, would you, Mr Church? Mind you, he's got a sly eye on 'im, Sarge. Wouldn't surprise me if he's played more than a little bit before."

"Lay off, Bates. Mr Church got a meeting first thing with the major tomorrow. Needs to be on his mettle."

"Oh, beg pardon, Mr Church. Next time you're up then."

"I could play for an hour," I said. "Couldn't I, Sergeant Oates?"

Five including me, but not Oates ("Lucky in love, pal"), sat down at green baize. I never played with less than a pair, never tried to fill a middle straight or a blue. I'd had four quid on arrival in Belfast and after an hour I had added seven and sixpence to my cash in hand.

"The sergeant . . ." I said to Bates, although I felt bad about walking out when I was in front. "I did say an hour."

"Let me see where's he's got to," Bates said and left the room.

The steward, unobtrusive as a phantom, placed foaming bitter at my elbow.

"Stepped out, it seems," Bates shrugged, closing the door.

"Time of the evening for 'is Irish crumpet," said one player.

"Right regular for 'is oats," said another and everyone laughed.

When I was dealt three tens, a knave and a queen I experienced the triumphant blood rush that all gamblers recognise as the prelude to a big win. Discarding the knave, I bought the fourth ten. "Church?"

Only two others remained: the opener (bought one card), and the dealer (three).

"I'll bet five bob."

"I'm out," said the dealer.

The trooper with openers sucked his pipe.

"Hmmm," he said. "Your five bob with ten."

Twice earlier I'd seen him caught trying to fill a run; now he'd managed it and thought by my one-card buy that I had done the same.

"Your ten with a pound," I said, all business.

"Your pound," said the opener, "an' my two."

"Your two pound seen," I said, trembling. "And I'll raise you twelve and six."

It was all I had.

"Seen," said the soldier and put in.

"Four tens," I said, unable to keep the grin from my face.

"Sorry. Four kings," said the soldier and scooped the cash across to his side.

In came Sergeant Oates.

"Ready whenever you are, Mr Church."

"Is there a nice moon tonight, Sergeant?" asked Corporal Bates.

"A lovely, crescent moon, Corporal Bates," replied Oates, "an' twice as nice believe me when you see 'er upside down."

I knew they were laughing at me. Dazed, I went out with Oates and was sick.

"Good to purge the system, I always say," said Oates, lifting me into his jeep. "Gets all the badness out and believe me there's always a lot waiting to come up. Like to clean your shoes with this, pal? There we are. All in a day's work." We tilted away. "Ah yes, I leave the cards to you chaps wot has the brains an' all. Too dangerous for the likes of me. I see some wot loses a whole year's pay in a bad night. My oh my. Well, here we are. O-eight-'undred hours, the major said. Think you'll find your way all right in the morning?"

Propped on the bedside, the tide of beery sherry tipping my co-ordinates however I lay, I awoke in the cold pre-dawn to unutterable desolation. Major Elmes seemed not to notice. He raced through the reports and quantities, getting up from his desk every so often and strolling, hands joined at his back, to the window.

"Well, I shall see you then in a fortnight, Mr Church," he said turning around with the light behind him like the beatification of Christ. "Did Oates look after you last night?"

"Yes, sir."

"Good man, Oates," the major nodded. "Tidy man. Boxes for everything. These reports. Quantities. Information. Everything where I can find it."

Within me, nausea fought with despair.

"Nobody knows about the boxes but me," glided the mellifluous major. "And those who supplied the information for my boxes, of course."

I craved water.

"Not that I expect to fill my boxes for nothing, or all of them at the same time either, that's not what we're about. Information accumulates you know, Mr Church. A word here, a name there. It's like a picture. D'y'ever see one of those painter chappies at work? I daresay. Stroke by stroke they build the thing up, y'know. Unbelievable. It's the same with my boxes."

Meaning came, like a barge from fog on the Monument river.

"It's a question of from which side you see things. Chap like you, for example, a Catholic, you're presumed to be one side. But you and I, I think we know each other a little better. Standards. Values. A way of life, am I right?"

Profound relief was the sensation I best recall.

"Just like two officers having a chat in the mess. One chap might say, I say, this might not mean anything, but last week this Irishman came to stay the night where I dig. I could not help overhearing him mention blah blah blah. The other officer might say, that's jolly interesting, do you have a name, and so on. Remember the chappie painting the picture. So the officer listening would then say, that's jolly useful, old boy. By the way, here's something to have a wet on your way home. Bird never flew on one wing, eh?"

We were at the door. The deft major tucked a folded five-pound note into the breast pocket of my jacket.

"Nothing gets out of my boxes, Mr Church. Believe me, you're safe as houses with us. And by the way, I haven't forgotten your request. Army's a big place. Bit like a ship. Hard to get on board initially, but once you're on, you're on. Carry on, Mr Church."

My baths were often taken on Sunday mornings when the twins were gone since first light. Steam worthy of a locomotive shot from the gasping tap and enveloped the sagging plaster of the ceiling. Speculating on when Major Elmes would come up with a place for me in the army and wondering the use to which he was putting the scraps of information I brought him, I lowered myself into the water, then lay back, and the roof came in.

With the detachment of shock, I stared at the sky – the sky! A period, almost peaceful and without clear boundaries of time, followed. But then the doughty Mrs McDevitt was babbling between sky and me, crying, "Ach, you poor wee lad and not a pick on you," and suchlike expressions of solicitude. A rug laid across my shoulders, she sat me in her kitchen and sponged blood from my face. The warm essences of her bed clung to her as, attired only in a cotton gown, she made me tea and added whiskey, one for her too, Jesus our Lord, what a thing to happen, and had me drink it quickly whilst she made two more – I'm in a state of shock meself, I don't mind tellin' ye, Chud – fussing with delight, allowing her plump hands to tweak my back for reassurance and going every so often to the open door of the bathroom where rifles were littered like umbrellas. Perhaps, used to dealing with the great weight of her husband over the years, Mrs McDevitt bore me upstairs as if I were no more than feathers. I remember no more than her singing me the first stanzas of 'The Londonderry Air', for when I came to it was noon.

Like a plain girl who has suddenly put colour in her cheeks, so the autumn made gay the drab Tyrone countryside. Concrete blocks were made and laid, engineers urged their foremen to get lathed and felted before the winter set in.

"Don't suppose you want to play cards again tonight, pal? Not bein' tired after your journey an' all."

Sergeant Oates drove me to a little country pub a mile out from Belfast. There in a back room was Major Elmes.

"Ah, Mr Church! What a good idea, Oates. What'll it be, Mr Church?"

I drank bitter, the major neat gin. Oates went quietly out and I heard the door of the jeep slam.

"Consider me standing, the king, God bless him," said Major Elmes.

"God bless him."

"Difficult business, you know, war. Puts a nation on its mettle."

"That's why I'd like to join up, sir."

"Handsome is as handsome does, Mr Church. One step at a time. Little boxes, remember?"

Just a name seemed to satisfy the major.

"And the brother, the twin, what does he do?"

The beer sat happily on my stomach, the more so since I never bought a round. Next morning after filing my buildings' reports I claimed expenses and they came across, fifteen shillings, with two quid extra.

"Bird never flew on one wing," chirped the major.

I smiled to myself. What I had told him the night before the major could have learned in Omagh from dogs in the street.

I did go to Monument for my four-day leave that Christmas. By a succession of cold, railway stations where we sat awaiting coal, through tiny towns and villages where people seemed all to be hastening home, on a long day mostly of darkness with bitter winds from the east, when talk of snow was on everyone's lips, past the comforting light from oil lamps in cottages, some of them, like the tracks, put down in the midst of midland wildnesses, down the length of neutrally secure, famished Ireland I zigzagged in my long homecoming. I walked down frozen Long Quay, my breath steaming. The people I knew and smiled at walked straight past me and my familiarity with my surroundings was as if it had been gleaned only from the pictures in a book.

As I cut through Conduit and up O'Gara Street to The Knock, I remembered the terror of my last day on these streets. The block of years that had passed had altered my perspectives, of the house (smaller), of the shrubberies (bigger), of the nearby invisible canal (smellier) and of the night sky from St Melb's (yet lovelier). Pausing by the conservatory, I could hear the piano being engaged in a tune known only to my Aunt Justina, a discordant but endearing ditty. Then, through the window I could make out a group in an attentive semi-circle, although they could not see me. In a way I had always been out here, all the time I had been growing up and even when I was away, above all then. Outside was my destined place. Part but separate. Unseen but still able to see Mr Gus with his happy, empty face, and Faithful Tadpole, in many respects like me, sitting to one side, not in it really, and the warm faces from the kitchen – where was Mrs Finnerty? – and Uncle Mary fast asleep and scowling Aunt Margaret. And in the centre . . . Where else? At sixty-seven she sat straighter than any of them. Through her foxy hair now shot sprays of white, but Ma Church was still a woman of the most striking beauty. She stared straight out into the night at me, frowning, and although she could not have seen me the force of her intelligence was such that I knew – as I had always known – that she did not need to see me in order to be aware of me, and that this ability in her was unaffected by distance.

Creeping in by way of the kitchen, I saw with relief the four-square shape of Mrs Finnerty at the range. I touched her shoulder and she whirled, open mouthed and walloped me across the head with a rolling pin. I awoke in a cot with a red-haired child looking down at me.

"Who are you?"

"Buddy," he said.

"Buddy who?"

He examined me strangely. "Buddy Stone." Then he ran out.

He was Olive's son, now aged eight and living here with his mother. So crowded, those few days. It took me months really to digest them, so many snapshots. Ma Church was still omnipotent, yet I could not fail to notice the tremor in her right hand, and the peering as she read, and the stiffness in her sitting down and getting up. And sometimes, even in company, she strayed, maybe back to her past, possibly into the future. On Christmas Day when we had fed on beef and goose, and Aunt Margaret had begun to weep as she always did after port wine, and Uncle Mary was snoring and Mr Gus was fitting on paper hats whilst his mother watched him with renewed resignation, I found Faithful Tadpole sitting outside my bedroom door, smoking.

"Hello, Chud."

Her face skin lay in white, leather-like patches and beneath her tinselled hair her scalp shone pink. But for the fact she spoke, she could have been an effigy.

"Ma says there's a place for you here, after the war."

"If it ever ends."

"I know. Once a war went on for a hundred years." She looked at me curiously. "You've been in my dreams, Chud."

I did not want to be in Tadpole's dreams ever again. "What now?"

"You are always going to sleep in the arms of an older woman."

I gaped. "Come on!"

"She loves you, but you don't love her. You want your mother, though, so you put up with her."

"You've lost your touch, Tadpole. How long is it since you've seen me?"

"I don't know about years, Chud, I know only about days."

"I don't want to hear more."

"Listen to my dreams, Chud. They may help you in the times ahead."

In Omagh, knowing I was coming home, I had begun to long for Rosa. I imagined that I might see her with other sisters from her convent, collecting money outside the cathedral, or just in for their Christmas shopping. Of course I never did see her and although I considered cycling out to Leire, I baulked at the thought of facing her in her convent. The day before I was due to return, horse races were taking place near Eillne. I would never have said so, but I was glad to be leaving. Monument, excluded from the drumbeat of history, seemed dull and stagnant for all its beauty, whilst Omagh, grey and shabby, at least seemed to march in time with the greater world.

"Mr Bensey!"

Paddy Bensey, attired in matching check cape and deerstalker, turned around from his place beside the upturned tea chest from which his employee was bawling odds.

"Chud Conduit."

"Church, now, Mr Bensey. Have you not heard?"

Despite the years that had passed I did not find Bensey's eyes any more giving than I remembered.

"You've changed," he said. "You're the same, but you've changed."

I touched my sprat-like moustache. "Soon be as big as yours, Mr Bensey."

"What are ye at?"

"Joining the British army, Mr Bensey."

I could see his eyes calculate the odds. "Some chance."

"Lay me odds, if you don't believe me."

"Hah, you haven't really changed much, have you? A trickster at heart."

"Afraid you'll lose again, Mr Bensey?"

"That'll be the day." I could see him looking for a way to wound me. "D'you know Jack Santry is an officer now?"

"Jack?"

"Captain Jack Santry, Royal Engineers," said Bensey.

"How is Rosa, Mr Bensey? Is she really going to be a nun?"

Paddy Bensey looked at me. "Rosa's going to make her own decisions without the likes of you knowing."

"Well, tell her I was asking for her."

I turned my back on him and walked away before I could hear his reply. Rosa was now three years in the convent in Leire and for this derailment of his plans, I knew Bensey would forever hold me responsible.

I now see the war as a stasis for us all: me in Omagh, Jack in England and Rosa in Leire. Over the years I learned bit by bit how she survived there. Perhaps over morning coffee in the Commercial Hotel, someone or thing would catch her eye, such as a girl dusting wainscotting, and Rosa would remark, "I used to do that in Leire." I was so absorbed by her that I never let such revelations pass without milking them for every last detail, hungry for anything which might show her in a novel light and add another dimension to my never jaded appetite. I thus succeeded in collecting enough impressions to form a picture of Rosa in Leire, beginning with the months after Delaware.

No member of the convent in Leire was as pretty as Sister Rose, nor as angry. In refectory and choir her perfect face was blank and ungiving. If spoken to she answered coldly. During the first cropping of her head when other girls broke down at the sight of their former glory on the floor around them, Sister Rose swept her dark tresses up and threw them in a bin with eggshells. In free time, although the rule of the order was to walk with the first sister you happened to encounter, the sinful opportunity for particular friendships being thus limited, Sister Rose preferred to walk alone. She soon abandoned walks entirely and regardless of weather sat alone on a cliff promontory staring out to sea.

Legends formed around lovely Sister Rose. (Rosa was too ornate for purposes of self-mortification.) Nuns hoeing a drill whispered from the sides of their mouths about sailors in Monument and girls who went aboard. One tiny novice came from a farm near Sibrille, where her father trained a racehorse and so this miniature religious knew of Paddy Bensey, the bookie. She said the dowry Sister Rose had brought with her for Christ came to a thousand pounds. The truth was known by Mother Crescentia, the not a little scheming superior of Leire's wind-blown nunnery. She knew all about the Santrys and the Churches and the events of that day at a mountain pool outside Monument. She accepted the bookmaker's donations and waited for the years to do the work of taming which the word of God had not.

Every month in the early days, usually on the first Sunday, Paddy Bensey was driven out to Leire. He brought hampers of the best black market, but when subsequently he saw his offerings lying unopened in Mother Crescentia's office he took his gifts home, Rosa's rejection lying heavy on his heart. It was not all Bensey brought home. Mother Crescentia handed him sheaves of unopened letters which she had tied with black ribbon. They were all from Jack to Rosa. At home, the bookie read each one, then put them away in a chest like treasure trove, which is where they remained for forty years until they made their way into my ring-binders. (R-B: 4)

On those visits father and daughter walked by the sea or, when the weather was too vile, sat alone in the visitors' parlour, where the bookie's attempts at conversation rebounded between the parquet floor and the high ceiling.

"There's not an orange to be had for love nor money in the whole of Ireland," Bensey said. "Hitler's stopped them all. But if you'd like me to, I can bring you half a dozen. Rosa?"

Rosa looked at him without expression.

"Do you know what I heard the other day?" confided Bensey as if this at last was a topic that would ignite her interest. "They're sweetening parsnip up in Balaklava and selling it as banana! I said, by golly, what next? I can get you real bananas, though, the real thing. Rosa?"

Bensey, not understanding the nature of Rosa's pride, had assumed that when time enough had elapsed for gossip to subside and for other scandals to transfix Monument's imagination, that Rosa would come home. He sent Father O'Dea, the young curate in Eillne, to talk some sense to her; even though the priest had made the long journey by bicycle, she declined to see him. Bensey soon began to regret his pre-emptive action which had sent Rosa here in the first place.

"I have spoken to Mother Crescentia," Bensey whispered. "She has no objections to you coming home to me for Christmas, Rosa."

Rosa turned her head away.

"I've had your room painted," said the bookie. "Mrs Church helped me choose the colour. You'll love it, Rosa. Paint is as hard to come by as hen's teeth, you know."

No curtains adorned the four windows of the visitors' room. November rain washed down the glass.

"There's a time and a place for everything. You go on in life, you don't stand and look back over your shoulder. What's done is done. We all make mistakes. You have, I have. Even your poor mother, Rosa, made mistakes."

He took Rosa's long, cool look in his direction as curiosity.

"I shot a rabbit once years ago, Rosa, before you were born. I brought it down to Mama – we had no servants then – and I says, we'll have this lad for dinner, Phyllis, then off I goes to work. When I came back at twelve o'clock, there she was in the kitchen, tears running down her face. D'you know what she'd tried to do? She'd tried to pluck him!"

Bensey threw his head back and howled with laughter at the recollection of his dead wife's misery.

"You see, she'd made a mistake, Rosa. But it didn't matter. I showed her how to skin the little bugger and your Mama made the nicest stew of him with pearl barley I ever ate."

When Bensey's car came two days before Christmas to Leire, it returned without Rosa. Ma Church, knowing the bookie would be on his own, invited him to St Melb's for his Christmas dinner, but Bensey declined. He sat at the head of his own table, laid out in all its silverware, and defiantly consumed his goose and port wine.

Rosa's anger abated over the years to an inner whirlpool of chastisement. She hated no-one but herself. She had fled her shame in Monument, but it went hidden within her, creeping out like fever even on the coldest day and burning her head. Although she despised her father's mediocrity, she knew she had betrayed his trust. For all his conniving ways and transparent generosity, he was still her father and however tawdry his outlook on life he had devoted it in large part to her happiness. Rosa raged. When she sat alone overlooking the sea, it seemed to her that only by leaping to the rocks fifty feet beneath would she ever find the distance from herself she so ardently sought.

What chided her most was the fact that she had been so stupid. Knowing that Jack and I would confuse virtue and vengeance, she had nonetheless made us do it. Rosa shaved her head and strapped her breasts until they hurt and twice each day with a painful brush scrubbed her body, including her face, until her skin was raw; but nothing she did diminished her despair. Because she spoke little, it was assumed that Rosa's dialogue was with God, that her solitary disposition arose from the wish to expunge past sin in isolation; but Mother Crescentia knew otherwise. In her private discussions with novices, during which the entire sweep of human foibles was put on display, not once did she detect in Sister Rose a nuance of contrition.

But Rosa's anger, when it burnt out, left her empty and exhausted. Alone in her cell at night, pressed down by the weight of misery, Rosa yearned for the merriment of Delaware. How long now since she had laughed? She could hear Jack's laughter at my remarks; she could see the three of us lying helpless on our rock, after Jack, at my suggestion, had done a take-off of Fleming the butler. She clung to these memories, for although Delaware in name would never be regained, neither would its spirit ever be extinguished, and this awareness, not a *rapport* with God, was what sustained Rosa through the years of the war.

Mrs McDevitt knew with the precision of guilt the times when her husband and his twin would return from their outings.

"Oh, you're the bonniest wee trout in the whole world."

She liked me to sit on her lap and to suck her prodigious breasts in turn, something that made her electrically pink all over.

"Ach, my wee lad."

"Where have they gone tonight?"

"You don't want to be asking dangerous questions. Here, sit this way, dote."

"They might come back, that's all."

"They'll not come back before twelve and this is only seven. Oh, look at you that big, precious. Have you no shame sitting here with your poor mother?"

"I'm nervous. They could come back."

"Have they ever come back before when I said they wouldn't, have they?"

"We're taking a big risk."

She put my head between her breasts and lay back on the bed, catching me between her knees.

"You're always asking questions when questions is nothing but trouble," she whispered, grasping me. "My wee tiger boy. You're just a cub, a cub, my lovely tiger cub. Lovely. Oh Jesus. Lovely. Oh Jesus. Oh Jesus. Kiss me. Oh God. Oh God. Oh God. Oh that was grand. Grand. Oh, look at you all wet, sweat running down your poor back. Don't get cold, sweetness, precious duck, don't get chilly."

Later she told me the twins had gone to their sister's in Lough Foyle. They'll all get their heads blown off one day, said Mrs McDevitt, serve them right, wouldn't it, my lovely chicken pie?

Into the foreman's attitude to me crept the shadow of doubt. It grew. I could see it feeding inside him. Perhaps his wife had removed her affections. Perhaps in bed with her at night the big man's nostrils were tinged with foreign scent. One night creeping out from my room to relieve myself, I walked straight into him as he stood outside my room, brooding like a hayrick.

"How are you, dear boy?"

"I'm – I'm fine, sir."

"You look tired."

"I just hope they don't think I'm coming up here too often."

"If they do, we'll just move you to another garrison, don't worry."

"I think the foreman suspects."

"The husband."

"Yes. He gives me these looks."

"Yes, but you would, wouldn't you, if you were he?"

Major Elmes went to the little hatch and came back with two more beers and cigarettes for me. Outside in the jeep sat brawny Oates, man and vehicle solid and reassuring.

I asked, "Have you considered my request?"

Major Elmes dragged on his tobacco, a process that created a tiny declivity in each rosy cheek.

"It's being processed. These things take time. Leave it to me to work in your best interests. The army is a wonderfully complicated place."

"I want to fight, sir."

"Of course, of course."

"Before the war is over."

"Yes, yes. Now, consider me standing, the king, God bless him."

"The king."

"Ah, it's not like the bitter in Warwickshire, but it's not that bad when all is said and done. I like your twins."

75

"You like them?"

"Yes, silent, committed types. Non-drinkers. Regular fanatics."

"Sir?"

"For their wretched cause, you know. It's interesting that the crates that fell on you – last year it must be now – it's interesting they never reappeared."

"Maybe they're afraid of me seeing them again since I know what's in them."

"I don't think so. If they were afraid of you to that extent you would not still be living in their midst. No, I doubt it."

"They'd have – got rid of me?"

"No, no, not in that way," chortled the major from the hatch. "I think they'd have found a reason for you to change your abode. No, what I mean is, I think it shows discipline that those crates never reappeared. Discipline marks out the professional from the amateur. Your twins could well be far more important than we thought."

"They're out a lot. Sometimes they don't come to bed at all."

"Mention where they've been?"

"Not to me."

"I shouldn't imagine. But in conversation to one another?"

"I heard Pigeon Top the other day."

Elmes nodded. "Good, good. Now, a bird never flew on one wing, Church."

The little pub beyond the Black Mountain, its wood-panelled walls, its cosy isolation, became as familiar to me as the away port to the captain of a tramp steamer. As did my friend, Major Elmes, the sort of gentleman I had been brought up to expect an Englishman to be. The life pattern of the twins, of their extended family, of the men they played cards with and with whom they went to fight their cocks, or so they said, this great, interlocking web of people's names, their relationships and the places they lived in, visited, drank in, bought their victuals, went to pray, or to watch a horse run, became part of me and me of it, except that I alone was painting its mirror image for Major Elmes.

A man appeared one Saturday. Small, dark and wiry, he had the McDevitt intensity. He ate his tea, sitting opposite me and never dropped me from his sights. Next evening Mrs McDevitt served me fish.

"The best food you could eat," she soothed. "Good for your teeth and the oils in your lovely skin."

The twins would be absent until the wee hours, a certainty attested by Mrs McDevitt's croonings and cluckings and by the fact that although it was not yet six she was attired in only a satin robe.

76

"All the way from Lough Foyle," she purred, leaning over to serve me another portion. "Lovely fish come all the way from Lough Foyle."

"A long way to swim."

"Ach now he didn't swim, did he, scrumptious?" she said, and then, in the shorthand of our relationship, putting aside an asset that could be used later, added, "But I can't be telling you how he got here, can I now?"

His name was Devoy, I learned during the course of that energetic evening, married to a McDevitt sister living on the banks of Lough Foyle. Never comes without his fish, Devoy, and what a waste that is since none of my two men here will touch it. Isn't it grand I've got you, Chud? Isn't it grand I have someone to fry Devoy's fish for at last?

Major Elmes pricked his ears.

"Now there's a name. Be a good chap, describe the fellow again."

I did.

"That's very good work, Mr Church. You don't know how good."

"Who is he, sir?"

"A blackguard. Family are all smugglers, but this is a real bad 'un. Been inside here. And now this link to Omagh. You've done well, Mr Church. Drink up and have another."

"Thank you, sir."

I could see the major racing his fingers along the edge of the hatch as he waited for our halves of bitter to be served.

"This visit took place the weekend before last?"

"Last Saturday week."

The major held out a brace of cigarettes in a "V" like the sign Mr Churchill made.

"Look, this is important. If this blighter turns up again I want you to go to the barracks straight away and ask for Captain Johns. You know who I mean?"

Captain Johns, a staff officer, was known to me by sight.

"Just say to Captain Johns, 'The fish has arrived.'"

"The fish has arrived."

"That's it. 'The fish has arrived.' Just that, but straight away, you understand? Immediately. We've waited a long time to nail this 'un."

"You're going to . . . ?"

"Don't concern yourself with our procedures, Mr Church. You just go to Captain Johns. He'll know what you mean."

"What if he doesn't know who I am, sir?"

"He knows exactly who you are, Church," the major said, then smiled hastily. "After all, you're one of us now, aren't you?"

I seized my opportunity. "Does that mean you've got me in, sir?"

"Ah, I think we can say that we are now moving in the right direction."

"I need more than just the right direction."

"Do this and you're in."

"Is that a promise?"

"You have my word, Church."

My hand shuddered.

"'The fish has arrived.'"

"Exactly," the major said, and still in the animal kingdom added, "Bird never flew on one wing."

On the way home I spread out two fivers from my pocket where the major had put them, tightly rolled. I was almost in the army. How proud of me Rosa would be.

"Where do you go in Belfast, precious?" purred Mrs McDevitt.

"To Victoria Road," I said. "With my reports."

"And what sort of reports is they?"

"You know the sort. Buildings."

"As long as that's all, pet."

"Did the foreman ask you to ask me that?"

"Ach, look at you all upset over nothing."

"Did he? Did he?"

The woman began to cry and all the bulk went out of her. "Don't do anything foolish, Chud. I've told them you're a bonny lad and so it's both of us'll be in trouble if you're not."

The smell was what came first that Saturday evening. To a Monument man used to Oscar Shortcourse taking off his boxes from trawlers on Long Quay, it was immediate. Descending the stairs, dread infected me. From the room where meals were eaten I saw, out in the kitchen, the back of the head of a man talking to the foreman. They went out.

"Just the two of us tonight," prattled Mrs McDevitt, bringing in from the kitchen a teapot and fried liver. "You must be starved waiting, look at you, goodness. White as a shroud. There."

No-one now stood in the kitchen, even the stench of the fish had been purged for the moment by the pungent liver. But the fish had arrived.

Through the kitchen I floundered, deaf, to the bathroom and bolted the door. Beyond the frosted window stood three men, one tidy, two sizeable, the evening sun behind them. In awe of myself I crouched, separated from them by no more than inches, then they drifted off, their voices lingering even when they were no longer there. I flushed the bowl and rinsed my hands. Doused my face. In the mirror, splintered since the roof came in, someone had taken a meat cleaver to my face.

"Men's all the same," chattered Mrs McDevitt. "Soon as you put up their tay they're gone." She lifted the saucepan lid from my plate. "I was promised an egg and I thought I'd have it for you as a treat, like, when the others were off on their affairs. But neery an egg was there to be had when the army had done their buying. So I said to myself, you'll have to make it up to your wee lad some other way."

"You have fish."

"Ach, yes, and you liked it that much the last time, I haven't forgotten, lamb. Tomorrow with the grace of God we'll have it, ay."

"The fish has arrived."

"Ay." She looked at me and smiled and caught herself under her bosoms. "I know what you likes, precious heart."

A hank of liver impaled and bleeding on my fork, I left the house. It came to me that once before I had felt myself so impelled, controlled by a greater force, and that then life had also been at issue. Children were kicking a ball at the bottom of Abbey Street. It rebounded to my feet and I tapped it back. Ten minutes later as I made my way home one of the boys passed the ball in my direction, but I was blind to it.

"I don't know what's got into you tonight," said Mrs McDevitt. "I think you're sickening with something."

"I had to take some air," I said. "I walked along the river."

"Then you didn't walk very far," said the woman, removing my untouched supper. "I never came across the like." She reappeared, armed with her usual determination to seize any windfall. "What you need now is to go straight up to bed, chicken. I'll bring you up beef tea, you said once how you liked my beef tea, and then I have put away for just such a thing as this a little jelly of calves' foot, ay, you'll need that on your chest, poor wee duck, I know you will surely."

She was right, I was sick, but it was all in my heart. Consumed by my own worthlessness, I allowed myself to be taken upstairs and undressed. I had no other request of God Whose attention I suddenly wished to engage than to be transported home intact to Monument where I would, I swore, work as hard for my grandmother as I had for Major Elmes. I no longer wanted the army. I yearned for the sight of the old stagers in their seasoned bowlers, for the comfort of my grandmother's wisdom and for a chance to begin my life over.

"No," I said, as Mrs McDevitt eased her warm flesh in beside mine. "They'll be back."

"They'll not be back, chicken pie."

"I – I can't. I'm sick."

"Ay, an' I'm going to cure you."

79

She propped herself on one elbow so that her breasts slithered across my chest like infants just born. Dipping her finger beside the bed she brought it up with a shimmering cap of jelly which she began to work into me. Never further from desire, I nonetheless realised she was my only ally.

"Ah, will you look at his royal highness and him asleep in his own thatch."

I changed my prayer. Please God, they won't be caught. Let Devoy go home to Lough Foyle. Just let them escape. The woman heard the latchkey.

"Oh, Jesus – whist!"

She could move fast. I grabbed her arm and saw the alarm in her eyes, but she must have seen mine too.

"I never went out!" I hissed.

Had she taken it in? I heard her bedroom door close, then movement underneath.

"Hannah?"

The voice of the foreman. Where was the twin? Or Devoy?

"Oh, is that you back already, Patrick? I was just up here doing a bit of tidying thinking you was all gone for the evening. The kettle's not long boiled."

She went downstairs, her words spinning the web for her escape. I heard them move into the back room. I heard the foreman's voice, low and identical to how it had sounded two hours beforehand when he was one of three standing outside the bathroom, reassuring as the thrum from a hive. I felt relief gush within me. The strength of one man's prayer. Silence came next. You could hear the movement of the house itself. A slate.

"Dead?"

Mrs McDevitt's voice cut mercilessly. I began to dress, jelly in blotches on my shirt. Sitting on the bed, pulling on my shoes, my eye caught movement outside through a gap in the curtains. Below, heaving for breath and looking up at me was the twin.

"Anything wrong?" I asked, coming downstairs.

Mrs McDevitt was sobbing in a chair beside the fireplace as the foreman stood over her and the twin, a pistol in his hand, was holding the centre of the room, wild and dazed like a man lost in a storm.

"What . . . ?"

"Trapped!" the twin hissed at me. "They were waiting. And as decent a man as ever breathed is now with his maker."

It had never struck me that Major Elmes might have been wrong, that a person could at the same time be a bad 'un and as decent a man as ever breathed, depending on your perspective.

"A wife and four wee bairns," the twin said as air whistled from his nostrils. "What will they do now?"

Fear made me look him in the eye.

"You're brazen, you bastard!" he spat, lunging for my neck and shoving the cold snout of his gun into my cheek.

The foreman lurched over and, foam-flecked and trembling, said, "I don't trust you, never did. Coming and going. Al'ays there to see what's none of your business. You put them on Devoy, didn't you?"

"Tell us or I'll blow your damn head off," hissed the twin.

"You've all lost your minds!" cried Mrs McDevitt.

"Oh, this time no woman's apron will save you, boy," the twin crooned. "Who did you tell? When did you tell them?"

"I never left this house," I whimpered.

"Why don't we believe you? Why do we recognise a liar by the smell from his mouth?"

"Oh, Lord have mercy on us!"

"Ask her. I was here all evening."

"No, I won't ask her nothing. But why don't we ask the wee lads kicking their ball at the bottom of the barracks hill? Ay. That's who we'll ask."

The twin motioned his head to the foreman.

"I went for an egg!" I blurted. "Tell him, for Christ's sake! I went for an egg!"

But Mrs McDevitt was beyond telling. In a heap beside the fire she shuddered like a tent floored in a wind.

"Bring the wee lads up," the twin said. "You're a dead mon if you went into the barracks."

I could hear the foreman's footsteps on the hall's tiles. Mother Mary of God. Don't let him. How did you pray? So soon to have forgotten. What would Ma Church think? I began to cry.

"Ay. The traitor and the coward, two heads al'ays on the same coin," the twin said.

I heard the street door being opened. A tremendous explosion. The twin whirled. I pushed him in the chest and ran for the hall. Soldiers in battledress were jumping the foreman's body. I sank as a hot bar branded my neck. Went deaf. Two soldiers in a moving bridgehead scooped me up and rammed me ahead of them back out through the kitchen and down the steps. The silent sky. They caught me up one arm each and ran, dragging me like a corpse. Hefted me onto a revving jeep. Threw themselves on top of me. Evacuated.

I was in Belfast that night. And the next. And the night after, reunited with my belongings, I was in England, *en route* for an armoured engineer squadron, which I would enter as a second lieutenant. It all happened so quickly there was no time for reflection. But that's war, everyone said, you don't think, just do the job at hand, follow your orders. End of story.

One last piece of business remains from these years. Jack. His letters to Rosa which I have already mentioned and which were discovered among Paddy Bensey's papers after the bookie's death in 1983 give a unique insight into Jack at that time and show just how much Delaware had affected him. He wrote in a tiny hand like a man confined to postage stamps, or a spy. Look at them: the words run into one another and when he comes to the end of a page he doesn't turn it over like you or I would, he continues in the vertical margin and when this has been rendered impenetrable, takes himself to the top of the page where he chokes every last breath of space. Sometimes it's nearly too much for me to break open these concrete blocks of correspondence.

Early on, Jack described his father's reaction to events at Delaware. General Santry vaguely understood himself to have, if not a place in history, then at least a position in it. Insulated from most of life's atrocities, very few matters of common concern could pierce the general's obduration. The Santrys had procedures for most inconveniences. In the countryside around Main you encountered men and women with blond heads and a familiar look about them and in Sibrille there was an entire clan of Santrys who had changed their religion, poor people on a ten-acre farm, but they were Santrys nonetheless, Jack assured Rosa. Twenty-five years before the general's father, Captain Santry, had built a cottage outside the walls for a buxom hussy that the young general-to-be had made big as an owl, then, when his son had nipped off to Flanders, given her four more himself in quick succession. It was to precedents of this kind that the general cast his mind in all emergencies, including the one that had on a Sunday in June 1938 broken about his woolly ears.

He had been on his fourth whiskey when the superintendent of the guards had arrived and explained the events that had occurred in mountain foothills owned by Main. The general poured the policeman a drink, expressed sympathy, offered a donation of money, and dropped it in along the way that Jack had returned to England the night before. Apologising for his intrusion, the superintendent drank up and returned to Monument. The general summoned Jack.

Jack, devastated by what had happened, had prepared himself as best he could, knowing that candour and a direct approach were the surest means of success with his father, a man whose entire life had been

82

characterised by bluntness and for whom concepts such as diplomacy reeked of compromise.

"Shame on you, sir!" the general bellowed. "Shame!"

Jack tried to explain.

"Balderdash!" cried the general. "Love her, but leave her, eh, sir?"

"I can't leave her, sir," Jack blurted.

With the evening sun behind him, the way he'd sat sending slackers to the labour squads after Loos, the old man twitched.

"Ye'll bloody well leave her, sir, ye hear? Ye'll bloody well leave her or I'll horsewhip ye m'self into those bluebottles in Monument! They want yer neck, sir, y'understand? Yer bloody neck!"

Jack could not contain his tears. The trauma of the day had reduced him down to essential marrow and now all his fondness and fright came tumbling out, one on the other, in an unstoppable tide of love and anguish. Disgusted, the general strode from the room leaving his son and heir abject. That same night Jack was smuggled out of Main and in case the usual mailboats were being watched, driven two hundred miles north and across the border, and sent via the ferry at Larne to a Santry in the Scottish Lowlands whose village's postmark is on the early letters to Rosa.

Jack found himself free on the page in matters in which he would have normally been reserved, or mute. It didn't do for Santrys with great creeds of responsibility awaiting – to land, to inferiors and inevitably, to war – to go about displaying inner sensations; one had learned at the knee (usually the knee of a servant) that the best feelings were those that did not exist. Nonetheless love came like a warm, rolling wave to Jack on the page. When he got somewhat over Delaware – it took many months and letters to do so – Jack described for Rosa exactly how their life would unfold together in Main. He dealt with tradition as if it were a passing difficulty and not something on which a dynasty was deemed to depend. He confronted their differing religions and, whilst he thought it unnecessary that he should change, he professed himself content that their children be brought up Catholics. There was a house in the grounds at Main where they would live whilst the general was still game. In its upstairs room, which overlooked the mountains, their papist children would be conceived.

From the Scottish Lowlands, from Eton, from Sandhurst, from a camp near – – – in – and finally, from the end of 1943, from outside – –, Jack wrote his censored letters to Rosa. Writing on the campaign table his great-grandfather had used in the Crimea, by the light of a gas burner, with the bleating of sheep and the cough of foxes drifting in from nameless moors, Jack pledged his love. But the spoil from this love, the release of forbidden feelings, overspilled to other areas of Jack's soul. These feelings more than any other were proscribed for a Santry. Jack, softened by love, became afraid of death.

The mood of the regiment was one of eagerness to engage the Boche. Jack dreamt about the Boche. His tenacity, his wiliness. His accuracy as a sniper. Jack had listened to his father talking about the Great War and describing how all the stupidity had been on the side of the British. Even though the general seemed to embody the weakness he ascribed to others, Jack wondered how solidly the aspirations of the Empire were really based if the future of the battle was invested in men like himself. Read your history, the general had counselled, and Jack had done so. Death lay between the lines of history. Stupidity and death. Read Brooke, the old man had said late one night. Read Brooke on battle. Jack had.

And the worst friend and enemy is but Death.

Death kept Jack awake into the small hours, for it seemed to lie behind him – in his family, in Delaware – as well as ahead. As he was detonating paths of real mines or training beneath live artillery or experimenting with bombs rolled in drums from aircraft and bounced down the – – – –, it occurred to Jack that the dread he was experiencing had lain in the breasts of all his ancestors, but that he was the first to allow it light. The deliberate vagueness of a Santry, that feigned nonchalance, that extravagant courtesy to others at times when it was others who should have shown courtesy to you, Jack knew then that all these devices of behaviour were constructed so as to keep capped for ever the well of self-pity.

By allowing the flowering of his feelings for Rosa, Jack had uncorked his own cowardice. He wrote to her every other day, his fear hatching out like pox. He did not want to die, he told her, because he knew if he was killed in France he would go into eternity without her. He did not, did not want to die.

Jack's later letters were meaningless – and probably illegible – to the censors, who were looking for more technical stuff. His letters went unscathed to the convent in Leire whence, unread by Rosa, they were removed each month by Paddy Bensey. Bensey learned that the heir to Main loved his daughter more than duty. This must have at first surprised the bookie, who, like everyone else in Monument, thought of blind courage in war and a Santry as one and the same; but as each letter laid open ever more Jack's heart, Paddy Bensey swallowed his natural shock and began to concentrate on his opportunities.

Eight

MA CHURCH TOLD ME she had taken to having Uncle Mary lagged. The measure made sense on grounds of economy alone, she wrote. So she oversaw Olive wrapping the old man in a thick combination that Mr Gus had acquired from the master of a Portuguese merchant ship, one of the few that now sailed up the Lyle. Reminds me of a Stilton just coming right, wrote Ma Church.

Although I could not explain it, there was never a time during all the years I was away that I did not feel her proximity. I often spoke to her as I went to sleep at night, as if continuing a long-running conversation, or an argument. She wrote and told me how, all that winter, St Melb's took the brunt of the east wind coming off the river. The Studebaker now ran on coal, a nuisance that, but then she was still able to get around, even if discharging soot.

Some evenings when I read her letters, looking west across the Moray Firth to Easter Ross, I imagined I was in Monument looking up the Lyle towards the Deilt Mountains with the sun going down behind them. I was in the garden of St Melb's. If I listened hard I would at any moment hear her voice indoors, laying down the law for Mr Gus or Uncle Mary or cajoling a grandstand performance out of Mrs Finnerty for the following Sunday, when Bensey would be coming over for luncheon.

It had been a year since I had completed a twelve-week training course in Perth and arrived to join the Royal Engineers Armoured Training Battalion at Elgin in the battledress of a second lieutenant, cost to be refunded, on a pre-paid railway warrant. NCOs snapped off salutes when they encountered me, and in Elgin if intelligence officers like Major Elmes existed, then they did so out of sight. We studied how artillery fire could destroy reinforced concrete and wire and were taught the appropriate degree of aloofness to adopt towards civilians in France. Men returned from North Africa and Italy came and talked about 'Sniping – The Enemy and You', the use of the Ryde Night Illumination Diagram and how to operate the No. 38 Wireless Set. One night in early 1944 we sailed to the Orkneys and did a mock invasion, then lurched home down the North Sea in high spirits, laughing at the piece of cake that France would be.

I bunked beside a Lieutenant Sim from Bognor Regis, who told me that his father was clergyman to a parish east of Southampton, a widower who had lived his life in the service of others. I told Sim that my grandfather had seen action in his day and that I was heir to a military tradition. It was true in a way. Service to the Empire was common to Dr Church and me, even if I had discharged my duty by being a spy on my fellow Irishmen and my grandfather's greatest act of loyalty had been to purge the bowels of a lord-lieutenant.

In February we moved to Suffolk, where four squadrons of Armoured Engineers were billeted in the grooms' quarters of a manor house two miles from Otley. Sleeping with Sim, three other subalterns and two hunters, I was reminded by the rich smell of leather of the outbuildings in Main. The welfare of the hunters was the sole concern of the daughter of the manor house, or at least it had so appeared until one night I awoke and became aware that she was in bed with Sim. She did the round of all the subalterns, confessing to me when it came to my turn that anything at all to do with horses made her passionate.

Captain Ivory did not like me, I knew. Home for Captain Ivory was a Londonderry estate of three thousand acres, where the attitude to Irish Catholics was of long standing. Tall, carrot-haired, with a bulging forehead and springing walk that everyone said made him a sniper's dream, Captain Ivory remarked in front of my troop sergeant, a man named Quelch from Durham, that he doubted I could read a map, or understand the routine duties of my troop, or was suited in any sense to lead men into battle. Glaring at me from small, angry eyes across the spiked wing-tips of his carrot-hued, bat-shaped moustache, I often heard the captain inferring that intelligence had never been the strong suit of the Irish.

A letter came from Aunt Margaret, its tone, like its author, distant and uncomfortable. Mrs Church, as she referred to her, was too distraught and had asked her to discharge this duty. It was not easy for Mrs Church who now had only Our Lord Jesus Christ for a companion. It had been Olive who found her, curled up like a baby, still warm, smiling. Her little heart. Faithful Tadpole was an angel now, RIP.

Seized with the great dismay of distance, excluded, I read on.

Mrs Church had been greatly assisted by Tadpole's dreams in reaching business decisions so this blow was extra hard, the letter continued, however she had requested that certain information be conveyed.

Faithful Tadpole kept seeing me in uniform, fighting a battle beside the sea. I could move. Dead men were everywhere around. A man nearby was running up and down, turning bodies over, looking down at their faces. Faithful Tadpole did not know his name but his hair was fair, his eyes were blue. He got ever nearer, then nearer still. I shouted to him. The man smiled. And there the dream always ended. You are in our prayers, rest assured, yours faithfully, Margaret Church. P.S. She bequeathed you her musical chair. She said she wished you to have it. M.C.

Mid-March. Trees around the camp broke into leaf and swathes of daffodils made their appearance.

"It's good to be in England," I overheard Captain Ivory say.

The postmark on the letter was over a month old and no date was given for Tadpole's death, so she must have died well over a month before, most likely in early February, around the time we moved down from Scotland. I felt comforted by the description of her dream, although I could not say why. The feeling persisted, as if, apart from the musical chair, Faithful Tadpole had left me something of value.

They have taught us that one of the chief factors for success in battle is the human factor, Jack writes to Rosa from Scotland. They tell us that the British soldier is easy to lead, that once you have gained his confidence he will never fail you and that the final result can thus never be in doubt.

Oh to be so sure!

Jack noticed as he put his pen down that his hand was atremble. He crossed his legs on his bunk and cradled his hands behind his head. The three other officers with whom he shared the hut accommodation were on twenty-four-hour leave and had gone to Dundee. Jack lit his pipe.

He felt he had by and large gained the confidence of the men in his squadron. There were times when the blood flowed between them as if in common veins and when that occurred, when he and his men were moving as one, Jack felt elated. But there were also occasions when he faltered, crucial moments when he stopped to consider the meaning of the word, kill. In those moments Jack's doubt backwashed and he knew that his men deserved better.

Blow out, you bugles, over the rich Dead!

His troop sergeant was a brawny Cockney named Speechley, and his batman, Hadfield, came from Derbyshire. Jack felt Sergeant Speechley's eyes on the back of his neck during manoeuvres and at odd times, such as outside the officer's dormitory hut as the shadows gathered.

"Off to your Uncle Ned, then, sir?"

"Good night, Speechley."

Sometimes it needed all the courage Jack could summon to look Speechley firmly in the eye and to give the order necessary, which he knew the NCO had anticipated beforehand.

A discreet knock came at the far end of the hut and Hadfield appeared with a mug of cocoa.

"Thank you, Hadfield."

"Will you be needing anything else, sir?"

"No, that's splendid. Good night."

"Good night, sir."

Jack swung his legs out and sat on the side of his bunk to sip from the steaming mug. In his letters to Rosa he wondered if the officers with whom he had an easy but not a comradely affiliation thought as much as he did about what awaited them on the coast of France, not just the wire and mines and ramps and other German fortifications, but the fields of fire they would have to pass through, that many would never pass through. Jack picked up his pen again. He tried to concentrate on his doubt, as if by applying to it techniques learned at Sandhurst he might come up with an engineering solution to what he recognised was a problem of spirituality. In an effort to harden his soul he had tried to forget Rosa, but that made him recall with obsession. The fact that she had turned her back not only on him but on life and that none of his now tens of letters had been replied to, tortured him through the lengthening days and silent, Scottish nights. But get her out of his mind he could not.

> *I had rest*
> *Unhoped this side of Heaven, beneath your breast.*

Jack realised now, he told Rosa, that there once had been another time when in the face of a challenge he had felt nothing but doubt and trepidation, when he had feared that he would let the side down, would fail to do his part. In the early days of Delaware, he confessed, Rosa's beauty had terrified him. Her poise contained none of the studied manners he was used to among women of his own class. She spoke like the Irish, without attempting to round words up and down or borrowing lazy Anglo-Irish tricks with consonants. These differences made Jack unsure of her. Then Chud Conduit had come out to Main, wrote Jack. He had felt a new courage. Chud had been an agent of sorts, odd that, like one of those chemical formulae one is given to learn. If only a similar chemistry could be found for the days ahead.

A week later, the last in March, as Jack put aside a soup plate after mulligatawny and was listening to a discussion as to the battle-worthiness of Americans, Speechley came in and saluted.

"Begging your pardon, sir."

"Yes, Speechley, what is it?"

"CO would like a word, sir. Asked me to convey the message."

The command hut built of split fir beams was twenty paces distant.

"Ah, Santry," said the colonel, a rather tired man with silvering hair who had seen the tail-end of action in 1918.

"At ease, Sergeant," he said to Speechley, who had remained in the background. The colonel looked at Jack. "You in good, ready shape?"

"Ripping, sir."

"Very good. Just had a telegram up from Suffolk. From the CO of one of those got-up armour regiments, don't you know."

Jack felt Speechley's eyes on his neck.

"Seems one of their squadron commanders was injured a few days ago. Leaves them in a bit of a hole. Think you could manage to sort them out?"

"Without a doubt, sir."

"Very good. Be sorry to miss you here, had looked forward to our bashing Gerry together. Ah well. Take Speechley. There's a train in the morning. An adjutant will telegraph them you're on your way. Otley's the place. Know it well. Any questions?"

"No, sir. Thank you, sir."

"Very good, Santry. And good luck. Dismissed."

Racing beneath sparkling, vernal canopies, in the back of a jeep with Captain Ivory and followed by eight sappers in a pair of trucks driven, one by Sergeant Quelch, the other by a lance corporal named German, I tried to imagine military action in an unknown land; but French beaches, let alone the Boche, despite months of briefings and hectic manoeuvres, eluded me. Battle had no part in this hopeful countryside, it lay in the realm of books. I glanced at Ivory. The captain's moustache had been flattened by the wind, the wings of the bat clung to his cherry-red cheeks.

We trundled off the road and down a dirt track for a mile, arriving in the yard of a sawmill where shrieking timber was being fed to a saw the size of the big wheel on a locomotive. From the dust swam a bare-chested man, tipping begrimed fingers to his head.

"Carry on, Church," Ivory yelled.

The output of the mill had been requisitioned for making fascines, bound bundles of poles carried by tanks and dropped into enemy ditches, which could then be crossed. I nodded to Sergeant Quelch and the sappers began loading mostly even-sized posts and stacking them in piles. Sunlight shone through the dust in bright channels and made the faces of the sappers and the bare arms and backs of the woodmen glisten. The sappers stooped two to a post and tossed them upward to another pair in the truck. The woodmen stooped six to a tree and hefted it in one movement onto the metal saw table. Along a steel gully they guided the tree to the teeth and the air was replenished with a fresh spigot of yellow shreds.

From the corner of my eye I saw Ivory strolling about, hands behind his back, now venturing the toe of his polished boot into a mound of orange-coloured, redolent wood chippings as if to inspect them, now tilting back his head and savouring the air as if this was an arboretum on his estate. I wondered if this was what it would be like in battle, me trying to lead my men, Ivory hovering around the fringes waiting for an excuse to criticise. Now he was peering into a doorless shed, but whipped around suddenly, catching my stare and then cocking his head to one side in an attitude of disdainful interrogation.

Verity and Hames, the sappers nearest to me, were stooping, catching and pitching, working their way swiftly through the pile so that now they were almost finished. The screaming saw removed one entire dimension from the setting, so what remained appeared in mute tableau. My men. I felt pride. We would fight shoulder to shoulder up the beachheads, whatever they turned out to be, smoothing the way. It would be different, over there. Quelch produced a docket book and pointed to where I should sign.

"Six 'undred and eighty-seven, sir!" he bellowed into my ear. "Left firteen aside as unsuitable! Sir!"

I nodded, amended the docket to the new number, wrote my name and was looking up again when I saw Captain Ivory. He had ambled across towards the devouring saw, a vacant smile on his face like someone come alone to a garden party. He halted, acknowledged the team of workmen, then turned his back to them and stood there in a penumbra of sawdust and uproar as if to prove that an officer trained for war could certainly adapt to these conditions.

I knew what was going to happen a full five seconds before it did. (Sim said later that shock affects you like that, that your mind shivers so violently that it resets, as it were, so that when you look back you *think* you saw what happened in advance.) Nonetheless, as a blot like a doodle-bug appeared in the halo around Ivory's head, I saw the outcome. A pioneering wasp it was, strayed into this great cosmos of debris and now I watched in fascination as it made to land on Captain Ivory's moustache. I shouted, but even if Ivory could have heard me he would not have understood since his full attention was fixed on conveying to me the difference between our ranks and status. I stared. The corner of Captain

Ivory's mouth began an upward spike of condescension. I opened my mouth again, but this time no sound came. Captain Ivory frowned. The wasp settled. Captain Ivory's eyes snapped into his nose and he flapped with one gloved hand at the intruder. This drove the wasp deeper into the sculpture of hair. Ivory stepped back, swatting at his face. His heels caught the edge of a spar. Flailing, Ivory fell backwards, exactly onto the blade as I had known he would. Beneath a bright red fountain he lurched out again minus everything below his left armpit, and fell to his knees, eyes fixed on my face.

It was a harsh reminder of the sudden tragedy that would be encountered in battle, said our colonel, an honest man from Lincolnshire named Wildgoose. No warning, Gerry always there to pounce on your slightest mistake, no point in mooning, you had a job to do, you carried on. The system was there to look after the chap that had bought it, damn shame, said Colonel Wildgoose, but damn shame that Gerry has brought us into this in the first place.

After we got back to Otley and Captain Ivory, between life and death, had been dispatched to hospital in Cambridge, I was ordered to send my men back to the sawmill to look for the arm. But by then the chippings had been removed as bedding for ponies. It would not have done, we all agreed, for the army to turn up at some little farm where the apple blossom was coming out and to go rummaging in stable droppings for an officer's arm. We were put under the temporary command of an officer from a neighbouring regiment whilst a replacement was found.

"Wonder who our new 'and will be, sir," grinned Sapper Verity at six o'clock in the morning, slogging home from night manoeuvres outside Bury St Edmunds. We had been acting as German patrols in a war game as other squadrons, using charts that showed the hourly progress of the moon, had tried to cross their tanks over open countryside. At the manor house, Sim caught me on my way to breakfast.

"You're to go over sharpish to the colonel," he said.

An officer was sitting, his back to me, in discussion with Colonel Wildgoose.

"You wanted to see me, Colonel?" I asked, saluting.

The new officer turned.

"Oh, hello Chud," Jack said.

Jack had not changed, or rather, if he had it had been in step with my expectations. Frail, with a little blond moustache, distant, of startled expression, if I had not known Jack I might have thought he was not glad to see me. Perhaps he was just circling me with caution, or perhaps he now felt guilty. I expect I embarrassed him, for I knew all there was to know about him, down to the mole in the small of his back and the shape of his circumcision. Whatever, he put me at arms' length for the first weeks and kept me there, the technique coming naturally to his class.

I could see two people in Jack: a somewhat awkward officer who worried more than most about the war, whose lack of dash was made up by his concern for his men in small things; and Jack from Delaware in an army uniform, looking as if he needed fattening. I can imagine how he saw me. Still lean but now dark-jowled from daily shaving, I was often taken for thirty-five although I was only twenty-one. I wanted, suddenly, to discuss the past, to talk about the day that had shaped our lives and was continuing to do so. I tried to approach Jack, but he stopped me dead. He managed to see that we would never be alone together and declined my suggestions of us taking a drink. Once or twice I thought I caught him looking at me, but if ever I made to open up the moment he would turn his attention elsewhere.

I began to think of Rosa almost immediately after Jack's appearance. It was as if she had jumped out from hiding, for now, in the first weeks in April when we struck camp in Otley and took ourselves and our truly overwhelming equipment down to a village near Petersfield, not far from Portsmouth, I could see her everywhere and think of no-one else. I once asked Jack if he knew anything about her circumstances, or had contacted her, but Jack answered curtly that Rosa was still in Leire and that, as far as he was concerned, there was no more to be said about the matter. I guessed, of course, that his attitude to me was all to do with Delaware and that time was needed for Jack to come to terms with me again.

I saw Rosa in the sky and in the countryside and in the armour plating of Churchill tanks. On the eve of what everyone said would be Man's greatest battle, my mind was filled with the image of a beautiful girl, now a nun, and nothing else. I began to write her letters. She would not be allowed them, I felt sure, but neither could I send them to her house in White City, for Bensey would certainly be alerted. I decided to write, nonetheless, and at some unspecified, future time, during leave, perhaps, to get them to her by means other than the post. Rosa would understand, I knew, and thus I wrote to her every day but kept each letter in its envelope, dated and sealed, which is how I found them forty-five years later.

April 2nd, 1944. Dear Rosa, I trust this finds you well. I am now in the British army, training to be one of the first men into France.

I have spent the last six months with the equipment we will use for the invasion. There's so much of it, you'll laugh. The big Churchill tank, for example, unmodified, weighs 41 tons, the size of a cottage – but with a swivel turret instead of a chimney!! It's modified to do different tasks on the beaches of France and is known as an AVRE which stands for Assault Vehicle Royal Engineers. I want so much to see you again. Will I ever be able to? Your old friend, Chud (Conduit) Church. P.S. I have changed my name to Church.

I wanted to build an image for her, of me going into battle, so that when she thought of me she could place me there, the same way I knew she placed Jack in Main.

April 5th. Dear Rosa, Things are hotting up here for France and most days we have map-reading sessions that send everyone to sleep. We keep hearing about the French beaches, but all I can ever imagine is the sea near you in Leire. These beaches – beginning a hundred yards' seaward of high-water mark are rows of outward jutting concrete ramps surmounted by mines. Where these ramps are not concrete they are made from twelve-foot logs, eight inches in diameter, lashed together and set in the shore facing the sea. Behind each beach are sand cliffs and dunes, up some of which you can drive a tank but not a vehicle with wheels. The Boche have put down anti-tank ditches and traps with steel teeth and concrete walls to stop us. Or so they think!!! I think of you constantly. Your loving friend. Chud (Church).

She was my sudden, overwhelming need. I knew she would still find me vital, that the years would not matter, that I could bring new colours into her day, make her smile, draw a certain look into her eyes. I was still the one who would be the cause of her untying her hair and shaking it out behind her, or of pinching out the fat of her tongue between her teeth as if suppressing the urge to laugh at me and Jack.

April 10th. Dearest Rosa, I think of you every moment as the time for the invasion approaches. Our training is as good as over – now we are concentrating on having our equipment in tiptop shape. Our AVREs, for example. Have I mentioned AVREs? Instead of guns, AVREs have petards, fat spigot mortars to hurl killing explosive charges at point-blank range into German bunkers. Bang! Carpet-laying AVREs lay log carpet between their tracks for infantry and wheeled vehicles. AVREs with timber fascines lay

93

their bundles into gaping ditches. AVREs with bridges carry steel platforms for placing over dikes and gullies. A giant revolving drum with chains protrudes in front of some AVREs and the chains flail the ground for mines as the tank proceeds in the wake of great explosions. Baroom! We call these Crabs. Your loving friend. Chud.

What would Rosa now see in Jack, I tried to imagine? Jack was not just himself but all he represented. Rosa loved Main and would have been mad not to. She loved the role that would come with Main. And where Jack was vulnerable she was strong and strong women are drawn to vulnerable men. I knew she would never have me. She would conclude that the season for infatuation is a short one and she would choose Jack. Her father would always damn me and I knew how much Rosa valued her father. All her uncalculating excitement must have come from her mother. Her mother must have been a rare beauty, I thought, like my own.

April 19th. Dear Rosa, You can hardly imagine the equipment each AVRE will be required to carry onto French soil. It's ridiculous! Not just shells and additional small explosives such as petards and grenades as well as the standard pieces of essential spares needed for a Churchill, that is, spare bogey wheels for the tracks, spare track plates, tieplates and pins, plus the tools necessary to fit them. In addition, since our job, being first in, will be to clear paths and to make beachhead gaps for the infantry, those gaps and paths will need to be marked. With signs such as, "Verges cleared to 10 ft!" By pennants with different colours for each troop and each beach, so that everyone will know who's who, and with red flags to warn if a building is about to be demolished (for the plans envisage there will be many), and with windsocks to allow the gunners at sea to fine-tune their artillery as they pound the Boche inland. Do you ever think of me, or about Delaware? I do, every day, at least a hundred times. I am, by the way, a 2nd Lt, which is an officer. Your old friend, Lt Chud Church. (Chud Conduit, that was.)

I was so proud of what I was doing that I could not imagine her being less than infected by my purpose.

May 1st. Dearest Rosa, Is it wet in Leire? It's rained here for a week, which makes the work we have to do all the more difficult. Since an AVRE with four men and its ammunition is already full, means have had to be found to store the assorted stoops, shackles, bulldog clips, blow plates, winches and cables, and thus welding teams directed by officers – like me! – are working shifts seven days a week to fit hooks, brackets and bolts to the hulls, sides, turrets and bellies of the big tanks. Do you know what a bulldozer is? We intend to land them in France, but they too need innumerable brackets, hooks, pegs, bolts, slings and cradles welded to their structures, though no-one envies the poor sods who are going to launch these dinosaurs from the moving platforms of landing craft into enemy shallows. It's you I'll be thinking of when we go in. Your loving friend, Chud.

I have met Chud Conduit, or Church as he is now known, writes Jack to Rosa. We are in the same regiment, in fact.

Jack's Otley letters ignore me at first, for he must have feared that by mentioning me he risked re-awakening Rosa's interest. Rather, Jack's attitude is one of perpetual complaint, which I now recognise as having me as its source. His sergeant, Speechley, has an offensive and insubordinate nature. This is evidenced in the way, off duty, he speaks to Jack in rhyming Cockney slang. Apples and Pears, Arry Stotle, Trouble and Strife. The way Speechley has of looking at Jack makes Jack doubt himself the more. Not that Hadfield who is diligent and loyal, or Corporal Fowles who picks his nose, or the sappers Tully, brothers, or Bruce or Rowe are not all fine chaps, doing their best in these thrown-together circumstances, ready to risk death for their country with a cheerful grin, but do any of them really understand the sheer magnitude of the task ahead? Have any of them read history? Or Brooke? Jack doubts it. He supposes that ignorance is a virtue in the face of such miserable odds, but as an engineer he can deal only with the known and his knowledge fills him with unease.

But a tone creeps into the letters which, like the season, is slowly warming. Jack can bring himself to tell Rosa he has seen me. He means, he is glad to have seen me. A spring enters his words. He laughs at Speechley, searching the Apple Pie for German planes. Sapper Rowe is discovered to sketch a good likeness and one of the Tully brothers, Jack can hardly tell them apart, is a genius with an engine. Sleep too comes peacefully and without torment. Jack tells Rosa he dreamt he rode a white horse through clouds, ate jelly with the king of England and put a match to Main.

> *And think, this heart, all evil shed away,*
> *A pulse in the eternal mind . . .*

All part of one creation, neither life nor death is important, Jack explains, only love, because love transcends both life and death, it beats eternally, as Brooke has, in fact, said.

Saw Chud Church cutting a bit of a dash, Jack reports in early May. Probably up to no good as usual. Put on some condition. Grown older somehow.

Yes, he was glad that I was there, as once he had been glad before.

We moved our AVREs and tanks the short distance to Portsmouth Harbour on special transporters. It rained most of the time, making the piers slick underfoot. Sapper Renshaw from Glasgow fell in the dock, upon which it was discovered he could not swim. We fished him out, then threw him back in again till he could manage. The huge harbour bristled with activity. Naval ratings worked on deck landing craft and infantry regiments lined up to carry on their bicycles. This exercise had been so long in the preparing and the waiting. We manoeuvred our AVREs off their transporters and down slips and reversed them through the squat, square bows of the landing craft, where they were covered at once by camouflage nets. The sea outside the harbour got up so bad it rocked the landing craft within. France for breakfast, Corporal German said. Then we were told that what had been on was off, because of the sodding weather, we were told, just when spirits had been at their height.

I found Sim, wet, sitting astern his craft, in tears. His father, the rector, was gravely ill as a week-old letter from the old man revealed, you could see death in the slant of his hand, in each tortuous scratch of ink, a father's final effort for his soldier son.

"If only I could be with him," Sim wept. "This cruel world."

The south of England had been transformed into a military pen and passes out of it were hard to come by.

"Captain Santry is going to Gosport to collect winches," I told Sim. "He'll take you to see your father."

"No, he won't," said Sim, already lost to grief.

An hour later I drove us, one wheel on the grass verge, past a long line of military vehicles heading for Portsmouth.

"Slow down," Jack said, "and that's an order."

"Have you heard from Rosa?"

Jack glanced to Sim in the back. "I plan to marry her, Chud." When he was stiff, Jack was very much a Santry.

"Have you asked her?"

"Yes. No. Can we leave it now?"

"What makes you think she'll want to marry you?"

"I have my reasons," Jack said.

"I suppose the general is overjoyed."

"The general isn't getting married, I am. Now slow down, damn it!" He put his pipe bowl into the cave of his hands and sucked it alight. "By the way, has anyone ever told you to mind your own business?"

"Paddy Bensey wants Main, that's what Bensey wants for Rosa. Main."

"Paddy Bensey is a dreadful person, but unfortunately he is the father of the woman I love."

"You should hear yourself."

Jack decided to take refuge in silent dignity.

"What would you do if she refused?"

Jack said, "I'll get another driver and dump you and your friend back in barracks, if you wish."

"Or if she decided to marry me?"

Jack turned to me.

"Is that a possibility?"

"Who knows? Perhaps it is."

"If that is your position, which of course clearly makes us rivals, then I think as a fellow officer you should declare it."

I could see Sim's pale, preoccupied face in the rearview mirror. "I just asked."

"You ask too much then," Jack snapped. "I've a good mind to order you to turn this vehicle around. I'm already breaking regulations on your behalf. Typical."

The sky was split between blue and black, the way it was sometimes over Monument.

"Has she written to you?"

Jack took a patient breath. "She's in a bloody convent."

"I've been writing to her."

"*You've* been writing to her?"

"Yes."

"Damn you, Chud, that's no way to treat a friendship."

"You haven't asked her to marry you, you've already said so."

"I'm very sorry I was ever posted to this bloody regiment," said Jack.

We came upon the rectory – desolate, rainswept – beside its church and trees, a knot on a wide plain. The house gates were chained. Sim immediately knew. He ran to the churchyard, weaving through its headstones, and fell on his knees before the fresh mound of earth and its flowers, faded, where in rain squalls he wept.

"You lived your life for others," he cried, his fingers making paste of the clay.

Jack and I stood back, our shared callowness suddenly a force between us.

"Your wife died when I was five. After that, apart from me you had no-one. The world was your family after that."

A woman would have known what to do. Rosa would have known.

"We picnicked here," Sim cried. "You loved the history of this place."

"How old was he, Simmy?" I asked.

"Eighty-seven."

"A good age."

"Had I been there I might have made it easier for him. This bastard army. This cruel world."

Rain ran down the back of Sim's neck.

"Lieutenant Sim?"

"Sir?"

"Take this, would you?" said Jack and handed Sim his topcoat.

In an inn where Sim was known, the one-eyed landlord opened up and sat us at a fire and brought us tea and whisky.

"When exactly do you think it's going to happen?" I asked.

"Next forty-eight hours or never, so they say," Jack replied.

Thunder outside made the landlord close his shutters. Sim matched us drink for drink, the steam rising from our tunics.

"I will die in France," stated Sim.

"But you will be buried here," said Jack with tact.

"In this churchyard."

"Beside your father."

"*With* him."

"Sorry, with."

"If they find me."

"If."

"If they find any of us," I said and went to the counter for whiskys. "Here's to the men who will find us."

"You know," said red-eyed Sim, smacking his lips, "although he's dead, he did have a life, albeit lonely and lived in the service of others."

"He lived eight-seven years, Simmy."

"We won't live half that. Quarter."

"Your father's the one who should be drinking to us."

"Yet, he did live his life for others," Jack said correctly.

"In that case," I said, "let us salute a man who lived his life for others."

In the heat of the fire and the womb-like embrace of the tiny inn the happy whisky slid down.

"Be so kind, bring the bottle," Sim said to the landlord.

"Mr Sim."

"He joins my mother whom I never had the pleasure," Sim said after time had elapsed.

"Nor I," said Jack.

"Oh dear," Sim laughed. "His sermons. He'd spend all week from Wednesday on them, every night. Then he'd try them out on me. Deuteronomy was his favourite. Do either of you know Deuteronomy?"

Jack, ever polite, searched.

Sim said, "The Fifth Book of Moses?"

Jack cleared his throat. "I'm certainly aware of it."

"Good for you, Jack," I said.

"'I command you this day to love the Lord your God and to serve him with all your heart and with all your soul,'" Sim said and burst into tears.

"More whisky, Simmy. It'll make you feel better."

Sim, in an unreachable place, cast for meaning in the hot coals and drank whisky.

Jack took a profoundly troubled breath. "Snipers are going to be our main threat," he said, thumbing lumps of shag into his pipe. "Read the reports from Italy. Read the dispatches from the Great War."

"At least you'll never feel it," I suggested.

"They infest whole areas. A German sniper can kill a man at quarter of a mile. They look for an officer."

"So there's no point in worrying, is there?"

"What a bloody stupid thing to say!"

"What's the point in worrying? They say it's like being run over by a bus."

Jack puffed with fury so that the landlord behind the bar was all but lost to vision. "A sniper as good as knows you. He's waiting for you to stretch your arms out of the turret, or to step from shadow into sunlight."

"You worry too much, Jack. Doesn't he, Simmy?"

"I shall love mine enemy," said Simmy, with a hint of truculence.

The landlord put another bottle on the table.

"D'you know," said Sim, seizing it and drinking from the neck, "d'you know what I'm going to do when I get to France?"

I blinked at him through Jack's pipe smoke. "No idea."

"Picnic," Sim said, all but over-toppling.

"I'll join you, Simmy. Remember our picnics, Jack?"

"That'll show them," Sim said.

"In Delaware?"

"Homemade mayonnaise," Sim said.

"I don't recall mayonnaise – do you, Jack?"

Jack puffed and his eyes locked unseeing on the fire's brightness. It was the first time in nearly five years that Jack and I had been alone, if the presence of Sim and the landlord was not counted.

I said, "D'you ever think about it?"

Jack started.

I said, "You know what I'm talking about."

His breath came ragged. "I'm sorry. Sincerely."

"I saw his face."

"You saw . . . ?"

"His face. I saw it."

"God. You mean . . . before?"

"Just before."

"Oh, God."

"God our Father in heaven," muttered Sim and sank unconscious into a warm hollow between the table and the fire.

The whisky seemed to clarify everything, including the old images.

"He knew what was happening. I've never been able to forget that."

Jack closed his eyes. "I'm very sorry."

"It doesn't really matter now, I suppose."

"You don't believe me."

"I do."

"You . . ." He looked at me. "You, you know, you . . ."

"I what?"

Jack cleared his throat. "However, one has to go forward."

"His face, Jack!"

"The past is the past. What matters now is what lies ahead."

A low groan rose from below the table. Jack poured himself a stiff one and threw it back in a single gulp.

"I have to know!" he gasped, crashing the glass down.

"Jack?"

"Fuck you, Chud! You know what!"

"Give me a hint."

Jack said, "The odds are one of us won't make it."

"Hah! What do you know about odds?"

Jack lurched over and caught my wrist. "Read history. Read Brooke."

"You're standing on Simmy."

"You're a shit. You never bothered to write to her until I arrived in Otley."

"Is that a crime?"

"It's true, then?"

"So what if it is?"

"It's an offence against our friendship."

"Rosa always said you were pompous. You've become a pompous old fart."

Jack sat back and ran his hands in claws through his hair. "I want to marry Rosa Bensey. Dare you or anyone stop me."

"Marry her, then."

"Not if I get killed in France, I can't."

"A mere detail."

"Please!"

"Look, Jack, I can get killed too."

"Y' prob'ly won't."

"I'll drink to that. Cheers."

"So I think you should now state what you want. Like a gentleman."

"I want to marry her too."

"Too?"

"I mean, I, too, want to marry her."

"For Christ's sake!" Jack stood up, took half a dozen involuntary steps backwards and careened off the mahogany bar counter. Sunlight shone through chinks in the shutters and lay on the floor like new knives. "I'm going back to Portsmouth before Wildgoose tumbles."

"Sit down."

"Fuck you."

"Jack . . ."

"What is it now, *old friend*?"

"Let's toss for her."

"Beg pardon?"

"Toss. Whoever wins. What could be fairer?"

"Can't be serious."

"Why not?"

Jack took a series of deep breaths and came back, ponderously. "What about her?"

"She's not here. We're here. We're sailing for occupied France."

"Hah."

Jack shook out a cigarette and the rest of the packet fell into the fire or onto Sim. Jack flared a match and scorched the length of his cigarette, then leant back. From the gloom the landlord's eyes shone like fireflies.

"Wouldn't work," Jack said.

"Why not?"

"Might work at a time when there wasn't so much uncertainty. Say we do as you suggest, settle it with a coin, and you win, then you buy one –"

"You mean, get shot?"

"Snipers," Jack said.

"At least she was mine until then."

"Where would that leave me?"

"Assuming you don't get shot as well."

"Then there's no problem."

"I think that's the best solution – for both of us to be downed."

Jack, fighting to concentrate, stated, "If you win her then you win her, full stop. She doesn't fall to me, I don't inherit her."

"Why not?"

"I don't want her by default!" Jack shrieked. "If she's yours, she's yours, live or die."

"Whoever wins her wins her."

"I dislike the term."

"It's the bet."

"If you win I promise you as a friend and an officer that you shall never hear from me again on the subject of Rosa Bensey, so help me God," Jack said.

"All right."

"And if you die in battle that I shall not approach Rosa, nor entertain any approach. If you win."

"I have no problem."

"I want you to agree likewise."

"I do."

"Then say it. As a friend and an officer."

"You win her, that's the end of it. Dead or alive. Me likewise."

"I think I should toss the coin," Jack said. "Since you made the suggestion."

"Bugger that."

Jack looked to Sim, now snoring, then turned round and saw the landlord as if for the first time.

"Would you be ever so kind . . ."

"I think there's someone at the door, sir."

"Door?"

"A military vehicle."

"Fuck the door, toss a coin."

"As you wish, sir."

I had the vague feeling that this was not the stake to win, that luck would be needed more in the coming days than here in a pub near Southampton. A fist was hammering for the door to be opened.

"Toss the fucking coin!"

The man flicked the coin up into the pipe smoke still curling in the rafters. The door crashed inwards.

"Tails," I said.

"Thank heavens I've found you, sir!" cried Sergeant Speechley.

Nine

ROSA LOOKED BACK ON Leire in that early summer of 1944 with almost tender fascination. In particular, she remembered Father Joseph, a mournful man who came alive only when he spoke of Christ's love for us. The blunt knobs of Father Joseph's cheekbones strove to be free of their restraining flesh, a metaphor for their owner's philosophy.

"Happy the man in his shroud, happy at last. Happy in the arms of his own true love, Jesus Christ, Our Lord."

On a sunny morning a taxi with a roof-mounted gas burner brought Father Joseph to Leire for the retreat. A mighty sea thrashed the cliffs, its spume rinsing the air and relegating the sun to a dim, orange presence in the distance. He ate dinner at one with Mother Crescentia in the guest parlour. TB had left suffering, or its memory, lurking in the watery porches of Father Joseph's eyes and in his broken-winded chest.

"You will need a sister to attend you, Father," smiled Mother Crescentia. "There is one girl. Difficult. She may learn from your example."

If you were a woman wanting to live with God, Leire had no equal as a setting for such an aspiration. Once the home of a Victorian lighthouse keeper, the convent clung to a table of cliff on whose three sides the Atlantic churned, or heaved, or deeply soughed, or in an offshore wind merely slapped the distant foundations. The lawns and gardens were not the usual rich beds of model convents but had been mercilessly scoured by wind and salt of all possibilities of issue. Inside, no corner or nook existed that had not over years been dusted and polished without remorse. To see parallels between the place and its inhabitants was unavoidable. As he set off around the promontory on a wheezing, after-dinner tour, the huddled faces that peered at Father Joseph with fallow curiosity would have seemed to him, were he not himself drained of such interest, of neither one gender nor another.

The majority of those who had chosen Leire as the last rendezvous on earth between woman and Maker belonged to a great middle age, women who would bring some vestiges of their arrested youth into the very winters of their existence. On those nights on which the sea was subdued, piteous sobbing pervaded Leire, but otherwise it was a providential haven for the lost, the bewildered, the timid and for those otherwise dislocated by life.

Where Father Joseph thought the cliff had ended a path appeared, leading further out and down to a shelf above the sea to which an iron seat had been bolted. Sitting to regain his breath, Father Joseph beheld the great swelling mass of green water, a symbol affirming or denying fertility, he could not decide which. In his youth he had been a hurler, running from deep within his own defence, his sandy hair bobbing, the *sliothar* stuck to the tip of his stick, to the excited roars of his parish. Now his hair had thinned and faded and where muscle had gleamed his bone shone in lengths. He closed his eyes and for a moment allowed himself to imagine the throat of the sea as the voice of a crowd, surging with excitement every time he made a run.

Stooping forward, Father Joseph beheld a speck amid the rocks far below him. His eyesight had declined so he had to narrow his streaming eyes to confirm his impression. A sister, yes. Steady as a black diver in the driving breath of the sea, every so often the wind rustled out her garments around her like pterodactyl wings.

Later, Mother Crescentia was followed into the parlour by a taller, younger woman.

"Father Joseph, this is Sister Rose Bensey of whom we spoke. She will attend you for the course of the retreat."

The name meant nothing to Father Joseph, who came from the friary in Drogheda, but he thought he recognised this young woman from the rocks, although he would never mention it, his whole life having been dedicated to the curtailment of impulses.

For five days, when to yearn for any more than for your coffin would have seemed profane, the sisters in Leire lived without speaking, cleansing their souls for the life to come. Rosa's role was to prepare Father Joseph's vestments and mass chalices in the tiny sacristy, to serve at his mass and to then return everything to its place. Father Joseph wheezed from any effort and the altar steps took great toll on his stamina. He slumped in genuflections, then dragged himself back up to drink from his chalice. When he turned to the congregation to expose the Host, Father Joseph's face was troubled and his hand shook. There were moments when Rosa wondered if he was going to pitch forward, scattering the blessed wafers on the ground and creating in the process a procedural crisis. When his heart and lungs settled back into step, Father Joseph carried the heavy chalice down to the waiting row of modestly bowed heads who one by one raised their closed-eyed faces and presented a range of tongues. Other than Father Joseph's tired voice, the only sounds in Leire for five days were those of the wind and sea and of the occasional pot banged in the kitchen, where Rosa was charged with preparing Father Joseph's meal.

Otherwise, when not praying for a happy death or preparing the soul for the aftermath of death or gathered in the assembly room to hear about some fresh benefits of death hitherto overlooked, Rosa went alone, as she had done all the years since she had come to Leire, and sat on the rock beside the never quiet sea.

In the course of this retreat she, like everyone, had been urged to think of death as the final escape and this was what Rosa now dwelt upon. She could not separate her misery from the character of the sea. Although she had come to hate the ocean that lived eternally in her ears, she was nonetheless drawn to it as if, like her wretched self, it was not something she could escape. Then, as without warning the mist lifted and bright sunshine transformed the sea from ink to blackbird's egg blue, Rosa understood what the sea had been all along inviting. To launch herself into its cold arms and be drawn down quickly and mercifully by the tent of her clothes. Rosa stood up. Father Joseph was right. She drew in her breath to jump. The sun went in, the ink returned. On the other hand this was the ultimate sin, Rosa thought, sitting down again. She would be buried – were her body found – in unconsecrated earth. Shame in death after shame in life. Her father. No, the message of the ugly sea was too ambiguous. Rosa needed a clearer sign before she exchanged this hell for the next, something had to show her the way and when it did then she would know.

On the final morning when the sea was flat, the wind having gone about, Father Joseph dropped dead at breakfast. Standing beside Mother Crescentia, he said the grace, then during the rumble of chairs he fell, cracking his chin against the mahogany table and breaking his neck, although perhaps he was dead from the outset. Rosa was in the kitchen. The first she knew was when a sister burst in, eyes bulging in her retreat-bound, balloon-like face, and pointing to the refectory.

"Sister?"

The sister flailed her short arms. Rosa ran out.

Each sister stood frozen at her place. Because he was a man, albeit one worn out and now dead, Father Joseph's gender guaranteed the little area of quarantine around him. He lay most uncomfortably, one leg twisted around an upturned chair, his head pitched over like an up-rooted red cabbage. Mother Crescentia stood to attention, defying anyone to move.

"We must get a doctor!" Rosa cried as thirty pairs of eyes disdained her.

Mother Crescentia was ashen, the refuge of silence preferable to the articulation of a decision.

"For God's sake!" Rosa said and strode from the room.

Having sponged several sisters' remains over the course of five years and been the one to come upon the oldest member of the order dead as mutton in a toilet cubicle, Rosa well knew death when she saw it. So, setting out for the post office five miles away to telephone to a doctor, she knew that since no doctor could help Father Joseph, something else had sent her on this journey. The scents were of gorse and of woodbine, of grazing cattle and of tar curling in the heat. Rosa came to the brink of a hill and free-wheeled down it shrieking, her habit swelling up around her. At a narrow bridge she got off and wandering into the verge which was soft with ferns and warm with shingle, kicked her shoes off. Red weals stood out on her feet. She lay. A bird of yellow breast landed on the stonework and cocked a look at her. Rosa dragged off her headdress and for the first time in years allowed sun at her scalp. Sunshine poured over her face as if to embalm it. Rosa unpinned her starched collar and undid the buttons of her habit and lifted it, black and heavy, over her head. Then the halter. Then the coarse fabric knickers. The sun filled her and over-flowed into the earth. Spread like a star, Rosa listened. The voices of the countryside were so layered you had to reach separately for each one: the nearby brook's music, birdsong, a grasshopper, the munching of beasts in meadow, the whistle of a man a mile off, the answer of his dog. Rosa suddenly realised she could no longer hear the sea.

"Thank you," she whispered to Father Joseph whose spirit, mixed with the perfume of the day, she knew attended nearby. "Thank you."

The same hackney that had so recently left off a man with a small suitcase in Leire could now, from outside the front gate, be seen to have its back seat laid out with reverence for the return trip to Monument. The sisters had straightened Father Joseph out as best they could and joined his hands around the black beads of his rosary, but they had been unable to correct the painful angle of his head and so, although most of Father Joseph lay along the seat, his head hung into the void of the footwell, where some of the sisters had placed a cushion between the once sandy head and the mat.

"He'll hardly notice the odd bump, Mother," said the driver, who had pocketed his pipe during the loading process.

"Ensure we are informed of the arrangements, mind," said Mother Crescentia.

A cluster of weeping sisters stood to one side of the hall door whilst the windows held presses of pale faces. Father Joseph was the lucky one; not only was he dead, but he was leaving Leire. The hackney pulled away and was lost in clouds of smoke from his roof-mounted gas bag.

Out of the gate and around the first bend a youth stood by the roadside, bag slung on his shoulder, sunlight reflecting from his short-cropped hair. The hackney pulled over.

"Are you going to Monument?"

The youth nodded.

"Will we give him a lift, Father?" asked the driver, glancing over his shoulder. "Whatever you say. Hop in, so."

Rosa remembered that trip for the unending chatter which the driver uncorked on her cloistered ears and for her first sight in over five years of a newspaper, the *Monument Gazette*. "Invasion of Normandy!" shouted the front-page headline as they breasted a hill and Rosa, tears in her eyes, saw the Lyle.

Ten

ONCE, A SHIP'S CAPTAIN, anxious to impress Ma Church, had taken me in his tub for a spin down the Lyle only to meet squalls at the bend and be forced home in lumpy water. I have never forgotten the sensation of utter luxury when, terrified and porraceous, I stepped back onto the granite quay in Monument. Now, looking out at the rolling armada of which my landing craft was just one fleck, I would have given anything to relive that homecoming. It seemed impossible that the sheer weight of so much steel could not subdue the English Channel, yet my craft might have been battling all on its own in a grey sea which every so often broke over us like dew.

We had begun to ship water through a loading door as soon as we cleared harbour. The crew bailed all they could, but we developed a list to starboard which refused to right. Pitching, we ploughed on and within an hour everyone, including the naval ratings was sick. I told Quelch to issue tablets.

Hoved to within clear sight of England, slap of water on the hull, fumes from other boats drifting across in smoky wedges, the tank stays creaked with each brace against the chop.

"We will all do our duty," Colonel Wildgoose had said when he had come aboard an hour before we left. "That is what the German can never devise a weapon to overcome. For over four years the free world has endured the most atrocious tyranny ever foisted upon mankind and now it is our duty to end it."

How proud of me my grandmother would be, I thought, and my grandfather, too, were he alive. Whatever the past, I was now an officer, leading his troop into the greatest battle ever known. These thoughts, not to mention seasickness, made death unimportant. Hames would be first off. His AVRE with fascines would tow ashore an ammunition sledge known as a Porpoise. Sergeant Quelch would be next in a Crab. That left myself with Sappers Verity and Renshaw in an AVRE carrying a bridge and lastly, Lance Corporal German, who would land a bulldozer. Our orders were to make a gap at the head of Queen Red beach and then to make the ditches and deep culverts behind the beachhead suitable for crossing by an army. The disclosure that we would land on Queen Red hardly came as a surprise since weeks had been spent in studying the defences on Queen Red and in swotting up from photos taken at wave level. It would have been like memorising the London to Crewe timetable only to learn that your destination was Bath, Sim had said. I had seen him a few moments before, standing at the gunnel of the craft under his command, his eyes towards France, or towards where France was said to be.

At twilight we began to sail in formation, south-east. The men were either huddled around hydra burners or retching over the side. I watched Verity vomit until he could no longer stand; Sergeant Quelch wrapped him in a blanket. My head split. As I broke open dry rations, a big seagull came to perch on the bridge. It, too, looked towards France, as Sim had, perhaps still was doing in the adjacent boat, although I could not see that far now. I found a length on the inner tank track and, pulling my sleeping bag up around me, imagined Rosa.

Jack's D-Day is recorded by him over five pages, headed 'SUMMARY OF LANDING AND BREACHING OPS BY CAPT SANTRY RE 4 TP 39 ARMD SON RE' and filed in the regimental archives in Chatham under '5 ASLT REGT RE – SUMMARY OF ACTIVITIES D–D + 4'. (See R-B:4 for copy.) Knowing Jack as I do, I can read between the lines here and there, and, based on my parallel experience a few boats to starboard, follow with some certainty his frame of mind during those hours.

As Jack's landing craft slopped around in the Channel darkness, men groaned in sleep. Sergeant Speechley in particular had been voluminously ill, but Jack had remained unaffected. Not that he had sailed much other than the odd time in Penzance at house parties, it was just that motion of this kind did not upset him. On the bridge beside the chief petty officer, he smoked his pipe and boned up on his French in an attempt to banish from his mind the doubts that hatched there.

Jack was part of something so large, both militarily and in the sense of his own, newly secure place in the plan of things, that he should have been able to see nothing other than his own beckoning future; but all he saw were the parts of himself that were lacking. He made his eyes lock on the phrases.

French at Eton had been a lot to do with classical texts, as far as Jack could remember, and had little in common with MoD suggestions of how to ask, for example, to be brought to meet the mayor of a town.

"Emmenez-moi tout de suite chez la mairie."

Every town in France it seemed, had a mayor, a rum arrangement. Jack put the pamphlet aside.

"I wonder what's going on out there," he asked, staring into the ungiving darkness.

"Our lads are out there, sir," said the chief petty officer, his hands never more than fondling the wheel. "Minesweepers. Running up and down in front of us, clearing the approaches. And our paratroopers have been dropped in France by now, securing our flanks."

"God bless them," Jack said, surprised he had said that.

"He'll bless us all, sir, don't you worry," said the other man, tilting lightly with the action of his boat.

"I know," Jack said. "I don't."

The chief petty officer glanced at him. "Plenty as was in Dunkirk might have doubted 'im then, but not for long. I mean, otherwise what's the point, I ask myself? You do your best, you fight for what you 'ave. He knows that, that's my motto."

"I'm to be married. Afterwards."

"Well, there you are, sir, see what I mean? There's a plan, isn't there? We're all part of 'is plan in the end of the day. Makes you laugh, really, when you look back and wonder what it was we was worrying about."

Jack strained to absorb the comfort of the cosy wheelhouse, the other man's simple peace, but the truth was that he believed in none of it. The nearer they inched to France the more he became prey to old fears.

"Not goin' to grab some kip while you can, sir?"

"Not really tired."

"You might need it tomorrow, sir. Or today as now is."

"I might catch an hour shortly. Thanks."

He would have liked to talk some more, but feared appearing irresolute to the chief petty officer, and so he had to make do with the other man's silent presence and the knock-knocking of the Channel against the hull beneath them.

Overtaken by events as our pub wager had been, Jack nonetheless now wondered what had made him insist on the absolute terms which he had made a central part of the bet. As he had tried to insist, if he got killed in a few hours' time no-one would be happy. He would be dead, I would be debarred from Rosa. Jack was overcome with regret. Poised between freedom and tyranny, he realised that in his pettiness lay the root to his own self-doubt and weakness, for if he could not be magnanimous to others he could never achieve the big gesture needed to redeem himself. Conversely he wondered, had he shown me the generosity he lacked, whether that might now staunch his creeping funk. Too late.

One of the ratings brought up to the wheelhouse messages decoded from morse. The chief petty officer checked charts and measured his position with the aid of a shrouded light. It was two a.m. Jack nodded off once or twice, but each time jumped awake when he dreamt of me being the first man to die in Normandy.

Quelch woke me. The pounding in my dream had been rain drubbing the battlements on Cattleyard and all the roofs beneath it down to Long Quay.

"O-five-'undred, sir."

Very dim under the tank but squinting bright when I crawled out. Everyone looked miserable.

"They should eat."

"Sir."

I took a look either side of the boat. I still had that sense of our being on our own, even though the early sun made steel on the starboard side glint to infinity. Salty. I ate my last biscuit as un-ship-like, distant shapes began forming. I ordered Quelch to begin the final check of vehicles.

The target known to Jack from a hundred briefings as Burlington Bertie's villa was straight-away familiar. It had a steep and elongated roof whose eaves came to within twelve feet of the ground on the west side. Blackened Tudor-type beams defined the walls. A nest of vipers, rest assured, the briefing officer had said of Burlington Bertie's villa.

Jack strapped on his metal helmet and gave Speechley the order to have the vehicles' restraining shackles readied for casting off. He had shaken hands with the chief petty officer before he left the bridge. Comfort in the man's big, warm hand. In his briny smell. Jack wanted to say something about how they would meet later, whenever, in England. Something about God that needed to be further discussed. He didn't even know the man's name. Speechley was calling something. The landing-craft number would do to trace the sailor.

"We've a loose bogey on 1A, sir."

"Then you'd better see to it, Speechley."

Speechley's expression, always searching Jack's face for a chink of weakness. "Sapper's doing that already, sir."

"That's Burlington Bertie's villa, isn't it?" Jack said.

"Coming in on it now, sir."

"Let's have those shackles off, Speechley."

Rockets whistled overhead followed by the boom from the ships' guns that had discharged them. Steel now thickened the air. I ordered tanks started. A house stood out, even in the tar-like smoke, on the coastline less than half a mile away. Tide was running fast east to west, bringing

Sim's boat rapidly nearer and causing the wheelman on ours to lurch to starboard.

I gave the order to mount tanks. At my own turret, watching the shore sliding sideways now at an alarming rate, I heard an explosion. A great spout of water. Then again. Naval rockets were colliding overhead in sunbursts and plunging down. Sparks flew from the bridge of Sim's boat as if from a forge. Smoke. A black plume of ignited diesel. I heard the roar as Sim's craft went full astern. I felt us check. The water ten feet aft blossomed with fresh naval debris.

"Whose side is the bloody navy on?" cried Hames.

The house that had moments before been at the top of the hour now lay at a quarter past. Even rougher in here, the sea, another mystery. I saw Quelch out of his turret shouting to the bridge, but his words were lost in the screams of rockets. Sim's boat, invalided and rudderless, was being washed in broadside between us and the beach and we were on course to ram her. Our stern swung and we clipped past Sim's dead boat with our ramp dropping.

As we touched down we shook, hit. Two planes with British markings came low out of the dust cloud on the French coast. I waved. They swooped and dropped bombs, one just outside our port bow which lifted us up and flicked us west along the seashore. I could feel us going over, then we hit hard. I watched as a tank track swam up and smacked my helmet. Sprawled on my back, blood from my nose ran into my throat. Catching at a wet, steel handle of something solid I pulled myself to my feet and spat out tooth splinters. Left hand numb. Visibility confined to a tiny theatre of grey beach framed either side by groynes and confirming earlier notions of isolation. The bomb's impact had sent Hames's AVRE skew-ways at the top of the ramp, where it was wedged by its fascine bundles. Sea water washed in, sucked out.

"Cut his holding ropes, dammit!"

From his own tank Quelch vaulted onto Hames's, straining to right its position. Quelch's knife sliced ropes and as Hames's fascine bundles began to fall away in sections, Quelch jumped to deck between Hames's tank and the hull. Hames's tank, uncorked, leapt back on one track and filled the space in which Quelch stood. Then, freed, Hames lurched off into the chop.

"Verity, take charge!" I cried, marvelling even as I said it, at my response.

Sergeant Quelch from Durham, open-mouthed and dead beyond question in place of the man who seconds before had been vitally alive, was my first sight of death that day. It meant nothing. I should have felt awe, grief on behalf of a family unknown to me in Durham, rage at fate, puzzlement. The truth is that several days passed before I even thought of Sergeant Quelch again and when someone told me that his body had returned to Portsmouth on our landing craft, I was surprised.

Two ratings dragged Quelch aside as Verity, wide-eyed, mounted Quelch's Crab and followed Hames. I gave the order to my driver. We hoisted our steel bridge ahead of us and plunged off. This was when we might drown, everyone knew. The tide was higher than we had been told it would be, but the sand dunes were much nearer than I had expected. I could hear Renshaw reciting the Lord's Prayer. Ahead, Hames discharged mortars from his petard. Dust. Verity's Crab had now passed Hames and was already flogging straight up a dune whilst we were still in four foot of water. Our AVRE shuddered as the bridge, twice the length of our tank, took a partial hit. As we passed Sim's boat, I was aware of confusion there. Resting at a right angle to the beach and with each wave being flung over further on her side, her ramp was down, but nothing was driving off.

We cleared the tide in the tracks of Hames and made twenty yards. Halting, I directed windsocks to be put up. Much more like dusk than dawn. As Renshaw and Sapper Ewer, nineteen, from Middlesex clambered down I saw Verity's Crab near the top of a steep dune leap as it caught a mine with its left track. The track peeled. First two sappers, then Verity and lastly the driver came out of the turret and began to run to us. Ewer saw them. His windsock in place he was crouching around the side of us, but when he saw the running men he stepped outside the track marks to urge them on. The force of an anti-tank mine ripped through the AVRE.

"Jesus," said Verity, ashen. "Ewer . . ."

Tears on Verity's cheeks.

"Nineteen," I remember saying.

Verity's tank was now blocking the most obvious place in the dunes in which to make a gap and bring the bridge through.

"Where's German?" I asked.

I looked back through the upright teeth of the obstacles through which we had just weaved, but which I had not noticed. Our landing craft had already put half a mile between it and France. Infantry craft were inching in. Our bulldozer was sitting, unmoving, waves breaking over its upper structure with, slumped in plain view in his cab, Corporal German.

"Deep tank ditch just over the brow of the hill," Verity shouted. "We'll need your bridge."

"Tell Hames to get your Crab off that dune!"

I had no sensation in my left hand, but it did not bother me. Myself, Verity and the others still alive moved as one with a clarity of purpose previously unimaginable. It was a good feeling. It beat most other feelings into a cocked hat.

Hames had jettisoned his Porpoise and his sappers had clipped winches onto the wounded Sherman Crab. They dragged it down the sandhill, and the Crab slewed off to one side and set off another mine which blew it further out of the way and dragged Hames's tank at a right angle off the intended path. I gave the order and my driver went for the gap. Our bridge was hit again and swung so violently that the Churchill spent seconds off its tracks. But we were perched now, atop a dune above a yawning ditch on the other side, looking across flat, featureless countryside. A hundred yards away I saw the gable end of the villa.

"Drop her!" I shouted.

One of the hawsers must have got damaged because although the bridge dropped down and lay at an awkward angle across the ditch, it did not release. I saw Hames come up on foot with wire cutters. Obstinate. The tank could feel the weight lift as the bridge was freed.

"Where's Ewer, sir?"

I looked at Hames.

"Fucking bastards," he said thickly. "We'll pay them back."

Back down the beach lay two Crabs in the water either side the botched ramp of Sim's vessel. As I watched a bulldozer appeared, pushing an AVRE in front of it.

"I bet that's Simmy," I said. I turned to my wireless operator. "Tell them we've made the gap and dropped the bridge," I said.

Jack saw Colonel Wildgoose hit. Jack saw him pirouette on the bridge of the command vessel to port, then fall backwards, his head hitting the steel cupola before he disappeared. It would later be confirmed that a single bullet, a shot from a position at least half a mile distant, had killed the colonel, although at the time Jack thought it was navy shrapnel.

He couldn't hear anything but shelling and mortar fire. The tide was concertinaing landing craft further and further west, away from their designated sites. Nor see: Jack could barely make out Burlington Bertie's villa. Twenty yards out a violent impact to their bow. As they went full astern Jack could see a drowned AVRE forward of them, although from what boat it had come or how it had got there he had no idea. Going out again, he saw a line of landing craft lying between their position and shore and all of a sudden wondered if they might fail to disembark. Which thought disorientated him for a moment, allowing space to the baser feelings he had fought to contain. Then they were going in again against the race at an angle of forty-five degrees.

Ahead of their lowered ramp stood a steel hedgehog topped by a shell. Jack ordered the petard fired. The obstacle evaporated. Jack's AVRE was first off.

He didn't want to close the turret. He feared if they were hit the turret might jam and they would drown. He tried to see forward in his periscope but could see nothing and had to risk head and shoulders up in the hatch. Water broke over him, he could taste salt. Success with the petard prompted him to have a go at other hedgehogs along high-water mark. Speechley, too, was using the gun on his Crab, disarming the mines on concrete ramps. Behind, Jack saw the dozer lumber off like a khaki hippo and begin to push debris in its path to one side or the other. When Jack turned around again, he was steaming up the beach.

As Speechley began flailing up to where they would gap, Jack saw the gun dug into the dunes, fire belching from a horizontal slit. He looked back for his second AVRE, but he could not see it, saw instead on the shore the driver of the bulldozer lying curled as if asleep by the track of his machine. Jack knew he should send a sapper to take over, but he could not, could not send a man back over open ground. Speechley's Crab, turret reversed, chains flailing, was beating a track up the beach. Jack then saw his second AVRE, inching sideways in the breakers, unable to come ashore. "He's lost steering," Jack said to his gunner, and as he said it saw the men in the stricken tank begin to climb out. A shell from the German gun hit them above the waterline just when the corporal, a man from Somerset named Fowles, appeared. The white of the explosion cleared the air of all dust for fifty yards either side, then a new, orange cloud went up like a balloon.

"Hit their Bangalore," Jack tried to say.

In mid-beach, he was too far from the German gun to use his petard. The gunner knew what he had to do and climbed up behind the Besa and fired it at the tongues of flame.

"Sappers Tully and Bruce have bought it, sir!" cried Sergeant Speechley, materialised in Jack's tank, as if from the air.

Three men, was Jack's first thought, not two, because the Tully sappers were brothers. Then as he began to wonder why Speechley was here, not in his own tank, Jack saw Speechley's Crab twenty yards short of the German gun, entangled, turret shattered, and he began to understand the magnitude of the disaster that had engulfed his troop.

"Get the gun!" Jack yelled.

A little dip hid them for some yards and Jack's driver used it to change by a few degrees the point at which they might be expected to emerge.

When they did so, Jack could see the Germans' epaulettes and their 75mm swinging around. Jack's driver gave all the throttle he had. Petard and gun fired on a common trigger.

Jack felt nothing. He came to after no more than thirty seconds could have passed, lying beneath the body of his wireless operator. The upper infrastructure of the Churchill, the part where the plate all round was thinnest, was buckled inwards. Smoke, thick as black wool, was unravelling. As Jack pushed himself up he could see that his driver, too, was dead, his neck broken. Speechley and a sapper named Rowe were struggling upwards for the hatch like men trapped under water. Jack climbed out after them and jumped down. A crater where the German gun had been. His Churchill had its entire right-hand track missing, and some of the bogeys were still revolving. A sapper named O'Hara, his uniform in tatters, stood swaying, a strange look on his face.

Sergeant Speechley, bloody-faced, held a revolver.

"Come on you bastard."

A bare-headed, fair German was staggering from the ruin of the emplacement. He dragged his right side and could not see. Speechley shot him through the temple. The sappers cheered.

Renshaw had tried to use our Bangalore to blast a hole in the wire leading to the villa, but had not been successful. The house was still fifty yards away, too far for the petard. I could see a party of men approaching along the back of the dunes a hundred yards west. Protected by Sim's bulldozer I watched as one of them fell to a shot from a sniper. Now they were pinned down. Between gaps in shelling, bullets pinged off the dead man's helmet as the sniper used his head for recreation.

"Where the hell is Jack?" I wondered aloud to Sim.

Jack could hardly bring himself to look at Speechley.

"Mark the beach up to here!" he cried. "Then we'll join up with another troop. Look lively there, Speechley!"

Speechley ordered Rowe and O'Hara to fetch out markers from the wirebound Crab. They ran down the beach at a crouch, placing symbols either side of the cleared path. Then Jack led them up to a sandy track behind the dunes. The din of war, a constant, went almost unheard now, and the vistas, recently of limitless sea horizons and long low coastlines, had shrunk to small, almost private, patches of sand and dune. Speechley and Rowe advanced with a mine prodder. In dense, choking smoke it took thirty minutes to cover ten yards, locating each mine on the path and blowing it.

"Where's O'Hara?" asked Jack.

Speechley straightened up, his face exhausted from concentration. "Poor silly bastard," he said.

Sapper O'Hara was wandering in open ground, thirty yards away.

"O'Hara!" screamed Jack.

O'Hara turned right around, then flipped backwards before he fell, as if springs were involved. And Sapper Rowe now fell. Jack threw himself into pampas grass and belly crawled as Speechley pulled Rowe, the mine prodder still clasped in his hands.

"Rowe?"

Speechley turned the man over.

"Oh, God," said Jack, turning away.

"Bloody hell!" cried Sergeant Speechley and checked the chinstrap to his helmet. "They're going to kill us, those bastards in that fucking Bertie house!"

Two men a hundred yards west of our position are my clear memory now, two men pinned down between the narrow, metal track and the sand dunes. They got up, one beckoning the other. Banks of artillery smoke were drifting in from the sea, making visibility intermittent but also difficult for the snipers. The man in front looked over his shoulder, stopped, waved his hand to urge his companion on. Another ball of fumes enveloped them. When it cleared, he was still there, holding a revolver.

Not until I was forced by circumstances to recall these minutes was I able to do so, but then, when I did, it was as if just hours had passed.

I ordered covering fire and for what it was worth the remains of Sim's command and mine potted at Burlington Bertie's villa with rifles, pistols and a single Bren gun.

"Now!" I begged as the smoke lay in a big, black wad between the distant pair and the villa. "Now!"

The man in front looked back over his shoulder, stopped, again waved his hand for his companion to follow. Another ball of fumes enveloped them. When it cleared, the soldier was still there, holding a revolver. Then he went down into a rut.

"I think it's the captain!" shouted Verity.

Six inches of sand stood between Jack and death. He felt the grains of sand in his nose and teeth and if he could have dug deeper with his chin he would have.

"Come on, sir! We can't stay pinned down!"

Now that it had arrived, the terror that is, in full flower and recognisable, it was something he surrendered to. An incontrovertible fact. It was bound to happen, he should have arranged matters otherwise, but he had not, and now he was damned by his own futility. He could summon nothing to his rescue and that made his position even more pitiable. The sum of his life meant nothing, it had all been for nothing.

"Sir! Are you hit? Come on, damn it, or you'll have us both killed!"

He did not want to die, and he would die, as he had always known he would, in a sniper's field. Cold perspiration held him in a clammy film and he smelt of shit. Jack shuddered as Speechley leapt from where he had been flattened and landed beside him.

"Are you all right, sir?"

Jack turned his face to Speechley, which was enough.

"Jesus Christ, you're in a funk!" swore the NCO and lay on his back. "Look, we've got to join up with the troop that's at the other side of this fucking house. You understand that? You're not hit. You're alive which is more than can be said for the other lads. Now are we going to make a run for it or am I going to take out my fucking little gun and ram it up your fucking Khyber Pass? Sir?"

Smoke had cleared like sea mist and sunshine now bathed the arid ground, the part-hidden men, the eaves of the villa. Dust kicked up from a little ridge above the men's outline as the snipers tried to drill them. Then both of them were on their feet again, weaving towards us in ragged steps. A mine went up sending a jagged yellow spear of brightness through the smoke. As definition returned I saw the body of one man sprawled and the other again pinned down beside the track.

I looked around for Sim.

"Don't go home without me."

In the cab of Sim's bulldozer, I revved its engine. Raising the shovel level with the cab, so that although I could not see neither was I a sitting target, I edged out for the villa. Sim came up.

"Come on, then!" he cried.

I floored the pedal. We met the wire at the spot where it had been weakened by our Bangalore and flew through it, wire whipping.

Although the distance between us and the villa was shrinking by the second, something happened in those flying moments. Time expanded. Or stopped. I don't know, all I do know is that something happened, because out of all the other many events of that day and the days either side, nothing stands out as clearly to me as that gap across which

I drove Simmy and myself on his bulldozer. (Sim experienced no such phenomenon, he said.)

I felt I was pushing the utmost end of a long line. At this frozen moment I was pushing further than anyone before me had ever pushed. Behind me stood my mother, and my father whom I have always felt I have known, and Ma Church whom I loved, and my grandfather, another person I had never met but with whom I had always been on familiar terms. And behind each of them stood long, patient lines of faces who could now mock death because of this moment. They had dwelt in English ports, in misty Irish villages and in districts of Naples. Their faces were more visible the closer I looked, nor did their numbers end where it appeared they might, but stretched further back and further, into Gaul and Rome and south-west facing Irish midland hills so loved by druids. Each and every one of them had waited for this caught moment in Normandy, some for millennia. Time in such a context was meaningless. Thousands of years and handfuls of seconds fused under the weight of the trust converging in me. A speck of time that lasted without end.

"*Brace!*"

Simmy brought the shovel down to ram. Windscreen cracked, webbed. We hit the gable on its corner and that entire section of the building collapsed around us.

Quiet.

"Simmy?"

"Here."

Then Verity's voice, leading in sappers.

"I think we got them," Sim said.

As we crawled out, behind us a man was being carried from the dunes. Jack stood there, holding a revolver.

"You all right, Jack?"

"My sergeant stood on a mine. Had his legs blown off."

His fingers sprang about as he tried to open the pocket of his tunic for cigarettes.

He said, "I have high casualties and no armour. I'm going to have to reform the squadron around what you have left, Chud. What happened to your hand?"

"I think I broke my wrist."

From the villa came a series of explosions as Hames finished it off with his mortar. Out of the dust appeared a group with hands in the air, herded by a sapper with the Bren. Five, I counted. But other than one grimed and bloodshot man in his fifties, these were boys.

"What is this?"

"Snipers, sir," answered Verity. "And gunners."

"Are you sure?"

Verity turned to them. They looked young enough to have come out from school. One had red hair and Verity caught his tunic collar to show me the jagged, divisional flashes.

"They're the real thing, sir. There's no-one else in there. These are the ones who've been potting at us."

"We should deliver them to the infantry," Jack said.

"Verity."

"Sir."

"Take them down a safe route until you find an infantry battalion. Then rejoin us here on the double."

The red-haired German caught my eye. His were green. He said something to me, I still wonder what it was, although I now have a fair idea.

"What did he say?"

"Did you say something, Fritz?"

The boy, pale, turned his head away.

"Carry on, Verity."

My wrist began to hurt. Jack was talking to Sim about equipment as Verity marched them off. Jack was choosing a point for a squadron rally. Asking the wireless operator to connect him to command. The sun came out. From the nearby dunes came the prolonged rattle of the Bren. The wireless corporal looked up. Jack and Sim both turned to me. The noise paused then restarted, like someone running a stick at speed along railings. I looked at the dunes.

"What a bloody awful day," Jack said.

We linked up with survivors of other squadrons, salvaged what tanks we could from shore and tide and with Jack in command took the little hamlet behind the beach in what would later come to be known as the Battle of Riva Bouche. It was scarcely a battle. It was over at noon and ninety-seven Germans surrendered. But later, when the press came to focus on Ouistreham and on the activities that took place there and when the many facts began to harden into something capable of comprehension, it was Captain Santry's taking of ninety-seven German prisoners in the Battle of Riva Bouche that stayed in the mind and the earlier parts of the morning were forgotten.

I liked when it was all happening, at speed, when you were so up that you couldn't feel pain, running flat out along an edge so thin that stopping would mean you were finished. I even liked the noise, the sound of the ships' howitzers, the rockets, the German guns and the Moaning Minnies.

All these parts of war filled up spaces. It was the happiness of instant fulfilment. Coming ashore, beating up the beaches, beating death. In a sense we beat death every moment we breathe, but it's not the same as D-Day. On D-Day we walked through death. It lay on the beaches. We landed, walked through it and came out the other side. Or some of us did. After that, space grew like a cold stain. By afternoon nothing was unknown in the way that it had been earlier. By afternoon death was commonplace. Its unconscious acceptance in everyone's mind devalued the general hold on life and went by the name of courage. So many had died without even having touched the French soil they had come to liberate. Colonel Wildgoose. Sergeant Quelch. Corporal German. Sapper Ewer had touched it and it had devoured him. So much death affected men in different ways. Some like Sim it made heroes of, some like the German boy, grew pale and went to embrace it mute. Verity saw an opportunity and took it. Hames, you suspected, would have performed in the same, dogged way in heavy traffic.

In the years that followed there was no-one with whom I could discuss those crucial hours. Describe them, yes, to people who had not been there, but not *discuss* them. For a few years I badly wanted to get back at the kernel of that morning and find what it was made of. Life at both its worst and best, I suspected, which was confusing but still made sense. A vital sensation that I never had experienced before and never have since. It became a loss that I could never accept, a form of grief. As I grew older the failure took on a taint of shame and in that way was at last forgotten.

In the early years I tried to keep in touch, but I found that the people, like the memories, defied permanence. In our regular regroupings before and after taking Caen and then in the slog up northern France and through the Low Countries, there were dozens of new names and faces, but the ones I have always kept in my mind were those I landed with at Ouistreham.

I received a letter from Renshaw in the early 1950s. He was applying for an office job in Glasgow and needed a character reference. I obliged by return. Some months later I followed up, suggesting we meet, but my letter came back saying, "Not at this address".

Hames was wounded in the Rhineland and shipped home. He had a brother who told me when I inquired that Hames had gone to America and that the last he, the brother, had heard was that Hames had been divorced. Verity died the year after the war of a burst appendix.

Sim became a quantity surveyor, married and settled in Bristol. He did not reply to correspondence. During a business trip I made a point of coming home through Bristol and found Sim in a small office with a heavy-set woman, his wife, doing reception duties. The parson's son was cold and ungiving. Perhaps it was all those years of listening to his father in the rectory near Southampton. He did not even suggest that we go and have a pot of tea and when I did he said he simply had too much work to do.

RING-BINDERS
5 - 6

Eleven

PERSISTENT RAIN IRRIGATED MONUMENT. Come that morning from the delta of the Lyle in thin, slanting lines, it washed down every roof and window with diligence. The tiered character of the town, its almost amphitheatrical plan together with its underlying sewers, drains and sluices put down by, first Cromwellian, then Georgian, then Victorian engineers, allowed expression to rain not possible in other, more recumbent towns. From slates of Balaklava, from gutters and downpipes of Buttermilk, rain swelled sloping gullies and conduits in Mulberry, troughways in Palastine, courses and culverts and pipes in Half Loaf and in Pig and Litter. It purged underground races and made whole districts rumble. Where trickles had meandered now rapids rushed. The children of Balaklava, in a tradition reaching back into the very nub of history, launched paper boats in the little Venice of their streets, then ran headlong to watch them discharged into the river opposite Bagnall's Lane six minutes or so later. Rain made a series of ornamental lakes and waterfalls on the steps of Priest's Way. It hissed from battlements, clefts and nicks and came shooting from embellished spigots. In an ever-widening arc it dispersed in melodies over Skin Alley, Pollack Street and Moneysack and then, the river in its sights, brimmed over the cobblestones of MacCartie Square like a shimmering, ever-shedding skin, washing litter before it as it had done offal and dung for centuries and giving today's street sweepers a transient satisfaction in their station.

I wore galoshes down The Knock between St Melb's and O'Gara Street. Also a brolly. On the bend where once had stood a huckster's shop now two houses had been knocked into one and sold newspapers and provisions.

"Will it ever stop, Mr Church?"

"Never. Thank you."

Paper tucked inside my coat, I carried on downhill, allowing the rain at my face. To bathe it. Damp had swollen the office door: it gave with a squeak if you came to it sharply with your shoulder. Flapped my brolly, toed off the galoshes, stood them heels up to the wall. Wasting time. In a cubicle observed through an internal window sat Miss D'Arcy at her switchboard, smoking Craven 'A'. She smiled. In the main office Buddy Stone was entering invoices in the debtors' ledger.

"Filthy."

"Down for the day."

It had not changed. The white-faced mahogany clock. Over the fireplace on a nail the bank's calendar that had been placed there in January without its predecessor having been removed and the same before that for nine years, each January, starting in 1951. On the mantelpiece were gathered the seals of the Church companies, hunched like large, feeding insects. For Buddy a rolltop desk, for myself Ma Church's old desk surmounted by rows of pigeon-holes. The desks faced one other so that when seated their occupants communicated as if from bunkers.

The opened post lay on my desk. Cheques, two, had been placed by Buddy atop a thick foundation of bills and other correspondence. Into my diary Miss D'Arcy wrote incoming calls, a line for each one.

"Who's 'A lady'?" I asked into my telephone.

"Wouldn't leave her name. Said she'd ring back."

Unlikely my wife would go to such lengths to speak to me, though not impossible. I replaced the cheques, picked up and revolved between my fingers Ma Church's tortoiseshell fountain pen. Rain swam down the face of the window, a curtain to match the lace one inside. Taking out the newspaper, I opened it at a deep page, closed it again. Above my head documents nested in the rows like kittiwakes.

"Talk of them dredging up beyond Small Quay again," said Buddy, now a disembodied voice.

"Where did you hear that?"

"I met Matt Luther yesterday after mass."

"Hm. What did he have to say?"

"Luther's all right, Chud, he has his uses. He says they've told him to start dredging next month."

"Let them," I said. "It'll silt up in the first spring tide."

Buddy was now standing off to one side, journal in hand, a little chewing going on at the corner of his mouth. Basic concerns. Shoots of carroty red hair and the blotchy face of Olive, his mother. Engaged to a girl from Captain Penny's Road, he thought a job in Church Land was as good as money in the bank.

The telephone on my desk jingled.

"That lady again," Miss D'Arcy's voice said.

"Thank you. Hello?"

"Chud?"

"Who is this?"

"I wish to see you," she said and, stating a time and place, hung up. Buddy was scrutinising me.

I said, "I'm going out."

I walked back along the Monument river to collect my car. No barges had sailed here since 1955, the year Mr Gus died, not that any connection existed between the two cessations. I had come up here after the war, in my first years home in Monument, to try, as now, to think. The unused, once sooty waterway was now a curd-surfaced pill. And yet the very presence of water, albeit filthy, made the rainy bank perversely peaceful. It would be so easy to imagine, I thought as I walked along, that Mrs Finnerty was still in her kitchen, Uncle Mary was asleep in the front room and Aunts Margaret and Justina were still waiting in dread of their mother's arrival to inspect their embroidery, not lying beside their father and brothers in the adjoining grave.

Mr Gus had first faltered on the very day on which Ma Church had married Paddy Bensey. Indeed, at the wedding breakfast. Drink, his mother had raged, and sent him home in a taxi with his sisters. He was dead in four months, cancer of the pancreas, never left the hospital. The nurses wept openly, for he'd spent a fortune on chocolates for them and had never been happier than when he was so doing.

Mrs Paddy Bensey she might have become, but Ma Church was still overseeing the running of Church Land then. I admired her more than anyone, even when she became aware of my fondness for a bet.

"Ah, Chud, you break my 'eart! You 'ave a wife an' child to think of, you cannot go on takin' the bread from their mouths to sop up your own boredom. I really thought the war would make you. I was wrong."

She didn't understand. I wanted to tell her about the war, but all I could do was shrug my shoulders in what, I knew, must have seemed to her like utter fecklessness. At the war's end, when I lay in a hospital in Greenwich with half a pound of German shrapnel in my leg, she had come over. I remember her hat, her perfume, and one enchanting July morning we spent together surrounded by roses and watching shipping on the Thames.

I had been demobbed early in 1948 and come home. Straightaway it was all business: the discharging of fruit and timber, steel and wine, hogsheads of beer and boxes of industrial explosives. The loading of terrified cattle. One day our wharves – the best in Monument – might be working sweet-smelling Pakistani jute bales, another snowing bags of icing sugar from Rouen. "Before the war" was like another country. And since happenings in another country were seen as having no bearing on our own, the circumstances under which I had once left Monument never reappeared as an issue and I, as you might expect, was happy to assume that this would be the case for ever.

Then, a week after my return, I saw them. It was Rosa's elegance – from their car as she and Jack drove down Long Quay; she didn't even see me – that turned me inside out. Of course I had heard talk of "Main" and of the "new Mrs Santry" in St Melb's, but I had not yet had time to absorb its significance. Now I knew at once that my life would not be complete until I possessed her, which I knew I could not, but logic has little to do with fascination. The fact that Rosa was now married to Jack did not, as it should have, imply new boundaries had been drawn and that for me to seek out their company, her company, would entail danger. The war had bred in me a certain attitude, for if you land at dawn on the shore of a continent and actually take it by force, you are inclined ever afterwards to doubt the merits of caution.

Without delay I became an expert on her activities and could tell the day and the hour when she would arrive to place her order with Wise, or go up to Shortcourse the butcher in Balaklava, or take the time to drive up Dudley's Hill and out to White City to pay her respects to her father. I could anticipate, as she left her car, the way she would walk, or turn her head, or look up and smile, or transfer from one hand to the other her shopping basket, or in a shop put the basket on the counter and with both hands reach up to adjust the pin in her hat, a gesture that made me weak with longing and nostalgia, because that was how she had squeezed out her wet hair at Delaware.

I went to a hunt ball in the Commercial Hotel because I knew she and Jack would be at it; and spent the whole night at their table. Following that, I was invited out to Main for supper, once, and although Jack seemed not to notice, I spent the whole evening gazing at Rosa, so much so that I was not invited out thereafter.

I would wake to deep longings. At the expense of the office work I was meant to be engaged in, I would spend hours contriving to bump into her, which meant hanging around the places I expected her to appear, much as I had done in our years of growing up. She went to nine o'clock mass on Sunday as a rule, but this was not always the case so when I heard she sometimes went to eleven I made sure to be there too, gaining in the process a groundless reputation for piety. I ached out of sight of her. I envied others in her company whose appreciation for their good fortune could never match mine. I took up golf so that in a round, on those holes that hugged the boundary with Main or ran along the road, I might glimpse her out driving, or walking in a wood, or exercising her cob, or on her way into Monument, in which case I would abandon my game and dash back to town pleading business commitments.

She was aware of me, of course. At first I presented no more of a threat than other, similar men who yearned for her, beautiful women knowing by instinct how to weave through such hazards. Then, as she would later admit (see R-B:5), she began to feel unexplained sensations.

Rosa knew her position and loved her husband, but her new feelings led her to be restless, and short with Jack, and flustered when calmness was hers by second nature. Sleep began to elude her, yet she had ever been the best of sleepers. Sometimes she went alone to another room in Main, pleading the need to sleep, and managed it, only to awake in the grip of a powerful arousal which she knew had nothing to do with the man she had left across the corridor. She found herself flushing when, in society, something touching me came up, and had to run from the room in a riot of embarrassment, which left the company looking knowingly at each other and assuming she was pregnant again. Eventually, in her sober moments, she began to speak about me with disparagement as the only means by which she could govern her emotions. This led her in turn to act towards me with increasing coldness in order to justify her hurtful words.

I, of course, blamed Jack. I considered it unworthy in the context of what we had been through for him to have married the woman he knew I also loved as I lay recovering from wounds in an English hospital. Conscious of every small alteration in Rosa's demeanour, when I saw her turn away from me and laugh to whomsoever she was with as if to decry my existence, it cut me to my pith, but since I could not bear to attach a fault to Rosa, I blamed Jack. I began to compile a list of his shortcomings which might one day justify her switching her affections to me. Criticism of a Santry came easily to a Church. I began to scorn the way of life Jack clung to, the manner in which he dressed and walked and spoke and the fact, rich coming from me, that everything he owned had been handed to him. Malice overcame me. I detested the attitude I imagined Jack held towards me, which I was sure had lamed Rosa's natural affection.

But Rosa's campaign had its own effect, for although I might have in the short term kept her image sweet and impugned only Jack, over the longer haul this stance had sooner or later to bleed out and include Rosa. I no longer trusted her. The fact that she could so turn against me bred in me a deep contempt for her weakness, and although still hypnotised by her presence, in my own defence I began to wonder what type of a woman would reward genuine feeling with such fickleness, and counted myself lucky that I had found out in time. I began to resent her readiness to be so manipulated by Jack and became scornful of her attacks. Never daring to be the first to turn my back just in case her mind had veered again in my direction, I nonetheless became angry at the very thought of her, and began to speak about Jack's lack of taste, and was always the first to put in a bad word for the Benseys, not that that was difficult, until I reached the point that if I ever thought of Rosa Santry it was with bitterness.

What Rosa could not avoid, however, was her own tendency to compare Jack with me, especially in those inevitable moments when the wisdom of a recent marriage stands, if not in doubt, then at least in suspense. To her, Main and Jack exuded a common monotony. She tried to provoke him, first with insults, then coquettishness, but he was like a fish under the deep bank of a river, he never rose. She wondered if something of the war still kept him hostage and was the cause of his often blank and empty eyes, but never once did she succeed in getting him to tell her anything about the actions for which he had been decorated. Critical of my well-known raffishness, another barren tactic since Jack never reacted to gossip, Rosa found herself thinking of me again in this very context. She despaired of Jack. He was not a person in the normal sense, he was a scion of a great place, inseparable from it in the way of a king and his country. History made him immutable. The only time he had seemed to float free of his inherited environment had been with me, a forbidden thought, since it brought Rosa back to the very source of her frustration. She could flare up with him, but it never led to a similar reaction, since Jack was predisposed to treat women as ornaments. Worse, when she deprecated me to Jack he invariably defended me, provoking Rosa to greater heights of invective. These she would later regret and force herself to make a retraction. But this, no more than her attack, never aroused Jack to more than polite murmurings. Which incensed Rosa. Unable to succeed either by attacking or defending me, Rosa took to attacking Jack himself, but Jack just smiled as if the whole thing were a manifestation of woman's whimsy. In the end, unable to penetrate the edifice of Jack, Rosa rebounded from it onto me.

At first she allowed herself to think of me as a revenge upon Jack. But when the level of her ire had fallen a self-pity overtook her and she began to justify her indulgent fantasies on the basis of her impoverished circumstances. She was after all a woman just in her mid-twenties who deserved more than marriage to a man who acted twice her age. Although leaving Jack or Main was not a possibility, Rosa felt that life in certain areas had cheated her. Even on nights when Jack turned to her in bed, often he could not complete what he had begun, pleading exhaustion, although what might have so exhausted him Rosa had no idea. She was sure it was not the bed of another woman, for in this matter as in others Jack appeared to have broken with tradition; but sometimes Rosa wished it could be the case, for if, even in the realm of fantasy Jack could sleep with another woman, so too could Rosa with a different man.

She began to imagine me in the same relationship with herself and Jack as that which had once prevailed in Delaware, which included me and Jack in acts of open affection, but now, in her fancy, it was to me she turned the most. Circumstances were contrived in her mind to throw us alone together, in Monument, or when Jack as he sometimes did had gone to Deilt to buy cattle, in Main. She told me that once she went to sleep with this image and preserved it to her dreams so that at some point in the night she awoke as she thought to a transformed reality and reached out for Jack, believing him to be me, until he shrugged her off and resumed snoring and she lay there, conscious of her self-deception and crying like a waif. In the end, fantasy could not put bread on her table and so Rosa found herself seeking me out.

She was at first shy. But when my response was favourable hope soared in her and she was swept by relief. Now at home she could relish more than the simple work of her imagination, she could construct a series of careful meetings to which Jack was always a willing party. When I began coming out again to Main, Rosa fussed over me, inventing shortcomings in my dress so that she could pinch a thread here or dust a speck there whilst Jack stood, hands behind his back, absorbed in a test match on the wireless. She listened with rapt attention to anything I had to say and responded with enthusiasm to developments in the Church business empire. Now when she came into Monument, whether with Jack or alone, it had to be at a time when I was available. If we met for elevenses in the little snug of the Commercial Hotel, she would ask me what had happened earlier in the week when she had come in as usual but I had not, and when I explained that I had told her I would be in Dublin that day, she would sit back as if Dublin was a woman and not a place, but then just as quickly reach over and touch my hand, saying it was her fault, that she had forgotten.

She began to live for these meetings. She insisted I be in our place, so much so that the hotel kept other people out and our pot of coffee ready. On Saturdays I went out to Main and on Sundays Rosa came into mass in the cathedral, not caring any more what her father thought if she and I after all these years shared a pew.

But just as fantasy could not itself satisfy the emptiness in her life, neither could mere conversation or contiguity. She began to itch, even when we were together, and stamp her foot for no reason and look away. Her chest hurt. She drove home to her husband in a more diminished state than that in which she had set out.

She had evolved from a beautiful girl into a beautiful woman. Yet it was not her beauty alone I wanted to possess, it was something far more primal, as if Rosa represented a lost part of myself.

"Do you ever think about Delaware?"

She looked at me. "I try not to. Do you?"

"No," I told her.

But Delaware was a code that neither of us would give up and which, for good or evil, would continue to shape our lives whatever the risk, whatever the price.

We became indifferent to the signals we were sending to the community, Jack alone excluded, needless to say. We began to touch cheeks on meeting and parting, sometimes in the street. I now looked forward not just to her company but also to the feel of her cheek to my lips, and of her lips below my ear, two separate sensations. And then one morning having spent the night striking off the minutes till eleven, I contrived to be in the hotel early with our coffee in place, so that we would not be disturbed and when she came in she would have to sit beside me and perform our greeting in that position; which she did, but I then put my hand to her neck and steered her head so that our lips touched, turning the previous two sensations not into one but into one hundred, and tasting her mouth as I had not done in nearly ten years.

As these meetings increased, however, I could not help but consider Jack's position. Although not meaning to, he was driving his wife at me. Never a week went by when I was not in his company, as Rosa's arrangements made sure. On these occasions Jack could be amusing, his well-known vagueness already flowering into something of a trademark, so much so that I sometimes wondered if it were not a ploy to entrap me. Nothing less likely was imaginable, of course, and so I had to decide to stop seeing Rosa as the only means of upholding my respect for Jack.

Rosa had come to the same conclusion. In her case it set her off on a fresh round of self-recrimination, of snubbing me, of damning me in front of Jack, of realising that Jack actually liked me, of re-contrasting me to Jack, of putting herself once again in the way of seeing me, of re-establishing our mornings, conversations, greetings and touchings, our kissing, until at last she reached the point again where only Jack's vulnerability stood between us.

These first months of 1948 were what went through my head twelve years later as I drove out, as Rosa had telephoned to say I should, towards Eillne.

I can't say I was too familiar with the holy well on Captain Penny's Road to Eillne. Whatever its origins, it would gain brief fame in the 1980s when women would claim they had seen the head of Christ looking up from the water and candlelight vigils sprang up and rosaries were recited round the clock and people from Balaklava came out and sold trinkets and light refreshments to pilgrims, some of whom had been bussed down from Armagh. But in late April 1960 it was just a trickle of water in a pile of rocks inside a wrought-iron gate on a quiet country road.

I sat in my car with the window open. The countryside lay with the peculiar quietness that comes from sun after rain, not quietness in reality but the constant susurration of heat-hatched insects that rules out all other sounds. I turned off the car radio, where they were discussing Russia. What did she want? I could no longer imagine, or even fantasise, that her phone call had sprung from incorrigible want. With the exception of one visit to Main the year before, a visit I would prefer to forget, we had not spoken.

I looked at my watch. She had said holy well, and even I knew there was only one in or around Monument. There had, of course, been other women in my life, apart from my wife, I mean. Following business trips, ladies had rung me from Rouen, from Trouville and Le Havre, and the lady from Baton Rouge was not speaking from her home in Louisiana but from a B & B in Dublin. I couldn't even remember her. She must have thought my qualities lyrical to walk out on her husband and two children and find herself telephoning me from Amiens Street. A car appeared from the bend behind me, a Morris Minor, with a bird-like woman in her sixties at the wheel. She kept on for Eillne. My wife Joy's sister had come home once from Australia, where she had left her husband minding their outback farm and during the month of her stay with us had confirmed everything I had often heard of her pioneering spirit. Now only photographs came, at Christmas, showing in each successive picture her family growing up around her like a new plantation. One of them, maybe, was that summer's child, I could not tell, but she had left two weeks early, no recriminations, kissed me on the mouth, said, "This one will be my memory," and returned to the outback with haste, no doubt to conjoin with the waiting farmer and early the following spring to have a baby four weeks' premature. For a few years I'd thought of going out there, for ever, of leaving everything behind. Just a thought, but one which sustained me on bad evenings when other men went to tie one on. Then I'd find the Christmas photograph and realise she was a stranger, yet another, just as she had been before we'd met.

"I think you should get out."

I started. Rosa was looking in at me through the window on the passenger side.

"I've been waiting in there for fifteen minutes."

I said something by way of greeting, but she had turned and gone back in the little gate through which she must have just come out without me seeing her. I followed her in and down the path to the well. A few small, pewter cups attached by twine to rings fixed in the rocks allowed visitors to sup from the spring. Rosa held one of these as if about to drink.

I asked, "How did you get here?"

"You shameful bastard!" she hissed and tossed the cupful into my eyes, then, as I stood there blinking, slapped me as hard as she could with her open hand.

In shock I reeled to the well and sat down, gasping and dripping.

"Why?" she demanded.

"Why what?"

"To think you once told me you loved me."

My mind was straining to find reason in her words.

"What did he do that day that you can now bleed him for? I don't care, I want to know."

I looked at her. Even through nausea and mystification, the magnificence of her rage was coming through as a consolation.

"Who . . . ?"

"I had hoped we could discuss this like adults."

"Rosa . . ."

"Don't you dare try and touch me, you serpent!"

"Rosa, you're mad."

"Perhaps I am. But if I am, why am I? Because you have driven us to this edge through your own greed."

I looked up at her and all I could think of was her distress.

"My father had you summed up from the first day."

That stung.

"Fuck off," I sighed and dipped one of the mugs into the water to take a restorative drink.

"You do understand, I have no doubt, that what you are engaged in makes you a criminal."

Mine is the type of personality that can never be quite sure if I am a criminal or not, although staying out of gaol proper has so far been one of my few realised ambitions. I tried to make out where in the canon of my ramshackle activities there existed one that involved Rosa.

"Who's 'he'?"

"What did you say?"

"I have no idea what you mean. Who is 'he'? You said, 'What did he do?' Who? Tell me what this is all about, for Christ's sake."

Her eyes widened for a moment, but only for a moment.

"Very clever. I expected you to be devious, which of course was always the case, I should have remembered."

"If you mean by that what I think you mean, then please also remember that what I did that day in Delaware, I did for you, Rosa."

She sneered at me. "Don't try and twist this around."

I stood up.

"I'm sorry. Whatever it is I've done, I'm sorry. I'm going back into town now."

She grasped me by my arm.

"'Whatever it is I've done'? 'Whatever it is I've done'? You think you can walk off just like that, back into your office? Well you can't, you know, you . . . you blackmailer!"

Then she spat in my face. I caught her wrists and pushed her back against the stones and as she kicked me, made her sit in the place I had just left. I was angry.

"I'm going to call the guards!"

"If you don't behave yourself, I'm going to hit you."

"You wouldn't dare!"

I hit her. She caught my hand and tried to bite it. I had to envelop her with my arms and also wind my legs around hers to contain her needle-like heels as she squirmed and scratched and cried out until I began to fear the arrival of foot pilgrims from Monument with their bottles for holy water.

"Rosa . . ."

"Bastard . . ."

I caught her jaw in my hand and squeezed it until she moaned in pain, then turned her thus distorted face into mine.

"I don't have the slightest bloody clue what you're talking about!"

She fell limp. Now it was her turn, fighting for breath, rubbing her mouth, to drink from the well. She leaned in and I saw for the first time that she was wearing a silk dress which, as she bent to the water, tightened around the lower part of her figure so that the shape of her most glorious bum and its relationship with her long legs was ratified like an article of faith.

"You don't mean to say . . ."

"I didn't come here to say anything."

"You are blackmailing Jack for money."

I took a deep breath. "Why do you think that?"

"Hah!" she cried and tossed her head, but the gesture was too dismissive, it was contrived to disguise the doubt whose foothold she had suddenly felt.

"Tell me. Please."

She looked at me with a mixture of bitterness and bewilderment. "He tried to kill himself."

"How?"

"Does it matter how?"

"Please."

"I found him in a shed putting strychnine into a glass of lemonade."

"That's terrible."

"I'm glad you think so. He denied it, of course, but I could tell. So I began watching him and going through his belongings and his desk, something I'd never do in a thousand years. That's how I found you out."

"Go on."

"You're unbelievable."

"Please go on."

"He's paid you over two thousand pounds."

"How do you know?"

"Because who else would he be paying? Who else does he know who is so desperate for money? Who came out last year to Main and begged for a loan to pay off his gambling debts?" She took from her pocket a piece of crumpled paper. "I copied it word for word. Jack has no idea. Read your own words, if you dare."

I read.

> We all know what happened in the a.m. of 6-6-'44, don't we, Colonel Jack Santry MC, my old friend? but just in case there are them that doesn't I've written it all down very neat. You shall be hearing from me. Cheers. Your old mate.

"Where did you find this?"

"Surprised? The poor man keeps it in his trousers' pocket. I found it when he was asleep." Without warning she began to cry. "What did he do? I really don't care because he's a sweet, loving man who wouldn't harm a fly, but this has eaten him out, it's taken his manhood. So what was it? What was so bad that he wants to die before he'd let anyone know?"

Dread seized me, for Rosa, for Jack. The greater the love the worse the dread.

"Where did he pay the money?"

"Why go on with this?"

"Tell me."

"What's the point? You already know. Some address in England."

It made quiet sense in a perverse way. I'd wondered now and then over the years why he'd dropped the rank, why he'd never gone to a regimental reunion or the like, or accepted invitations – and there had been plenty – to speak about the war. Not that I'd ever done any of these things, but I wasn't a hero. Up to that morning I always imagined Jack and myself in the same mental picture, marching on Riva Bouche and accepting the surrender of the German garrison. That was the history. But now I was forced to reconsider that impression and accept that there was also a period that morning when we had not been together.

I sat down beside Rosa on the rock.

"Can I speak?"

She looked at me tightly.

"It's not me," I began.

Twelve

ONE DAY, TWELVE MONTHS before our holy well encounter, I had found myself crossing the Thom and driving between the granite piers of Main. The black cattle were still there, and the green pastures, and the spreading oak and ash. I emerged from rhododendron for the final climb.

It was Jack I had come to see, not Rosa. Since the beginning of that year, in a particularly unlucky patch, I had lost two thousand pounds to a bookmaker in Dublin. The man, who in any other walk of life would have been classed a criminal, had come down to Monument with a pair of his associates and I had written him out a cheque on Church Land, intending when he left the office to pick up the phone to the bank and stop the payment. But the bookie had taken the cheque around by hand whilst his associates had remained in my office, one of them with the telephone beneath his buttocks, the other trimming his fingernails with a flick knife.

I had to put the money back before Ma Church found out. I didn't have it. My bank manager, a stiff-collared anachronism, would never pony up two grand. In the face of our upcoming audit I had tried to touch another bank, without success, and a shipper I knew in Dublin, a mistake when I saw his reaction, and I even contemplated Paddy Bensey before coming to my senses. And so, as a last resort, I had driven out to Main.

The previous time I had been out here was the day we had buried the general. Cold had enveloped the mourners like ether. We brought the old man up through the estate on a gun carriage to the cemetery looking out on Dollan. Six men, working in teams, had taken a day to dig out the grave; the coffin went in and the earth, glinting like silver, was shovelled after. Back down in Main we gulped hot whiskey as fast as the kitchen could make it. Only a crude padlock attached in haste to the door of the gunroom gave any suggestion that beyond the door a week before Santry tradition had been adhered to.

That day Rosa's eyes when they met mine were cold and disinterested. She was punishing herself as well as me, I knew. She was now consort to a war hero of whom Monument was proud. Did I tell you they named a bridge after Jack? The one that crosses the Thom before you reach Main.

It was swept away in the rains of 1954, rebuilt by the local authorities and, amid suitable fuss, opened by a junior member of the cabinet and named Jack Santry Bridge.

In a little oasis away from mourners I said, "I remember when there was one lad who did nothing but clean the windows."

I watched a little smile tug at her eyes before she resisted.

"Give your wife my regards."

"What's your boy's name? You didn't call him after Jack."

"Kevin. And your little girl is Grace," said Rosa.

"Yes."

"I'm sure she's lovely."

"Rosa."

I avoided her. If I thought she might be in a place, I passed it. There was never an hour she did not stray into my mind but to meet her, to smell her and hear her voice and then to have to suffer anew the distance between us was more than I could bear. Now and again I saw Jack in Monument. He was becoming another general – so to speak because Jack was only a colonel – in his bearing and vague manner and the stiffish way he picked his steps down a street like a man who has just dismounted. But until twelve months ago I had avoided Jack too for fear that to resurrect our friendship would plunge me into fresh contact with Rosa.

Main was such an enormous house that no mere change in regime could impact upon its character. There was no way, for example, in which a young wife could fling on a dust coat one Monday morning and decide to paint the hall, for the hall alone contained galleries rising three storeys in height, alcoves the size of average living rooms, walls that required scaffolding in order to take down portraits for cleaning, and cloister-like corridors that led to distant libraries, drawing rooms, studies and a ballroom.

A girl in uniform made the tiles of a long passage resound as she led me to Jack. The mournful eyes of Santrys gazed down from all sides, still lamenting the fickleness of their ambitions. Over twenty years since these surfaces had tasted Fleming's chamois. The last standing butler in Main, never replaced. Nowadays when they entertained the Santrys hired in the head waiter from the Commercial Hotel. The library, whose layered rugs we now traversed, had volumes on all the great military engagements of history, walls of soft morocco glowing like embers. The natural world too had its place. Captain John Santry (b. 1826) had loved birds, flowers and fauna and had travelled extensively to begin the library to which his successors had added with varying diligence. Two years before a man had come from London to maintain the collection and three months after he had left all the plates were discovered missing from the volumes by Audubon. The snooker room beyond the library also housed the butterfly collection, a fad of Jack's great-grandmother, who had begun acquiring these exotic insects in the pleasure gardens of the Romanovs. Reflecting on the ability of the Cecropia moth to survive where entire dynasties had vanished, I stood by as the maid knocked on a door recessed between stands of cues and said, "Mr Church, Colonel."

"Chud! Come in, for the love of God!"

The little room overlooked an internal courtyard.

"Sit down, sit down. Mary! Good girl, bring us some tea, would you?"

As I sat the curtains rustled and a boy of ten or so slithered out.

"Kevin, this is Mr Church. Say how do you do. Mr Church is a very important man."

"Ah, so this is Kevin."

He was fair like the Santrys, but his brown eyes, like my own, spoke of olive groves and business done in togas.

"Why are you important?"

The Anglo-Irish bluntness.

"Mr Church fought in the war with me, Kevin."

"Have you got medals like Daddy?"

"Only a little one."

"Mummy told me you were coming. She said you're a rogue."

"Kevin! I'm quite sure she said nothing of the sort! Say, 'I'm sorry, sir,' to Mr Church."

"It doesn't matter, Jack . . ."

"I'm sorry, sir."

"Now please remove yourself."

Dwelling on me, but with his back to his father so that only I saw his distaste, the child then left the room just as Mary returned with the tea. The girl did well not to drop the tray, but its jugs and pots overturned and hot tea streamed over one edge causing Kevin to yelp.

"Dear oh dear oh dear," Jack sighed. "Kevin, try and be more careful."

"She never knocked!"

"Get out! That's all right, Mary, it's not your fault. We shall forget about tea. Whiskey, Chud?"

I had not studied Jack at such close quarters for ages. Apart from the tendency of his class in Ireland to apotheosise relics, which in Jack's case meant a herringbone tweed jacket gone in both elbows and a full two sizes too big for him, he seemed part of a generation senior to my own. A question of attitude. The fussy way he was now setting out two glasses, the manner in which he was pouring, trembling, the way he came over, almost at a crouch, with my drink. Jack seemed to have slipped through a keyhole of age.

"Your health. How is Joy?"

"Well, thank you. And Rosa?"

"Not a bother. You've a little girl, I know. Remind me . . ."

"Grace."

"Ah yes. Doing well?"

"She's down with something at the moment, Armstrong says half the town is sick."

"Ah dear. I'm sure it's nothing."

He had once loved me and perhaps a part of him still did, causing the thought of illness in one loved by me to pain him. It was, of course, that part of Jack I was hoping to exploit.

I said, "She'll be fine."

"They're all we have," Jack said, looking towards the door and bestowing posthumous forgiveness on his son. "And how are you?"

"I'm . . . OK."

"Best foot forward, is my rule."

"Do you ever think of the past? We've been through a lot together."

"I'd say."

"Not to mention the war."

Jack blinked. "You got wounded."

"Jack, I need to borrow some money."

Jack stared at me as if I had just materialised in front of him.

"You?"

"I need two thousand pounds."

"You own the biggest firm in Monument."

"I've . . . lost some money. Things are difficult. I'm worried about Grace. I'm in the shit."

"I don't have that kind of money."

"You have access to it."

Jack winced. "I'm just a farmer. My chap told me last week how many sheep we have. Eleven thousand, including the ones on our mountainage at Dollan. I cut trees and must replant them. Tens of thousands. I always try to keep a mare and have her in foal to a half good horse."

"It's only for a few weeks."

"You see, Rosa runs the accounts. There are still a hell of a lot of people working here, she's the expert on how many, but it's all money out once a week, believe me. I'd love to help you, but I don't see how I can."

"Jack, I once helped you."

Jack squirmed within his outsize jacket. Just as surprise had been replaced by evasion in his face, now it was the turn of guilt to make an appearance followed closely by fear.

"Life didn't change for you, Jack. You went away to school as you were always meant to. Rosa went to Leire, but she could have come home and chose not to. I took the blame for everyone."

"You're living in the past," said Jack with a touch of defiance.

"Sometimes I wish I was."

"Two thousand is a huge sum."

"I'll pay it back."

"Rosa writes the cheques."

"Then tell her to write me one."

Compassion is such a self-destructive emotion. Jack leant across and put his hand on my wrist.

"Let me talk to Rosa," he said. "I had no choice."

"I heard you weren't here two minutes and the house was in uproar."

Jack dropped my arm. Neither of us had heard the door. We stood up.

"Did Kevin . . . ?"

"Rosa."

Although she was smiling, there was also an air of inquisitiveness to her.

"How is your wife?"

You live and you learn to winkle hope from the tiniest clefts in life's armour.

"Well, thank you."

Within "your wife" was a studious level of disinterest, but one which had only jealousy as its root. A deadly sin jealousy may be, but to my ears the distancing of my wife and the mother of my child from Rosa's mouth brought nothing but comfort. She wore a loose pullover, and jodhpurs and scuffed leather boots, their straps undone.

"Chud's daughter is ill."

"I'm sorry to hear it. Nothing serious, I hope. Now, I have actually managed to arrange tea."

Two women sailed in with elaborate trays of silver pots and dishes and set them down under Rosa's direction. She issued plates and napkins and forks and then poured tea through a strainer and lifted lids to uncover hives of sandwiches and sausages in glistening shoals. Yet something tense lay behind all the activity, which my egotism, or lust, at first interpreted as desire suppressed, but which, as the ceremony proceeded, I had to concede lay in a more general disapproval of my presence. But within my analysis of the mood I also sensed an unevenness between her and Jack, a shorthand that exceeded the mutual presumption of marriage. In Rosa's case it took the form of an absence of admiration for Jack and in Jack's a resignation, as if their relationship had a hollow core and all that bound them was this great house. Nothing in Rosa's attitude to me, however, suggested I could profit from this perceived estrangement.

"We're most honoured that you haven't forgotten your way here," she said, looking at me like a sniper over the rim of her cup.

"How could I?"

"Easily."

"We were looking at the past," Jack said, wary.

"The past does not exist," Rosa said. "It's gone. Have a sandwich, Chud."

I understood that despite everything, love once born never dies outright and that Rosa too knew this and so had long set her mind on how she would react in such a situation as this.

"Chud's in a spot of bother," Jack muttered.

"What sort of bother?"

"I need money. I need two thousand pounds."

"And you came to find it here?" she asked.

Although I would have fought anyone to the death who impugned her, if ever Rosa's attraction was capable of being tarnished it was in those rare moments when she became like her father.

"People think just because you live on a large estate that you have money to burn, but I'm sure you understand that Jack's commitments mean every shilling has to be accounted for."

She could never hate me, but I believe she hoped that her blunt rejection would at least make me hate her.

She said, "I'm sure Jack would say exactly the same thing."

Jack was the picture of misery.

"It's not a gift, it's a loan. I'll pay it back in a few weeks, or a month at the most."

I loathed my abasement, but not altogether. There came with it an element of bondage where Rosa was concerned and so, concurrent with shame, I felt a tickle of gratified lust.

"What you propose is impossible. The decision of course is Jack's not mine, but Jack can't alter the facts. There is not that kind of money here."

Jack said, "I'm sorry."

Steps needed to be taken which would allow the three of us to make a dignified pretence that the previous ten minutes had not happened and for me to leave other than as a vagrant in the making; and thus Rosa led us in an unbroken excursion around the many people we knew in common, avoiding names that might trigger further explosions of embarrassment as if it had been she who had negotiated German minefields and not Jack and myself. As she gave her impressions of the new grocery premises just opened by Mr Wise, its glass-covered counters and stalls of exotic fruit, I began to undress her from her throat. I knew the two big bones that fanned out to her shoulders, and her wide shoulders, their luminous rounds, and their taste, and how as I licked the base of her throat out to those rounds, what it felt like to gather her close and to then run my hands down her wide back into her spine. She mentioned the new rector of Main – a superfluity since Jack alone of us worshipped in the reformed faith – and his wife, as I caught her boots and eased them from her feet and then with little tugs to the heels of her jodhpurs exposed the thighs which I had never forgotten, their startling, feminine bigness, their ability in my never quiet mind to contain between them the entire canon of bliss.

"You know Love?" I heard her ask me. "Bernard Love?"

So many points existed at which to begin making love to Rosa that no part of her body could not immediately outrank its peers for allure. I tried to consider the most unlikely, and settled on her heels. They would be hard and yellowish and made from tough, rigid skin. In some heels I had observed – in the army, for example – ridges of fossilised flesh had formed on them which I had no reason to believe were not universal. But Rosa's could have bled and it would have made no difference. I at once imagined that her stony heels were grinding me unsparingly, and apart from the sheer joy of the experience which sought to pummel my groin and all that lay in it to sweet powder, the antipodal nature of our positions necessary to such an exercise sent me off on a new arc of longing.

"Mrs Beagle found a dead wren in her bag of tea, imagine. They say there may be a case against Love."

"Chud isn't interested in Mrs Beagle's tea, Rosa," said Jack, standing up.

I said, "Thank you. It's time I was off."

Still sitting, her knees coming in from the wide angle of her hips to kiss each other through their pads of Bedford cord, she looked up and I, poised as I would always be to tumble into her dark eyes, gazed down and saw in her face an expression of wilful satisfaction.

"Are you going now?"

I looked to the door. Kevin had been standing there watching us, his face white as albumen.

Jack's frame of mind in 1960 comes to us as you might expect in the form of letters written to Rosa, but not till twenty years later when he was in the United States does this come to light. (R-B:8) In the usual Jack fashion – large pages turned into tenements by their crowded words – he set out his dilemma at that time with great candour.

Jack looked over to where Rosa in long gloves was picking gooseberries and wondered if, in fact, he existed. In some men this surge of doubt might have led to an excursion into philosophy at least, but for Jack it merely confirmed what he had long suspected. He sat down by the sundial in the walled garden and took out his pipe.

The sun shone from the afternoon sky with unambiguous promise, the grasses within the warm walls crackled with preoccupied insects, fruits where they grew debouched and flowers blossomed, yet all that Jack was aware of was his own unreality.

"Underneath, Kevin, the fat ones are all underneath!"

His wife, his child. His mansion on his estate. He should have been easily able to deal with the viper that unknown to anyone but himself had crept among them, yet he could not, could not bring himself to tell. Foundations, that was the problem. The whole thing was built on no foundations.

How could that be, since foundations were just what Santry and Main meant to the outside world? During the war he had come upon his inner self with cruel surprise, discovering the vice that no Santry had ever been associated with. The truth was that in those moments of self-discovery he had never been happier, not just because it had come to him through his love for Rosa, nor in the sense that a demon had at last been confronted, but Jack had discovered transient yet glorious happiness in finding his true nature. Not bellicose or crude but gentle and compassionate. If only he could have built his life on those moments.

He watched Rosa and Kevin work their way away from him down the row of round bushes. But was it true to say no Santry had ever felt this despair? If not, what had driven his father, the general, in a copy-book mimicry of Captain Santry in 1911, to take his life? The general had tried variety as a way to staunch the black dog: Jack met him in London after the war and suffered the acute embarrassment of watching his old man being mounted by a tart near Paddington. (Discomfiture was a feature of that, the general's last innings in London. They stayed together in the old man's club opposite Green Park. Each morning, following a breakfast fit for a general, they walked in lock-step down Piccadilly, the objective being the toilet in the Regent Palace Hotel. Like, one suspects, many of the general's aims, they never made it, not once. As a rule in front of the Ritz, or sometimes outside the Royal Academy, General Santry would halt on the pavement, crimson, jaws to buttocks clenched, and Jack would have to load him like a concrete statue into a taxi.)

In Monument the general's malaise was put down to drink, to which in the end he became a slave, proceeding up the stairs every night on hands and knees, ranting, with a judicious servant following behind, a vivid tableau that Jack remembered, a swineherd driving a mad old boar. The general too, Jack concluded, knew all about no foundations.

Jack walked from the walled garden by way of wired pear trees, out through the tack room and the comforting, real smell of horses and dung, through the yard and over the back avenue to a point where, through semi-transparent canopies of leaf the Deilt mountains could be observed. Untrue to say no foundations whatsoever, he reflected. Three hundred years could not be dismissed, nor the evidence of one's eyes any more than the product of one's loins. Yet what had *he* ever done that was in keeping with the integrity that he knew lay at his core? Twice he'd been tested, twice failed: once, years ago at Delaware – the very name now made him shiver – and once . . .

He was not himself but an entailed successor of great and varied obligations. He lived in a country of which, in the main, he knew nothing but which he loved, representing a defunct class and Empire which he embodied but detested. In 1946 he had returned to Monument with a rank, colonel, and a decoration for bravery, the Military Cross. He had wanted nothing more than to forget his entire past and to be reborn from the fertile acres and forests and running waters of Main – but he stepped off the train into blizzards of confetti, streets decked out with bunting and the uproar caused by two thousand people and a brass band.

It was all Paddy Bensey. The civic reception, the speeches, the ostentatious banquet in the Commercial Hotel for which the bookie wrote the cheque.

WELCOME HOME COLONEL J. SANTRY MC

How could he have turned his back on it all without hurting Rosa? How could he explain that he felt not pride but shame? He could never explain without knocking everything and beginning again on new foundations.

Looking at Dollan, Jack wondered at some men's ability to find solace in a God. He remembered how once he had been drawn into that orbit on a ship, or at least crossing water, but he could not cut through the fog of his dread to identify the moment, just its transient comfort remained, at once valuable and unsatisfactory. He had become a shell. On the outside was Colonel Santry of Main, the hero of the Battle of Riva Bouche, the husband of the most ardently beautiful woman in Monument and the widely recognised summit of local society. Inside was

There was nothing inside. But if so, then where was the real man, Jack the shell wondered. In his gut. Yes. Down there beneath all the leaden weight of his misery, compressed for ever, coming out every so often in mild farts of compassion, but in essence, lost, doomed like all in the entrails. Where was the engineer, if he had ever existed? Or the man who clasped Brooke at night like a brother?

Tenderly, day that I have loved, I close your eyes,
And smooth your quiet brow, and fold your thin dead hands.

Rosa, Jack knew, was no different from her countless predecessors in coming to terms with the fact that she had married not a man alone but an institution. It was just as well. Main with its commitments, which had devolved to Rosa, diluted for her the burden of being married to someone without a soul, Jack imagined. He frowned at the thought and fixed on Dollan's peak. He had never ceased to love her, and now their son, but now his love was inseparable from his misery, his knowledge of his own emptiness and his certainty that Rosa more pitied than loved him and that their only child thought him a fool.

Jack had had a long-term plan, a description so ornate for what it represented that even he had been amused by it. It went something as follows: one day – ah, one day – he would begin the dismantling of himself. Not alone, but with Rosa. It would entail much pain, but in his case the pain would be no worse than he felt anyway, and for Rosa, well, he could not say for sure, but for the sake of the plan he imagined she would endure it out of a sense of duty. But the joy that would come with the sweeping aside of pretence would flood them. In transformation worthy of an alchemist, his weakness would turn into his strength. It could be done.

Outcast and doomed and driven, you and I,
Alone, serene beyond all love or hate . . .

Begin again. That had been Jack's plan.

Had been. His hand touched his trousers pocket and felt there the piece of paper he had carried around for six months, not daring to leave it separate from himself. Like everyone on whom disaster falls, Jack swore to himself that if he could just once escape the burden that the page in his pocket represented, then nothing more would ever stand in the way of his personal reformation. But as each further month had gone by he had come to realise that his way of dealing with the problem was just another manifestation of his weakness. Looking back, he realised that at the very moment the contagion had struck a perfect opportunity had also existed to begin his rebirth. But he had lacked either the necessary nerve or imagination. To tell Rosa everything. To bare his chest to Monument and the world. He could imagine the faces turning away in the street; the mean post that lacked invitations; the looks across February fields during point-to-points; the rods and guns no longer reciprocated; the Monument Historical Society of which he was patron, for which every year he held a garden party in Main, to which in four weeks' time the most senior field-marshal in the British army would lecture on "Aspects of Gaul in York – Today and Yesterday"; no-one would ever forgive him for failing to embody their own aspirations.

He did not even feel hate for the writer of the letter. Rather, he accepted the situation in all its baseness with a resignation born of guilt, a feeling that it was not only inevitable but due, and a certain weary relief. That the catalyst should be a blackguard mattered none, because deep within Jack was the belief that no-one was blacker than he. Proof of this was hardly needed, for he thought of little else than the one, old incident to which he was nailed; but if, for diversity, he wanted other examples of his own lack, all he had to do was to consider the manner in which he had dealt with the letter. The ready way in which he had dispatched funds. How he had justified it on the basis of another's misfortune. How, as the demands had increased he had failed to confront the threat but had used his guilt as an excuse for further compliance.

Just as it must have dawned on Jack's ancestors, so it came to Jack with a certain, sly satisfaction that there was a way out. The fact that the solution was established as something of a family tradition facilitated it greatly, since people were less likely to inquire as to a specific cause but would rather take in their stride another accident at Main, just as they accepted that Santrys always went to Eton. Minimal investigation would follow. A Santry never left a note, melodrama being tactless. A Santry knew when to go.

The first thing that had struck Jack when they broke down the door of the gunroom and found the general was not the mess – so bad that six years on you could reach for a box of cartridges and still come upon another nugget of brain – but the smell of drink. Three empty bottles of the Macallan lay on the floor, themselves a testament to sheer capacity. The old man had pulled the trigger roaring. Jack rejected a re-enactment, not just for the stiff task he would leave Rosa and a mortician, but he held an old, if now devalued but nonetheless narcissistic, view of his own body and in particular, his head, that he could not bear to contemplate in giblets.

With a sigh Jack got up and began to walk back to the sheds and offices that housed tack and tools and items stored in locked presses for use in different situations on the farm. He retained an image of death that pleased him. The year before he had held on his lap the rigid but still breathing body of his dying setter as her moment drew closer. She did not appear to suffer or even to be conscious and died quickly and, most important, intact. Jack closed the door. The strychnine seemed to advance death with admirable efficiency as these things go, bringing with it the *rigor mortis* first rather than later, a bit like getting death on appro, then sliding away without pain, the body side of things having first been dealt with.

"In the basket, darling! Put the goose-gogs in the basket!"

Jack opened the press with a master key.

"Oh, *Kevin!*"

Jack took a deep breath. Her eyes (the red setter's) had been glassy and Jack did not believe she had been able to see him, but that had been at least an hour after she had eaten the meat, so it was reasonable, he felt, to anticipate a certain gradualness in the process, like going to sleep as a child in spite of the light outside, and hearing one's parents at croquet, and the evening chorus, and steps on gravel, and cattle, and insects, and the distant fall of mountain water.

Thirteen

I SOMETIMES LOOK BACK and ask myself, what was my life? It's not clear. Despite my cutting and pasting, there are too few points of connection between the now and the then. For example, I still have that photograph of me, the one commissioned by the seafarer, Uncle Giles, but it seems inconceivable that what I now see in the mirror could have evolved from the bright-eyed youngster in my ring-binder, looking with such hopeful curiosity from the other end of the century. The same is true of the army snaps where I am wearing my cap at a jaunty angle and grinning out. Where was the line drawn? Where did the one person finally cease and the other begin? With Grace, I believe.

"I think you should come upstairs and have a look at Grace," said Joy, appearing at the door of the breakfast room, wherein I was installed for its stated purpose on the first Wednesday in June. Some days you remember. The Epsom Derby was always run on the first Wednesday in June.

"Is she sick again?"

"Why don't you come and see for yourself?"

Joy, who had never known how to be firm with a man, had in its place discovered obstinacy. We went upstairs to the little bedroom that had once been Faithful Tadpole's. Grace, who should have been getting dressed for school, lay in her nightdress on the outside of the quilt, looking at me from black orbs.

"Grace?"

I sat beside her. Times had been – and since – when I blamed her wanness on the atmosphere in St Melb's. I loved her more than my life, but not enough, it seemed, to show her mother the necessary affection.

"Do you have a pain?"

"No."

"We'll get you a nice breakfast in bed." Kissing Grace, I made my way from the room. "Ring Dr Armstrong," I said, although Joy, once a nurse, needed no telling.

Only the week before Dr Armstrong had identified a lack of thriving as the problem, but I knew more now, don't ask me how. I had tried to breeze into Grace's presence with contagious cheer, but her mother acted as ballast against any such levitation. Now I just knew.

"Rain's easing up."

"The wireless is giving sun."

"Will I put my shilling on Lester, Mr Church?"

"Lester knows Epsom."

If I went up the Amazon for a year and came back I knew Buddy and Miss D'Arcy would still be at their posts. To some people that might seem reassuring. Buddy was on creditors' invoices, stacks of them. I sometimes envied him his bookkeeper's mind, which was gratified by the balance of opposing equals. I sat, hypnotised with fear. Licking my lips, I sniffed Buddy's pipe tobacco and yearned for something I had never experienced, then pushed to one side the fresh-faced post and rested my head on my desk.

The only thing I knew about in life was death and I had gained that knowledge without ever experiencing grief. No longer. Death is like a tone. It comes down the wind from miles off in a world of utter silence. Death is a vector of harsh light that shines down the mouth of the river.

And grief? I didn't know it. Even Delaware had not revealed grief to me. And later, with men I knew and had drunk and whored with lying warmly dead beside me, classic battlefield cadavers with their eyes open, I had felt only glad it wasn't me. Now I wished it was. That's grief.

In the pit of despair, head on my desk, all but seized up with dread for Grace, my only balm was the thought of Rosa. In the five weeks since the holy well, I had with the utmost difficulty restrained myself from contacting her. A rare example for me of standards outweighing want. She had left me with her accusations unretracted; she would have to discover for herself that I was blameless. Nonetheless, during this time of waiting I had run riot imagining my taking advantage of her predicament, of Jack's successful suicide and Rosa's widowhood, of my uncoupling from Joy and living with Rosa. Then I would be ravaged by guilt on account of my regard for Jack, which despite all the rubble that had been tipped between us remained warm and true at base. I wondered not just for what he was being blackmailed, but if in fact he was being blackmailed at all; whether it was all a warped ruse of Jack's to get Rosa's attention; that Jack, unlike me, harboured notions of guilt about the war and was now manifesting them in letters to himself. Unlikely. Unflinching, that's how I remember him that day. Shaking the hand of Riva Bouche's mayor and then cocking an eyebrow towards an adjacent orchard as five feet away an American soldier crumpled to a sniper's bullet.

"Mr Church."

Miss D'Arcy had left her switchboard burring like a dentist's drill and made the journey all the way from her office to mine.

"Mr Church."

"Miss D'Arcy?"

"A lady," she mouthed so that Buddy would not know.

The slim threads that bind us.

"Hello?"

"Chud, I'm so sorry. I've wronged you terribly."

The unchanging fact of Main must often have bolstered faltering Santrys in their resolve, even when that involved self-destruction. The back avenue along which we now spun, the mare stepping out smartly, half a dozen strides between each great beech, was as broad and straight as a boulevard. On one side lay the mountains whose easterly aspect was unique to Main, on the other the walls and roofs of the house, extensive as many a town.

"He's bringing cash over to England and then presumably posting it to a person in Manchester. I saw the envelope. I went there myself last week. The man's name is Speechley."

"Speechley!"

"I think he was a sergeant."

"He was Jack's staff sergeant. I thought he'd been killed."

"He's a cripple."

"What?"

"I saw him coming out of his house in a wheelchair."

Pears hung like teardrops over the tan bricks of the walled garden.

"Where is Jack?"

"In England. Watch the peacock plops."

Rosa threw her hat and veil on a table as she walked in and eased her gloves off and made one bundle of them before tossing them on a chair in the hall. The drawing room had two sets of French windows, both open. Rosa went to a box for a cigarette.

"You don't?"

"I gave them up."

Amongst the shelves of books and portraits and vases of gladioli I tried to imagine what my life might have been in different circumstances.

"How is your little girl?"

I couldn't answer that, not to Rosa.

"Oh, Chud." Cigarette unlit in her mouth she sat there and caught my hand in both of hers. "Oh, God."

"It's . . ."

"Don't."

All those years, lost, and still I could never blame her.

"Does Jack know you know?" I asked.

Rosa lit the cigarette.

"Absolutely not."

"And has he gone to England to meet Speechley?"

"I have no idea. All I know is, it's like cancer. It's worse, because it's killing me too. And it must be true, I mean, he must know something, why else would Jack pay up?"

"I can't imagine what it might be."

"Weren't you together?"

All the many cracks that had been filled over in the retelling, not that I'd retold or even much told for that matter, other than to myself. Times were, I remembered them now, when I would wake at night to the green eyes of a young German. Or trying to recall Sergeant Quelch, and failing. Or Sapper Ewer. Then I'd turn on the bedside light and go back to sleep, thinking of Rosa.

"Ridiculous, but I can't remember."

"Try, Chud."

"There was a period of four hours. More. Nearly five."

"When you weren't together?"

"Between the landing – "

"And what?"

"Jack was on a separate landing craft."

"What does that mean?"

Red admirals were mesmerised by a potted geranium.

I said, "I broke my wrist."

Rosa stared at me.

I said, "I'm sorry, I don't even know why I mention it. Jack noticed it, I think."

"Speechley's letter refers to specific events that happened 'in the a.m. of 6-6-'44'. The morning. What could have happened?"

"Anything is the answer."

Rosa closed her eyes. "It's not fair to you, I know. Especially now. It's just . . . I just don't know anyone else to ask."

It was the most natural thing in the world for her to have turned to me with her problem, forgetting, like a child, how she had recently seen me as the root of it.

"I suppose, now that I think of it, I didn't see Jack from the time we left Portsmouth Harbour on the Sunday night until noon on D-Day, when we took an enemy position above the beach we'd landed on."

"That's when you met up with him."

"It's all in the dispatches."

"There's not likely to be anything helpful in the dispatches since he went on to get a Military Cross."

"How much has Jack paid him?"

"As far as I can make out, over two thousand."

"And you have his address."

Rosa bit her lip, nodded. We sat in deep wicker chairs just inside the French windows, where you could feel the heat but not be in the sun.

"Give it to me," I said and took the scrap of paper.

You fall in love. You pitch headlong, beyond balance or reason, time and again. Slowly Rosa leaned forward. Because of the angle of the chairs only our heads could meet, yet the very limits imposed by our positions enriched the feasible. She teased out half her tongue, glistening, so that I could see what I was about to taste. At first she commanded my mouth, steering with unambiguous intent into its deep reaches, then withdrew, closed-eyed and moist-lipped. Now me. I asked her mouth to yield one section at a time. Then as my desire began to run like a spring fish, I could see the exquisite elongation of her neck.

She stood up, still joined to me at the mouth, then led me out across the hall and up the stairs past the, I thought, acquiescent gazes of her in-laws. As if to set herself the most direct route to infidelity, she led me into the first bedroom we came to, and drawing the light summer curtains as if she were on a tour of household duties, she took off her shoes, then bangles on her wrist plus rings and a watch, making a heap of them in a ceramic dish before turning her back to me, her nape bared as if for execution. I kissed the little, final rises of her vertebrae, stepping up them with my lips into the wide valley at the base of her neck. She leaned back and held me. Easing out the silk over her bra straps until the rounds of her shoulders shone like lamps, all my strength drained into a single point and my legs went so that I slipped down her as if down the bole of a tree.

Beneath her silk dress was further silk. Kneeling, I crept up her legs, sorting and probing. Turning, she remained on her feet but lifted her clothing so as to include me in it. I felt her step from one leg of her fallen knickers. Born all over again. She took her breath in big shudders. Shifted to allow me more. Not just reborn but reabsorbed, a concept that led me ever deeper.

Light intruded. She had taken off her dress and slip and as I looked up removed her bra so that her breasts inquired at me like a doe. I stood up. I favoured braces in those days and one by one she unleashed the leather eyelets so that my trousers fell like a regimental flag. She tugged me backwards, spancelled. I managed one trouser leg off, dragging it

156

inside out and my shoe with it, but she had me two-handed now and her face was riveted.

"Oh, Jesus."

"You . . ."

"Oh."

"You . . ."

"Oh, *Jesus!*"

Some straggling part of me still on sentry duty heard the noise. Rosa was burrowing down, heaving with urgency, and I was committed more to our fulfilment than I was to life, wrenching up my heavy clothes and igniting within myself further boosts of sensuality; but the door behind us had clicked open. I wrenched around. Kevin, Rosa's young son, was standing in the doorway.

A week to the day Joy came running down The Knock and burst in terrified to O'Gara Street, for once oblivious to protocol or her own perceived dignity. I led the way back home. I thought at first Grace was dead, and that might have been more merciful, but crying out I scooped her up unconscious in a blanket and ran, my weeping wife behind me, all the way to Dr Armstrong in Binn's Street. That night she was in Monument Hospital and the next day in Dublin. Never once, not for a moment, did I feel a sting of guilt regarding my reborn relationship with Rosa.

With an old person the cancer ebbs their bulk from bones, but a child of ten, like a flower, just fades. Most of the time she didn't know me. Her mother sat for five weeks by the bed, holding her hand, whilst in a room provided by the hospital I slept. So much that I could not sleep and they gave me pills and I slept again. The room had no windows so that days and nights were lost to me and I began to think with a certain gratitude that nothing further in life would be demanded of me than sleep in this small, warm room. I awoke one night or day, I had no idea which, and went to the ward. Dawn. Grace's bed was by a window. Flowers and toys. Cards. A colour photograph of St Melb's. Joy was holding her hand as Grace slept and slipped. My wife looked up and saw me. I'll never forget her face. I turned and went back to bed, wondering how I had created such desolation.

Once I drove to Monument but had barely set foot in my office when a call came through from the hospital that I should return immediately to Dublin. Which of course I did, but she actually rallied when they all expected her to go, and when I got there she and Joy were both sleeping and I, dizzy with exhaustion, lay down in my room, so that when

I reappeared I do not believe my wife knew that I had even got up that morning.

Strange, still is, that even in the presence of such love I could find no room for pity. I could not bring myself to touch Joy. Perhaps I was jealous in some warped way of her total attention for Grace, or maybe Grace whenever she came round – and these moments came less and less – saw just her mother since I was usually either asleep or pacing up and down the street or trying to telephone Buddy in the office. Stripped by approaching death of even the need to be civil, Joy and I met only across the dwindling body of our child and saw what both of us had always known.

I even missed my daughter's dying. A nurse beside my bed, a tiny moment of confusion in my mind as to her intention, then a run in stockinged feet up the steps and into the ward where I could see no window because they'd drawn a curtain around the bed as if death could be contained by fabric. They'd taken away her drips and tubes and she lay there, her small hands joined as if she was sitting in St Melb's on the musical chair.

"She's dead now," her mother said.

It was the middle of the day. It was the middle of the summer. Outside someone was cutting grass and I wondered for a moment if Grace, like me, could smell it.

We had nothing to say to each other, Joy and I. Her aversion to me was strength to her. When she knew I was listening she described to a nurse Grace's last hours in the way in which we enshrine those moments, as if they somehow outweigh the life which they conclude. When she had last opened her eyes, looked at her mother, smiled. Her going. One last big breath. We brought her back to Monument in a white, maple coffin on the back seat of my car. I carried her in myself to the cathedral and sat in the front pew with Joy and her family, the Littles, on one side and Ma Church with Paddy Bensey on the other. Father O'Dea asserted that Grace was the luckier, a notion that I, dizzy from alternate bouts of misery and unaccountable elation, was close to agreeing with. More than a thousand people watched us bury her. We went home and my house was filled by the Littles, who had, it seemed, rallied to us their own weight in lemonade and sandwiches.

Ben Little's name was a byword for hard work. Having borrowed the thousand pounds to acquire Six Half Loaf from my grandmother before the war, he had manufactured lemonade night and day for three years until the debt was extinguished. He scavenged the countryside for the scarce glass bottles he needed, brought them home, rinsed them to a shine, filled them with his sweet cordial and then transported them by horse and cart to shops and pubs as far away as Deilt and Baiscne. All his sugar came in through our warehouses and you could look back over the Little, Son & Co Ltd account and see the growing tonnage. Mad, everyone said he was in 1946, when Ben Little pulled down the old shed beside the house and put up a new one with machinery that washed the bottles and refilled them with Little's Lemonade. Who was going to drink all this sugared water? Ben disappeared for three weeks and then a month after he came back, on the steam vessel that weekly brought the barrels of beer and stout to Monument from Dublin, he consigned ten gross of Little's Lemonade for the return trip to the capital. He'd got the shipping space for almost nothing, since the boat's owners had been delighted to bring back something other than fresh air.

Ben and Laura Little had one son, Billy, and two daughters, the youngest called Joy. Billy would take over the business in the 1950s and build the Little's Drinks factory on the Deilt Road and in the 1970s pass on the business in turn to his son, Benjamin, who within twenty years would make Little a brandname in thirty countries. But at Christmas 1948 Billy was still loading bottles at his father's elbow and his younger sister, Joy, a nurse, had just turned nineteen.

Joy Little looked at men as if no higher calling could exist than to please them. Older people spoke of her gentleness and acts beyond the call of duty, their eyes hazy with gratitude. Small, dark, slightly round, pretty-faced, nice complexioned, somewhat awkward of movement, attentive but demure, Joy was the type of girl whom men instinctively take advantage of. All that stood between the hotter bloods of Monument and her ravaging was the fear of retribution by her brother, Billy. Thus, at nineteen, although much admired, Joy remained unattached, the accepted wisdom being that whomsoever would first cross Joy Little's threshold would emerge alive only with her as his wife.

A marquee had been put up behind Half Loaf. In the sloping field behind the house were parked the cars and bikes that had come that December evening. A little chill blew from under the north star and as the moon rose it laid down a skin of nickel on the Lyle. Joy, in a long, white dress with a necklace of gold, stood between her parents and received her guests. Preoccupied since my return to Monument with the eternal stew of emotions in which I was embroiled with Rosa, it was only because I knew that Rosa would be there that I had accepted Ben Little's invitation in the first place.

"How is your grandmother, Chud?"

"Well, thank you, Mr Little."

"Give her our best. Sorry she could not come."

Joy looked at me with great giving.

"I'll be expecting a dance, Chud."

"You can count on it."

As you might expect there was no shortage of lemonade, but one of the Loves was tipping from a pewter hip flask into the reddish glasses. Dance tunes were played by a six-piece orchestra. Ben and Laura Little led the waltz, but when the music quickened to a foxtrot the hardworking lemonade manufacturer left the floor shaking his head and smiling as if to say, you had to draw the line somewhere.

From the bar I watched Rosa dance with Jack. She made them both look the height of elegance, the fan of her patterned skirt in the turn, the poise of her bare arms, the delight of her shoulders and neck. Jack's blond hair had begun a tactical retreat, but it was still a good, thick mop that ducktailed aristocratically over the stiff collar of his evening shirt. We were in one of our opposed phases, in that Rosa was rising from a cycle of despising me and I was on a downward curve of envy and stale lust. Which meant we were cool but correct rather than overtly hostile. Jack, blithe and cavalier, sailed by with my whole world in his grasp.

"Chud?"

Joy was waiting.

"Of course."

To the merest suggestion from my hands Joy adjusted her body whilst her face remained smiling and apprehensive. Aware though I was of her white, soft and rounded eagerness, its very existence served to distance rather than intrigue me. I could imagine her changing my bandages, or at a push, bed-bathing me, but not watching the moon upside-down. The body with which I was obsessed was gliding across my line of vision in its stark, black bodice.

"I would like us to dance a whole night together, Chud."

"Thank you, Joy."

The dance was guillotined and a Paul Jones called. Hoofing around in the outside circle, I saw Rosa skip towards me but when the tune stopped, although she was not strictly opposite, I nevertheless abandoned convention, leaned across and took her by the wrist.

"That will have been noticed."

"I don't care."

"Why should you? I'm the one who's married."

My arms now contained an altogether different proposition. With Rosa you were conscious of a separate force which either you mastered or else risked destruction from. She lengthened her stride so as to make me seem clumsy, but I was her equal.

"I thought Joy would melt with gratitude."

"It's her party."

"She's a good catch. Ben Little's money."

"Rosa."

As we danced she began to pinch me with steel fingernails. My back, my arms. Her face maintained a look of serenity.

"You know you're hurting me?"

"Good."

She snared me across the shoulders and burned a mark that must have been an inch long. Showing her teeth as we passed the bandstand she scored me all down the outside of my right arm.

"Stop."

"No."

I tried to deflect her by holding her into me more, allowing myself the bone of her hip, but she used the new formation to attack previously safe areas. The small of my back. My ribs. Everywhere my rind was punished.

"Why?"

"Why not?"

The firm muscles of her back beneath her dress. I caught a knob there and twisted till I heard her suck her breath.

"Bastard!"

"A truce."

We swirled towards the centre. Now I needed her to be close because I feared the whole of Monument becoming aware of my obvious discomfort. Rosa caught me with an excruciating twist to my nape.

"Jesus."

As we swept past Ben Little, his admiring wife and abandoned daughter I thought she'd had enough, but as soon as she judged me off guard her crab-like nipping recommenced. I clamped her hand, but no sooner had I done so than her other, up to that moment a model of decorum, set out. Releasing the original offender, which at once resumed as if starved of a victim, I went to her upper arm to capture its under flesh and bruise it, which I did.

"Ahh."

"Next dance, please!"

"Thank you, Rosa."

"I need some air."

We headed up the sloping field. She was frantic. She reefed my shirt all up the back and dug in and when I caught her two bare rounds beneath her skirt she gasped and her legs gave way.

"Come on!"

In along the back seat of someone's car, her legs locked around my waist, me kicking off my shoes and trying to wriggle pants down, Rosa, in one overhead motion, in only bra, and not for long either, dragging me on top of her.

"Bastard."

"Rosa."

"Come on!"

"Jesus."

She came at me out of the leather seat, firing. Her tongue. Her throat. Further exploration was limited by the chrome door fittings pressing into the backs of my legs. I pushed her back and she caught me double-handed.

"I have . . ."

"Go on!"

"I have . . ."

As if by enveloping her I could imbue myself with her redolence, I did not want to leave even a thumbnail of her unfelt. We rolled. Now, on top, she threw back her head and groaned as I ground her breasts. Such was the pressure of my heels on the window that the mechanism collapsed and my feet shot out. I thrust up and made her head hit the roof. She bent down and, my ear in her mouth, drove the point of her tongue into the pith of my brains. Way off I heard a drum roll.

"Is . . . Jack . . . likely to . . . come looking . . . ?"

Rosa went still.

I said, "Not that he'd find us."

The ripple of her thighs as she eased off me.

"Rosa . . ."

She made space, sat up and began to grope for her clothes.

"Rosa?"

"This is insane."

"Rosa, not now."

"Don't. Please."

I reached to her breast. "Rosa . . ."

"Don't!"

With great efficiency she dressed, found her shoes, slipped them on and got out. As the door closed I was left sitting alone on the leather seat, florid and crazed.

My need went beyond the merely sexual. The blood in me had washed away all picket fences of containment or the consequence of my actions. As I stooped back towards the tent, it was as if the survival of the species depended on my successful decanting. I heard no dance music, just the roar of my own surf. Never again would I doubt the extent of the forces of nature. And as in all natural disasters, fate too played a part, for at that precise moment Joy Little had decided to leave the tent for a refreshing breath.

"Chud?"

"Come here."

She was a nurse. All she wanted was to give herself in the letting of pain.

Now what I remember most about that night is the moon. Lying later beside Joy on the seat of the same car, whose I never discovered. Wondering what the moon thought. Watching its pale beams embalm us. Wondering if its streams of light were sealing our bodies with a blessing or a curse.

Fourteen

AUTUMN CAME TO THE river with uplifting significance. At dawn herons carved their ways between the turning banks in slow movements of prehuman grace, as into the dispersing mist leapt silver arcs of seagoing mullet. Teal clung to the fleece of the river in scurries to beat the tongues of sun. Heat made the trees shed their dew and for an hour they did so in cascade, and then, as the day ripened, beneath them wild mushrooms hatched out in succulent white knots. Only in the day's final phase could you see the dying leaves and grasses. On clear evenings as the water slept, the Lyle seemed to be bleeding from its heart.

The wonder was that all this beauty could co-exist with human grief, with the fever of the soul. As Monument still slept I walked the river in an attempt to find some antidotal scrap of love for Joy. Bound to her only by grief, I would rush back from the river as if I could outpace my fallowness and burst upon her and beg her to respect the shared moments of our past. The trouble was that all those moments lay in the shadow of my very first violation. I expect to Joy I reeked of infidelity as I blubbered by her bed. Even had a spark of outrage kindled between us it is possible that in the heat of blood something might have been born, but as it was I always withdrew to the bedroom now called mine, wondering if grief might not be preferable to indifference.

There is always a catalyst. Sometimes it can be hate but more often it is love. I went out to Main. Rosa swept aside the complications from my previous visit and set about the business of curing me. I do not mean taking me upstairs. I mean allowing me to cry with my head on her breast. I mean just sitting with me through the autumn evenings.

I became aware of Jack. I realised that although I had assumed the world had shut up shop the day Grace died, in fact it had continued on in its mirthless way using objects like Jack Santry for sport. Since grief actively seeks out cases more pitiful than its own in order to find balm in the relativities of fortune, I began to feel more anguish for Jack than for myself. It was heart-breaking. His courtly rituals, his innate grace. His murmurings of genuine distress for my loss, whilst all the time he himself was being bled of life because of something he had – or had not – done. After lunch one Saturday, sitting outside in sunshine with Rosa and listening to the occasional bump of an apple falling in the orchard, the door to the library opened and Jack came in. He had not been at lunch with us. He did not even know I was in Main or that his wife and I were sitting just a few yards away. He came in, heaving, and stood there, staring at the ceiling like a man contemplating his own gibbet. Neither Rosa nor I could speak. I'd seen men after battle in that attitude. Jack remained there for all of two minutes. Then he walked out again, leaving us with tears in our eyes.

It was a week later, I believe, that as I made my way back into Monument, instead of turning left out of the gate of Main I turned right and drove up into the foothills. Stopping at the flat rock I got out. I knew I had to act, as I had once before. Dusk had captured the mountains, but through some trick of the dying sun's reflection Delaware shone below me like a fleck of gold. I knew something had to be done if we wanted to keep Jack. I went to the pocket of my jacket and there found the piece of paper that Rosa had given me that day months before when we had made love.

In a Manchester street called, for some reason, Waterside, terraced both sides in identical, two-up two-down, red-brick houses, in one such house in whose short front garden grew a palm tree, through whose creaking gate the woman left every morning, from whose chimney flue oozed bluish smoke morning and evening, into whose gate pillar had been incorporated a piece of scrolled masonry, "Brock Villa", lived the former Sergeant Speechley.

I came in on a November evening, a business trip, leaving Buddy in charge. Told Rosa nothing. Booked into a new hotel behind the renovating city centre using some made-up name, cash in advance. The skyline beneath which Speechley lived, thirty minutes from the hotel, was dominated by a gasometer. Each road was laid down straight and even as a rule. I wasn't even sure at first if he was Speechley, but he was, the postman told me next morning: "'Arry Speechley? Two-two-eight. Na'atall."

At eleven he came out of his gate, strong arms spinning the chair wheels, cigarette jutting from his teeth, and rolled down to the corner shop. I didn't remember him, he could have been in the chair all his life judging from his bulky torso. Ten minutes later, a neighbour pushing, he came back, a newspaper in his lap, a fresh cigarette on the go.

Would a man already so reduced fear prosecution? I had planned to threaten the law, but now was unsure of my strategy. In Monument it had seemed straightforward. Before my arrival I had been prepared to expect that the blackmail was founded on a bluff, but the spectacle of Speechley bowling down the footpath under his own steam somehow precluded such a likelihood. He had married his nurse, the man behind the corner-shop counter told me with a wink. Crafty ol' 'Arry Speechley.

Of what was Jack guilty, I wondered during the bus journey back to my hotel? On the morning of D-Day, during those hours in which life itself had been a cauldron? Did even Jack know? I doubted he had murdered anyone on our own side, which in a way was the problem; Jack wouldn't, not even to save himself.

A young woman was checking in as I collected my key. Smiled at me with big, white teeth. A dining room and a bar with a few home-going businessmen, the lobby, that was all there was to the hotel. I took time in a bath. What must it be like to spend your life in a wheelchair? To be bathed? Married his nurse, a Manchester woman, moved north into her house. A lot of women want that, a child for ever. Women I'd met on my way through Belgium and Holland, I couldn't count them, wanted to keep our wounded, have their babies. Some succeeded. I looked down over the various islands of myself. Rosa and I had never been away together, a bathroom like this, a bed. Room service. Big, white teeth.

Downstairs I ordered a steak and ate it with onions and drank two tankards of beer.

"Haven't seen you here before."

She had stopped at my table, twirling her key.

"That's right, I'm new. What happens in Manchester on a Tuesday night?"

"Same as every other night. Very little."

Glasses. Long hair the colour of jute sacking. Nice mouth, though.

"Must be a little pub."

"There always is."

Don't ask me her name, any more than mine, that night. Twenty-one, a traveller in legal stationery, married, yes, so was I. Always easier when laws are broken in common. Great grip as if she'd once done something else with her hands, like rock climbing. Good little breasts. Why all this? Patience. She left my room at five having told me her life story, twice, and described without rationing her taxi-driver husband's anatomy.

Next morning I was seized by panic as I entered Waterside. Perhaps the Speechleys had children. I paused a hundred yards from the palm tree. Could a man like Speechley do it? If so, what better arrangement than for him to mind the child whilst the wife worked? I couldn't bear it. I couldn't humiliate even a man like this in front of his child.

I made my way towards the green fronds. I would ask for the money to be returned, but only as a negotiating ploy. He had to have a better nature, Speechley, we all do. What purpose would it serve Speechley if Jack drank strychnine? No-one had tended the garden, the palm tree might have been growing in a tip. What if he told Jack I had been here? Something I hadn't thought of. The gate creaked. The bell. Where was there any evidence of Jack's money? Rosa had got it wrong. I almost turned.

"It's not locked!"

Smells the same as those from the beds of the aged in the wards of the County Home. Medicine fringed with piss. I stood at the now open door to a narrow hallway, trying to overcome a surge of creeping insanity.

"Is that you, Terry?"

Was that the wife's name? I'd seen her leave at half-past eight, a strongly built woman, they have to be, all that leaning and lifting. It can't have been too easy to get a wheelchair through here and then I saw the scores of the wheel hubs just above the skirting. Steep stairs. Did she carry him up to bed? I stepped in.

"Sergeant Speechley?"

A front room, which I passed, full of china junk including in porcelain a life-sized dalmatian at the sit.

"Who is it?"

A kitchen. Whiff of gas. Two doors to a back garden with a ramp. He sat, staring at me, clasping the arms of his chair whose leather arm-pads I could see were in tatters.

"Speechley . . ."

"Don't tell me, don't tell me," he said.

From the breast pocket of the tunic thing he wore, he took Players. A gun-metal lighter lay on the kitchen table. Speechley reached for it, but missed. I stared. His hand flapped up the table to the lighter.

"My oh my oh my, sir," he said, breaking out into a smile. "I didn't think you'd have the guts."

His head went back and he began to laugh. The sinews in his neck stood out. It had been the newspaper the day before that threw me off. Without sound I moved two steps to my right. Speechley's eyes were still locked to where he thought I was.

"I said, 'e'll keep posting you the money, 'Arry, but e'll never dare show his nose."

He was blind. He thought I was Jack.

"Well, we'd better put the kettle on, 'adn't we, sir, to mark the occasion, like?" he said and, oozing smoke, spun to the sink.

"Let me . . ."

"Thank you kindly, sir, but 'ow d'you think I manage on the days you ain't 'ere?"

Although the wheelchair was too low for the enamel sink, a vice-grip was clamped onto the cold tap so that Speechley did not have to reach in. He dropped the tin kettle into the sink, biffed the vice-grip with the back of his hand, snatched the kettle out again and bumped it onto the gas ring. He took a spark gun from where it hung and popped a cheery, blue flame to life.

"I'd like to talk to you about . . ."

"Don't be in a rush, sir, please sir, take your time. I mean, we've an awful lot of things to say to each other, don't we? And I daresay it's most unlikely that you'll be inviting me over to your place for the return visit."

He took cups from the draining board and milk and sugar from a press.

"But who knows? Maybe a little outing is just what I need. Meet your missus and you'll love mine, fine girl, looks after me a treat. Have you got children, sir? None here, I'm sorry to say."

I could have looked into his wizened, pitted face for a thousand years and it would have meant nothing to me.

"Nursed me for three years when they brought me home. Never left me after. Name is Phyllis. Grandest lassie in the world. And yours, sir?"

"Rosa." I spoke her name the way Jack did.

"Rosa," said Speechley leaning back with a lascivious grin that made me want to throttle him. "Nice, that. Rosa."

"Speechley . . ."

"So you came at last, sir," he was now saying, unerringly pouring two cups of tea. "D'you come over this morning?"

"Yesterday."

"You should 'ave told me. I would 'ave 'ad the red carpet out. Why don't you sit down, sir?"

"Thank you."

Now I could inspect Speechley without inhibition. Nothing of him existed beyond the edge of the seat, but his chest, shoulders and arms strained with compensatory strength. Jowls of flesh had waxed heavily over the years, obliterating any neck and making him into a malign Humpty Dumpty.

"Well, cheers, sir. Sorry not being able to see you, but the memory is very clear, believe me."

"That's what I came to talk about, Sergeant."

"I don't bother with the rank no more, sir, if you don't mind. And you never called me anything but Speechley, did you?"

"It's going to have to stop, Speechley."

Back again went the head and now from close quarters I could see beyond bad teeth and down the back of the throat.

"Oh, it's not going to stop, sir, sorry, sir, it's not going to stop. Oh my oh my oh my. It's only just begun."

At least if I needed confirmation, now I had it.

"I am very sorry for your position. But what you are involved in is a crime."

"Permission to disagree, sir. I look upon it as my right. Fair repayment for what was done at the time. Natural justice, if you like, a bit like Nuremberg."

The hall door opened and closed.

"Is that you then, Terry?"

"'Morning, 'Arry. Just thought I'd . . . Oh, beg pardon, didn't know you 'ad a visitor."

A man of at least sixty with thick spectacles and a long tweed coat had appeared.

"This is Terry Horrocks. He can't 'ear no more than I can see, poor old bugger, but he helps me do my pools and with the odd piece of correspondence. Terry, come and meet a friend of mine," Speechley bellowed parade-ground-like.

"Oh, I can see 'Arry's looking after you," Terry said as he left down a parcel. "Brought you up a nice piece of cod, 'Arry."

"Just put it down there, Terry," Speechley said. To me, "Silly old ass, brings me fish no matter 'ow many times I tell him I hates it. Thanks, Terry. Is it rainin'?"

"Caught last night only, make sure you 'ave it for your tea, lovely in batter."

"Why don't you drop back this evening?"

"That's the way I like it, I must say."

"You can push off now then, Terry."

"Is that the time already, goodness. I'll drop in later when you're not so busy. Always nice to meet a friend of 'Arry's. I'll see myself out, should know the way by this stage. May see you later, ta-ra till then."

As Terry left a white cat materialised and cut a graceful crescent in the air as it sprang for the table.

"Get off, puss!" cried Speechley. He seized the parcel and threw it pinpoint, up onto a shelf. "The wife eats it. Shall we, sir?"

As I carried a kitchen chair out through the double doors I understood Jack's despair. A steep concrete path sloped down to a tiny pond. Speechley fumbled with a wall-mounted valve and a feeble fountain appeared from the centre of the pond. Surrounded by torpor, I realised that Speechley's only energy came from his persecution of Jack. He started another cigarette.

"Can feel the sun, can hear the water. What more could a man ask, sir?"

Perhaps I should have felt compassion, and perhaps Jack did, but the longer I remained in the presence of this predatory invalid the deeper would be my detestation. I sat beside him as with a strong thumb he clicked the brake of his apparatus.

"I am sorry, Speechley."

"Are you? For what?"

"To . . . find you like this."

"Is that all? Not that it matters."

"You'll have to tell me."

"D'you know how many years it is? Sixteen, sir. Sixteen years. You could come over 'andy enough now, sir, when it suits, but it took you sixteen years."

Smoke scored his sightless eyes.

"I always 'ad you down with a question mark, right from the beginning. I said to myself, ''Arry, watch this bloke, he'll let you down on the day,' and my goodness, sir, was I right."

"What exactly do you mean?"

"Hah! I can understand, sir, I've listened to all the reports, I know 'ow you came through it after, the Battle of Riva Bouche, the campaign up through them Low Countries. You see, for some like you it's like a big motion, if you'll excuse the language, sir. The fear, I mean. I've seen it. Once you've passed it, it's gone and you're as spunky as the rest."

Other than the pond and fountain, the back garden was no more inspired than the front. A tangle of cats lay in sunshine at some distance.

"The fun it must 'ave been, that campaign. Goodness me, I often sat 'ere and imagined I'd been with you all, me legs under me, me eyes looking down the sights of me Besa. What I wouldn't 'ave given. We beat the bastards, sir, and I wasn't there. That nearly killed me, to think that after all the waiting 'Arry Speechley didn't make it past twelve o'clock on D-Day. And all because of you, sir."

"Tough decisions had to be made, Speechley," I ventured. "No-one is perfect."

"Don't tell me about tough decisions, sir. Or 'ave you forgotten? I doubt it. You see, I understand 'ow your mind filled up with all the weeks and months that followed. Goodness, you even made it to Berlin. But understand my mind, sir. No weeks or months to fill my mind. Just hours, sir. Just bloody hours. I'm sure you well remember those hours, sir."

"They . . . went by very quickly."

"Selective memory, eh, sir? Can't say I blame you."

"I'm sorry, I really don't remember."

He shook his head, then smiled. "You're 'avin' me on."

"I'm afraid I'm not."

His hand, now shaking, went to the breast pocket of his jacket from which he jerked out a picture in cellophane, ejecting his cigarettes and lighter onto the concrete.

"D'you see 'im, sir? Tell me who you see."

A man in the uniform of a sergeant standing in front of a tank, smoking a cigarette.

"It's . . . you."

"Was I 'andsome, sir?"

"A fine man."

"A fine man, sir, thank you, sir. A fine man. And you don't even remember."

He shoved the picture back and then realised the cigarettes and lighter were gone. Gripping with one hand he swung down like a chimpanzee and swept his fingers back and forth over the ground. There was a moment when his weight threatened to overbalance him, but he had innate understanding of his circumstances and just as the whole structure began to tip he lurched back up again, lighter and fags held aloft.

"I know what you're feeling, sir, and it's not pity. You 'ate me, but there's more. 'E disgusts you, this fat little blind ball with no legs. 'E makes you sick. You'd much rather be at 'ome with your Rosa than sitting 'ere with this damn monkey. But you can't because you're afraid of him. So understand this, Captain, you feel no pity for me and I, sir, feel no pity for you."

He went through his lighting-up routine and took a drag of such magnitude that the sides of the cigarette collapsed.

"We took out their big gun with the petard on your Churchill. Killed every bastard but one. Blond 'un. I had 'im." Speechley ran his tongue out to capture an errant grain of tobacco. "I always thought after, at least I 'ad one of them, at least I came 'ome and 'ad a wife and a life, which is more than 'e 'ad."

"The time."

"Must have been o-eleven 'undred give or take. Took me an hour to flail up from the water and I thought I'd done it in thirty seconds."

"And I was . . ."

"You really don't remember, do you, sir?"

I shook my head. Then, "No."

"You were there, with us, your troop. You had Sappers Rowe and O'Hara – remember them? – mark the beach."

"The rest of the troop were . . ."

"Dead, sir, all dead. And every tank dead. We had to regroup the squadron smartish with your Irish mate from 'ome. They were the other side of the sand dunes near that villa. We 'ad to cross a minefield under sniper fire, sir. Remember now?"

"A little clearer."

"Good. Then the rest will start coming back to you, too, believe me. Because it weren't the mines that bothered you, sir, oh no, you actually led us into the mines. And I thought, dear me, I was wrong, the gentleman's got his dander up and God help Gerry. That's what I said to myself."

I did remember, suddenly. Men in the dunes. I remembered it so abruptly that I felt fright.

"Someone fell to a sniper. Gerry potted his helmet," I said.

"Well done, sir. That was O'Hara, poor silly bastard. So you remember the snipers, sir?"

I remembered the snipers and the villa because now I remembered that the snipers had been the reason we had rammed the villa, to stop them potting the men in the dunes. As if the time between the taking of the beachhead and the ramming of the villa had fallen into a cleft only now rediscovered, out it seeped, intact.

"The villa snipers, yes."

"Then you remember Sapper Rowe."

A cheery-faced lad popped in and out of my mind's eye. "I think so."

Speechley's head was cocked to one side like a cat at wainscotting.

"'E was what did it for you, weren't he? His 'ead."

"His head?"

"The dog's dinner, sir. Come on. Gerry's bullet took the back of his 'ead clean off. I dragged him down off the road. That left just you and me. Didn't look good, sir, did it?"

Two men. East of our position. Smoke drifting in across the dunes like banks of fog. I'd ordered covering fire.

"Go on."

"We couldn't stay there. Dust and artillery smoke were giving us a bit of cover, but when the wind cleared it we were going to be ducks in a row. We had to try and make a run for it. For a moment I thought you'd been hit, sir. I was actually wondering how I was going to carry you.

Then I saw your face."

All I could think of was Jack. Poor Jack.

"I'd seen funks before, we got them when we started training along the Caledonian with live ammunition. But never one like yours. You were rigid, like as if you was in another world. I should have shot you." Speechley pinched the bridge of his nose. "Why didn't I? Have I asked myself that question a thousand times? A million, more like. I should have drilled you one and gone on. I was within my rights to do so. We were under enemy fire and my commanding officer was a lily liver. Why didn't I?"

Poor Jack, poor Rosa. Sun high over suburban rooftops coursed down through the defiant fountain. Beside the pond a cat stretched, its claws sprung.

"Because you was an officer. Because I knew I was better than a thousand like you. Because at that moment I realised that the whole thing was a fucking sham, the airs and graces, the decent NCOs like 'Arry Speechley running and lifting for the likes of dirt like you. I was going to show you up for what you were. I was going to march you up through that minefield and when we rejoined our lads make sure you were never put in charge of anyone again."

His cigarette had burned right down to his fingers, but it didn't seem to matter to him.

"What happened?"

"I dragged you to your feet and then began to prod along, fast as I could. I remember thinking, only a few more yards." Speechley sighed. "Suddenly I saw a dozer going for the villa. I turned round to see if you'd seen it. I'll never forget your face, never. The terror in it. You see, yours was the last face I ever saw."

Bus brakes shrieked and children cried out from another world. "I said, that does it. I shall 'ave to march the bastard in." Speechley went quiet. "That was it, sir. That was my life."

Not in all the years had anyone evoked the war's images for me like Speechley. They were his daily view, as fresh now as then. Those of us who'd been lucky and come home had put other images between us and war, but for Speechley the ugliness had been sealed inside his head at the height of the inferno and now made him what he was.

"I'd like you to try and see it from my position," I said and bit my tongue. Then, "What happened to you is a tragedy beyond words. I can say I'm sorry a thousand times, but it won't change things. And I am sorry, Speechley, sincerely."

"It were a crime. A criminal act. If things 'ad worked out different, if

173

I 'adn't trod on that mine, you'd 'ave been court-martialled, perhaps shot. But as it 'appened, I'm the one who got sent to a dark room for the rest of 'is life and they gave you a bloody gong."

"And that's where you want me to be, too, isn't it? With you in that dark room for the rest of my life? Well it's not going to happen, Speechley."

"You put me 'ere and now you can pay for it. You think this is easy? A few quid benefit to buy fags? We'd be on the street if it weren't for the army pension. Look at this dump I live in! I've never seen it, but I know what it's like. My wife 'as to work 'er knuckles to the bone to keep us in food. I'd like to buy 'er a proper cooker and a cold refrigerator for 'er kitchen. I'd like to buy myself a proper one of these. Christ, I'm going to spend the rest of my life sitting in it. Who's going to pay for it all?"

"What have you done with the money I've already sent?"

"It's hid where not even Phyllis can find it, and that's where it's going to stay, so you just keep sending those registered letters. Then one day, when I've saved enough, I shall take 'er on a cruise. I've given 'er nothing all the years, you see, sir. She's been like an angel and I'm going to take 'er away where everyone'll be lifting and carrying to 'er as if she were the queen. And that's what she is, too, 'ave no doubt. Oh, your money's safe, sir, don't you worry a bit," chuckled Sergeant Speechley.

We were and always had been, I now understood, beyond discussion. He would always drain Jack of everything, including courage, as once he had before.

"You talk about crime. What do you think you're involved in? Blackmail is a crime and the fact that you're a cripple won't save you. Now we're going to settle this today, once and for all."

"Oh, 'e's got a rush of blood, the gentleman 'as. D'you think I care? But my bet is that you do, sir. And maybe deep down that's what I want to 'appen, for you to report me, because if you do, then I shall 'ave to explain, shan't I? And I want to explain, sir, blimey do I what. Go ahead, sir. Cheer me up. Take a little cripple to court and see the fun and games there'll be then!"

As on so many other occasions in my life, I wished I had had a plan. It was nearly noon.

"Listen, a man can only take so much, do you understand what I mean, Speechley?"

In a movement that was truly over before I knew it had begun, Speechley had, from somewhere in the seat of his wheelchair, reached for and was now readying a nine-inch knife.

"Come on, sir, I'm ready! I've it all worked out, I've 'ad years to do so.

Not much of a contest, you probably thought, you against a cripple. But I know where you are every second. You see these? These ears are poor old 'Arry's eyes. I know just where your 'eart is for I can 'ear it beating twice as fast as mine."

"You're a bad bastard."

Speechley frowned. "My, you 'ave changed. Almost a different person, by the sound of you there. Where did you find that spunk? Don't tell me, don't tell me. What's 'er name? Rosa, that's it. Rosa put steel in your back, and elsewhere too, I fancy. Is she nice? I'll bet. Would she do it for me, sir? If I said I'd forget everything, would you send Rosa over here and tell her to put steel in old 'Arry Speechley's rod?"

"You little cunt."

"My oh my, I think we're getting somewhere after all. My Phyllis is a regular old darlin', but I can tell she's no beauty, how could she be, endin' up with the likes of me? I'm sure she 'as her little flings. I don't blame her, but it's been dreadful lonely 'ere for all these years, so an officer's doxy might be just the thing old 'Arry needs to cheer 'im up."

It was hard to believe he was sightless, perched with his knife presented, facing me sideways from his chair. I reached out my foot.

"I'll know if you get up!"

I brought my toe to the brake clip.

"What are . . . ? Why you . . . !"

I almost didn't make it. I snapped down the steel lever as his knife hand was whistling for my leg, but he had already begun to roll. Only half a dozen revolutions to the lip of the water. He tried to stab his knife into the spinning spokes, but he'd gained too much momentum and the blade was wrenched from his hand. He never uttered. I watched cats scatter as the chair whacked into the base and Speechley was decanted headfirst into his ornamental pond.

Peaceful. Speechley's curious rump was alone visible. I walked down and put both my hands to it. A minute would cool him off. From the water came a deep eruption of trapped air. He began a mighty struggle so I pressed down with all my strength, then reached for his hair and pulled his head up. Water streamed from his glassy face. I plunged him back again and heard his head crack the base. I hadn't realised it was only twelve inches deep.

A creak. Substantial parts of a second were needed to extract the sound from the other distractions, then identify it. From the front of the house. The gate. I legged it in through the kitchen, into the sitting room with its china clutter, and spied the front of the house through an imitation lace curtain. Phyllis Speechley was standing inside the gate, a shopping bag in hand, chatting to another woman in a scarf. I thought not of Speechley, as I should have, but of my incriminating cup and chair lying outside. Our instant facility for self-preservation. Phyllis had taken out a fag. Fully expecting to be confronted by Speechley's venomous face I sprinted back out through the kitchen, seized the cup, thrust it into the pocket of my jacket (fingerprints), and dragged the chair back inside. I was again at the front-room window before I realised that I had seen nothing of Speechley. But now Phyllis had taken two steps towards the front door, puffing smoke, still chatting, but putting space between herself and the other woman.

The implications of each further second fell heavily around me. I readied myself for another dash out back, this time to rescue Speechley, but then so did Phyllis take another step nearer her door. It would take me thirty seconds to heave him out and get back, I reckoned. I was in the hall when I heard the rattle of the latchkey. I dived back in again and cowered behind a cloisonné totem. Yet still the women lingered as if joined by an umbilical cord of gossip. Swept by an old and once more familiar terror, one that predated the war, I realised the outcome. The fact of justice being done flickered at the edge of my conscience, but my overwhelming feeling was one of awe. As I crouched, as Phyllis dallied, here in grimy Manchester one man's life was ending whilst in Ireland another's, although he did not know it, had rebegun. It happens every moment of every day although you are rarely aware of it and never, I imagine, in the way I was then. It was the very hinge of creation.

The hall door opened, closed. Whilst up to now a certain serendipity had attended events, now I began to pray that she would not save him. There's no stopping fortune once she's on a roll; instead of going to her kitchen, Phyllis Speechley's footsteps could be heard on her stairs.

I did not go back for a final look. I was up the path, out of the gate and fifty yards up the road without once exhaling. I was in the airport by two and within sight of the Lyle that evening as the Angelus was being dealt out by the cathedral bell.

You look for comfort where you can in these things and I found it, or some of it, in the fact that when she had come home Phyllis Speechley had gone straight upstairs. It confirmed something to me of their relationship. He had become the monster: to me as Jack, to deaf Terry Horrocks, and I imagine, to Phyllis, his wife, whose loyalty he had not hesitated to impugn given the opportunity. She'd not gone straight to him when she came home and that to me spoke volumes.

I would never tell Rosa what had happened. Simply suggest she watched Jack for signs of improvement. A sweet glow of anticipation began to form in my guts as I drove along Long Quay. I parked my car inside the gate of St Melb's. I would ring her tomorrow.

RING-BINDERS
7 - 9

Fifteen

Rosa used to shop for all three of us, an activity which took her out around the town, meeting people and, she said, keeping her limbs green. Not that she moved with any less grace than I remembered, more if anything, so that from a distance I could still imagine her a girl. She made no secret about preferring life in Monument, although she had spent and loved almost forty years in Main. O'Gara Street, built of thick walls, was and is cosy and private and yet within minutes of Long Quay and MacCartie Square. There are river views from the upstairs rooms.

But I'm running way ahead of myself, jumping from Manchester in 1960 to O'Gara Street in 1986, locating Rosa and Jack with me in Monument and leaving out the reasons why we were all together in the first place.

Church Land had become a big company by the late 1960s. Four warehouses, that is, three on the Monument river below St Melb's and one, designed by me, on the southern end of Long Quay, between the Monument river and Oxburgh Street. We owned the best river frontage in the town. Within the ambit of our wharves and warehouses an entire, self-contained universe existed – boats that plied to us, most of them from Liverpool, men who took bagged goods from their crane slings and loaded them onto steel-wheeled trolleys for our warehouses, riots of paperwork spawned by each boat and requiring in turn armies of checkers and clerks, and watchers and officers of the state with indelible purple pencils, checking and double-checking manifests, entering their findings into books and onto forms in quadruplicate. I couldn't take it, however hard I tried. I saw men thumbing through their molting tariff books and imposing levies and all I wanted was to be elsewhere. I could not be elsewhere since I had a business to run, and so only in gambling could I escape the monotony of stamping bags, of calculating tonnage, of identifying names of consignors and consignees, of statistics. My personal balance sheet comprised, on its credit side, solid warehouses full of other people's goods, and opposite, horses that went down by the shortest of short heads. Except that it wasn't in balance. My slow horses outweighed entire shiploads.

Ma Church had grown old. It was not that Paddy Bensey was to blame, or her leaving St Melb's, or the fresh demands which marriage imposed;

my grandmother, I think, relaxed for the first time in memory, took her eye off the office in O'Gara Street and forgot the tide. It didn't suit her. Within a year of her retirement what I had never thought possible was a reality. Ma Church had stepped into the final phase of her life as if through an open door.

She tried to keep in touch with events through daily reports. She must have known. She must have seen the bank balance and realised what was going on. Gambling was her essence too, after all. To quit the feathered if storm-tossed nest as the paid mistress to an earl, to bet her life on an impulse and walk down the gangway, to wager everything on a town and country and with a man all of which and of whom she knew nothing, what were those if not the actions of a gambler? And since we're talking about gamblers, what widow would have plunged headlong into a business about whose prospects her only inkling was the cupidity on the faces of men? This is some dame we're talking about! Bequeathing me Church Land was her last roll of the dice.

These reports. They were delivered to her in White City by Buddy Stone, whose devotion to the ha'pence of business made him shine in my grandmother's eyes. In at eight each morning and still there twelve hours later, if ever he heard a boat's captain blowing for the tide – for that meant our gangs had been slow in loading – Buddy would leap to his feet like a man electrocuted, sprint riverwards cramming his bowler hat down on his head, and march up and down the wharf screaming obscenities (which later he would confess in the cathedral, he once told me). I trusted Buddy with all the details – he was like my brother, after all – and I thought of making him a director and giving him shares in the company in which his life had been invested.

I could sense him hovering.

"No luck with the bank?"

"No."

"We're right up against our limit, Chud."

"I know."

"We could try and sell some land to the Commissioners."

"I know."

Buddy sank from view. The phone on his desk tinkled. Buddy said, "He's not in."

I could blame no-one but myself for the debts, nor even now claim that pleasure had attended their incurring. Thought did not come to me clearly. What were the moves? There had to be moves, yet I could not grasp them. Poor Ma Church. She must have hoped that some instinct for survival in me would have outweighed my vices.

If asked what, if anything, I did well during those years I would in honesty have to answer, I loved a woman. Nothing existed that took up my mind or my purpose more. I had no other friends or pastimes. When I should have been focused on the great evolving of my inheritance, I was planning my next few hours with Rosa. First I would smell her. In the same way as garden smells are released by rain, or kitchen baking by an open oven door, so she grew out of the atmosphere without needing to be seen, the best moment, I often thought, because I knew she smelled me as well, she told me so. As if we existed only in terms unique to both of us, our essences embraced. I would keep sight of her till last, the same way I still isolated the yoke of a fried egg, delayed the first sip of sherry or the last chapter of a worthwhile book. How could a woman resemble a note of music? I had no idea, but she did. Her beauty resonated. Her tautness had now run into something quieter. Except her eyes. They still changed as often as moonbeams on running water.

Details of Rosa's clothes in those days still fill me with longing. A blue shirt she wore out riding, a Jack cast-off, was frayed white around the collar, and where the threads were splayed they touched the skin beneath her ears. She often wore gloves, black and of kid leather, into which I could only, to her amusement, fit the first three fingers of my hand. Country life being what it is, her jackets and skirts were often serviceably bulky, concealing her figure, but as if to reward my patience she would on the summer nights I came out for supper wear an airy, cream dress with straps across her bare shoulders, confirming that none of her skin's lustre had been lost to the Irish winter.

In those early days we met in our cars: at the holy well, in Sibrille and with, for Rosa, delicious irony, in Leire. Sitting between my legs as distant, black figures scurried through the sea mist, she fantasised that I had scaled the cliff and torn her from the staring refectory. One evening when I was working late she came to O'Gara Street and we went upstairs to an unused room and made love on old invoices. If a number of lines were being drawn, this one was bold in the extreme, for after that encounter I lit a coal fire upstairs and we bothered no more with cars. Of course, Buddy and Miss D'Arcy came to know, and of course I knew they would; but having embraced happiness at last neither Rosa nor I was prepared to negotiate it, even at the expense of the scandal leaking out beneath the door of O'Gara Street.

Since there was never any question of her abandoning Jack, the impropriety of our relationship was not gall to us but spice. We uncovered the lost years and laughed and sometimes cried at the zigzag paths that had taken us back to where we had started. I left the office every morning at ten-thirty and walked by way of Conduit out onto Long Quay and down to the Commercial Hotel. Into our snug. One such morning as I came in Rosa smiled and I leaned down and kissed her on the mouth just as the door of the snug opened behind me and Billy Little, Joy's brother, appeared, agog. I thought for a moment he was going to have a swing at me and in a way I hoped he would.

"Billy."

He took long breaths, like a man about to duck dive. Then he went out, still staring, as if to offer me his back would risk a knife in it.

On Rosa's insistence I had gone back to Main, since Rosa believed that the more I postponed re-encountering Kevin the harder it would become and the greater the original irregularity would grow in the child's mind. He had a cold look, a remodelled version of Jack without the heart. More than once, as Rosa and I took tea in the porch, or outside the doors of the library, I fancied that in shrubs fifty yards away a blob of yellow hair was conducting a surveillance.

"Chud." Rosa, looking out at me over the spectacles she now used for reading. "D'you ever think of what happened in Delaware?"

"Yes and no. When I went away then I thought nothing of it at all, nor during the war. Now I think of it more."

Rosa put down her book. "Why do you think that is?"

I didn't want to tell her what I believed, which was that however much you try to forget them the people you have truly wronged will never let you. But I said, "I don't let it bother me. Nor should you. It just happened. We were young."

"D'you know what I think?"

I shook my head.

"That one day it's all going to come back on us," Rosa said. "Silly, maybe, but that's what I think."

"In what way?"

"Hard to say. Maybe we should all talk about it, the three of us."

"Maybe."

Frosts deepened in November and from the upstairs window in O'Gara Street, despite the fire, stark but pretty cobwebs fringed the narrow view to the river.

"Tell me, who owns what and all?"

"You mean . . . ?"

"Your business. Property."

So she learned the details of my business, and the problems. I said, "Times are difficult."

Rosa winced. She would never try to hurt me by verbalising my unsuitability for business of any kind. She asked, "St Melb's?"

"In Joy's name."

Rosa's eyes were darting in thought.

"And this place?"

"The company."

She lay on her front with her ankles crossed, like something carved from a stripped, tawny branch. Taking out a cigarette, she lit it, a process which, even when she was not naked, I found arousing.

"Stop. I'm thinking. How much is it worth?"

"What?"

"Here. This office, house."

"Ten thousand, maybe."

"You've got to get it for yourself."

"Why?"

"Chud, I love you. Because your wife doesn't live here."

A ship's masts crossed a distant square of brightness, sailing upriver. I wondered, was she bound for us.

Six weeks later, with money given to her by Paddy Bensey, Rosa through her solicitor purchased O'Gara Street from Church Land in trust and when the sale came to be closed, my name was inserted as the new owner.

Ma Church never shrank in the way of the dying. I have no doubt she could have been buried in cascading black silk with dramatic insertions of white valenciennes and nothing, not a stitch, would have needed altering. She fainted one morning before she left her house in White City and so began an eight-month descent, during which such people as Dr Armstrong assumed a central role in our lives.

I say "our", because my grandmother's illness transformed Joy from a moping, self-pitying appendage into the efficient, tireless nurse she had been when first I met her. Out came her old uniform and newly starched she went rustling out of St Melb's every morning. Joy in uniform assumed an aura of power and authority that had me wondering whether Ma Church's illness might not have all been for the better.

Life is a rat-bag of surprises, but sometimes they are pleasing and in this twilight saga one of the revelations to which even I will admit was Paddy Bensey's dignity. His love for Ma Church could deny her nothing, sweeping aside his own dislikes and in the process making him something almost likeable. To ensure her happiness, not even the sight of me in his house twice and sometimes more each day gave rise to objections from

Bensey. He would even agree to my grandmother's going down beside Dr Church, a statement of her priorities that must have pained him.

So the final months – they telescoped into exhausting days and nights – caused Joy to breeze into Ma Church's bedroom and, utterly unlike the woman I was married to, exclaim, "Ah, Chud is here and your happy face says it all, Mrs Church! I'll just ease you up a little, you stay where you are, Chud. There we are! My goodness those are the most beautiful flowers. Don't tell me, I'll guess, Chud. Would you not manage just that little last piece of toast, Mrs Church? Never mind. Give a little ring of the bell if you need me."

I beat a path every day over Balaklava and out to Paddy Bensey's, where evergreen trees had been planted too near the house and had added to the overall crisis of proportion.

"Chud."

"Ma?"

"I don't want to die."

"You're not going to die, Ma."

"Ah, Chud, you were always such a liar."

I thought she was sleeping, but she opened her eyes.

"I came up that river," she whispered, "and I knew I would never go down it again. Before ever I met him, I knew 'e was 'ere." The legacy of our history.

"Tell me, Ma."

For five days during which she neither ate nor slept nor woke Ma Church replayed her entire life in an unpunctuated monologue. I heard of lords and earls and Cowes and the Hebrides. She spoke of a telephone call, of the cold of the night, of hot whiskey and thoughtlessness and perjury and her husband the poor doctor, a man who would leave the arms of his wife and his warm bed and go out in any weather if he thought he could lessen pain. She lamented the infamous misdeed that I, as a child, had been a part of, and in a seductive tone she made my case all over again to Beagle. She called out for all her children, dead and alive, my mother, Hilda, included, and for poor Gus, and for Uncle Mary, and for Faithful Tadpole, for whom she wept from unseeing, open eyes. She died at six in the morning on August 12th, 1967, with just myself and Paddy Bensey beside her.

Huge funeral. Bensey shone that day. He walked alone after the coffin down the aisle, leaving a gap to the rest of us, and out into the cemetery as if she had been in his safekeeping for this moment. The like of the flowers had never before been seen. An entire cartload was sent from London from Giles Church, the proprietor of Church's, the ship's chandlers. Later we went back to Bensey's for drinks, Rosa, Jack and myself, Miss D'Arcy, Buddy and many from Monument's business community. Later, as I was leaving alone, Bensey buttonholed me by his stone pillars.

"A word."

He was in fact ten years Ma Church's junior although to my eyes he had always seemed much the older.

"Mr Bensey?" I wondered was he drunk.

"D'you see that gate?" he said, pointing towards the road. "When you go out that gate today, don't ever come back in through it again."

Monument is a town where each season finds full expression. I know cities where on a dull day the points of the compass are as much a mystery as the time of the year; but not Monument. Wedded to its river, a symbiosis is evident in the way of long-enduring couples where you need only to read the face of one to understand the disposition of the other. You will see harbingers of the first snow flurries across the surface of the Lyle or in the voice of the wind over Cattleyard; you will read all the changing seasons in the ever-moving rigging of a ship, or in the cheeks of the old stagers on Long Quay.

Certain features of St Melb's always recalled the old days to me: the thick knit of winter-flowering jasmine cut square around the windows, the sudden sight of the Monument river as you rounded the gable, the steep pitch of the one-sided roof above the porch. In truth it was only in its evocation of the past that the house still sparked affection in me, for the recent years of my tenure had witnessed nothing but grief, estrangement and suspicion.

Coming up to Christmas, I drove to Dublin with Buddy to meet someone from whom we wished to buy a crane. It was still the year of Ma Church's death, but if she had hoped that her passing might inspire me to give up the gambling which was draining Church Land, then she had hoped in vain. At eight Buddy dropped me at the foot of The Knock and I made my way, hat brim snapped down against the cold, to St Melb's. Despite the fact that coal barges no longer used it, the Monument river still harboured a sooty demeanour and, I fancied, smell. I could just about make out in the dusk the top of the original Church warehouse. It recalled the past to me with acuity and reminded me yet again of the downward slope I seemed incapable of leaving. My key refused to turn. I rang the bell. As my hand went once again to the bell, the door opened and the light over my head came on.

"The lock is broken," I said aloud.

"It's not broken, Chud."

In the doorway stood an unyielding, black figure.

"Father O'Dea?"

He stepped out, keeping between me and the door.

I said, "I've been in Dublin."

"I know. I'm afraid you will find a lot changed since you left this morning."

"What's wrong?"

The priest sighed. "Oh dear, Chud. You were never far from trouble, were you?"

"I . . ."

"Arrangements have been made for you in the Commercial Hotel."

". . . What?"

"I'll drive you there now in fact and we can talk on the way."

"Look, this is my house! I want to go in."

"In fact it's Joy's house. The deeds are in her name. You made them over to her some years ago."

"What in the name of Christ is this about?"

"Blaspheme at your peril. Joy is under heavy sedation. The scandal is consuming the town. I can only pray that God will show both of you the sinful nature of your ways and that you will realise that it is never too late for true contrition. But in the meantime I cannot allow you into this house."

In the following order it occurred to me: to be sick, to sit down, to ring Rosa, to go to my office, to see Jack. However, I said, "I want to see my wife."

"That's not possible."

"Who are you to say so?"

"I am her priest."

"I want to see my wife! Get out of my way!"

"Is that him?"

"It's all right, Joy, he's going."

She was in the porch. The light, maybe, but her hair looked grey. In a dressing-gown, with her brother Billy beside her.

Billy said, "I'm going to kill you, you bastard."

"Billy!" Father O'Dea spread out his arms behind him as if to contain the ocean. "Remember what we agreed!"

That made it worse, to realise that the forces joined against me were acting to a plan.

Joy spoke. "I know you didn't love me, but did you have to tell the town? Did you, Chud? I know what you think of me, but does Grace not deserve more?"

I shook my head as if trying to wake up. Joy was lurching towards me, fingers rasping.

"D'you see this speck of dirt? That's what you've made me, Chud! A speck of dirt."

"Joy, I'll see to this now. Now, please, Chud."

"I should have listened to my father! He told me all about you years ago, Chud! He told me everything!"

"Joy . . ."

"Let me kill him!"

"You're finished! We're going to take every stitch off you! Every brick and every perch. What will you and your whore do then? What hole will ye crawl into?"

Father O'Dea stepped up into the porch and eased my weeping wife back into my recent house. In fact it might then have been any house for its relevance to me was all at once empty. To wait for the priest to re-emerge and make further pronouncements was more than I could suffer. I walked out of St Melb's. It was not the first time, I reflected, but a slowly gathering wisdom told me it was the last.

The Littles had become a force in Monument. Billy Little employed more than two hundred people and his sister was Mrs Joy Church. For a bank to pull the rug on Church Land might risk offending the Littles. Worse, perhaps some uninformed sole trader, unaware of who Mrs Joy Church really was and upon hearing of a collapse at Church Land might refuse the inhabitant of St Melb's her normal credit for hen's eggs or tripe. The Littles might not be amused. Worse, worse, perhaps in the subsequent impugning of Mrs Joy Church's credit-worthiness the Little empire itself might, by free association, come under a shadow in the town. Who knew what might then happen? A run. Traders refusing to cash Little's Lemonade cheques. Creditors shifting their tenuous buttocks. Sugar credit refused. Widespread unemployment. So easy for forty years' diligence to perish in an epidemic of ignorance. So my severing – it was known everywhere in two days – allowed the bank a clear target. Nothing like a jilted woman to clear the air.

I set my sights on merchant bankers in Dublin, men who lunched in clubs and in some cases, like myself, had seen action. In the same way that people at sunset will draw their chairs into the last wedge of sunshine, it is fundamental to the life of a hopeless case that the focus be on the wealth, however shrinking. They listened politely to my predictions for increased trade and noted carefully the values I attributed to my assets, but their eyes grew small when it came to lending money.

Only my trips out to Main kept me sane.

"Chud."

Her cheek. The inside of her arm as it held the teapot in midair. How could a clutch of sinews and bone tantalise a man poised over such an abyss? Even if her money from Bensey had not been tied up and Rosa could have saved me, I don't think I would have let her. I now lived in O'Gara Street in the house she had bought for me. Enough. In a way I felt relief at the approaching collapse, the psychosis of the doomed, if you will, but a liberating one nonetheless. To be rid of so much.

One afternoon I came back into O'Gara Street from Main like an aviator returning from the world above the clouds. Buddy had decamped, to where I was not sure, given two weeks' notice and never worked it out. I didn't hold it against him. He'd repaid whatever ancient debt he felt was owed by his family to the Churches. Still. It was lonely without his invisible presence. I went up the misty Knock and down by the Monument river. Through the error of a clerk, when St Melb's had been transferred for the sake of financial prudence to Joy, a skelp of adjoining land up here amounting to three acres had been omitted; and during the various mortgagings of company assets the same land had been wrongly assumed to be attached to St Melb's. It and O'Gara Street were all I would end up with. Remembering Uncle Percy's ancient solution, but recalling also his swollen body and rejecting the tactic on grounds of pride alone, I sucked in damp air, broke the skin of my knuckles against the door of our warehouse – my warehouse! – and reeled on down the path in alternate waves of dread and elation. Back in my office with only Miss D'Arcy for company I sat, day after day beneath the white-faced mahogany clock as if engaged in a stand-off with time.

Like the final advent of death (I imagine), the collapse was swift and decisive. It involved the serving of statutory instruments, the changing of warehouse locks, the impounding of records, of goods, the crystallisation of affairs, the publication of notices, the general suspension of credit, the alienating of my few remaining loyal customers and the open feeding of the rumours coursing through the streets.

My reaction on hearing that Buddy had been given the money by the bank to buy Church Land was one of happiness for him.

Sixteen

KEVIN WAS DIFFERENT FROM every previous first-born Santry, beginning with his name. From the time he could walk, Kevin had to run the gauntlet, morning and night on stair and in hall, of his ancestors, whose high foreheads, fair hair and curling upper lips persevered in the child, but not their first name. Rosa had liked Kevin, and Jack, having at the time forsaken Santry rules to marry Rosa, abandoned yet another. The child was named Kevin Patrick Bensey Santry. He had gone away to Eton with "KPBS" embroidered on his shirts.

Kevin Santry excelled in class, a fact that caused the older housemasters who remembered Jack to shake their heads in amazement. Establishing early on that he had no intention of entering the army, he forged ahead with his studies and went up to Oxford. Kevin would continue to break all the moulds which his naming had initiated, leaving Oxford with a first in history and returning to Dublin in 1971, where he became articled to a solicitor.

Kevin, as he would later famously admit, never managed to come to terms with his conflicting feelings for his mother. As he grew into manhood he came more and more to admire her exceptional beauty and grace. Side by side with this infatuation existed a rejection of Rosa and everything she stood for, dating from the distant year of his discovery of her with me upstairs in Main. Kevin's feelings for his mother provoked in him long interludes of guilt. Only by exaggerating his contempt for her could he manage these feelings. Whereas indifference was the most Kevin could muster for Jack, for Rosa he nurtured a highly charged field of love lost, jealousy and exculpatory hate.

Kevin formed an early and you might say instinctive alliance with his grandfather, Paddy Bensey. Kevin was all Bensey upstairs, an unpitying calculator of human odds. The bookie did not so much as blink in 1974 when Kevin proposed the purchase of Beagle & Co, the biggest solicitors in Monument. Bensey wrote out a cheque for a reputed one hundred thousand, and thus with the stroke of his grandfather's pen, Kevin Santry, the scion of Main, also became one of the most important men in Monument.

But more than cold logic or common blood bound grandfather and grandson. Rosa knew, but she never mentioned it. For on that night on which he had come in upon his mother and myself, young Kevin had afterwards gone missing. His bicycle was not in the shed. Rosa, determined not to surrender to panic nor to burden Jack with her anxieties, went out around Main on her horse and searched every copse and gully and hedgerow and rode down to Delaware, and up the foothills on the far side, calling as she might to a lost hound, "Kevin! Come on, Kevin! Kevin, Kevin, Kevin!"

Stabling the horse and checking the stables, she searched all the garden sheds, tack rooms, feed and machinery stations, hay lofts, grain lofts, byres and coops. She went into every quarter of the grooms' and gardeners' lodgings – still in use in 1960 – and then into the greenhouses, and down into the boiler houses of the greenhouses, and out into the concrete sties for the pigs – a Jack project – and even looked up behind the dovecote, in which Kevin sometimes hung out when he was picking off rats from under cover with his airgun.

The telephone was ringing as Rosa, exhausted, came in, resigned to have to concoct some rigmarole for Jack and to put out a more general alert.

"Hello?"

"Rosa, my pet, this is your father."

"Oh."

She feared the bookie in the same way in which she would come to fear her son.

"It's all right, Rosa, the lad's here with me."

"I see."

"The size of him and the quickness of his mind," the bookie went on. "No fear of that lad, none at all. He'll stay here with me until the mood takes him to go home. Isn't that the best, Rosa?"

"Yes," said Rosa and put down the phone.

She knew he knew. And she knew that binding Bensey and Kevin Santry from that day more even than genetics was their mutual loathing of me.

For Kevin's manner alone people disliked him, but there was a fixity to him, altogether absent in Jack, that ensured he got his way. Six months following his purchase of Beagle & Co he married, and a daughter, Annabelle, was born in 1975. The Kennel House at Main, a residence by custom used for those widowed or in waiting, was replumbed and rewired and became the home of Kevin and Brigid Santry.

She had been Brigid Bell. Kevin had first set eyes on her, a long-limbed nineteen-year-old with an exotic tinge to her skin and tilt to her eyes, during a summer charity concert in Dublin. She was one of an undergraduate dancing troupe and her legs had made the young solicitor weak with longing. Brigid was tall (like Rosa) and blonde (like Jack). Kevin stayed on in Dublin, the next night securing a more prominent seat in the stalls; and kept it for the remainder of that week. He sent flowers each night. On his feet, he led the applause for the dancers. Brigid did agree to meet him, outside the theatre. She thanked him for his enthusiasm and generosity, but revealed her commitment to another young man, a student she had known since her early teens. She shook Kevin's hand and walked away, her hips the embodiment of grace.

The show moved to Kilkenny. So did Kevin. Informing the chief clerk in Beagle & Co that he would be absent until further notice, he bought his customary prominent seat, so that when the curtain went up in Kilkenny, Brigid could not believe she had changed venues.

He wore her down. Away from home – and from her teenage sweetheart, if he ever existed – Brigid allowed herself to be fêted. From a modest background, when she began to understand who he was, she could not but be flattered by his attention. She never went home. She came straight to Monument where, in a private ceremony conducted by Father O'Dea, she married the heir to Main.

To me, she seemed like a pleasant girl, athletic, determined, quite attractive if you liked intensity, which Kevin clearly did. In the early years, when Brigid and I met in Main, or on the street in Monument, and exchanged pleasantries, I thought I detected a trace of hostility towards me, but I put it down at the time to something she would have picked up from Kevin.

Around then, which is to say the mid-1970s, Jack began to drink. Other Santrys, like Jack, who had fought but had not died in action and limped back to their beautiful estate, had in most cases ended life in their cups. Major John Santry had accepted the surrender of Minorca in 1708 and come home to Main, which he had set fire to one evening when drunk. (The Main we all know rose from those ashes.) Port wine had been the downfall of Captain John Santry, present in 1748 at the signing of the treaty of Aix-la-Chapelle. For forty years afterwards, barque-loads of good vintages sailed up the Lyle from Porto. No fewer than three Santrys had died in ensuring the defeat of Bonaparte (two at Vittoria, one, Colonel John Santry, at Waterloo). The line had been carried on by a brother too young to fight, Lionel Santry (1799–1865), (a rare Santry who was neither a John nor a drunkard), who fathered Captain John Santry (killed in the Crimea), himself the father of (likewise) Captain John Santry, father in turn of the general, whose leglessness was a matter of legend.

Jack fell into his new ways without a murmur, as if drink was yet another inheritance to which he had submitted. He felt he was the victim of some need which he was unable to explain, for once lunch was over he would begin to yearn for his nip. Neither the management of Main nor the majesty of the Deilt Mountains – regarded by the Santrys as a personal possession – could divert Jack's thirst. He went to Monument. When drink-emboldened barflies tried to elbow their way into his confidence, Jack would move onto another pub where it might be assumed that this was his first drink of the day, and so on, until hours later, a solitary figure – Colonel Jack Santry MC – he would set out for Main afloat on gin and malt whisky.

He attempted to conquer his new tendency, saving Monument until Fridays and on other days stepping the land with the rising sun, walking out to Delaware and far beyond before breakfast, warming with the earth and as the day went on engaging with enthusiasm beside paid hands in jobs to do with crops and animals of which a Santry was expected to have only a textbook knowledge. Even so, odds and ends were always required from Monument – a new handle for an axe, a can of DDT, a roll of sheep wire, a pound of staples – and soon enough Jack was gunning in for his old haunts. Whereas once Colonel Santry of Main had been taken for the incarnation of sobriety, now it became accepted that after a certain hour, usually half-past five, he was drunk. Blood always ran true, people said. If you saw Jack Santry coming out the Deilt road against you of an evening, the chosen course of action was to pull well into the ditch on your own side and hope for the best.

It got worse with the years. Only cognac gave Jack five consecutive hours of sleep. Otherwise, after fifty minutes he would sit bolt upright, shrieking, believing for those first muddled seconds, as he told us later, that a snake was wound around his legs and had begun to burrow up his rectum, or that a child with a beard lurked in the corners of the room, or that a two-headed cat was perched on the window architrave. Once awake Jack's only recourse was further drink, often tumbling asleep in the library and being heaved up the stairs by whomsoever was to hand in a faithful re-enactment of history.

Sex had never been a high priority in the marriage of Rosa and Jack. Jack's sexual appetite – and I never discussed this as such with Rosa; these are my impressions – seems to have peaked during adolescence. Although clearly he managed to produce Kevin, no urgency, no brimming desire attended Jack after the war. He would on the great majority of occasions fall asleep between Rosa's breasts, acceptable after *coitus* but not before. Whatever flicker might have been left in him, by the time we're talking about came around, had been quenched by drink.

Jack's decline was a gradual phenomenon and only dramatic to people who encountered him now and then. He continued to be Jack, whatever his condition, which is to say, a husband full of kindness, a considerate and caring (if unheeded) father, generous in his actions, the benevolent squire of a large estate, a man vague in his opinions, solitary in his ways and more and more adrift in the autumn of life.

Kevin began to take closer interest in Main and its affairs. Main was entailed and therefore no uncertainty existed as to its devolving, yet Kevin now began asking to see accounts and questioning his mother about his father's fitness to be in charge of seven thousand acres. But Rosa of all people knew a Bensey when she saw one.

You must, if you have not already, grasp the nature of Rosa and Jack's relationship to understand what follows. Rosa's high valuation of her own independence has already been established. Her natural integrity did not allow her to hold one outlook on life for herself and impose on others anything less: Jack's life was his own, just as her life was hers. It was not her practice to manage people. Saving them from outside attack was another matter, however, and she had shown in the Speechley episode all the magnificent and protective hackles that one might expect.

At Christmas 1979 Kevin Santry, aged thirty-one, reinstated the Boxing Day meet at Main, a tradition that had lapsed with the general, and didn't even bother to inform his parents that he was going to do so. He came out mounted on his father's horse and was to the fore in an eleven-mile point to Eillne, the best day's hunting anyone could remember. Jack's struggle to keep up the shoot at Main had waned: Kevin, on the eve of the New Year, invited every client of Beagle & Co plus anyone who mattered in the county, rounded up urchins from Deilt and Baiscne, brought in dog-men in droves and killed in one morning two hundred and six brace of pheasants, forty mallard and three woodcock. At the lunch, to which his father was not invited but which Rosa was damned if she was not going to attend, Kevin was toasted in a manner that would only have been appropriate had Jack been dead.

Rosa knew what Kevin was at. Playing him along, pretending to share his concerns for Jack and Main and to sway off her track of family loyalty, Rosa began to love her threatened husband with fresh vigour. Having made the relevant inquiries, early in the New Year she travelled to Dublin.

"My husband is an alcoholic."

"If you say so, madam."

"He drinks two bottles of vodka every day."

"Fair enough," the doctor conceded. Small, bald and benign, he was called Dr Tate. Over his shoulder Rosa could see distant, north-facing, cold January mountains.

She asked, "How is he cured?"

"He stops drinking."

"He won't. He can't."

"Why won't he? Why can't he?"

"I don't know."

"And neither do I, madam, for if I did I'd be a millionaire."

Rosa realised that her impatience for a solution was cutting no ice with this man and so, with a sigh she began again.

"I'm sorry."

"Mrs Santry, I am unneedful of apology. What is required is information. Would you care for Earl Grey?"

If Dr Tate had other appointments that day then he swept them aside. Rosa had that effect on men. Under the psychiatrist's skilful and no doubt love-struck questioning, little by little she gave him the low-down on Jack. The Santry family, the military tradition. Jack's war. Speechley. What Dr Tate referred to as the "domestic situation" was teased out despite Rosa's blazing cheeks. By half-past four, as the Dublin mountains were lost in shadow and the lights of double-decker buses made a flickering buddha of Dr Tate, Rosa leaned back with feelings of betrayal and relief.

Dr Tate produced and lit himself a cigarette. As if to signal that proceedings had reached a more informal stage, he stood up, drew the curtains and switched on the lights.

"Your husband is an alcoholic," Dr Tate said, "an observation which you shared with me some five hours ago, my dear Mrs Santry, and one which a less astute client might give me little thanks for now making, considering the exorbitant level of my hourly fee."

Rosa smiled. She had come to a warm opinion of her day-long companion, admiring the skill of his approach and noting along the way his gaily spotted yellow dicky-bow that seemed to glow in the gathering shadows, the way his lips fluted to the rim of his many cups of tea and the configuration of his waistcoat buttons, arranged in pairs, symptoms of a pedantic but endearing vanity.

"Imagine the contents of a baby's mind on the day it is born as a single piece of thread," said Dr Tate, regaining his desk, "spun in a way unique to that child, but all the same just a piece of thread. On its first day it experiences mother, milk, sounds, sensations and a second piece of thread grows and weaves round the first. Subsequent days produce yet more strands. After a year it is a twine. After ten years, a rope, and after twenty or more, a hawser. Now imagine further, dear madam, these threads as living fibres and as is the case in all biology that the health of the whole depends on the health of each of the constituent parts: and then imagine that along the way some of the threads in our cable were contaminated. The result? A thick rope that is decaying from the inside out. We need to get at those ancient, contaminated threads, for they are the cause. But they are lost from sight. How do we proceed?"

The psychiatrist clasped himself contentedly about his midriff like a man whose cables and hawsers strummed with good health.

"We must thank our friends from Vienna for the way they have given us into the heart of the rope," said Dr Tate, "the painstaking reduction of this impenetrable whole until the source of the illness has been laid bare."

Rosa said, "I thought you'd say he'd have to be locked away and given electric shocks."

Dr Tate raised an admonitory finger. "Undoubtedly the case if he submits himself to an Irish institution. Practices change but slowly in this wonderful old country of ours. A fatal correlation exists between guilt and certain types of illness. Retribution is a common prognosis but not one, I'm sure, to which you or I subscribe."

He twinkled at Rosa and she shone back for him. She knew, and he knew that she knew, that he would leave his rooms that evening and drive home to Donnybrook or Rathgar and that his bubbling good humour, for which Rosa was responsible, would manifest itself in displays of courtesy to his wife beyond the norm, in perhaps a glass of special sherry together, and even, if his timing was right, in an interlude of intimacy after lights out which would be all the sweeter for its surprise.

"Your position is as follows," said Dr Tate, now with an air of urgency. "Your husband is a man of considerable standing in a small community. His illness is neither admitted nor discussed. Were he to confront it, he would in a sense be letting everyone down, would he not, for societies prefer not to imagine that they are led by drunkards."

Rosa winced.

"Jack, if I may so call him, drinks in order not to remember, but he cannot now remember what it is he drinks to forget. But from what you have told me, Jack is being devoured by guilt. For what? I'll tell you for what. For the past."

Rosa said, "The past."

Dr Tate nodded calmly. "Jack must be liberated from the past to be cured of his physical and mental debilities."

"Mental debility," repeated Rosa.

"He must not just be dried out but cured, dear madam. For his own happiness, and most important, for yours, he must be cured of the past."

"He must go to where the best treatment is available."

"And you are in the fortuitous position whereby the means to acquire such treatment are not an obstacle," murmured the acquiescent Dr Tate.

"I presume you mean London," Rosa said.

"What I have in mind," said the doctor, "is New York."

Seventeen

I WAS ENJOYING AN interlude of peace at the beginning of 1979. Some of my time was spent dealing in bits and pieces of my land along the river in cahoots with a red-faced, cute-eyed, white-haired and overweight member of the Monument Town Council Planning Committee, named Matt Luther (a visiting Germanic sailor father, a Monument girl, the usual story). Twenty years before, when I ran Church Land, Luther was skipper on a mud dredger that kept open the Lyle for shipping. He had moved on to dredge elsewhere, as it were, every year or so facilitating the re-zoning of my land and other people's in exchange for bribes, in my case allowing me to sell on and use the proceeds to pay off my debts to banks and bookmakers. Why hide the truth? I'm lucky in love, you see. And two years before my uncle, Giles Church, the famous chandler and society queen, had died in London and willed me the income from a small legacy. His last testament referred to me as "the little angel whose photograph I have carried on my person through my life". I cried for that lost child, who, for fifty years, had represented innocence to a lonely man.

Rosa never contemplated going to New York with Jack. Main demanded too much for it to be left for the two months' minimum Dr Tate had prescribed, and Rosa had no intention of handing over its management to Kevin. Jack, hammered down flush like a nail by drink, took to the suggestion with relief. He simply asked that Rosa write to him once a week, got into the car and was driven to Shannon.

It was only two in the afternoon, but the heavy skies already abbreviated the mid-February day as men with shovels scattered sand in arcs on the slope of Oxburgh Street. I crept into the ghost-filled foothills thinking of the three weeks that had already passed since Jack flew west. I had spent the first in Main, and most of the second, and a few days of the third. Kevin Santry had encountered me on two separate occasions and had chosen to ignore me. Rosa smiled as I propped up on Jack's pillows.

"He's not getting Main," she said, meaning Kevin. "Jack will be cured and we'll stay here till we're a hundred."

In the first week I had seized without restraint what I had so longed for. Her body. Her company. To be able, when she had sent the staff home, to eat together in the evenings and not have to wonder where Jack was;

to go hand and hand up the stairs of Main and sleep in the big bed and wake up with a whole further day ahead of us.

"You're a light sleeper," Rosa said, stroking my chest.

"I was looking at you." And I had been. Hour after hour, by the light of a night-light, at her face in sleep, and when she turned at the full length of her back.

"I was awake too," she confessed.

The snow confined us indoors, unlike in Monument, where you could get out whatever the weather. In winter for reasons of economy the Santrys lived in very few rooms. If Rosa was not in the kitchen she was in the small room off the library, or in the hotpress, the only truly cosy place in the house, where she dressed. The common areas required at all times a topcoat. Even then hands froze without gloves and gloves indoors seemed the limit. The books in the library, including those of once fabulous illustration, were springing with mould and in a distant bathroom into which once I strayed, I found gigantic mushrooms growing proudly from the water cistern.

"If you haven't lived in a house like this in the winter it takes a bit of getting used to."

"I'd live under a bush with you if I had to."

And I would have in those first weeks. At the very beginning we were both too fascinated to surrender at once to sex. Not that we hadn't been enjoying each other regularly, both here and in O'Gara Street, but this was different: Jack was gone. When we did give in we spent hours laughing like children; and yet, towards the end of the second week, there was an evening when Rosa came at me all business, but for some reason I could not explain it was not the night for me. I recalled how before in similar circumstances I would have kissed her and murmured, "Jack's looking a bit lonely tonight. I think you should . . .", and Rosa would have accepted my wisdom, not to mention my concern for her husband, and shooed me home. But now Jack was gone, leaving me to plead fatigue. Rosa left without a word and joined me in bed only when I was asleep.

But that was the sort of thing we put down to our new situation.

"We're like a honeymoon couple!" we laughed.

In normal times I might have had supper out with Jack and Rosa on a Monday, and on Wednesday when Rosa came into town to shop she would come over for a cup of tea. Then on Friday my phone would ring asking if I had anything planned for lunch on Saturday because if I had not Jack and she would love to see me. Over twenty years our behaviour on these occasions had acquired its own protocol. Rosa and I, although we kissed on meeting and leaving whether Jack was present or not, never flaunted our closeness in front of him. Thus, in Main, we made do with a variety of places and became experts of the clandestine rendezvous. O'Gara Street was better, lacking the pressures of Main, but Rosa was a woman who liked it quick. She liked pulling up her dress to me in, say, the back hall of Main, and getting up on me hot and furtive as she looked over my shoulder and letting it all happen in a glorious white water of fifty seconds. Even in O'Gara Street she often pleaded that she had another appointment, or would say that Jack needed the liver fluke dose she'd come in to get, so that she could kiss me as if time were scarce and in the same way unbutton me and proceed, often surrounded by bags of shopping. There was no denying a woman as attractive and as ready as Rosa. And although the always attendant illicitness made me come on hard immediately and deliver, I did fantasise over the years about more leisurely circumstances. Now with Jack gone we had them. And yet . . .

And yet I missed him about the place. Hard to explain why since he was so often in Monument when he was there, so to speak, and when at home he was either drunk and morose or asleep. Rosa wrote to him every week. We talked about him, wondered how he was coping, laughed about his likely attitude to America. But our relationship had become like a sport played under altered rules. The objective was still the same but I lay awake afterwards remembering other times and listening to the void which might once have been filled by Jack's footsteps.

"I think I bore you."

She was looking at me over her glasses as she said it, ten to ten in the little room whose fire was dying.

"You what?"

"You know what I mean."

"Not in this case."

She looked away. "Perhaps it's all too much at once. Jack's not being here . . . changes so much. Doesn't it? Between you and me, I mean."

"It shouldn't."

"But it does."

"That does not mean that you bore me." I knelt beside her and went through all the motions to do with captivation, and we then had it there and then on the cord rug, something to which next day my raw knees attested. But next night I had to stay in Monument because a plumber was installing a shower – Rosa's idea – and the one after that I stayed home too, pleading the state of the roads, and lay awake in my own bed awed by the possibility that I had heard the truth spoken.

* * *

Snow had re-formed the landscape. I crossed Jack Santry bridge, then, rather than drive in the gates of Main, went on uphill to be alone with the mountains, something I might well have done on my way home from Main but never on my way there. I wondered whether I was being pulled away from Rosa. The peaks of Dollan, Ferta and Mecha and Laeg, seen so many times, yet as never before with each new visitation, gazed at me. In the pellucid air all their distance was lost. I felt I belonged among these mountains, the way some people feel they belong in a church.

Yet Main too was memorable in snow. Car tracks marked the avenue and I wondered if Rosa might have tried to meet me but that I had missed her due to my diversion. When Jack was at home I always rang the hall door, but in the last month I had been coming in through the kitchen.

"I thought I might have missed you," I began.

"Chud, this is Miss Delitsky," Rosa said. "Unluckily she has come all the way from America to talk to Jack about the war."

Before I left St Melb's I had managed to scavenge a few bits and pieces with which to furnish O'Gara Street. Joy had allowed this only because anything that resonated with personal significance for me she deemed filth. Thus I had come to O'Gara Street with my bed, with Faithful Tadpole's musical wicker chair, with a box of decorated glassware used by Ma Church in the old days, some books, the kitchen wireless, and all the photographs that had begun with the birth of photography, of my dear grandfather, his wife and the line they had created.

Now I took down these photographs and dusted the side table on which they stood, then the picture frames themselves. My upstairs sitting room was drab, so I had acquired two bright throw rugs, and flowers, expensive in midwinter, but well worth it for the freshness they breathed into the room. I had even trimmed my moustache that morning when I had shaved and then, having begun what I could not complete, I had gone out and had my hair cut.

I understood she was from an American university – researching a thesis about D-Day. The year before she had come across papers which detailed the taking of Riva Bouche on D-Day and Jack's part in that. She had written to him, she reported, stating that she was coming and had even rung him once so that no chance of confusion remained.

Rosa had asked, "What time of the day did you speak to him?"

"I guess it was night here."

Rosa and I looked at each other.

"Chud can help you, I'm sure. He knows every bit as much as Jack."

"That's wonderful."

She was tiny. She could have fitted in an incubator. Or a television.

"Where are you staying?"

"In a little place called the Sailors' Rest."

"Oh," Rosa said.

"Mr Church, do you mean to say that you were involved in the landings?"

"Well, yes, I suppose I was."

"Don't be ridiculous. 'Suppose I was.' The man was in the thick of it."

"Oh my God!"

I'd never seen so many black curls. Or such white teeth or bright eyes, the colour brown. Not recently, at any rate, save on television. She could have been no more than twenty-six or twenty-seven. I knew no women of that age nowadays, if you excluded the girls in shops and offices around the town who called me Mr Church.

"I mean, when you told me that Colonel Santry, your husband, was in the States I could have screamed. But this is incredible! I mean, Mr Church, I'd appreciate it so much if I could fit in around your schedule."

Yet for all her smallness nothing frail suggested itself. Despite the season, her skirt showed most of her thighs – glossy, healthy, muscled – and her jumper strained to restrict her breasts. It was as if a world of perfect miniature had become reality.

"I'm sure Chud has everything you need," Rosa had smiled.

I didn't drink much at home, or at all, but Americans on television seemed to be addicted to gin martinis so I got a bottle and tonic and a box of prawn crackers that not until I got home did I realise needed to be processed first, which I attempted, filling the house with fumes and ruining the effect of my earlier labours.

"I don't drink, but you go right ahead," Brandy Delitsky said, sitting right down on Faithful Tadpole's wicker chair. "Oh my God!" she cried as the last bars of a Strauss waltz were initiated beneath her from an ancient winding. "Where did this come from?"

"It was always in the family."

"It's worth a fortune," she said, pronouncing the last word as if I could only lip-read.

Outside was freezing. All the windows looked as if they were made of moth's wings. I drew the curtains, though it was only four.

"Mrs Santry is beautiful, isn't she?"

"Very."

"She'll be beautiful when she's a hundred." Miss Delitsky's legs were not crossed, I couldn't help noticing. "How long have you known her?"

"All my life."

Rosa knew all about this meeting and anyway we had both agreed that we needed time apart.

"And Jack?"

"The same. Always."

"How wonderful. I guess he's in the States on business."

"Yes." She did invite candour. "Sort of. He's being dried out."

"Oh, Jesus, I'm sorry. But, you know, I understand. I have some idea what you guys went through."

"How?"

"Books, movies. I've interviewed over forty survivors from the American beaches. We know nowadays what war does to men, especially to the survivors. We knew nothing then."

"I never think about the war."

"That is a problem. And, you know, I don't feel you should now either if you don't want to."

"What does that leave?"

"You."

"Me?"

"Sure."

"Why?"

"You mean, why do I want to talk to you about you?"

I nodded. "You never heard of me before yesterday."

Brandy smiled. "Because I want to be your friend."

I can never think of Brandy without gratitude. Were it not for her I don't think my ring-binders would exist. She gave me the idea of how a life might be classified and provided the impetus that has kept me going ever since.

It must be said that a lot of what followed between Brandy and myself now seems like one long and endless day – not the many days and several weeks which, in fact, she spent here. I realised, of course, that Rosa must have understood what I was up to, since my trips to Main dried to a trickle, but I now believe she saw it as marking time until Jack returned and normal circumstances were re-established.

"Where would you like to start, Mr Church?"

"Chud."

"OK, Chud. D'you mind if I sit over here beside you?" She tucked her legs beneath her in a lithe movement. "Any ideas?"

"Not the faintest. I'll rely on you."

"Do you mind if I smoke one of these?"

"Is that one of those . . . ?"

"You've never tried one?"

"I've not smoked for years."

"This is mild. Just take it down halfway and hold it. No big deal."

"I suppose I'm too old to become addicted."

"To what?"

We laughed, or rather, she laughed and I coughed up a grey cloud of smoke and spittle that left me dizzy.

I had known in the kitchen in Main, in the very opening seconds of our laying eyes on one another, what would transpire. It's something that happens to us all, an animal thing. In my case, I distended like a horse and thought of nothing else until the moment she came up the stairs in O'Gara Street twenty-two hours later.

Yet I was fearful of my own capabilities, a wry reminder of how late the hour. I knew Rosa like I knew myself, but Brandy was new and I dreaded not being her equal.

She took a little thing from her bag and put it out on the table, then a red light came on. "Are you afraid of me, Chud?"

"Yes."

My need was deeper than simply physical. It went to a level at which nothing was more prized than youth or mourned more than its loss. Mere appetite did not do justice to my want. Taking another drag, I began.

"My grandfather was the county doctor. He was a mighty, handsome man if those old photographs behind you tell the truth . . ."

During my first night with Brandy I cried like a child. It was not usual for me, someone for whom the great interplay of death and life had been like theatre from my earliest years; it was the marijuana, Brandy said. It took you like that if you were not prepared, in my case in tears of utter desolation in her arms. I suppose all tears in the end are for yourself, but that night I wept for all those I knew beneath the earth on which I felt I balanced. Then I slept, or rather sank to the depths in a mimicry of those whom I had just lamented. Once, I burst from that deep place, involuntarily I thought, like a firework. Noon next day when I awoke Brandy was sitting up in bed beside me.

"You slept real well."

"Yes."

"Is everything OK?"

"I think so."

Her chest was brown except for a lightly tanned oval the size of a duck's egg around each nipple.

"I think I said a lot."

"It was wonderful."

"And was . . . ? Did . . . ?"

"You were wonderful." She melted down beside me. "I mean, wonderful."

Afraid that Rosa might drop in, although she hated driving in snow, I arranged that some of my interviews be conducted in the Sailors' Rest. In a small back room on the second floor, I told Brandy what had been done that day in Delaware.

"Jesus. H. Christ," she whispered. "You guys did that?"

In the days that followed, as her transcripts would reveal, Brandy heard about Omagh and Major Elmes and Sergeant Oates. She came to know Lieutenant Sim on our trip to the Orkneys, and Sergeant Quelch from Durham, and Hames and Verity and Renshaw. The past expanded and was unpacked onto Brandy's tape recorder. I told her about Jack and Speechley.

In a colourful, silk-like robe with exotic birds springing from the rounds of her hips, Brandy slid onto the bed. She said she came from New Orleans, where her grandfather, a preacher, had raised her.

"All that interested him was the second coming," was all Brandy would reveal. "Give me your foot."

At one side of my head the long tongue of the drug still licked.

She had learned feet from old Creole men on beaches. Total pleasure was in their mastery, for it was said that once encountered the only orgasms that mattered were those incurred at the behest of your instep.

"I see all your history here. You have lost a lot, Chud."

"My foot says?"

"That you are a gambler."

"The foot is right."

"You live for the moment and nothing else. Your impulses are you. You will turn a new corner and within ten seconds bet your whole life. It's not money you're after, it's excitement."

She married Casper when she was seventeen, a minor dealer in dope and stolen goods operating on a three-block patch which started at West 103rd Street. Sometimes their apartment would be crammed with radios, other times with electric shavers, or gold watches, or fancy torches with blue strobe lights, or silk scarves in bales of one hundred, or cartons of women's cosmetics, or racks of tortoiseshell spectacle frames, or, on one occasion when Casper had been stoned, a sweet pair of racing pigeons that someone had sold Casper for a grand.

"You come from such a big family."

Each little bone in my foot was having a day out.

"I'm an only child."

"You remember your parents?" Roll a joint the size of a sausage with one hand, Brandy could.

"What if they smell this downstairs?"

Brandy looked at me. "I bought this shit downstairs, Chud."

Ever bigger pulls sank now, no effort, to fill my lungs big as spinnakers. Yellow light in shoals of minnows swam through the curtain.

"Sure."

"Mama was . . ."

"Beautiful. A butterfly. Spent all her life in one room."

She grew out of my naked lap, so perfectly small, impaled.

"That's so lovely. Her name."

"Hilda. Hilda Church."

"When did she die?"

"I was a child."

"Were you sad?"

"I think so. We never really knew each other, you see. I'm sad now."

She understood how information, like blood, can only be given a little at a time. More, that it must flow both ways. So Casper's supply, I learned, came through a dealer in Queens and although Casper personally preferred Colombian gold there were times when Mexican red and brown and Panama red and gold and African black and Santa Marta red and even Jersey green were produced. This city is like a fuckin' rainbow, Casper said.

"I see a strong mother."

"Grand. Mother."

"Likes to travel."

"Not a native."

"Strong woman, strong love. Her love is still in you."

Exquisite reserves of pleasure were being eked from beneath the carapace of my foot's outer ridge.

"She was once a tart. A hooker."

"No woman can love like a whore. A good whore has conquered sex, it's her stock in trade, it doesn't ever bother her. That's a rare thing, to put sex to one side. It leaves you free to love."

I couldn't put it to one side. I sometimes woke in the cold morning in O'Gara Street having come home from the Sailors' Rest just two hours before, anticipating a visit from Rosa, or because I had gone out to Main from a sense of duty but had come home when it became obvious to both of us that my mind was elsewhere – or missing entirely, as was sometimes the case. Those small hours when I woke cold and alone I jumped from bed and, barely clothed, drove across town and was admitted by the woman who now ran the place, cigarette laconically adroop. Brandy never minded. Sometimes I had to have her with my trousers still around my ankles. I had to have her. My need reared from nowhere in the middle of short, dark days. Life tilted on a new axis whereby I revolved hallucinating and insatiable.

"Man, you've just fucked my mind," she whispered when I told her about the landings.

Shortly thereafter she became more aggressive and began to throw me around the bed like a sack of beans. With the points of her elbows she hammered my rib cage and drove her fit knees into my chest and groin. I had to have her, but she wanted me to fight for her. Her head of black hair was like a bag of squid. Pulling it back so that she gasped I caught her on the soft flesh beneath the thigh and immobilised her. She bit my ear and drew blood. I shouted out and someone in the next room, a client of one of the residents, roared abuse. Chewing Brandy's throat I hooked my toes into the bed-end so as to secure my weight on top of her and went in. And Brandy, crying with pleasure, bleeding from her throat and, it seemed, her mouth, voided herself onto the bed to my bellows of rapture.

I seemed to be on a tether to the drug. Once Rosa appeared in O'Gara Street, bright and determined with some news of Jack, and I could not bring forth her name.

"Are you all right?"

She appeared to have legs like saplings.

"Chud? What are you doing?"

"In'erview."

The sputum on my chin was spring tide washing up the Lyle and, gloriously spread-eagled, I was giving birth to a calf.

"Chud!"

Brandy at that moment walked stark naked across the ceiling from the bathroom and when I looked up again eight hours later Rosa had disappeared.

My dear dearest. I suddenly miss you more than I ever imagined and had I known before you left that I would feel like this, then there is no way I would not have come with you.

Rosa's letters to Jack in New York are the only lengthy examples I have of Rosa's handwriting, let alone of her emotions set down. On blue paper, in a big, looping hand, they only become love letters after the middle of February. After Brandy appeared. Before Brandy, they are weekly letters at the most and deal with events in Main in much the way a loyal retainer might report to an absent master. The birth of early lambs. A marauding fox. The damage done to the lawn (a field of eighty-six acres) when the hunt came through, the hunt's proposals for compensation, the weather, the lengthening days and the fact that I was keeping everyone's (ie Rosa's) spirits up. Mid-February. Nothing about Main any more, not a word. Nor of me. And now the letters are every day.

My darling. Although you are the one who has gone away to be treated, I think I too have, in my own way, been sickening for years, something of which I cannot have been aware of, but now that you are gone and I have time to myself, of which I am deeply ashamed. I have, I realise, been seeing too little of you and too much of <u>other people</u>. I don't know why this is, there is no excuse, I am sorry and as I write this I cry. *[Such a statement would normally call for a tear blot or at least a smudge, but none are evident – C.C.]* We will both be far the better for this awful separation, for when you come home, and I hope it is soon, we will both begin again and laugh at the misery of the past. Your loving, loving wife, Rosa.

And so on. If I were to be critical, I suppose I would say that Rosa, aware of me and Brandy, was overcome by the necessity to consolidate her position with Jack. A most needy tone is what is loudest in these letters, a fear almost that she has sent Jack off and that now, for some reason, he may not come back. But that is too simple an explanation.

I believe that Rosa's chemistry was the mirror of my own, that with Jack absent her interest in me was no greater than mine in her. We were always three. Had Jack died, for example, I do not think that we would have married. I don't mean by that that all she wanted me to be was a fancy-man; no, what I'm telling you is that Rosa never made love to me without thinking of Jack. What she didn't remember in her letters was that every time she saw Jack she also saw me. And if you accept that no sooner had Jack gone to New York than my ardour for Rosa began to shrink, then I think you'll understand what I mean when I say that our chemistries were each other's mirror.

Brandy's black curly hair, when wet, was gathered in a tail down her neck. Casper used to cut her hair in summer, real close, and she kept it like that until the fall, after which she let it grow out for the winter. A sheen of very fine hairs on her forearms, an even finer variety located in a delicious swoop between her shoulder blades, her eyebrows, her pubic and under-arm hair, the tiny and altogether arousing stippling on the insides of her thighs, in each area with the clarity of the disturbed I could count the stems.

"I get recall when I smoke. I go back in my mind, I'm a child," said Brandy, swallowing and passing it back.

"I love you."

"I know the inside of my mother's womb like I know my hand."

"Let's get married."

"I look down at my hands and I see two Egyptian dogs asleep there. Cairo, you understand what I'm telling you?"

Brandy laid down my liberated, free-flying toes and took up on her lap my other hoof which weighed a cement block. Never dealt with both feet the same way, one of her gifts. Now she began at the heel, a region as dense and impenetrable as the ice cap, and with infinite persistence began to coax out its shy treasures.

"Peace and love, nothing else's worth a crock of manure, Casper says."

I knew him well by now, an old pal. Not a ripple of excess fat was housed in his torso, remarkable since he never took exercise. Brandy spun the top from a bottle of cooking oil.

"How can you love others if you don't love yourself first? You can't, no way. Casper loves the living and the dead. I love myself and I love my neighbour. I love you and I hope you love me. Here, you want to do my back?"

Under my hand oil swam out on the shell of her shoulders as like a cat she arched.

"Come on!"

Held her close beneath me, pillow beneath her pelvis as she lit a Gitane.

Sometimes, when I was flaccid, she liked to take me in her mouth, all of me, then, thus incubated, I would slowly fill till, one bit at a time, I was reborn from her lips. Not knowing the hour, some days my head swelled with the Great Tintini, and I stood up and went to the window, often unable to place my surroundings. Nightbirds flapped on strange phone lines. Monument, it must have been, slept. No dream involved, or any that I could remember. Once, it must have been in O'Gara Street, Faithful Tadpole began to sit in her wicker musical chair; I put it in a cupboard. Tassy puffed fags, her head thrown back in glee and defiance. Tobacco. Visits began from the McDevitt brothers and I awoke to a powerful surge of lust caused by Mrs McDevitt's clucking buttering. German soldier with green eyes. And one night, for which Brandy apologised, putting it down to a line of bad shit, I evidently tried to head-butt my way from the small room in the Sailors' Rest, to escape the one-armed man with blood spouting from his stump trying to kill me. Came to with women sitting on me either end and Brandy cradling my head and crooning like a small, shining hen.

She took my foot, supple and soft and guided it between her thighs.

"I never met someone like you. Did you ever know you were a hero? I'd heard that the heroes are always the quiet ones, now I know."

My aim was to be entirely absorbed.

"I just want you to be real happy," Brandy said.

Everything for her was in the giving. The power in her hands, her beauty, her sex. She came astride me like honey and I never moved a muscle.

Uncle Percy, Aunt Opalene and my mother Hilda all appeared one night, as real to my purblind eyes as the far-off bed-end. But the person I was dreading most was Ma Church, because she'd hardly agree to be left out, and when it was her turn I doubted very much if, having taken the trouble to appear, she'd then disappear like the others. I faced a lot of explaining, sleeping here above her office (I think), her life's work carved up and fed to banks and creditors, St Melb's now home to Ben Little (they'd moved in), the dignity which she had embodied replaced with drugs and scandal.

Brandy's eyes were sly as she reached out slowly to finger the collar of my shirt and I watched her do so.

"You finish it."

But I didn't take the joint, just blobbed from a tube onto my tiny palms as she began to undo my shirt buttons. Pupils beat into the apex of her eyes like metronomes.

"What . . ."

"Come on, come on," she gasped.

Small voices in the heavens, probing out and upwards to all the grim, dead faces I also knew.

"I want a baby! I want a baby! I want a baby!"

I watched her smoking one afternoon as my doorbell rang. That's my mind's picture of you, Brandy, wherever you are now. A blue denim skirt tight over your bum, your hair growing out and caught by the pale sunlight. Thanks for my past, I owe you for that. I see you in a big city somewhere, at the other side of the Atlantic that I've never crossed. A lover's moon. You're in an apartment with Casper. Tell him I said hello.

"Chud?"

Voice on the stairs.

"Chud, I think we should have a chat," Jack said.

Eighteen

BRIGID SANTRY WAS LOOKED on with bemusement by languid Monument. A woman might ride a horse to a standstill after hounds in a January gale, but to run up the side of Dollan as Brigid did, or swim in the Thom, were seen as peculiar. All the tone and grace of the athlete were hers, the long, shining muscles, the sculpted arms, the strong back, the steady head. Perhaps it was this strength that allowed Brigid to keep her secret to herself for so long, or, at least, until the day she included all of us in her feelings.

She had married Kevin in 1974, eleven years before. She had at first been overwhelmed by the sheer size of Main and the eccentricities of her in-laws. Rosa sometimes invited her to tea, an invitation which Brigid, left alone in the Kennel House when Kevin went to work in Monument, gladly accepted; but it became obvious to Brigid that Rosa preferred to keep anything to do with Kevin at arms' length. Both Rosa and Brigid were independent-minded women. Too much energy attached itself to every move of Brigid's for Rosa's liking; and Brigid, as she came to understand what Kevin referred to as "the carry-on" in Main, was hard put to contain her outrage at what she saw as Rosa's treatment of Jack. Once there had been hare coursing near Deilt and Brigid had come along with Jack and Rosa, and me. It was an unexceptional day. Mild weather, a good crowd. Rosa brought a picnic. But much as Jack tried to include Brigid – helping her with her bets and introducing her to locals who tipped their caps and called him "Colonel" – the outing was not a success. None of us felt we could behave as we usually did in such circumstances, Brigid included. The picnic was had in silence. We left for home before the final match.

Of course Brigid understood that she was an interloper, and that she was unlikely to have much in common with people so much older than her. Neither was she the kind of young woman to let a mere afternoon get the better of her, but, like the athlete she was, used such setbacks to stimulate her towards greater achievements. Annabelle was born the next year and came home to great rejoicing. Even Rosa seemed to mellow at the sight of the baby girl and for a few weeks began dropping by.

But soon the novelty passed. What remained was the original

awkwardness, of which the failed outing to Deilt stood out as but one example. When it came to thinking of Jack, Rosa and myself, Brigid had begun to do so with a certain predisposition.

She surged from the river, dripping, stuck her toes into worn gym shoes, wiped her face with a towel and began to jog home steadily in the late afternoon heat. One of her earliest memories was her grandfather, an ancient man, calling his only son, Franco. Franco was Frank, her father. Could juggle six balls, or knives, or kitchen plates. Do back flips at fifty. Walk a tightrope. Worked most of his life on a Dublin milk round, bringing Brigid on his float even as a tiny baby, telling her over and over the old stories, of grandfather, whose name was something else, of fleeings in the dead of night, of dear ones who had died but whose memories never would. Of what had been and what might have been. Frank Bell had died ten years after his Irish wife and left Brigid, then seventeen, their only daughter, his few possessions.

She had intended telling Kevin all this, had looked forward to sharing it with him. Then she had seen Main. Had met the Santrys. Thereafter Brigid decided to allow Kevin to assume that Bell, with its ecclesiastical chime, had its root somewhere in Scotland.

Brigid cut down a track outside the back avenue of Main, past the circular pool which she'd never swum in, it didn't have the scope for the long, fluid strokes with which she propelled herself for a mile or more along the Thom starting at Jack Santry bridge. In fact the back avenue left Brigid with a strange sense of unease, and although Annabelle often begged to picnic at the pool and swim in it Brigid always brought her and her friends to other parts of the estate.

Brigid opened up along the back avenue, six devouring strides between each beech. In the empty stable yard – she hated horses – she stuck her head beneath a tap, then avoiding the front door of Main, struck out for the Kennel House. It had been her home since they got married. It was the place where one morning in the first year of their marriage, pregnant and restless, she had made her way upstairs to an unused bedroom (one of six) where were stored all the belongings that had come with her from Dublin. Her clothes, an exercise bicycle, school books (she was still only nineteen then), a box containing her mother's wedding dress. Her father's things. An hour later Brigid was sitting wet-faced, surrounded by his life. His meagre library of thrillers, his two sets of coloured juggling balls, a sack with a length of hemp and a greaseproof package containing copper bolts, clamps and wing nuts, a tiny derringer pistol, the ugly clock they'd given him for thirty-five years of milk rounds, and a cardboard box with dozens of faded photographs wrapped in old newspapers. Who were these people? Her ancestors, Brigid imagined as she leafed through them, but other than that she had no idea.

The photographs. A man with a heavy moustache stood outside a house, his hand on the handlebars of a bicycle. A big, blocky boy with a slightly sneering face rested his arm around the shoulders of another boy no more than five. A tall, powerful man with a moustache was dressed in the skin-tight, sequinned costume of a circus performer, a posed portrait this against the mountain landscape backdrop of a studio. Printed at the bottom right-hand corner was the word "Trieste".

Brigid was putting away in their newspapers these images of which she knew nothing, yet for which she felt all at once responsible, when one yellowed edge transfixed her. Terrifying foreboding. The name. Here in the old box come down with her from Dublin were ancient copies of the *Monument Gazette*.

Pieces of the yellowed paper flaked off beneath young Brigid Santry's quivering knuckles. Tenderly opening out the brittle pages she read the date: September 23rd, 1938. Then a picture: a man of deep eyes examining the camera: the same man who dwelt in the box with his bicycle among her father's mementos.

Mr Mario Belli
father of the deceased boy

Breathless, Brigid sprang to the next photograph.

Master Bruno Belli

Back to the box she found the original shot of two boys, hand in hand. The *Gazette* had cropped out the little chap, the no more than five-year-old, leaving the older one, now called Bruno, looking out to the next generations. Brigid realised that the younger boy was her father, Frank, standing beside this, his older brother, Bruno, not Bell but Belli.

With mounting awe Brigid read the *Gazette*'s story.

YOUTH KILLED
NEAR MAIN
IN CONFUSED
CIRCUMSTANCES
State Solicitor
Clears Anyone of Blame

Sorrow welled up in Brigid Bell Santry as she went through those old columns. The refugees who had put down roots in Monument, the gifted elder son, pride of his father's life, his tragic death in a bizarre but unexplained accident. But as she read on, the tone of the report began to speak evil to Brigid's ears.

Mr M. Beagle, state solicitor, referred to the coroner's verdict of death by misadventure. Mr M. Beagle said that Mr Belli, a recent arrival to Monument from Europe, although bereaved and understandably upset, would be well advised to let matters rest where they lay.

Since Frank had only been a child then, it must have been Brigid's grandfather, Mario, the recipient of the state solicitor's harsh advice, who had folded it and all his other goods away and left the town that had taken his son. Brigid wept tears of anger for her stricken grandfather, for his dead son and for her own father, robbed of the older brother he so evidently admired. She wept but she wept alone. To reveal to Kevin what she had discovered would have been to reveal too much.

Lives are defined in single moments: so it was with Brigid, so would she forever after feel herself directed by what she had found that afternoon. In the weeks that followed she recalled in fractions at a time the lore with which her father had imbued her: great plodding horses that drew loads the size of houses, lions, artistes that flew through the air. One phrase stole into her mind and stuck there, why she did not know: "Il Grande Tintini!" What did it mean? Brigid knew with mounting if unexplained certainty that a dark injustice had been done to her people. And she knew that she would have to discover what that injustice had been.

Then one day, by now heavily pregnant and alone in the Kennel House it came to her. The young Mrs Santry ran upstairs, panting with exertion and excitement, and hauled out the box. It was all so vague and rounded! How exactly had Bruno died? Who'd found his body? Who raised the alarm? Witnesses, although referred to, were not identified. In fact, apart from Bruno Belli, his family and Mr M. Beagle, the state solicitor, no-one else was named. Nor did urgency attend the *Gazette*'s report, even allowing for the foot-dragging standards of that journal. But, crucially, the report was dealing with an event that, at the date of publication, was nearly two weeks old. The previous edition was what Brigid needed! The *Gazette* of September 16th! Brigid got into the second-hand Fiat Jack had recently bought her and hurried into the Monument public library. An hour later the mistress-to-be of Main arrived back at her car, her heart in fragments. In the dusty volume in which the 1938 *Gazettes* were bound, the edition of September 16th had had its front page removed at the binding.

Had I known of Brigid's turmoil at the time, I do not think I could have suppressed a smile of admiration for Ma Church. What an operator! At the time she'd probably bought up every other copy of the paper too, for what parent distracted with grief as poor Mr Belli was would rush out to buy a paper in the midst of his crisis? The next week's perhaps, as the hum of grief remained but the sting receded, but hardly the issue that bore the news.

Brigid applied to the *Gazette* itself, but was informed that nothing went back before 1962, the year of the fortuitous fire from which the *Gazette* emerged with a brand-new building and presses. Most people would have conceded defeat, but Brigid Bell Santry was now driven by deep purpose. Discovering that the National Library held file copies of all provincial newspapers back to the last century, she went to Dublin and walked into the building on Kildare Street. The stack containing the *Monument Gazettes* for 1938 was produced. Trembling, Brigid turned to September 16th.

Boy Held in Connection
with Main Death

Weeping, Brigid learned about Delaware. She learned of the scenes of pandemonium in Monument the day Bruno died, events which one could never have guessed at from reading the successor edition. They'd put in my photograph too, the one Uncle Giles had so loved and which I have since regarded as the ultimate proof of time's cruelty.

Charles Conduit

No wonder Brigid always looked at me coolly whenever our paths crossed. She thought I'd murdered their champion, for God's sake. But up to the mid-1980s, which is the point we have reached, Brigid kept her shocking knowledge to herself. She was waiting.

Jack had come back different from New York. Physically he had recovered some of the ground lost to the drink. His hair, still fair, was closely trimmed and his face was tanned (he'd also been to Florida). You saw again his broad shoulders and a spring, a nervous one but a spring nonetheless, in his step. A bit of the old officer Jack was evident in the way he shook Brandy and me loose and, for all I know, put her on the road out of Monument.

"As a friend, I have to say that I think this fling has gone far enough," was all he had said.

It was not so much that I agreed with him, as that, from almost exactly the date of his return, I began to tire of Brandy. It was not that I didn't enjoy her, I did, but like a knife used over and over, the edge went off my infatuation and infatuation is all edge. I began to yearn for some variety in our encounters, to pray that she would not always fulfil my predictions. The parameters established by the elusive world of her drugs seemed to satisfy her, whereas I was never certain whether or not I had achieved climax, although it always *seemed* as if I had. She and I were never ourselves but our own reflections, thus devoid of any further responsibility. Jack's reappearance jolted me back to thoughts of Rosa, someone of whom it never could be said that she was any less than real. And whereas Rosa was dependable she was never predictable. A week after Jack's return Brandy had left for ever with the tapes of my interviews and once again the three of us took up where we had left off.

Jack was now seized by the need for action. In the course of a single month he launched Main into the horticulture business, into the selective breeding of sheep, into irreversible decisions which dedicated two hundred otherwise perfectly arable acres to the growing of Christmas trees, and he opened the estate to anyone who wished, for a small fee, to spend a day there. His insomnia had, if anything, grown worse. He declared war on thistles, buying a flail for fitting to the drive shaft of a new, £40,000 tractor which he himself went out on, sometimes before the sun had risen, and drove relentlessly up and down thistle-poisoned fields with the aid of headlights. When his own thistles had been scoured he took to scourging those of neighbours, not that he would accept any recompense for this activity, rather it was as if no minute of the day was safe from his newly sprung vigour. He decided to clean all the gutters in Main, a task that had defied his predecessors even in the days of unlimited labour, and bought a hoist, or at least, a device like a hollow concertina on which a platform rose on spindly legs, again from the back of the new tractor, and could be seen, often in gales, swaying close to daunting parapets, until Rosa commanded that the gizmo be taken down and packed away for ever. All at once Jack was everywhere, clearing out the undergrowth from copses, dredging ditches, cutting away dead trees, driving into Main on his new tractor pulling a trailer which carried an estimated fifteen hundred head of fresh lettuce and discovering that he could not even give away his produce, hunting out at the point of a loaded gun a raucous and drunken group of apparent trespassers whose bawdy picnic revels he had picked up on the wind and later discovering to his and Rosa's embarrassment that they had paid a pound a head to come into Main and were entitled to be there. They sued and received an out-of-court settlement of twelve hundred pounds, more than Main would make out of ten years of admissions, observed Rosa, instructing the signs to be taken down from the gates.

Jack had returned from New York imbued with an abhorrence for drink. It had not even been difficult to give up. Tucked away in a clinic on Long Island, he lived under the care of a psychotherapist, a gigantic woman with an attitude so positive that Jack simply plugged into her every day as into a nuclear reactor. She had his measure on day three. On day four she began the first of their twice daily sessions with the question, "What is a man?" Jack did not at first appreciate that this was not polite small talk but the bedrock on which her strategy for him was founded. Every day (*every* day) for ten weeks she pounded away, like a naval gun reducing inland defences. What is a man in war that he is not in peace? The same, a poor, petty thing, the incarnation of love, flesh and bones, the parcel for an immortal soul, above all, himself, insisted the unswerving therapist. Carpet-bombed by her invective, Jack's ego gave up and he babbled out his most densely guarded secrets. Nothing was safe from her, he told us years later. Delaware was described for her in every detail, not just the final day, but all the days that had led to it, our budding love of all those years before. Likewise, D-Day. She probed like a ghoul and Jack yielded. He came home shrived and with a new mechanism for facing life, a fresh grasp of his own past and place in the universe and a deep respect for America. Brainwashed, in other words.

Whilst he was ready on his return, not to mention eager, to make a new break of it with Rosa, Rosa, even in the light of her loving letters, was now more cautious about embarking with Jack on the froth of his New World enthusiasm. Not that she didn't appreciate the effort he was making, the truth was that Rosa, like me, had known a certain type of Jack virtually all her life, had married him and had his child, and was now not ready to jump horses, as it were, from the old, flawed Jack to this creation of a Long Island shrink. Neither, to her anguish, was she ready for the peppiness that now attended Jack in the evenings. Their occasional lovemaking in recent years had occurred at her instigation – the result of pity, guilt and desperation – and so when the new Jack made his first move, glass-eyed, grinning, and with a line of incomprehensible chat, Rosa felt she was being propositioned by a stranger. It was not as if she did not want Jack, she did, but who was Jack? (Jack, fresh from the "What is a man?" school might have leapt at this arrival of existentialism in Main, but Rosa never asked him.) They did get going once, with Rosa determined to see it through despite being told by Jack that she was cute, but just when Rosa began to wonder if this new Jack might not have after all something to recommend him, the old, tired Jack made a reappearance since the new Jack was unable to complete what he had begun. Rosa thereafter pleaded the usual clauses so that even the new Jack became half-hearted in his asking.

All his projects ran their keels onto the same dried-out beds of his optimism. The lambs of his new sheep were scrawny and he gave them away. Wind attacked the long, black plastic tunnels from which it had been envisaged all of Monument would be fed. Grass choked the Christmas trees and new bearings for the drive shaft of the tractor would cost £1,100 from a thief in Japan. Poor Jack. It took several years for him finally to stop bouncing. What was left was just the old Jack and an abhorrence for alcohol. No philosophy, no tricks. No jargon. Frantic energy was then replaced by lassitude. Rosa and he resumed their former sleeping arrangements and Jack spent twelve hours out of every twenty-four in bed, once every now and then waking in the dead of night, trying in vain to recall the great cliff of an American woman on whom he'd once thought his very existence depended, and occasionally asking aloud, "What is a man?"

These were the domestic circumstances prevailing in Main when Brigid Santry made her move against me.

Money is something I have never been able to master. Any time I think I have enough, a thousand projects and objects appear from nowhere and seize my small surfeit in hand. Concomitantly I live with the illusion, for I know it is an illusion, that one day I am going to clean out Art Bensey. I have lived the moment so many times, I have even gone to the trouble, years ago, of establishing in writing with Bensey senior that no limit clauses whatsoever exist in so far as my bets with him are concerned, because when the day comes, like the Day of Judgement, the walls of his temple will shudder under the weight of my victory. I can stand outside all this, of course, and recognise the magnitude of my self-deception. Like every punter in the world I must construct a basis, however fraudulent, to justify my activity. Mine is the conniving belief that everything I have ever lost is simply a loan I have made, secured against one inevitable day in the future. It is a piteous theory. Piteous but sweet. The world, after all, could probably not revolve if people accepted that fundamental justice does not exist and that God is a dolt.

It was a lovely May. The pain in my chest had been diagnosed as acute indigestion by Dr Armstrong and had gone away. Rosa, concerned for my diet, had found someone to come in and do for me, a pleasant woman from Balaklava, a good-looker in her day, named Mrs Tresadern. I had attended the funeral of Buddy Stone, who after a brave fight had died of rabies in a Dublin clinic. He had been bitten by a fox discovered in the hold of a ship being discharged at one of his wharves. The captain, impatient for the tide, had complained about the wait that an official exterminator would involve and Buddy, to whom demurrage had always seemed worse than death, now paid the ultimate price for his philosophy. In the almost empty hold he had brought down the skulking beast with the first barrel from a shotgun. Too mean to use the second cartridge as insurance, Buddy Stone, Olive's little red-haired baby, the wealthy proprietor of Church Land, much-loved husband and father of eight, and the near brother who had waited for thirty years to take my business from me, stood on the neck of the dying beast in order to choke it to death and received in exchange a mouth's load of saliva-coated fangs into the right calf. They say he died strapped down and beyond sedation, his eyes out like paperweights.

I was thus unmindful of anything except my own well-being that morning, a feeling confirmed by the sudden heat of the sun. I had begun a reasonably methodical editing of the masses of paper from the University of Houston, where Brandy had had transcribed our – you won't believe this – 480 hours of interviews. Four canvas US Mail sacks arrived, each containing a box which I could just about lift onto a table. A few days later came a letter from Brandy herself saying that she was to marry. A stockbroker from Miami. She did not think it wise to leave a forwarding address, and in fact she was now destroying mine, but it had been such fun, and so worthwhile, and I would live for ever in her heart because I was the only person in the entire world whom she really knew, as she hoped I too now knew myself, love always and goodbye.

Every day I put aside an hour or so and cut the heart from the green and white striped pages, pasted them up anew, then when they had dried, filed them onto numbered ring-binders. By the mid-1980s three ring-binders bulged with their pasted documents and still I had only reached 1941.

"God is in His heaven this morning, Mr Church. Just give me your squiggle there, that's grand."

The blue registration bands on the letter reminded me of the Cross of St George, or of some other icons of battles, at least. I opened it. The contents swam in and out of focus, yet once glimpsed they were recognisable ever after. It was as if in our brief encounter the postman had sucked from me all the sweet marrow of the day and taken it with him.

BEAGLE & COMPANY
Solicitors Commissioners for Oaths
12 Cuconaught Street
Monument

May 3rd, 1985

Charles Church Esq.,
7 O'Gara Street
Monument

<u>Our client: — Bank Ltd and You</u>

Dear Sir

We refer to the mortgage in the capital sum of £30,000 (say thirty thousand pounds) registered against the deeds of 7 O'Gara Street, Monument by our client. Our client informs us that despite numerous agreements by you to so do, no repayment of capital or of interest on this loan has ever been made. You have furthermore ignored all attempts by our client to contact you, nor have you so much as acknowledged the previous correspondence from ourselves, copies of which we now attach.

Therefore, under the terms of the agreement registering the mortgage we hereby claim repayment in full of the capital sum of £30,000 (say thirty thousand pounds) and accrued interest of £11,252 (say eleven thousand, two hundred and fifty-two pounds) within fifteen days. Failure to so discharge this liability will result in an action at law against you by our client.

Yours faithfully,

Kevin Santry
for Beagle & Company

Enclosures: 7 (Seven)

As mortal men we manage to live our lives without over-noticing the hopelessness of the human condition; why worry, then, about banks? I didn't and don't, until, that is, I can no longer avoid them. Then I rely on the gambler's creed, that something will turn up.

I found myself later that day driving out to White City. It was a measure of the dire pass that I actually called Rosa and asked her to have a word: but at the base of it all I convinced myself that after forty-odd years of mainly one-way business, Paddy Bensey owed me something.

Because he was no longer seen about the town, many people assumed Paddy Bensey was dead. Knowing otherwise, I heard from Rosa how Art, his nephew, still brought up boxes of betting dockets from the shop and how Bensey settled them with age-defying speed. He had picked up land going cheap over the years, some of it choice, and now spent his good days being driven around to inspect his holdings, like a baby loaded and unloaded into and from his mint new Mercedes. A cook prepared his meals and Rosa had brought nursing staff into White City and put them in charge of general hygiene.

A woman in a starched white coat requested that I wait in the hall. I could never get over the feeling of being a boy to Bensey's man, even now at sixty-four and eighty-six respectively. My skin corrugated. I could only justify the lack of dignity which this visit entailed by congratulating myself on at last taking advantage of him. I wondered if he recalled his instructions to me after Ma Church's funeral. The white coat re-emerged, smiling, and showed me into the room where once we had lunched.

If youth is all about courage then old age's theme is fear. Sitting by a fire, tiny and be-rugged, Bensey might try to glare at me over his bushy, snowy moustache, but he was afraid: of me, of offending Rosa, perhaps of the person in the white coat, and most certainly of the station at the end of the line which his train was fast approaching. I felt a rush of regret, not for him because I loathed him, but at being forced to beg in this manner.

"Very cold."

"Very cold, Paddy."

"How is your mother?"

I sat down.

The bookie said, "What am I talking about? No dockets for a week, that's the trouble. Very cold."

"Very cold, Paddy."

"I tell him to bring them up from the shop and I'll settle them here. He tells me they're settled already. As long as I'm settling, this is grand," he said and tapped his forehead. "You're married."

"Ah, yes."

"Who?"

"Ben Little's daughter."

"Ben Little's daughter."

"Joy."

"Have you a family?"

"One girl. But she died. Grace died."

He may actually have smiled. Death in third parties tends to be seen by the old as further proof of their endurance.

"But you're well," I said, with at least some sincerity. I wanted him alive, or at least until he had signed the guarantee of my liabilities which the bank had agreed as the price for deferring their actions for a year.

"Chud Conduit."

"Church, Paddy."

"How old are you?"

"How old would you say I am?"

He looked at me with complete mystification. "Haven't an iota."

"I'm sixty-four."

"Go way," the bookie said and shook his head, lost in prairies of his own making. Then he frowned and his eyes swam back into focus as if rounded up by a snapping thought.

"You killed someone."

"No."

"Chud Conduit was sent away for murder. The whole town knew about it. They could talk of nothing else."

"What did they say?" I asked, unable to resist.

The uncertain ground between the present and the past began once more to skid from under Bensey and his jaw dropped open like a cellar lid.

"That you killed . . . that you killed . . ." He cocked his head. "Who was it you killed at all that day?"

I shook my head. Then the whole, distant and confusing episode slipped away from Bensey and he shuffled himself back to more immediate and fixed concerns.

"D'you see Jack Santry at all?"

To his cute old mind it was the penultimate question, for if I was tipping his daughter then surely her husband would be the last person with whom I would associate.

"I had tea with him yesterday."

Bensey nodded, a little too eager. "And he's . . . all right?"

This was the final worry, that Jack had forsaken reason, for as long as a man had his wits about him, as far as Paddy Bensey was concerned, then he would hardly drink tea with his wife's lover.

"Never seen him better," I replied.

"The war takes a lot out of them."

"It does."

"Jack Santry had a good war."

"The finest."

"Colonel Jack Santry, MC. Centuries of it. They're bred to it. Not like . . . some others."

It was like old times, his disapproval of me. It was as if in this room a set piece was always performed whereby the Santrys were eulogised and I was disparaged, regardless of the facts. Reminded of his lack of feeling towards Tassy, I was suddenly seized by the urge to vilify this old scalper to his face and to redeem my pride; but that might have put at risk what I had come for and so I kept my mouth shut.

"He killed his fair share of them German yokes," Bensey asserted, his hungry rodent's eyes checking me and the room around me. "Did you fire a shot at all?"

"I just followed Jack."

"Humph."

It wasn't until the following year that I found Jack's war letters to Rosa and realised that the bookie all along must have known Jack's limitations as a hero. Colonel Jack Santry, MC, war hero, was in many respects the creation of Paddy Bensey the bookie.

"Jack had a hard time," Bensey frowned.

"Yes."

"Did he ever talk to you?"

"About what?"

The mind that settled cross doubles and accumulators performed before my eyes.

"About the letters he wrote to Rosa. When she was out in that convent."

"Never, Paddy."

The bookie looked at me, then he chuckled. "There's a lad that was afraid of nothing. Colonel Jack Santry, MC. You made one good decision, anyway. You picked the right man to follow and saved your skin."

It seemed incredible to me, as it had done on countless other occasions, that this man and the woman I loved could be father and daughter.

I said, "I think Rosa has mentioned the position, Paddy. I have a bit of land I'm developing, but it'll take a little time before I'll be able to sell it and pay off the bank. I need a breathing space. The bank'll play ball if you put your name to things. It's only for twelve months."

He was staring into the fire, making it difficult to say whether or not he had taken it in. Although he had given Rosa no more than a good wedding and a fine honeymoon, she would never want for anything and this was understood, even when her demands included me.

"How much?" asked the bookie suddenly.

"Thirty."

"You were never any good."

"You'll never have to pay a penny, it's just a guarantee."

"I said it to Mabel."

"A formality."

"It's only because Rosa asked me, but why she bothers with you I'll never know."

"I'm grateful to you, Paddy."

"A clown from the first day I set eyes on you up the town. Child of a sailor's doxy, what could you expect."

"What did you say?"

The regular tick of a pendulum within mahogany casing dominated the room. It was the only occasion on which I premeditated doing bodily harm and the only reason I restrained myself was because of what I owed. But Bensey must have seen the venom in my face.

"I'll go into the bank and do it in the morning," he cried and started to his feet as the rug in which he was wrapped fell like bark to the floor.

"Thank you."

"I'll soon be dead and then you'll all have to make do on your own," he trembled, the bridge of his nose coming to the middle button of my shirt.

But sin is all in the intent. I went back to O'Gara Street and rang the bank and told them that Paddy Bensey would come in the following morning. It was Mrs Tresadern who arrived bright and early, brimming with the news. He'd been found by his nurse at midnight, frothing at the mouth, he would never again communicate. In fact all that moved of him were his eyes, and they were two things no-one, believe me, no-one, said Mrs Tresadern, would want to see. What was wrong with his eyes, I inquired with a sense of doom? Mrs Tresadern went quiet and checked back and forth to emphasise the exclusive nature of her information. The nurse said she'd never seen an expression the like of it in them, Mrs Tresadern whispered. In the end, Bensey the bookie had been paralysed by fright. A tragedy for both of us, I realised, noting in passing the irony and, as on countless other such occasions which are sprinkled through my life, getting into my car a week later and driving out to Main.

Not that Rosa needed additional problems to tax her. Apart from her father's new condition, Main was now paying the price of Jack's projects.

"It's suddenly all money, money," she said, tossing an apple core out of a window in the library. "I've never had to worry about money until now."

"I didn't think it was that much of a problem."

"Main doesn't earn anything, it doesn't even pay the wages. Do you know how many lawnmowers there are in Main?"

"Lawnmowers."

"Eleven."

We laughed as a girl brought in tea and distributed it under Rosa's careful eye.

"It's actually quite serious. As Jack himself says, he hasn't been trained to do anything other than storm a fortified position."

"I never thought of Main as needing money. To me it *was* money."

"It seems we've been diddled by the steward, by every person working on the estate, by stockbrokers and bank managers. Do you know that it wasn't until recently that Jack realised that a ewe could have twins?"

It was hard to be serious.

"If it goes on like this everything will be taken from us. It happens. So-called county people living like paupers in huge mansions. They just disappear. End up living in boarding houses in Wales." She brushed her hair back with her hand, then bit into homemade shortbread. "Kevin will save Main, I imagine."

"Is that what Jack is hoping for?"

Rosa looked away. "This is all top secret, but he's getting it."

"Getting it?"

"Jack and I are to be his tenants, next month, I believe. Jack will have an income as a consultant. We are to live here as long as we choose."

What I wanted was nothing more than to sit and look at her, as I was now doing, no greater ambition than to relish the pool of cool silence that contained us.

"We mustn't mope," Rosa said. "And what about you?"

I recounted my new dilemma in the feigned, light-hearted manner of someone who believes that in a catastrophe things can only improve.

"God, what are you going to do?"

"I don't know. I mean, someone will buy O'Gara Street. Perhaps they'll allow me to keep it on for a rent."

"There are cottages all over the place here."

"I don't want to."

"I know. Still."

"It wouldn't be . . . comfortable, you know."

"A roof's a roof. There were once a hundred and fifty people living here, between everything."

"I like my walks. Starting out down O'Gara Street, Oxburgh Street, through Conduit, down Demijohn Street and into MacCartie Square."

"I often think of you doing that."

"Or I might go in the other direction, up through Binn's Street and Cattleyard, down across Pig and Litter and Candle Lane to the cathedral."

"Oh Chud."

"There's no-one left to put flowers on their graves. Jesus, it's incredible. There were so many of us and now there are none."

"A rent." Rosa was all of a sudden wearing her Bensey look, the one I usually disapproved of, but which now, in the circumstances, seemed to offer hope. "You could pay a rent."

"I have an income."

"I'll buy it as an investment and you'll pay me a rent."

"You already bought it in the first place. What about the money?"

"My poor father is one of the wealthiest men in Monument. Kevin will arrange it."

"It's Kevin who's evicting me."

"Yes, but on behalf of. I'll buy your house."

"Is it wise to tell Kevin?"

"He's my solicitor."

I had my doubts, but they never lasted for long around Rosa. She could sweep away all my problems, even an eviction. That was Rosa. Rosa could turn salt into candy.

The Kennel House at Main sat on slightly elevated ground in the north-east corner of the estate, a two-storey house of reddish, cut-stone walls and a slate roof. Built in the late eighteenth century for the master of the Main foxhounds, it overlooked not only the golf course and the distant river and its town but also, looking west, Main itself and its mountains.

"You won't believe what my mother asked me to do today." Kevin stood at the drawing-room windows, looking down at Main.

"As far as she was concerned, I'd believe anything."

"She asked me to buy O'Gara Street."

Brigid was sewing. "Is . . . he selling?"

"He's . . . I can't really . . . We're acting for the bank."

"And they're selling."

"There's a court order."

"I see," Brigid said, carefully studying her embroidery.

Kevin turned away from the window and stood before the unlit fireplace, his pale face stamped with years of anger. "There's no talking to her as far as he's concerned. Do you want to know something unbelievable? I'll tell you something. Twenty years ago Chud Church went belly up, both in his marriage and his business, but before he did my mother went to my grandfather, Paddy Bensey, and got him to give her the money to buy O'Gara Street. She bought the house from his company and gave it to him. 'There's a house for you.' Now that my grandfather is dying and Church is bust – again! – she's prepared to borrow money against her father's estate and buy Church the same house a second time!"

"I suppose it's better that he lives in Monument . . ."

"D'you know how long this has been going on?"

". . . than out here."

"All my life. From my earliest memory."

"Isn't it, Kevin?"

"I found him screwing her in broad daylight in a bedroom! I was only ten or eleven."

"You've told me that a hundred times."

Brigid had waited years for this moment, yet she knew that to reveal to Kevin her true feelings would risk taking him off the boil.

"He can't come out here to live. I own Main now. I won't have him in it," Kevin said.

"Your mother knows that. Which is why she's buying O'Gara Street for him. Clever woman."

Kevin saw references to Rosa's ability as a challenge, Brigid knew.

"That's hardly how I'd describe her."

"So where would he go?"

"You've no idea the mess they've left Main in."

"He can hardly end up on the side of the street."

"They have to heat up one entire wing of the house so my father has hot shaving water. I wouldn't describe that as particularly clever."

"You're going to make such a success of Main, and they know that. I'd say they can't wait to hand it over. Or partly hand it over."

"The County Home."

"What?"

"You asked where would he go. The County Home. Too good for him, I'd say."

Brigid put aside her *petit point* and went to the window and, side by side with Kevin, gazed down. She spoke quietly.

"You should buy it."

Kevin's steady breathing.

"You'd manage it so much better, like everything."

When he didn't reply at once, she knew she had won.

"There's no reason why I couldn't," Kevin said at last. "No conflict of interest. The bank just want their money."

"Property will rise."

"We put enough business their way."

"They don't care who buys it."

"I'll put it in your name!"

"Kevin."

"Turn it into flats!" Kevin was beside himself. "You can collect the rent!"

"You're a very clever man, Kevin."

"It's the Benseys!" Kevin laughed. "My mother says it all comes from the Benseys!"

Kevin, believing himself to have come alone to his decision, moved swiftly. The bank held the deeds of O'Gara Street against my debts, the court had made an order for possession, allowing the bank to recoup its money by way of sale; Kevin drew up a deed of conveyance, needing only the court order to execute my side of the transaction; the purchaser's name was Brigid Santry. The bank debt was discharged by Kevin and my house, without any reference to me, passed over like a soul in the night.

Rosa alone remained as a possible problem – (Kevin, unwisely as it turned out, ignored Jack's existence) – but Kevin was able to gloss over the facts by telling his mother, "We bought that house," which Rosa took to mean she had, and which Kevin hoped would tide her over until some other cause arose and make her forget about O'Gara Street. I, aware that I no longer owned the house but convinced that Rosa now did, could not have been happier. Rosa too seemed pleased by events, but when I brought up the subject of rent, all she would do was smile and say, "I've put everything in Kevin's hands." So when a team of builders arrived one day and Brigid with them, I took it that Kevin had, in turn, passed on the practical arrangements to Brigid and that she was now dealing with O'Gara Street on behalf of Rosa, at one remove.

Brigid explained to me how, by modernising the house into two, self-contained flats, or apartments, as she called them, my comfort would be enhanced. Proper kitchen facilities and oil-fired central heating for the Monument winters. New bathrooms.

"There won't be apartments like them in the town," Brigid smiled, and although she was a well-toned, attractive woman, something about her did not allow me to trust her.

I moved downstairs with my possessions as upstairs the builders gutted the roof spaces. They began early every morning, making it difficult for me to sleep late or when I got up to concentrate on my collating of the Brandy interviews. The renovations had to be costing a fortune, I thought, but just before Christmas Paddy Bensey died and laid out in his best check suit with a pair of Zeiss binoculars by his side, was buried in the cathedral grounds. His will was in the middle range of estimates, about £400,000 with duties paid, so Rosa had few worries, I reckoned, as I watched a marble bathroom suite in its paper cladding being borne upstairs on the shoulders of plumbers' mates. Early in the New Year Brigid announced that the time had come for me to take up residence. A clerk from Beagle's arrived with a lease. I could barely see the line on which I had to sign, let alone read the conditions, but I was glad that the position was now regularised. With a last and somewhat nostalgic glance at the rooms where the Church warehouse empire had been born, had flourished and eventually had died, I ascended.

I did not recognise the splendour into which I arrived nor understand, despite my training as a draughtsman, where all the space had come from. In a daze I went through a warm, wood-panelled living room of colourful rugs, low-slung metal and canvas chairs and spotlighting, into a stone-floored kitchen full of electrical devices with instrument panels at eye-level. I went to sleep – in my own bed, I had insisted – as daylight ebbed from curtains of *fleurs-de-lis,* awaking only when sledgehammers began to swing downstairs the next morning.

Over the next few weeks I began to wonder how I had managed before with so little furniture. I also enjoyed more space in my crafty upstairs apartment than I previously had in the entire house. Rosa said she would come in and see what had been done. She said Kevin was, after all, her son. Mrs Tresadern went on incessantly about the joy it was to work in the brand-new kitchen, and I, infected to some degree by Mrs Tresadern's enthusiasm, was stupid enough to wonder if I should not revise my opinion of Brigid Santry.

I went to answer my door in good form. The builders had nearly finished the downstairs flat and already Brigid was showing prospective tenants around it. My ring-binders were now in 1944 with its petards and grenades, spare bogey wheels, track plates, tieplates and pins.

"Hold your horses!" I cried to the shrill bell, a rare feature of the new arrangements with which I found myself in disagreement. Often the builders needed to come back up in order to go out on the roof or to feed wires through internal ducting and I thought this might be them.

"Mr Church."

It took me moments to place him, a man in his fifties, the eternal clerk type. Then I remembered. He was the one from Beagle's.

"What do you want?"

He'd been the office boy in the old days and had often dropped in envelopes to me with the smug expression of those who thrive on the destruction of others.

"Mrs Santry asked me to come up so that you rectify an error on the rent."

"I've paid the rent," I said, and closed the door.

"Mr Church." He had put his shoulder in. "Your cheque's in error," he said and now his crustaceous hand had pinned in it a rectangular piece of paper that could indeed have been a cheque.

"Here." I took the cheque, but now had to retreat in order to find spectacles. When I turned, Beagle's clerk was standing inside.

"What's wrong with it?" I snapped, having first ascertained that no banker's mark of rejection defiled it.

"The amount."

"The amount is twenty-five pounds," I said, handing it back.

"That's the error."

"What error? That's the rent. I signed a lease."

"Ah, this would be it," he said.

How mercilessly old age usurps hegemony. I felt afraid of this prawn.

"Here's the rent clause, sir," he murmured, able to switch at will between the menacing and the obsequious.

I'd glanced at it before I'd paid my rent, of course, and now, all too briefly, it appeared constant with my first impression. But then, like an act of treachery long obvious to everyone else but myself, I saw the "o" after the "25".

"This is a mistake."

"Hardly. It's stated in words as well."

So it was. "Two hundred and fifty pounds? A month?" I laughed, to conceal my alarm. "That's ridiculous."

"What shall I tell Mrs Santry? That you're sending a cheque?"

I felt the painful clutch of matters gone askew.

"Mrs Santry sent you here?"

"Yes." He looked at me insolently. "Not Rosa."

I should have hit him. Her name on his lips was blasphemous.

"Oh, Mrs Brigid Santry? You should have made yourself clear at the beginning. Not that she has anything to do with this. Now off with you, I'll deal with it."

"And I'll tell her . . . what?"

"That I don't take kindly to being pestered by gombeen men."

That stung him, I'm glad to say.

"You were once up there like a king, Chud," he said in a whisper from the spleen, "but now you're drowning in the shit like the rest of us," and he withdrew.

Rosa was not at home. I knew she had never countenanced such a rent, she would have known it was beyond me. Yet it was Rosa who had arranged the purchase of O'Gara Street. I drove out to Main and met herself and Jack clipping up the front drive in a trap pulled by a cob.

"I left all the details to Kevin," she said, sliding her scarf from her head. "I envisaged something nominal."

"It's outrageous," muttered Jack.

"It's his wife," Rosa said. "She's ambitious."

"Who owns the house now?"

"I assume I do."

"Did you actually sign anything?"

"No. Did you, Jack?"

"Not that I remember."

"The arrangements were quite clear between me and Kevin. I'll see him and sort it out. He'll do exactly as I tell him."

But there had been something in the set of Beagle's clerk that had told a different story, that spoke of shifts in power and of the drawing of battle lines. I spoke nothing of my fears to Rosa or Jack, for there was much more than my rent at stake, I realised. I thought the problem had gone away until one morning in May I was, for the second time in twelve months, served by Beagle & Co, this time with a notice to quit.

Few spectacles could match Rosa going to war. Her striking, blood-red dress clothed her like exotic plumage. Around her neck she wore a stole made of a fox's head, whose death leer sang of old routs and high stakes. On her head a black straw hat topped with an ostrich feather proclaimed the insignia of elite battalions. Jack drove her in the old maroon Bentley into Cuconaught Street. Kevin had to be there, Rosa knew, because the circuit court was sitting. I too knew this and quite separately had decided to confront Kevin in his office that morning. One further coincidence completed the ingredients for this disaster in the making. Brigid Santry had let the downstairs flat in O'Gara Street and arrived at her husband's office with her tenants, a young husband and wife, at the same moment that I rounded the corner on foot and Rosa and Jack pulled up in the Bentley.

Nothing is as daunting as enraged beauty. With Jack and myself behind her and with Brigid and the prospective tenants bringing up the rear,

Rosa walked straight through the staring main office of Beagle & Co and into Kevin's office, where her son was, we later learned, conducting the delicate, last-minute settlement details of an insurance action with a visiting solicitor.

"Mother . . . ?"

"We are here to *speak* to you, Kevin."

"Can you please wait outside . . ."

"We will not wait outside. We will not wait anywhere or at all. I suggest that if there are *others, they* may wait outside."

The visiting solicitor was cute enough to spot danger. Muttering something – perhaps a hasty and overdue settlement – to Kevin, he scooped up his files and made a loping exit. Brigid's tenants, with the trustful expressions of people for whom the inner workings of solicitors' offices are a mystery, allowed themselves to be shepherded out to seats in the general office. Brigid came back in and shut the door. She walked around the desk so that she and her husband could face us together.

"As this is a family matter, Chud, do you think you could spare us for a few moments?" asked Kevin.

"Chud will do nothing of the sort," Rosa said and tilted up her chin. "He is why we are here in the first place, so don't try that one, boy."

Little pink coins of outrage popped out on the high bones of Kevin's pale cheeks. "Perhaps we should all sit down," he said.

Rosa weighed up his suggestion for its tactical implications, then decided that to remain on her feet would be ridiculous. Everyone found a chair, except Brigid, who was left standing beside her husband. I got up again, picked up a heavy batwing chair and carried it around.

"Kevin, your father and I require an explanation."

Kevin could not remember when last he had had a conversation with his father, let alone a confrontation.

"As you wish. So to what national emergency do we owe this intrusion?"

"Chud?" Rosa was looking at me.

I said, "This notice to quit," and took it out.

"It's a standard form," said Kevin, flicking through the pages. "You won't pay the rent."

"The rent is ten times what I expected."

"Expected, indeed. You've never paid anyone in your life," Kevin snapped.

"What you want is to put our oldest friend into the gutter," said Jack unexpectedly.

"Out of my house," Rosa said.

"Mother . . ."

"I asked you to buy it, you bought it."

"But . . ."

"Under whose authority is this outrageous rent demanded? Not mine. Some clerk's perhaps. I'm sure that is the case, Kevin. A clerk has made this error concerning my house."

"The house is mine."

Brigid was trembling, but she'd said it. Kevin stared at his mother in victorious defiance.

"How *dare* you!" Rosa cried.

"You're not the only person allowed to own property in Monument, Mrs Santry," Brigid quivered.

"Don't lecture me, girl!" Rosa spat. To Kevin, "So you stole my suggestion, Kevin. Is that, what is the term, professional? If you steal from your mother, God help your clients."

"The house is Brigid's, bought openly and fairly for the market price. Nothing improper occurred. Your temper lets you down, as ever, Mother."

"You were always a devious child, Kevin, God help you. This is not just any house bought on the market for his wife by a wealthy man in the way you suggest. This is *Chud*'s house. But in another sense, it is also *my* house, since my father bought it for me originally and since I clearly instructed you to acquire it on my behalf from your wretched clients. It's not for you or for your wife to come along now and meddle in what has been a part of our lives for so long."

"I suggest, Mother, if you are capable, that you should curb your nature and for once where this man is concerned not let it shame you in front of your family."

"Watch your tongue," Jack growled.

"It may suit you and your wife to pretend you are on pedestals. It may seem to you in your grand office that you do not have to take account of the feelings of old people, even those who are your parents."

"Mother . . ."

"You may think that time gives you some licence to discard us and our lives and the people we hold dear. A bright young man you may be, but if you assume any of the things I have just mentioned, then you are not as bright as you believe. You can steal our house, Kevin, but you will not, believe me, steal our existence."

Jack nodded. "Hear, hear."

Kevin, floundering, took refuge in open documents before him.

"I deeply resent your allegations of professional misconduct. Brigid is charging a rent that will achieve a return on our investment."

"Return on investment!" Rosa scoffed. "What right have you to pretend one thing and do another? You are worse than a common thief!"

"Oh God," said Kevin. "Look, I suppose in the circumstances, if he absolutely says he cannot pay . . ."

"Kevin!" Brigid's two hands had seized the edge of Kevin's partner's desk. "What did we *say*?"

Kevin put both hands to his face and drew them down it as if he were holding a towel.

"If I had known," he said, revealing his face again, his eyes on me, "that the world I was coming into was going to be blighted by you all the years of my life, then I swear to God I would have chosen not to be born."

"That," cried Rosa, "is a blasphemous thing to say!"

"It's true!" Brigid snapped, so vehemently that Rosa blinked. "You see, I know who this man is. He is a murderer."

Brigid's words had the momentary effect of making everyone stare at me.

"Brigid, I . . ."

"I'm sorry, Kevin, but it's true. He's the devil."

"Old hat!" scoffed Jack.

Kevin's jaw had gone slack. "Brigid, be very careful what . . ."

"I won't be careful! I've known it since we married. It's true, isn't it? It's why you grew up in a borstal prison. I've done my research on you, Chud . . . *Conduit*! Look at your face now! The face of evil."

Kevin was staring at his wife as if seeing a woman quite different from the one he knew.

I said, with as much dignity as I could muster, "Your information is wrong, Brigid."

"Brigid?" Kevin asked, clearing his throat.

Brigid cocked her head. "The time has come to pay old debts, Chud Conduit. Get out of my house! Get out of Monument! For ever! Get out of this town the same way decent people once were forced to because of you!"

Our sudden silence seeped out under the door and into the main office and its suspended peck of typewriters.

"I think perhaps we should adjourn," suggested Kevin, ashen.

Rosa was the first to recover. "You're a clever little girl, aren't you, whoever you are. Let me just tell you one thing: you know nothing, d'you hear me? Nothing. As for Chud, on whose behalf we are here in the first place, he's worth ten of you any day, Kevin."

"Well then take him, all ten of him, damn and blast him! And you!" Kevin shouted and stood up. "If you can't see the fool he's made of you both in front of the whole town by now, then you never will! And while you're at it, take yourself and this senile cuckold *out of Main*!"

I thought Jack, at this, was standing up to leave. He did in fact turn his shoulder, but it was only to maximise his swing. The blow caught Kevin smack on the nose. He fell back with all his weight on his chair. It disintegrated.

"*Kevin!*" screamed Brigid. "*You bitch!*"

"Should have done that years ago," remarked Jack to no-one in particular.

The door burst open and an assortment of Beagle people, plus Brigid's new tenants to be, were revealed in all their horror and fascination.

"It's all right," Kevin said, a handkerchief to his face. He added, as he walked around his desk to close the door, "I just slipped." He sat down again, this time in an armchair. To me he mumbled, "You've really done it now."

"At least we all now know where we stand," said Rosa. "Thank you, Kevin, for your kindness towards your father and myself. We shall be leaving Main in the course of the next week. A year or two before we intended, perhaps, but in the circumstances, not a minute too soon. We can't wait, in fact, isn't that right, Jack?"

"Can't stand the place," Jack agreed.

"You can't expect Brigid to make the Kennel House available to you at such short notice," said Kevin.

"The Kennel House?" From Rosa's face her son might have suggested the asylum. "We're leaving Main, not just the house. Main. Do you think your father or myself would want to live on the same property as you and your wife after what has taken place here this morning?"

"And where will you go, Mother?" cried Kevin.

"Into O'Gara Street," Rosa said and got up. "Come on, Jack. We've a lot to arrange."

All three of us moved to the door.

Rosa paused. "And by the way, if you ever, and I mean ever, think of evicting Chud, then your father and I will leave with him and camp on the side of the road or wherever else we may be forced to."

"Mother . . ."

"Is that quite clear? I think that Monument will have very firm views about its so-called leading solicitor, who breaks every rule of his professional code and then puts his parents onto the street. Good morning to you."

What I remember most of our leaving is not the open-mouthed stares of the assembly in the office outside, but the sound of Brigid Santry's weeping.

Ten days later Jack and Rosa moved out of Main and into O'Gara Street, to the larger, upstairs flat. I moved back downstairs to where I had started. Jack had forsaken the last vestige of his heritage. He had left Main.

RING-BINDERS
10 -12

Nineteen

Mr and Mrs Kevin Santry
Invite you to celebrate the wedding
of their daughter
Annabelle
with
Mr John Love
June 6th, 1999

RSVP   *Dinner 8.00 pm*
Main   *Black Tie*
                                                          Fireworks

I can even say what I had for breakfast that morning. Kippers fried in butter by Mrs Tresadern, French stick bought on her way over by Mrs Tresadern in the new bakery in MacCartie Square. Butter, honey. Coffee black as hell from Costa Rica.

I never rose before ten, a subterfuge to shorten the day, spring and summer days in particular. Twelve hours is enough, often too much, but in the still-lengthening evenings it's capitulation to retire when everything outside is going full throttle; better to rise late. I rolled off my bed and, one foot at a time like infantry under fire, crouched for my bathroom. Crystals glistened, the plughole was already stopped. The odd night when I'd forgotten to give effect to these arrangements, Rosa would come down. Bit by bit I straightened in the hot water, although every morning took a little longer, or so it seemed. Weightless, I shaved without the expense of lather, the beard leaving my broiled cheeks the way I have seen chickens plucked.

Breakfasted, the alarm on my watch set, I made my way up O'Gara Street. The watch with its augural, electronic peals was Rosa's idea. She acquired it for me after the second occasion on which I had forgotten to use my spray and ended up in the intensive care unit of the hospital. Angina is like that, they warned me, an enemy on whom your back may never be turned. I strode up The Knock, past St Melb's. From an untended field of one acre – still mine – the dubious pleasure of sitting and looking at the Monument river could be indulged. If we were one of those towns where a prospect of sluggish water against the setting of a gasworks might be considered uplifting, this so called green-belt zone might have been worth saving. But this was Monument. Just around the point lay the whole length of Long Quay, where a real river flowed, plus an unequalled vista upriver to the Deilt Mountains. I turned for town.

I reached CityWise sometime after one. A multi-level development on the site of the old ice rink, CityWise teemed with moving walkways, escalators and lifts. Sitting outside a café with my paper, from the corner of my eye I saw Cyril Turner approach. I pretended not to notice him.

"Mind if I join you, Chud?"

A big, tedious man in his sixties, he settled down beside me, although the café had numerous other vacancies.

"You got a pleasant something through your door this morning, Chud, I bet you did," Cyril said, preening himself in the shop window opposite.

Some days he wouldn't even bid me a civil greeting, which to my mind was satisfactory.

"They're getting in a professional fireworks crowd from England," he continued as if this was a conversation. "It'll be some performance, have no doubt. But who am I telling?"

He ran a chemist's shop from the premises in Mead Street in which his father, a watchmaker, and his father before him had traded.

"Have you any idea how much those yokes cost?" Cyril demanded as a coffee was put in front of him. "I mean, if you want to do it right? – and knowing Santry it'll be done right. Ten grand minimum, I'm told. D'you want a coffee, Chud, do you no harm?"

Grunting refusal, I remained behind my paper.

"It'll be the old days again out at Main, by God, my father used to tell me about them. What a way for Monument to end the century."

I looked up. "What are you talking about?"

Cyril stiffened and went quiet, as if scenting game on the wind.

"Kevin Santry's daughter Annabelle is getting married to one of the Loves," he whispered in a voice that did not dare believe its luck. "The wedding's private, but there's a party out in Main on June 6th. The invitations arrived this morning, the whole town is asked. What time is your post?"

Letters were pushed under my door in time to be picked up before breakfast by Mrs Tresadern. "Two," I answered.

"Ah, there, you see?" Cyril said, knocking back his espresso thimble. He stood up. "Two o'clock? Of course you'll get one, Chud. It'll be there when you get home. Cheer up. This has put the whole town in good humour."

When I arrived home again I actually checked my post, a meaningless exercise. A demand that I renew my television licence. A begging letter from a hopelessly uninformed bishop in Africa. That was it, and Cyril Turner knew it too. Never forgiven me, though it was thirty years ago. He'd come back into the room when he'd seemed to be outside showing his other guests off and found his wife with her knee in my crotch and her tongue down the back of my throat. Cyril just blinked, then walked out. She never spoke to me again.

I looked at my watch, picked up the telephone, waited on the number, switched the television on. Four black youths and a man, all well dressed, sat in a living room, rolling their eyes in unison. I gave up on the phone and sat down. An unseen audience shrieked laughter.

"You see these cookies? These are supposed to be flat cookies. But look at 'em, they're inflated. You know why?"

"I don't know."

I pressed out the number again and listened. It was now after three. My appointment was set for four, but not the venue.

"It's not how the cookies look, but how they would taste."

I put down the barren phone, went to a shelf and removed one of my ring-binders. Once each day I take down at least one Brandy binder and once each day, when I do, I think of her. I think of Miami, a hazy, television-produced jungle of towering buildings and beaches, where she commutes between one and the other, one of the stockbroker's children by the hand, another in a sling over her shoulder, her well-muscled legs rippling under one of those gauze beachwear things that women on television wear over their swimsuits.

On the screen the black family were on their feet, clustered around a table whilst their hidden audience laughed helplessly.

"These cookies are puffy and bad because . . .", the laughter rose to the hysterical, *". . . I said for you all to . . ."*

"These cookies aren't just puffy and bad, they're puffy and disgusting!"

"I'm . . . I'm confused . . ."

Even the very tentative relationship that I, an old man in an Irish port town, had with a fabricated family of black Americans seemed to fill an otherwise empty sleeve, and so I clung on, putting up with the banal exchanges as if the people on the screen were tolerating me and not the other way around.

"I told you before, my blood sugar is low."

"He only gets one son and look at what he got . . ."

I looked at my watch – 3.35 – and to the phone, and it rang, causing me to start.

"Yes?" I listened, said, "I've been ringing all afternoon. What? Hold on . . ."

"The point is, if you go shopping, who buys all the ingredients? We're talking about . . ."

I took a step in the direction of the television and dropped the phone. "Fuck."

"You got any money?"

I lunged at the television, killed it, then picked up the phone.

"Hello? Oh, nothing, nothing. I just . . . the television. I have you now again. Go ahead."

I listened.

"Cattleyard?" I bit my lip. "All right, all right. It might be a quarter past before I get there. What? D'you think I'm coming up to Cattleyard for exercise? Yes, I have it and I'll bring it. Yes."

In the bedroom I listened for movement upstairs and wondered where she was. The mere sound of her was once enough. I ran my hand along a shelf of a dozen titles to the *Hardy Compendium*. Although I had done so six times before, now once again I shook out the bundles of £20 notes and counted them out. Twenty-five times twenty. By three. £1,500. I stacked the notes, wound rubber bands round each bundle, put each of them in an envelope, then made room for them in my pockets. My watch chimed four o'clock.

I left O'Gara Street and entered Binn's Street. A storm was forming somewhere out to sea beyond the mouth of the Lyle, you could tell by the dark pillars building up in the otherwise clear sky, by the little puffs of winds that rattled the wires between the telegraph poles. I patted my pockets and caught at my hat as a gust rose. I paused for breath in smells of piss and beer in Skin Alley, then I resumed my climb for Cattleyard.

Cattleyard is one of many terraces cut into the hill that is Monument, a square more than a street, a houseless outcrop faced with a row of mock battlements and with a great wall buttressing the rise behind it. People came here for a view over the town and river; a metal telescope on a pedestal that worked when you put in a coin had been placed at the battlements. In the embracing shadows of the wall I saw a man.

As he moved out stiffly towards me, he looked just as old as I did, something that pleased me greatly, because he had yet to reach his seventies.

"You weren't a minute. Stopped for a half one on the way to steady your nerves, did you, Chud?"

I ignored him. Dealing with Luther involved an irretrievable loss of dignity.

"Count it." I handed him the envelopes. "Where I can see you."

Luther's hands trembled as he hunched back into the wall and began to take the money out.

"I can't see you."

"I'm fucking counting it."

"I want to see you."

"You need new fucking glasses, Chud."

We made our way out from the shadows and over to the telescope, Luther clutching the money to his chest.

"When is the vote?" I asked as Luther began to count and my cheek was hit by a single pellet of rain.

"Monday night." Luther's hands were clumsy. He had trouble thumbing each separate note from the bundle.

"And?"

"And what?"

"What will happen?"

"There'll be fucking war, that's what'll happen. We're re-zoning a green belt where old bolloxes like you have rested their arses for a hundred years, that's what." Luther paused, bright drops of sweat on his temple. "I'm not getting half enough for this, Chud. For the risk."

"How much do you want to stick your paw in the air?"

"You always were a miserable old shite. You and your grandmother before you."

"Give it back so," I said and set my jaw. I put my hand out. "Give me back my money and fuck off home to Balaklava."

"Ah, fuck off yourself," Luther growled and continued thumbing.

Then this happened. A young couple with a pram appeared from the Half Loaf end of Cattleyard. The sky above them as I looked was evenly divided between bright blue and deep black. I glanced at Luther, from whose inept hands notes blossomed like purple cabbage gone to seed. I put my eye to the blind shutter of the telescope. "To your right," I muttered. Luther started around, his mouth slack with guilt. A mighty gush of wind enveloped Cattleyard and sucked the cash from Luther's hands into the atmosphere.

"Oh Jesus!"

We scrambled for what we could. Luther in his consternation had dropped the balance of the money and wind was whipping it from the ground, one note at a time, in the way of calendars in movies. I went down on it like a prop forward on a loose ball. I heard laughter. The couple with the pram were jumping here and there, snatching at £20 notes that floated above and about them like butterflies. I stuffed the pockets of my coat. Luther was staring helplessly over the battlements. Then, in copybook succession, the rain arrived.

Not just rain, of course, but a curtain of driving water. Luther was stepping in a lively fashion beside a stream that bore rafts of cash on its merry surface. Getting to my feet, trying to calculate how much had been lost – because Luther would never tell the truth – stooping into the swirling mud that had appeared at the base of the telescope and retrieving a lone, sodden £20 note, my watch chimed.

I went to one drenched pocket. Then another. I could not believe it.

"Hey! Chud!"

I was already at the end of Cattleyard. Fear allows no time for dignity. I looked over my shoulder. The evening sun had made a sheepish appearance behind Luther. I began to take the downward steps in twos and, as I did so, to pray in a disjointed way that it wouldn't hurt too much.

"Chud, you old cunt! Come back here!"

I would later – I hoped – despise the greed that had led to me leaving my can at home, probably on my bed. Sorrow would then succeed anger, and be followed by deep and merciless grief. Funny that, how even as you career along the edge of life, you can be so clear about such things.

"Chud!"

Oh, God. The last thing I needed was this episode. I stopped, chest heaving, at the end of Skin Alley. The peculiar silence that follows rain. One day this would kill me.

Jack was the first man in Monument with a satellite dish. Whilst far younger men were scoffing at the need for more than two television channels, Jack was sucking in pictures from the ether. The old engineering background. So that he could watch the test match from Australia, he said. That and Formula 1 racing, as well as snooker, and basketball games from American universities.

He was happy. Shrunk to an inch below my already degraded eyes, walking with the aid of a shooting stick and rarely going anywhere except out to Main and then only down the back avenue to Delaware, where he was left sitting in the car for several hours alone, he and I did not actually meet all that often, despite the fact that we lived on top of each other. Rosa tacked between us, spending the long afternoons with me as upstairs there was canoeing, but always combing out her hair and setting it correctly before the Angelus, and returning back upstairs to spend the night with Jack.

"Kevin's being difficult about the wedding," Rosa said.

"Oh?"

"The whole thing is the most vulgar display. I mean, he's being difficult about you, Chud."

"I'm not going to the wedding. I'm not invited."

"I can get around Kevin," Rosa said. "It's Brigid who's the problem. I can't really believe that she's so obsessed with that whole, old business. Never naughty with her, were you, Chud? She's an attractive girl."

"Rosa!"

She began to laugh and then to cough. She shook and her face went dark.

"Are you taking that stuff?"

"Of course I am, but it's useless."

"Then you're smoking."

"Look, I've made it clear to Kevin that you have to go. You're mine and his father's oldest friend. It's appalling bad manners, to say the least."

"I don't want to go."

"I want you to go. You have to now because I've told Kevin that unless he invites you neither Jack nor I will go."

"Jesus, Rosa, I don't want to go out and spend an evening with Kevin and his wife. What does Jack say?"

"Jack doesn't want to go either." Rosa sighed. "And the truth is, neither do I. But I'm damned if the whole town is going to hog it for the night in my house and I'm not going to be there. And there's Annabelle to consider."

Usually, by this stage of the day, my horses had gone down either by a short head fighting gallantly or had tumbled like cartwheels over regulation ditches. Overhead I could hear the volume surge as Jack pressed the wrong button on his zapper. Rosa stood up and went into the bedroom. When I came in she was already beneath the covers. Overhead, a motor race whined in its inexplicable revolutions.

The pleasure of her skin, its heat, the way in which it liberated my body, was a recurring wonder. Having engulfed her in my arms, capturing her entirely in one swoop, I then let my tongue find her throat. From the declivity at the very head of her breastplate, I went slowly to her breasts and then to her belly, round and warm and wondrous. She turned over and I kissed each knob of her spine. She turned back and drew me up and kissed me on the mouth. Her hair was everywhere. She had washed it that morning, I could smell the scents she had used. In the dimness everything was unseen. Her invisible guiding hand. As I roared she clamped my mouth with her free hand and then locked our ankles. And five minutes later as we lay there, an ashtray between us, she lit the only cigarette she said she would smoke that day, it being the other matter of which Jack was deemed to know nothing.

The collective ancestors of the Santrys might have blinked once at the sound of Kevin Santry's name, and again at his religion, but then they would have moved swiftly to raise their glasses and toast the financial acumen of the man who had secured Main.

By the time Annabelle came to be married, Main was not only safe (in the financial sense), but Kevin Santry had more personal wealth than any Santry since the end of the Napoleonic Wars. Having extinguished the debts of the family by the sale of a mere twenty-five acres of land, and not even land within the walls of Main, Kevin had at once rented the entire estate to a neighbouring farmer. This made twenty-two people redundant and those who, with their families, avoided emigration found themselves the target of insidious litigation from the offices of Beagle & Co in the matter of their tenancy. As each successive cottage became vacant, Brigid descended on it and within three months the same dwelling in which generations of Main dairymen, or handymen, or grooms, or ploughmen, or foresters, or any of the truly feudal sinecures without which a great estate had seemed unable to function, these tarted-up cottages were in the brochures of time-share operators in Dublin and London.

Kevin was a chameleon. To the Anglo-Irish he conversed in the hardened syllables of their race, taking an apparent interest in things British and never displaying emotion, the Anglo-Irish template for survival. But he could chat also in the soft burr of Monument to a strong farmer whose conveyance would mean one per cent, or even to the most modest shopkeeper in Balaklava if his will was to be notarised by Beagle & Co. He never missed Sunday mass in the cathedral, but he also made a point on the first Sunday of every month in seeing that he, Brigid and Annabelle shored up the eroding congregation in the little church outside Main. Whichever way you looked at Kevin you found something to please your eye. Beagle & Co employed twelve solicitors by the 1990s and Kevin grew even wealthier by buying up such swathes of Monument property that would have made his grandfather Bensey swell with pride.

He was a committee man like no Santry before him. He sat on the Chamber of Commerce, on the boards of the harbour commissioners, hospital, secondary school, library, Knights of Malta, tourist action group, Deilt and District Foxhounds and Saint Vincent de Paul. You could not imagine an event, any event, occurring in Monument without one or other of Kevin or Brigid, or more usually both, attending. No-one in or around Monument could claim the same stature – the same sheer damn importance – as Kevin Santry. In pursuit of funds for his various local projects he had even invited the reichs chancellor of Germany to come to lunch.

One thing, however, that Kevin (and Brigid) had not been able to achieve was a son. They could not have been accused of too much presumption, when after healthy, bouncing, eight-pound Annabelle was born, Kevin had cried, "And now a boy!" Brigid Santry was in boisterous good health. Kevin's sperm brimmed with fertility. (After two further years trying they had had it checked by the best man in Dublin.) Both of them gave up alcohol on one physician's advice and meat on another's. Brigid went twice a week every week for four months to a Chinaman in Deilt who told her she must unblock her *chi*. Lying with needles in her stomach and temples she thought of nothing else but the need to hatch an heir for Main. Her *chi* remained blocked and Kevin considered suing for the recovery of his money.

But Annabelle, leggy, beautiful and blonde – such a *Santry*! – grew up and Kevin despaired. It was *not him,* three further, very expensive doctors told him. *Neither was it Brigid,* asserted a clinic in Southampton, following tests that cost £1,500. It was just, there was no, you had to sometimes, damn it all he wanted a son! The last resort was a filthy old crone from Baiscne, brought in at considerable risk – for no-one, absolutely no-one knew about this problem – this evil-smelling old woman who lived with thirty dogs in a shack out on the bog near the site of the Deilt Ambush, this creature came with a dark green potion in a bottle which she insisted on personally smearing along Brigid's bare stomach, crooning gibberish as she did so. Such was Kevin's fervour for fecundity that he watched in frozen wonder as the stuff ran off his lovely wife onto the ottoman rug. That night they made love – washing was not allowed – and went to sleep in a happy, hopeful embrace, the sheets destroyed: but who cared if an heir for Main came after? Brigid's next period arrived like the clap of doom and Kevin began to ponder his options.

Annabelle was everything that any Santry had ever been. Tall, blonde, of course. Very Anglo and Santry in outlook, inflexible in fact in a way that Kevin never was or else he could never have toadied for money. Short of her taking up a gun and going off to fight a war, even in history you could not have found someone who could have better encapsulated the Santry tradition. Kevin found himself thinking more and more of Annabelle's potential. What a mother she would make! What a son she would one day bear! Annabelle would marry, Main would be entailed for her son and Kevin would still be young enough, well, seventy, when the youngster came of age.

And so with Brigid's connivance, a campaign of socialising and chats in the library at Main over glasses of brandy was initiated with young Johnnie Love. They'd known each other since they were children. Johnnie Love adored Annabelle. Love & Son, the tea importers, was a valued Beagle client. It was nearly over before it began. Johnnie Love could not wait to get his hands on Annabelle and Annabelle, although it had never been discussed, fully understood her father's strategy. Kevin was as overjoyed as if Brigid had given him a son. Annabelle's plumbing had been OK'd by two different professors in this field and Johnnie's sperm – although Annabelle made a joke of it – was as profuse as the universe, seen through the telescope at Jodrell Bank.

And thus the great celebration planned by Kevin Santry was not just to cheer the wedding of his lovely daughter to the son of one of Monument's oldest commercial families, it was also to consecrate the perpetuity of Main.

The church ceremony presented a problem. Many people thought that the Santrys were Protestants, except those clients to whom Kevin's Catholicism was an issue. Then there were all those Anglo-Irish clients who knew but preferred to forget. The Loves were Catholics too, but like the Santrys had, a century earlier, been Protestant, or at least their ancestor Sammy Love had been, but had changed horses in order to clinch his marriage. None of the Loves bothered with mass any more, leading some people to say they had reverted. Only in death did such obfuscation fall away.

Annabelle herself came up with the solution. She and her new husband would be married in the Dublin Registry Office. The next day they would return to Main, where, in the little Santry church, their marriage would be blessed by both the rector of Thom and Bishop O'Dea. Then up to Main for Kevin's bash. Such a *Santry* solution! Practical, incisive, strategically apt. Kevin sat down with Brigid and they drew up the plans for the party that would put the seal on three and a half centuries of hegemony.

"Circuses use tents," said Kevin, kindly but firmly.

Brigid looked away.

"Darling, what I mean is, space is not a problem."

"But the cost."

Kevin caught her hands. "To hell with that."

Early in the New Year painters moved in. Not just some lads with a couple of ladders, but an entire firm from Dublin, no-one in Main being able to satisfy Kevin that they could complete the job on time. It was a massive undertaking. The sash windows alone, the sole provenance of one man in the old days, required taking out for painting and in this exercise many were found to be rotten. Joiners in Monument worked flat out to replace them and a forge in Balaklava reopened specially to mint the window weights. All the wood panelling in the house required refurbishing, for to varnish, say, the ballroom and not the hall leading to it, would have created a disunity. Men with dust masks and acres of fine sandpaper crawled into every alcove. This required that all the portraits be taken down, revealing at close quarters a serious need for cleaning, varnishing and in some cases, reframing. Experts were brought down from Dublin, insurance policies were updated and the lonely men and women who over the centuries had silently observed events in Main were now taken away wrapped in bubble plastic.

Although entertaining on the scale planned by Kevin had almost become unheard of – four hundred guests by mid-March – the minds of the Anglo-Irish still flourished with robust delusions. Brigid had learned enough of big house procedures to understand that the Santrys never hired caterers. Staff yes, but never caterers. To buy in food was a hopeless admission that one was unused to entertaining. Brigid put her mind to the requirements.

There would be dancing, an eight-piece band in the ballroom, giving way to a discotheque at two a.m. It almost went without saying that dress would be formal, thus the words "Black Tie" at the bottom right-hand corner of the gilded invitation, although some *parvenus* among the Monument business class (like the Littles) needed to have it explained. Kevin, spending money like a pasha, went out and had a new, waisted dinner jacket made, for one of his fantasies was to stand with Brigid on the terrace of Main on the stroke of midnight, smoking a cigar, and watch his fireworks exploding over Monument, his enigmatic expression that of a character in a novel by F. Scott Fitzgerald.

Ah, the fireworks. Illegal in Ireland, of course, a matter the Anglos had always found incomprehensible. You needed the Department of Justice on your side to get a licence, but not a problem this for the chairman of Beagle & Co. From his schooldays in England Kevin knew exactly what he wanted and, licence in hand, found an operator in Brighton who would provide the climax to the evening. Sky rockets and star bursts. Serpents, torpedoes and cherry bombs. Pinwheels. Cracker bonbons and fizgigs. Flowerpots, girandoles, caps, squibs, snakes and whizz bangs. Main would light up the night over Monument. A century later people would look back and talk about the great night in Main. That is what Kevin thought.

Annabelle realised early on that this party was the venture of her father's heart and so, very practically, she let him get on with it. She was, in fact, studying fine art in London and spent most of her time there, returning to Main to sit and patiently listen to updates, to be fussed over by her parents and to see her fiancé. On one such weekend, having clambered up to her bedroom across dustsheets and the tea-stations of painters and French-polishers, and then clambered down again and suffered more of her father's rapturous embellishments to his plans, which Annabelle frankly thought juvenile, her eye had meandered down the guest list.

"Papa, what are these names in brackets?"

"Brackets? Oh, I see, they are the 'nos'. Could we concentrate on this question of loos, my darling. Your mother says we must hire portable things, but the question is, where do we put them?"

"This can't be right."

"The orchard is ideal, hides them completely, but the gate is too small. So we'll need a crane."

"Papa, why are Granny and the colonel with the nos?"

"Because they are." Kevin's back straightened. "Problem is, the crane will have to remain and hoist them out again. It's hardly the thing one wants one's friends to bump into in the orchard, is it?"

"Why are they?"

Kevin betrayed a brief, controlled contraction of impatience. As always, as it had ever been since as long as his memory served him, the same obstacle to his happiness now once again leapt out at him.

"Because, Annabelle, they are."

"That's not an explanation, Papa."

"I'm afraid it is."

Brigid walked into the library. "What are you two on about?"

"The loos," beamed Kevin in an attempt to create a complicity between Annabelle and himself and therefore kill off the subject that his daughter had raised.

"Mama, why are Granny and the colonel not coming?"

Kevin's head became restless. "Annabelle, there are some people . . ."

"Grandfather's too old," Brigid purred, "hates crowds, likes his comforts, his television. And she won't leave him on his own."

"But then we must make a special effort for them." Annabelle sat up and took an interest for the first time. Since she was a baby she had always, albeit from afar, adored her hero grandfather, Colonel Jack Santry, MC. She went on, "It can't happen without them. I'll talk to the colonel. I'm sure he'll come if I ask him."

"I've tried." Kevin's eyes shone with the fraudulent memory of the effort. "It's useless."

"Old people like your grandparents are set in their ways," Brigid said. "I know it's hard for you to understand, my darling, but I've tried everything and so now we must respect their decision."

Annabelle was far too astute to be press-ganged so easily. She'd had nearly twenty-five years of Brigid's poisoned darts and of her father's bitching about his father and the state of Main and his mother's scandalous lifestyle; Annabelle could read her vainglorious parents like a book.

"Was Chud Church invited? I don't see his name."

Kevin reacted quickly. "We thought it best . . ."

"He most certainly was not!" For Brigid it was chemical. "The thought of having that man back in this house . . . would make me sick!"

Annabelle said, "That's why Granny and the colonel won't come, isn't it? They want you to invite Chud Church."

Kevin struggled. "That's an oversimplification."

Brigid stamped her foot. "They're all in our house, in my house in O'Gara Street, like a colony of baboons. I know they're your grandparents and I often thought over the years how nice it would have been for me when I came here to Monument to have had nice, normal in-laws." Mouth atremble, Brigid crossed into the desert of her loathing. "All I found was my mother-in-law living in open sin with . . ."

"Brigid . . ."

". . . with a murderer!"

"That's not correct, Brigid, I mean, that description of him, at least, not technically, as far as we know . . ."

"And do you know what's worse? When I told your grandmother this, all she did was laugh at me."

"Brigid . . ."

"It's true!"

"Mama, even the Israelis and the Germans are on speaking terms! It can't be good for you to keep on like this!"

"I am entitled to my feelings!" Brigid shrieked. "They were *my* family!"

"Look, both of you, please . . ."

"I won't have him in the house! After all we've done for you, Annabelle, this is the respect you have for my feelings!"

Kevin found a handkerchief for Annabelle's mother.

"I'm sorry if I've hurt your feelings, Mama." Annabelle could become glacial. "But I've gone along with everything up to now. D'you know what I think? I think the whole production is ridiculous. I think it's vulgar and boring. I'd much prefer the money. But I'm going along with it because I understand how much it means to you, and especially to you, Papa . . ."

"Your attitude to your father is deplorable, Annabelle!"

". . . but it would be unforgivable to have my wedding party in Main without my grandparents. For goodness sake, they're your mother and father, Papa! And this is their house. They've lived all their lives in Main." Annabelle's cold, Cromwellian laugh. "You mean – no! – I don't believe it –", here Annabelle went to the stapled list, "– you mean to say, you're inviting – Cyril Turner? For God's sake! You think I want to spend an evening drinking champagne with that oaf while the only grandparents I have are watching television in a flat in O'Gara Street?"

It was the injustice that always got to Kevin in the end. The sheer scale of the injustice.

"They won't come," he said. "They won't come without him."

"Then ask him."

"Annabelle . . ."

"Kevin!"

"He wouldn't come even if we did invite him, so there's no point," said Kevin.

"There's no *question* of inviting him!" Brigid screamed.

"You're putting a lot into this," Annabelle said, alert to the shift in her father's position. "It's seen by everyone as an amazing gesture – which it is. I apologise if I seemed ungrateful, I'm not, actually I'm extremely grateful."

"Thank you."

"But the gesture will be empty, Papa, if your own mother and father can't share it with you. What are we talking about? We are in fact talking about inviting an old, quite ill man, if appearances can be trusted . . ."

"Annabelle, please . . ."

". . . who in all probability won't accept. Who even if he did is so old and feeble that all he'll do is sit in a corner for a few hours and then go home. What damage can he do? None. What are you frightened of? A scene of some kind? Ruin your great evening? Come on!"

"*Annabelle!*"

"Mama, rather than continue this old feud, rather than bring it into the next century, surely the adult thing to do is to be magnanimous and invite the old fool! Remove this shadow from your lives."

The shadow was so much a part of Kevin's life that the prospect of its removal was irresistible.

"I actually don't think he'd have the nerve to accept."

"I won't have him in this house! You can cancel your party!" Brigid yelled.

"Very well." Annabelle stood up. "Do what you like, but neither Johnnie nor I will be at it."

"Annabelle!"

"In fact," said Annabelle, standing regally by plundered volumes of Audubon, "in fact, we both said how much more fun it would be to go on safari in Kenya, which is now just what we will do."

As Annabelle began her walk to the door, her gun-barrel-straight Santry back itself a statement of unalterable resolve, it was clear to her parents that once she left the library six months' planning and a lifetime's fantasy would go with her.

"All right!"

It was, Annabelle later told Johnnie, like a play, everyone frozen in their positions penultimate to disaster.

"It's just one invitation," Kevin muttered. "He can sit somewhere I don't have to look at him."

Brigid sank down with a low moan. "You have just stabbed me in the heart. All these years. The one day we have promised ourselves. And you go and ruin it. A murderer. In the house I've worked so hard to make a home."

"For Christ's *sake*!" shouted Kevin. "What is it to you? I had to stand there and watch him screwing my mother."

"He's the curse of our lives," Brigid wept.

Annabelle slipped out, victory stamped on her handsome young features. The fact is, she was only getting married in the first place because she approved so heartily of Main and all it represented and thus she understood as only someone in thrall to history can the logic of her father's wishes for an heir. But whilst Kevin might be a power in the land, her grandfather was Colonel Jack Santry, MC, the true embodiment of the family history that Annabelle cherished. No way was she going ahead without him being there. In a way Annabelle thought of her father as something of a caretaker, like herself. She secretly hoped that the son she would soon produce would be a strapping Santry who would join a regiment and perhaps distinguish himself, if not in a British war, then perhaps in a conflict involving the United Nations.

This was the background against which, the very next morning, Kevin instructed his secretary to send me an invitation.

Twenty

I DON'T THINK OF death very often, but when I do I wonder if I will, to any degree, bring impressions of my town with me into eternity. How could there be a heaven without a Long Quay on a hot summer's afternoon? The town behind you, humming, and the river at your face with its working vessels. No breath of wind. Smells ingrained for centuries: pipe tobacco, hay from cattle boats, baked dung. Tea when Love's have a boat in. The heated serge of the old stagers' suits. The images of the world coming ashore, their feet with a listing spring heading for the spots in Balaklava and Dudley's Hill which they first heard tell of, perhaps, beneath a blood-red sunset in Panama.

"Chud?"

"Who is this?"

"It's me."

I had not recognised Jack's voice and then took several instants to appreciate that he was ringing me from upstairs.

"Are you busy?"

"Not particularly." I was studying the past form of racehorses due to run that afternoon in Redcar.

"Would you ever mind coming up?"

A proper, broad staircase of polished wood had been installed during Brigid Santry's renovations.

"A drink."

"Just the smallest one."

The enormous television set showed a man playing golf before a gallery. I knew Rosa was not in. The sounds of our house were imbedded like wiring in my mind so that I never needed even to think who was in or out, or if they had visitors upstairs, or if they both had gone to bed or just one of them. Jack, his head bobbing like a tortoise's, did his usual routine around the drinks, holding up glasses to the light, peering at labels and eventually, everything atremble, pouring me a whiskey. He took a tonic himself and we clinked glasses over the fireplace.

"I got an invitation," I said, because I assumed that was what was on his mind.

"Oh yes, I know," said Jack, his eyes drawn to the big screen. "Are you going?"

"I may," I said.

"All those Loves in one room," shivered Jack. "Gather the one she's getting hitched to isn't a bad sort, although you'd have to say the blood is murky. Bernard was a frightful man. This chap's Johnnie's son."

"Who's dead."

"Drowned in the delta." Jack cleared his throat. "Chud, there's something I think you should be aware of."

A most unpleasant sensation swept through me.

"Go on."

"Have you seen the paper today?" Jack asked.

I knew the racing page did not count. "No."

"I'm afraid you're in it."

I noticed the *Gazette* on the floor beside Jack's chair and a photograph that was vaguely familiar.

"Jesus," I said, crouching.

It was the me from more than fifty-five years before, an army picture: one dark eyebrow cocked, a smile cracking up a corner of my mouth, my officer's cap at a jaunty angle. I actually felt a moment of pride, followed by one of relief. I had thought Jack was going to bring up me and Rosa.

"What's it all about?" I asked, wondering for a moment if they'd run my obituary by mistake and, if they had, could I sue.

"You should have spoken to them," Jack sighed.

The print defied my straining eyes.

"I can't read the fucking thing!" I exclaimed.

"All these people want is scandal," Jack said. "I don't care one bit, you know that, and neither does Rosa."

"Jesus Christ." I was down on my knees, the paper spread out, as the fragments of words such as depravity and public accountability swam below me. And Luther. "Is it something to do with Luther? Jack, is it?"

"What a thing to do," Jack said.

"What a thing what to do?" I cried, giving up.

"Found drowned in his own toilet bowl," replied Jack, changing channels. "Evidently left a letter admitting everything." He looked at me apologetically, then at his watch, a man prey to programme schedules. "Don't worry. Today's paper wraps tomorrow's fish, eh?"

"The bloody fool," I gasped.

"Head down and it'll blow over," Jack said as on a clay tennis court somewhere very far from Monument someone young and golden served.

I'd had some inkling, it must be said. Luther had driven our last re-zoning through a council meeting at which one-third of the delegates had walked

257

out in protest. Corruption is a dangerous business, for it makes of those left in the minor venal league virtual crusaders of probity. And one afternoon the week before I had gone to answer my doorbell. Rosa had her own key and I was not expecting anyone.

"Mr Charles Church?"

A thin-faced young woman wearing glasses stood there, looking at me with curiosity.

"And you are . . . ?"

"Alice Toole, *Monument Gazette*. Are you Mr Charles or Chud Church? Formerly of Church Land Limited?"

Out of reflex I closed the door. Too many evictions.

"Mr Church!"

She must have sensed that I was standing inside.

"Mr Church, Matt Luther, the town councillor and chairman of the planning committee, has just resigned in the face of widespread corruption allegations. He's made a statement through his solicitors implicating you. Did you get that, Mr Church?"

I got most of it. My door was thumped, presumably by her clenched fist, or else what I heard in my ears was my heart.

"Would you not like to make a statement putting your part of the story, Mr Church?" Thudding again. "Mr Church? He's saying you've been paying him to give favourable decisions for thirty years. Is this true?"

"Fuck off," I said and went and lay on my bed.

Now, listening again to the pop of tennis balls on Jack's television, I knew with hindsight that I should have brought her in and made her tea and allowed her to infer by my general dereliction that a man in my condition could not possibly be at the root of Luther's allegations, or if I was, then I was no longer fair game. My mistake was that after all these years I truly did not believe that anyone was that interested in me. Now Luther, up-ended, dead, bloody fool. What was it Jack had said? Something about tomorrow's fish. I smiled as if a warm glove had been fitted around me. In the end, all you have is the ones you love.

A great river is not simply a stately run of water between wide banks, it is a living thing. I have often leant on the railings of Long Quay and seen the Lyle as a mighty animal, or a ponderous old man like myself, or a maiden set on changing her status, depending on the day and the season. I have watched the skin of my river change from being the slewed-off pelt of a snake to that of a salmon in the space of time it takes to blink. The river lives and one day, in some glacial meltdown, it will die, but in the meantime, like all the living, it enjoys, it suffers, it rises to new heights and falls in droughts to new ebbs. The river's system for self-purging shifts and its bed silts up, needing to be cleared so that the keels of ever bigger ships may discover this safe haven at the head of our estuary.

In recent years it had become clear that massive work on the Lyle was needed. Clearance up beyond Small Quay to allow square-bowed container ships, unknown in Ma Church's day, or indeed mine. More, the port needed new wharfage, and roads, and railheads running right to the berths. Application for the considerable necessary funds was made to Europe and Kevin Santry headed the Monument delegation to Brussels, making so many trips that the unkinder tongues in the town – and there were a few – suggested he had a woman over there. They soon got their answer. In the last week of April up the Lyle aboard the yacht of an Irish cabinet minister sailed the reichs chancellor.

The fuss! You could scarcely avoid it on television. Three boatloads of reporters, photographers and television people bobbing along in the wake of this ugly gin palace. Although it was a Sunday, every shop in the town was open. The modern kaiser came ashore into a special marquee set up on Long Quay, where the town dignitaries, Kevin Santry, president of the Chamber of Commerce foremost among them, received him. The entourage then sat down to darnes of wild Lyle salmon, followed by Deilt mountain lamb and Eillne potatoes, followed by ice cream. It was a golden afternoon. Cordiality flowed, so much so that a senior German aide, it was reported, spent most of the luncheon with his hand on Brigid Santry's knee. Then small children presented the chancellor with trinkets bearing expressions of love. No-one doubted that this Kraut – I can't help it – would float back out to sea, oblivious to all but the magnanimity of his hosts and itching to sign the cheque that would consolidate this outpouring of affection.

They said later it was the ice cream. Brought in directly from Naples by WiseMart, a small portion of it contained bacterially active frozen cherries which the great man could not resist. As he rose to thank the assembled burghers and to speak the eagerly awaited words of financial comfort, it was as if the great pillars of his legs had been scythed from under him. Young Dr Temple dashed to the scene and ordered the ambulance. The most powerful man to have recently set foot in Monument was rushed to hospital, where Dr Temple ordered sedation and a saline drip for three days. It lasted eight.

The press corps, in the chance that the plenipotentiary might die, booked into every hotel and guesthouse in the town and were joined next day by three times their own number of political columnists, colour writers, medical journalists, diarists, Bavarian lobbyists, not to mention clinicians skilled in the stomach disorders of the great. Monument ran out of beds – Mrs Tresadern let a cot in her front room for £50 a day to someone from Milan – and then out of food. As the pack settled in, I heard the price of bread had doubled and that old stagers were charging a tenner for their photograph. When the hacks had tired of writing sketches of the quaint town they had happened on, its quays and whimsical old men, its history and its name, its nearby mountains, river estuary, delta and coastline, one of them, or maybe more than one, at any rate after ninety-six hours all of them, discovered me.

The manner of Luther's death, its symbolic awfulness and the scandal which he would rather die than face, all made for great copy. In Monument, where Luther was known and generally disliked, people had taken events somewhat in their stride. From my point of view, the fact that the only proof of undue influence against me lay in Luther's semi-literate and mostly incoherent (he'd died drunk) suicide letter allowed me to speculate that the odds had shaded in my favour. But now readers in a much wider arena were served up the story of the hidden river town all sweetness and champagne and smiling children on the outside, whose guts were putrefied with rotten cherries, corruption and violent death.

In the days that followed it was a curious sensation seeing my younger self looking out from newsstands and, on one occasion, from the television, my cap at a rakish angle, the grin with which I had confronted the world. What had been so funny? Something lovable clung to the roguish charm of that youngster. He was like a language I enjoyed hearing but no longer understood.

"I thought you looked very well," Rosa said, setting out my cups on their proper saucers and pouring tea.

How at this juncture could her wrist alone affect me so? It did. The sight of her in the act of holding and pouring, the supple movement of her glistening wrist, churned up sweet fragments of desire.

She asked, "Did they actually come here? The press?"

"Some tried."

"How awful."

"I didn't speak to any of them."

It was mid-May. Five days earlier the chancellor had made a brief – some said, ungraciously gruff – appearance on the balcony of the hospital before being choppered home to the safety of Berlin.

"It's not as if anyone can do anything to you. After all, that wretched man is dead." A little smile teased Rosa's mouth. "How do you know such awful people, Chud?"

I was still her catalyst for excitement, her illicit conduit to the underside of life.

"It's not been a huge success with Kevin." Rosa put down her cup, reached her hands behind her neck, undid the clasp there, shook out her hair, then regathered it between her fingers and rewound it swiftly back into its knot to be clasped. "One would imagine that he was responsible himself for everything that happens in this town. He says the Luther scandal made the front of most tabloid newspapers in Europe."

She coughed and I shook with her. Whatever thing had crept into her lungs was attacking me too.

"I won't go to the wedding, if that's what's bothering him."

Rosa said, "After everything that's happened? Of course you'll go."

"I don't want to."

"But you will for me."

She kissed my cheek and went upstairs. She knew whatever she wanted from me she would always get. In fact, the recent carry on had given me an inexplicable lift, as if notoriety was a drug I had too long lacked. This had not been lost on Rosa. Even I have never considered myself respectable. Respected, perhaps, but respectability is a dull seed from the dead pod of conformity. Cyril Turner is respectable. I took out the results of my daily Brandy updates and was about to sit down with them when I heard the door. Rosa, I thought, come back for something she had left.

"What did you forget . . . ?" I began.

Three men, three too many, were standing there, looking in at me.

"Charles Church?"

All I could think of was Luther, dead.

One, red of face and topped with a bush of snowy white hair, stepped forward. "Dublin Castle, Serious Crimes," he said.

Rocked for a moment by confusion as to whether or not in fact I might have been the one who finished Luther off – intent! intent! – emerging from this time warp of doubt accompanied by feelings of unfamiliar fear, I blurted, "I didn't kill him."

Two of the three policemen, for undoubtedly they were all policemen, a small, bald man in a cheap, three-piece suit and a tall, morose man in a sports jacket and yellow waistcoat, exchanged glances.

"Didn't kill who, sir?"

The waistcoat had asked the question. In an English regional accent.

"I haven't seen him since Christmas," I said, cursing my habitual tendency to lie, even when innocent.

The smaller of the two stepped forward. "Charlie, my name is Inspector Fish and this 'ere is my colleague, Sergeant Fazakerley. Manchester CID."

Here he did the thing they do on television with his wallet. "We were wondering if you'd care to 'elp us with our inquiries?"

"You seem a nice, inoffensive sort of bloke to me, sir," said Sergeant Fazakerley cheerfully and leaned on my mantelpiece uninvited. "Is there anyone in particular you say you haven't killed?"

I could see my mistake now. I looked for support to the back of the room, but the Irish policeman's sandstone face told of an unwonted veneration to duty.

"D'you know this chap?" asked the bald Fish.

It took me a bit of time to find my glasses. "No."

"Absolutely sure?"

Someone in army uniform. "Absolutely."

"Or him?"

A faded cripple in a wheelchair. "No." But I began to slide down the side of my own internal glacier.

"Name is 'Arry Speechley," said Inspector Fish, looking at me intently. "Someone drowned him in his own fishpond in Manchester in or around September 25th, 1960."

"Bit of a longshot to ask where you was that day, I suppose, sir?" chortled Sergeant Fazakerley.

I said, "Speechley."

"So you know 'im."

"Is this a joke?"

"Murder's never a joke, Charlie," replied Fish grimly, "any more than a murder file's ever closed. You see, the coroner returned a verdict of unlawful killing. Someone 'ad to 'ave 'eld this poor bugger down, 'e'd not gone and knocked 'imself out or nothing, not on your life. Someone drowned him. File's as thick as a loaf of bread. Wife was the main suspect for years, but 'e'd given her everything, so there was no real motive, that's if you don't count their tiffs – the file says 'e could be a nasty little git when he so chose."

I felt a strange wave of vindication embalm me.

"You see," said Fazakerley, "the only thing that stood between Harry Speechley's old lady and a fifteen-year stretch was the insistence of a neighbour of Harry's that there'd been a stranger in the house with Harry when he'd dropped by."

Fish said, "This 'stranger' theory was backed up by the postman and a local shopkeeper."

"And Harry's old neighbour said he saw him in the kitchen," said Fazakerley.

"Not that 'e was much 'elp to anyone," remarked Fish. "Deaf as a post, it seems – but still. 'E said someone 'ad been there. Was it you, Charlie?"

"Sergeant Speechley," I said.

"You fought, we know that, sir," nodded Fazakerley, respect where it was due. He broke into the sort of grin men use in golf clubs when they're disparaging their wives. "You remember your ladyfriend the night before, sir? You must have been some bloke, no question about it. She remembers you clear as if it were yesterday."

I gaped at him.

"She'd even gone to the police at the time, after the crime, responded to their appeals for help. You know the sort of thing, sir. 'Police would like to hear from anyone who might have encountered someone fitting the following description.'"

You sometimes wish for death, as I did then. Their faces multiplied. I could just imagine their expressions if I dropped dead there and then. Please.

"Never thought she'd remember you, did you, Charlie?" inquired Fish. "Picked up 'er paper last week, nearly swooned, the old dear. Never forgot, that's the effect you 'ad on 'er. Picked up 'er paper and there's you from all those years ago, looking out at 'er bold as brass."

Fazakerley said, "Hell hath no fury, as they say, sir."

Fish was leaning over me, his eyes, like his suit, nondescript. "Did you kill 'im, Charlie?"

"Mr Church killed plenty in the war, I've no doubt about that, Inspector," said Fazakerley from the fireplace.

"Got a taste for it, did you, Charlie?" asked Fish, quickly drawing up a chair and sitting at my knees. "Do you know the road 'Arry lived on's no longer there? Not a bit of it. All the people gone, dead or dispersed. No-one even remembers Waterside. 'Is wife died in '78. All dead and forgotten, Charlie, except this one file that no-one's ever been able to unravel."

Except for my breath that leapt out in painful gasps, I had lost all feeling from the chest down.

Fish: "Had a row, didn't you? File says he had an 'orrid temper, 'Arry Speechley. Served him right, I'd say, ugly little bugger."

Fazakerley: "Give Mr Church a chance, Inspector. After all, it's been nearly forty years."

Even had I wanted to speak I would have been unable. I thought my eardrums were going to burst.

"What 'appened, Charlie? Tell us what 'appened! Please. Don't make it this 'ard, not now, not after all this time."

I was thinking of that hotel in Manchester. I was thinking, would she ever have believed it that someday she'd be called an old dear.

Inspector Fish stood up. "Some people just refuse to make it easy on themselves, Sergeant, don't you agree? Come to a court of law, then they expect us to put in a good word for them. Fat chance. Here, 'e's all yours. I'm going for a piss."

I saw Fish make his way out by the white-haired man, rooted like a hawthorn bush at my door. Sergeant Fazakerley looked around surreptitiously, then came and perched on the chair.

"Look, I'm going to do you a favour, mate, all right? If I'm caught saying this I'm for the chop. He needs this for his career, get it? It's not that it's anything personal, and he'll ask them for a suspended sentence – but only if you make it easy for him."

Familiarity that stank of danger. "Why should I?"

Fazakerley again checked over his shoulder. "Because he's got you like a trout in a net, Charlie, that's why. Look, mate, it's none of my business, but we know why you killed the little fucker."

"Why?"

"He blackmailed you, Charlie, didn't he?" Fazakerley hunkered in close, mates at the end of the day. "We know there was a letter, Harry's old neighbour told the police that he'd addressed some sort of a threatening letter for blind Harry, but until now no-one ever knew to whom. They found registered envelopes when they searched the house. That was how you sent him the money, wasn't it, Charlie?"

An arcing image. A cat springing to a table, lured by the smell of fish.

"I'm not going to judge you, Charlie, I never fought a war, mine's the luck. So who can blame you for cracking under the pressure? Not I, sir. Not I. I think I'd have drowned him if he'd blackmailed me. Is that why you killed him, Charlie? Is it? No-one will blame you if it's true. War is war. But we have to know, Charlie! We have to!"

The flushing sounds of my toilet filled the space anticipated for my reply.

"Just nod to confirm you killed him, Charlie!" whispered Fazakerley urgently. "Just nod. Go ahead before he comes back! You'll never regret it. The woman's evidence is cast iron. Nod, Charlie!"

I didn't nod. I laughed. I realised what they thought had happened and I laughed.

"Bloody hell, I never saw the like," sighed Fazakerley, standing up.

"Now this is interesting." Inspector Fish was thumbing through one of my ring-binders, I could not see which one, as he strolled back in. "Writing our autobiography, are we? Very interesting indeed."

"That's private."

"Oh, did you hear that, Sergeant? I'm reading something I'm not meant to. Why, Charlie? Is it because there's something in here that you're afraid of?"

I could not for the life of me remember whether or not the Speechley story had yet made its way into the pasted record. Pushing up from my chair I made to grab the red folder from the policeman. Fish took a step back, catching me by the throat as he did so.

"You uppity old fool." He squeezed hard and as I felt my knees go, he pushed me back hard to where I had come from. "You're going to die in gaol, Charlie!" he hissed, mouth at my ear. "How's your arsehole? They don't mind 'ow old you are, you know, as long as it's tight!"

Way off I saw the bush move towards the door.

I said, "I . . ."

"Go on, Charlie, get it off your chest!" Fazakerley had hunkered down again, like a golfer measuring up a putt. It must have been the waistcoat.

"I . . ."

"They'll be easy on a gentleman of your years, sir, won't they Inspector?"

"You killed him, didn't you, Charlie?"

"Charlie's going to nod once if he did it, sir, aren't you, Charlie?"

"I . . ."

"Nod that you killed that little bastard Speechley, serves him right, sir, and we'll agree with you."

"Who . . . ? Has Jack . . . ?"

"Say, I killed Harry Speechley!"

"He's goin' to nod, Inspector, he's just about to nod, aren't you, sir?"

"You're going to die in gaol, Charlie! Old and lonely, you're going to die!"

Both men heard the door at the same time. They drew slowly back.

"What in God's name is going on here?" demanded Rosa.

Twenty-one

I LOVE MAY: BLUEBELLS and runaway days, candle shrines to the Queen of Heaven, mother of my youth, evening hatch on the river. May finds old sweetness in me, the way pollen is found in fossils. May gets me out again around the town, away from Long Quay and MacCartie Square, into the old quarters where nothing much has changed, where all the gaps are those left by people whose deaths I no doubt registered at the time but whom I nonetheless still assume will be there for my benefit. I'm sure young people who see me cannot work out what brings me along Moneysack, along the windowsills which alone betray that families once lived here, or why an old man would walk daily up Plunkett Hill, past the Friary and the head of the Crusader, and then on up to Cattleyard. I feed off hidden images, a bit like a ghost, or like a swallow whose only knowledge of a journey is in its blood.

Dick Coad's offices were located in rooms above the shop in Milners Street, from which his sister still sold stationery.

"I'm sorry about the space," apologised Dick for the third time, looking at us across a desk piled chin high with files and court documents tied around with scarlet ribbons and a three-day old ashtray, "but I didn't expect all of you. Particularly not your good selves, Colonel, Madam Santry. I'm sure you're used to a lot more space out in Main."

Dick was in his late fifties, slight, bald and square-headed with the kind of mouth that hangs open. One of his limpid green eyes was forever breaking ranks and sliding off on its own into one corner of its socket, as if demurring. He was one of Monument's most enduring bachelors, having lived with his mother and sister until the former had died just six months before; an occasion which had propelled Dick off the wagon of abstinence on which he had ridden up to that point for eighteen years. Although now his drinking was said to be confined to Friday nights and Saturdays, it was generally accepted that his sister lacked the influence of their mother and that Dick's eccentricities, and they were many, were on the brink of a – from Dick's point of view – long-overdue revival.

"I've been through the grounds a few times, but never in the house," Dick glowed at Jack and took out a fresh cigarette. "Not since the general's day."

Up to this all Dick had ever done for me was help me thread a path across the byways of the planning laws, for which advice he was ultimately given the conveyance of the subject property.

"And never," Dick added for emphasis, "in Ernesto Delamarre's ballroom." He smiled expectantly and sat back as if he had just handed Jack a small but expensive present.

Jack looked in alarm to Rosa.

"The ballroom in Main," she murmured. To Dick: "We have lived in O'Gara Street for over ten years, Mr Coad."

"Ernesto Delamarre," said Dick, undeterred. "Came to Main in 1816, designed not only your ballroom, but the Monument People's Library, as it was then called, in James Place. Loved Monument, the river. Ernesto Delamarre." Dick looked wistfully out of the window.

Dick Coad had published at his own expense a history of Main complete with maps, etchings and black and white photographs which could be still purchased, albeit dog-eared and smudged, in various local bookshops and tourist offices. No-one knew how he survived as a solicitor since he spent his every spare moment in the cataloguing of Monument and its district's past. Perhaps this other-worldliness had caused him many years before to fall foul of Kevin Santry (in the matter of a simple action for damages); whatever, as Beagle & Co had grown, so Kevin had seen to it that Coad & Co would shrink, never passing onto Dick any of the crumbs that were in the gift of an outfit as big as Beagle, never failing to damn his colleague with faint praise or to exclude him from the main arteries of business life in Monument. To Dick's great credit he could separate the venal from the worthy, the latter being represented to him in history, and so the arrival in his offices of – in Dick's eyes – the true inheritor of Main, dwarfed all other considerations, including, for the moment, allegations of murder.

"Can you imagine what it must have been like to have had Bonaparte himself as an enemy," he said with a kind of insane fixity. "That mind! And yet, and yet on the 26th of December 1811 – wait, I tell a lie, the 29th! – on the 29th of December 1811, writing from Cairo after the Massacre of Mamelukes, Captain John Santry, as he then was, your –"

A break, as if Dick had been switched off, whilst open-mouthed he stared abstractedly out of the window and no-one dared breathe, ensued for almost half a minute.

"– grandfather's great-grandfather," he gasped and we all slumped forward, "– I think! – where was I? – ah yes! – wrote home to Lady Mary

Santry in Main predicting that Bonaparte would be finished in three years." Dick looked at Jack as if readying up the punch line of a *risqué* joke. "He was only a year out. Six months to be exact. Not bad, eh? Cairo, 1811," he tailed off, happily, "and now at long last, Colonel, we meet in Monument."

Jack sat hunched, the fleece collar of his coat turned up to his ears, but I caught him checking the office behind him for an escape route.

"You're someone I've always hugely admired, Colonel, if you'll allow me to say so," Dick babbled on. "My father, God rest him, always said that it was the proudest day of his life when you came back from the war. Colonel Jack Santry, MC."

Rosa said, "Perhaps we should . . . ?"

"The Massacre of Mamelukes," Dick said with extraordinary contentment.

I was beginning to regret this.

"Of course, of course." Dick made a grim mouth and shuffled the edges of the papers on his desk into line. "Now, Chud, I take it this is all a load of nonsense."

I looked at Rosa and she smiled back. Jack's blue eyes flickered with brief interest in my direction.

"Chud?"

I asked, "What's the position? I mean, with you?"

"I'm your – solicitor," Dick replied.

"As to what you hear from me, I mean."

"Oh." Dick pursed his lips and another, dreadful silence ensued, as if everyone there was listening for the voices, however distant, of rescuers. "Three ways to go, essentially," Dick exhaled. "You tell me you're innocent, which of course you are, end of story. We fight. You tell me you're guilty, purely hypothetical, we give in. Or third, you tell me you're guilty, but you want me to use every technical trick in the book to get you off."

Each time he finished speaking Dick turned from me and beamed at Jack as if my presence was a distraction.

"What does that mean," Rosa asked, "Mr Coad?"

"Hmm? Oh, I see." Dick met her with eyes aligned. "It means that if I know my client's guilty, I can't lead him on to perjure himself. But I'm sure this is going down the wrong road. No warrant has been issued, after all. Chud? I take it you're innocent of this alleged crime?"

I said, "I killed him."

Little sounds, such as a water cistern refilling in a nearby room, became amplified.

"Ah, ah, Speechley," Dick blustered, looking down at notes he had taken from me earlier. "Harold Speechley, yes?"

Just to clear the decks of other candidates.

"Yes."

More used to brinkmanship concerning property than scaffolds, Dick shook himself.

"Any reason?" he asked.

I looked at Jack and Rosa. "I can't answer that, I'm sorry."

"Egad," Dick said and lit up another cigarette.

I wanted to open the windows and breathe in lungfuls of Lyle air, to hear ships working, to look out downhill and find the spire of the cathedral.

I asked, "What happens now?"

Dick drew in a deep breath and let it out in merry pips of wind.

"You referred to journals . . ."

"I haven't pasted up that far."

Rosa and Jack were looking at me.

"That American woman," I said. "When she interviewed me."

Rosa shook her head in vexation.

I said, "We covered a lot of ground."

"An understatement," Rosa said and turned away.

"Am I to understand," Dick asked, "that you described this alleged crime in an interview?"

"Yes."

"Why?"

"We were . . . I was . . ."

"He was drugged for two months is what he's trying to say," Rosa snapped.

"One."

"For God's sake."

"Steady! Steady!" cried Dick. "Are you saying you had less than all your faculties when this interview took place?"

"In one sense. In another, I've never been clearer."

"Who's to say Chud had anything to do with these statements?" Rosa demanded.

We had never discussed Brandy, Rosa and I, never once.

"Interesting," Dick said. "It depends on the particulars. For example, if Chud's journals demonstrate a grasp of detail that puts him beyond doubt in the house in Manchester, for example, then they constitute strong circumstantial evidence."

"Chud can't possibly have a clear memory that far back." Rosa looked at me incriminatingly. "Neither can this . . . further woman."

269

Who would have thought that after forty years, as maggots of embarrassment writhed within me, I would be pretending to examine my fingernails at the thought of Rosa's knowing?

"The time factor," Dick said. "The time factor will be part of our defence," and, lighting a cigarette, turned his beam back on Jack.

In the end you slip into new realities without a fight. Jack started asking about drill, which to Jack meant everything laid down as procedure on any subject in the world between the covers of a book. And I caught some of what Dick had to say about UK bench warrants, about the Irish attorney-general and about "the other side" needing a case of *prima facie*.

"A policeman might well decide that this is the case to try and make a name for himself on," said Dick as if this were all theoretical. "Recall what sort he was, Chud?"

"Name was Fish," I said.

Rosa snorted. "Fish!"

My fate, it seemed, was out there in the great lottery of human ambition. Yet I was oddly happy. You might think I was relieved at last to have the opportunity to atone for what I had done, but you would be wide of the mark. I'd have gone again in the morning and done it over, believe me. No, my happiness arose from seeing the deep regard in which Rosa and Jack held me. No surprise in itself, but true love never reaches a point where it no longer requires to hear its name called.

We all got to our feet.

"You've said a number of things today that you may wish to reconsider," said Dick, smoke trailing in zephyrs from his nose. "This witness, by the sound of her, is a very bitter lady and at her age God knows her state of mind. We just have to hope for the best. The past is a tricky business, we know that better than anyone, Colonel. Eh?"

In order not to have to meet Rosa's eye I trundled down the steep stairs ahead of them.

"Chud is not well," I heard Rosa say behind me. "It would be out of the question for him to travel anywhere in the circumstances."

"That doesn't really have a bearing on an extradition," Dick was cheerfully replying. "For example, they bring war criminals into court in oxygen tents and Chud is ambulatory."

Dick shook our hands, the Santrys' with great enthusiasm.

"It's been my great pleasure to meet you at last, Colonel and Madam Santry. I've heard so much about you, know so much, if you'll allow." He stepped back and gave a Battle of Britain thumbs up.

"And good luck next week. I won't be there, as you might expect, but my heart will."

Jack looked to Rosa as if to an interpreter; and Rosa to me. I hadn't a clue.

"The wedding," Dick said. "The great day. Main's great day."

"Oh, that bloody thing," Jack said. "D'you want to go instead of me?"

If Dick had any truly analytical capacity it was now finally suspended, for he blinked his wild eyes very rapidly and the tip of his tongue darted out and quivered like a pink humming bird in his open-mouth way.

"Do you mean," he said, "to represent you?"

"Mr Coad, my husband has a most unusual sense of humour. Come on, Jack."

"I'm serious."

Rosa looked at me for the first time that day in a way that blamed me.

"Jack, you *have* to go."

Jack shrugged. "The dogs in the street are going to the bloody thing, I don't even know how we're meant to get there."

"My husband is obsessed with procedures and logistics," Rosa informed Dick. "He was an engineer during the war. Everything has to run like one of his tanks."

"Well, how are *you* getting there?" demanded Jack in exasperation.

"*We* are presumably getting there the way we get everywhere else," Rosa replied. "In a taxi."

"You see?" Jack might have been addressing a staff meeting. "Every taxi in Monument has been booked for weeks." To Dick. "If half the drink I hear's been ordered is drunk it's ambulances'll be needed."

"May I make a most respectful suggestion?" asked Dick, almost whispering.

We strained forward.

"Would you let me drive you out to Main?" He shot up his hands like people do in a hold-up. "I want to, I'd love to, nothing would give me a greater sense of –"

It must sometimes be like this in the womb. Utterly suspended. Dick crushed down his forehead on his wrist.

"– personal fulfilment."

"I don't care how I get there as long as I'm home for the test match," said Jack, turning on his heel and walking away downhill.

All the wooden bar snugs and other cosy features of the Commercial Hotel had been swept away, leaving open regions of bright, ill-chosen carpet.

"I'm sorry, Jack," I said.

Jack sighed. "I've always known."

"How?"

"Rosa told me."

"In that case, Rosa was jumping to conclusions."

Rosa reached over. "It was the most wonderful thing that anyone ever did for a friend."

Jack said, "I suppose it's never too late to say, thank you. Thank you."

He leaned across and we shook hands.

I said, "He was a horrible man."

"He was right, however."

"Oh, Jack," Rosa said.

Jack said, "He was correct in what he said. I funked. He should have shot me there and then. I would have, looking back, had the roles been reversed. No hesitation."

A boy arrived with whiskey for me, gin for Rosa and clear water for Jack. The three of us at our little table in the centre of the otherwise empty lounge, I imagined like people in a lifeboat.

I said, "You have no need to worry, you know."

Jack blinked.

I said, "They'll never know."

"Chud, please," Rosa said.

"Blackmail is blackmail. But I don't care what anyone thinks about me. Jack is another proposition. Did you hear Dick Coad? Dumbstruck that he'd finally met the famous Colonel Santry."

"We're not going to let you go to gaol!" Rosa was outraged. "Not again."

Jack was winding thread around a loose button on his coat.

"We're not going to let you go to gaol if telling them that Jack made a mistake during the war is going to keep you out of it."

I said, "I doubt it would make a difference."

"Of course it would. Don't you remember the effect all that had on Jack at the time?" Rosa turned to Jack. "I found you about to drink strychnine, in case you forget."

"Perhaps I should have."

"Oh, for Christ's sake!"

"I never wanted all that fuss." Jack shot a dark and surprisingly bitter glance at Rosa. "That was all your bloody father."

"Don't blame a dead man for your problems!" Rosa said.

Jack shrugged. "The truth is, I thought if the details became known it would have meant the end of Main."

"You overrate your own importance," Rosa said, still rankling on Paddy Bensey's behalf.

I said, "I think Jack's right."

"Chud, don't get involved."

"You are who you are. Jack is still Colonel Jack Santry, MC. It's best all left that way."

"It would really take the skin off Kevin's nose!" said Jack with sudden joviality. "He'd soon find out that he owed a lot to my reputation."

When it was all over, Kevin Santry described in some detail his feelings of well-being as the day of Annabelle's wedding drew nearer.

Main, beautiful in any season, was especially captivating in June. Cattle and horses browsed in the first flush of meadows. The morning light as it illuminated the flowering trees did so with exquisite tenderness. Kevin picked up his breakfast cup and strolled out of the open doors of the library. He sat on the warm step of granite and, eyes closed, allowed the satisfying sounds of careful planning to top up his meniscus of happiness. Brigid's firm voice drifted to him from the windows of the ballroom within which were marshalled the twenty-five serving staff who in two days' time would ply the guests with drink and food. She had become quite the Santry, had Brigid, Kevin smiled. Her clipped consonants, the Anglo-Irish method of dealing with servants. It was Main that did it, turned the women into Santrys, his own mother included, he had to admit, despite everything.

"Never ask someone if they would like *another* drink, Mary. Simply, if they would care for a drink."

Allowing his listening to soar over the great house, to the front entrance and its climbing driveway, Kevin could make out the voices of men and the rattling sounds of aluminium crash barriers being linked together as the great paddock known as the lawn, which lay below the house, was formed into a temporary car park. The arrangements pleased Kevin immensely. The great day was at hand and he had not had to, as he should not have had to, lift a hand. Guards from Monument and the police traffic helicopter from Dublin had arrived and were rehearsing, a nice touch the last one, since the local television station was sharing the cost, sending up a cameraman to film the fireworks so the entire county – even those not come to Main – could enjoy the display. Kevin sighed with contentment. The deep groan of the crane that had come late and was now lifting portable toilets into the orchard, not even this symbolic, albeit minor, failure of organisation could dent Kevin's sense of achievement.

Time was, not so long ago either, when this spot, which is to say, the doors of the library and environs, had engulfed Kevin with so much dismay that for years he had circumvented it. It had been the favoured place for his mother to sit, either alone or with . . . From the nearby shrubberies, whose dank reek still, dammit, triggered in him pangs of hopeless jealousy, from their cover young Kevin had observed his mother as . . . It was ultimately to this spot that Kevin had had to come, even as the father of young Annabelle, and confront the truly overwhelming memory of his mother here with . . . me. Kevin shook his head and smiled. Where now were the participants from that farce? In flats in Monument. And Kevin was in Main.

Not easy at the time, mind you. Something like that takes a hold when you're a child and the rest of your life is spent in its thrall. But as a grown man as much as a Santry he had realised that the work must start somewhere and thus, with the courage of his forebears for example, Kevin had made himself come out here, sit in the library with its open doors, on the step, even hide in the shrubbery and come to terms with the altered perspective and changed reality. After that it had been easier. Every part of the house that bled of me, such as the far-off bedroom and the coat-room behind the downstairs toilet where once he had also come upon me with his mother, one by one Kevin had confronted them and won. Until the entire house was his, rather as, he imagined, a defended territory might yield after a hard-fought campaign.

Kevin shuddered with pleasure. Standing, or sitting as he now was, at the summit of his life's achievements, the concessions he had been forced to make now appeared inconsequential, not concessions at all in fact, more like gestures of charity and magnanimity. It said a lot for the distance he had come, although he would never admit it to anyone. That he had, in the end, been able to invite someone for whom no word existed to describe the degree of abhorrence that he felt, was itself a triumph. Santrys must have frequently, over the centuries, conquered their own feelings for mere people, when, for example, they had accepted the surrender of entire countries. It was a hazard of warfare that sooner or later one had to associate with one's enemies. And then, in a series of manners that could hardly be learned, one did so with profound grace and dignity. For Kevin had won, there was no question. He was a Santry like no other in history and in two days up the drive of Main would come, or rather, be brought, his oldest, vilest enemy to make obeisance, to feed from the trough of Kevin Santry's bounty and to join with the town and county in the general acknowledgment of Kevin's hegemony.

Kevin opened his eyes and the figure of his lovely, English-educated daughter striding to him across the croquet lawn overprinted his fond thoughts like the seal of an exchequer. No-one, Kevin knew, could upset the approaching day and the night. No-one in the world. No-one. Not even

Twenty-two

MY NIGHTMARES TAKE A variety of forms. One of them is that my pump-action spray, instead of sustaining me with puffs of nitroglycerine is killing me by degrees. Another is, that instead of progressing steadily towards even older age and death, I am in fact going in the opposite direction, slipping through wormholes of time back into my own past, so that my end will be a reverse facsimile of my birth. The people I encounter during this journey are always dead and when, finally, the face of my poor mother, Hilda, appears, I know the game is up.

I awoke, feeling as if a head of chemicals lay between me and the day. It took some minutes to crawl to my bathroom and once there to float for up to thirty minutes, climbing from the scaly depths of my doomed unconscious, gradually assimilating the sounds of the so-called real world, including those overhead of Rosa's coughing.

Now that the day had arrived at last, all the antics that had preceded it, the schemings and stand-offs between O'Gara Street and Main, seemed irrelevant. Old age is all about reduction: of physical size, of remaining time, of the number of themes in which at any one moment one can be interested.

"What about a drink?" suggested Jack peering at his watch. You'd never have thought he'd not touched alcohol in twenty years.

We had not discussed the coming evening between the three of us, since discussing Kevin or Main or even the future where Main was concerned, was sure to rankle someone. I think, too, we were conscious of the fact that Big a Day and all as it was for Monument, something was inherently askew if going out to Main was meant to be special for Rosa and Jack. Or for me, for that matter. Nor did the marriage of their granddaughter to one of the Loves hold any significance beyond the normal for Rosa or Jack. They were fond of Annabelle, but – as Brigid had made sure – they had almost never seen her after they left Main and thus did not know her well. And yet, despite all these reasons, it *was* in reality a big day for the three of us, not just because we never went anywhere any more, nor just because we all knew that Kevin and Brigid did not want us and so all of us would be damned before we would give them that satisfaction; no, the day meant more than all these things together, because this, we knew, was the last time we all would together go out to Main.

"Whiskey, Chud?" asked Jack, holding up a bottle and trying to read its label.

Rosa came from her bedroom and eyed me up and down in my dinner jacket. "There isn't time, Jack. The car will be here any moment."

The fact that she hadn't bothered to dye out the grey in her hair was a statement that the black in it was natural. The swoop of her neck and inner sides of her long shoulder blades dived into the deep blue silk of her dress and became the dip and rise of her rump. Clutching a silver-flecked shawl about herself, she pirouetted.

"Doesn't she look a picture?" asked Jack.

I felt old surges of power that took me beyond the clutches of creditors or police authorities. I sat one side of Rosa on the big sofa they'd brought with them from Main; Jack the other. She reached for our hands.

"You boys will look after me tonight, won't you?" she asked.

Jack puffed. "Of course."

For him it can't have been easy, for love often appears a doubtful consolation. Yet, Jack, so far as I could tell, had come to like it around the town, the little he went, had got used to people calling him 'Jack' and may even have appreciated the great symbolism he represented. He was, know it or not, the nearest a Santry had ever got to being a native.

"We'll have to watch that old fellow. Especially on the way home. Got a bad eye," Jack said. "What's his name?"

"Dick," I said as the doorbell rang. "Dick Coad."

I heard Rosa's sudden intake of breath from the hall door.

"Mr . . . Coad?"

"Madam Santry."

Jack and I turned and stared. Dick Coad, if indeed it still was he, was in ink-black serge, his legs drainpipes, his waist agonisingly attenuated, his chest blossoming with rows of bright gold buttons and a bar of medals and his shoulders topped with gilt epaulettes. Flattened beneath his left oxter was a tricorn hat from which gold tassels and ribbons impended.

"Good Lord," Jack said.

"Colonel," said Dick, newly abow. "Your humble servant." Unbending, he stepped back, seized the tricorn in his right hand and in a pantomime flourish swept the air between us and the doorway. "Familiar?" he asked, standing erect over black shoes of bright, bulging toecaps.

We cast around to one another.

"Captain John Santry, Fifth Dragoons, Peninsular campaign." The merest sigh of alcohol reached me on the air. "Some years ago, using his correspondence with his then tailors and hatters, Bentyn and Lock & Co respectively, both of St James's, I had everything made up exactly."

Rosa giggled.

"The hour awaits. History has nurtured us for a moment such as this. Madam Santry, if you will."

We went downstairs in a little bunch, like three lambs ahead of a mad sheepdog. Through the hall door, as Rosa opened it, poured such quantities of evening sunlight that it was impossible not to imagine that harmony was at hand.

"My God!"

Dick had darted out and was holding open the back door to a car, long, shining and black as a shark.

"This is ridiculous!" Rosa burst out laughing. "It's . . ." She got in first and began to shriek. "Jack, it's bigger than our bedroom!"

Walnut trim reflected lights recessed behind cocktail cabinets built into the doors, and in the bulkhead separating the passengers from the driver, a small television was turned on with Sumo wrestlers in action.

"A television," said Jack brightly, loading last.

"The test match, remember, Colonel," Dick said from the kerb.

Jack looked at him in bewilderment.

I said, "Dick, this is all very well, but . . ."

"Chud." Dick had placed his hat on. "Please." As if he'd been born an equerry, he shut us in, then took the wheel.

"Just use the intercom if you need me, Colonel," said his disembodied voice.

"The intercom!" Rosa cried.

"Fellow's pissed as an owl," Jack muttered.

As we moved off I sank so that my knees were higher than my chest and I could see Rosa and Jack in the opposite seat, Jack frowning, Rosa hugging herself like a child, both of them framed between the gap of my knees like the people on a screen.

"Hmmp," said Jack.

"What's *wrong* with you?" Rosa asked.

"Reminds me of a hearse."

"Time enough. Oh, look! There are the Turners! Blow the horn, Mr Coad!" She seized the curving, intercom pipe. "Blow the horn!"

"Don't!"

But Dick honked out a tune and I shrank down as, above its readymade dicky-bow, Cyril Turner's big, easily vacant face followed our magisterial progress down Long Quay.

"Looks as if he's seen a ghost!" Rosa laughed.

We rolled out along Small Quay and into the first foothills. Nothing unforgiving exists about old age. Instead of savouring the beauty of the countryside, the three of us were thinking of the other trips we had made out on this road, all the years that were written into every turn, all the dead faces.

"I wouldn't live out here now if you gave me a million pounds," Jack said as we crossed the Thom.

The stubborn illusions of misplaced pride, that's all you have left in old age. Traffic was backed up a good half mile before the church and every few moments a helicopter thrashed overhead.

"So noble," Dick said when we reached the church, speaking over the intercom. "In a letter to his son, written in 1780 during the Siege of Gibraltar, Captain John Santry described in detail where he would build this church when he came home and how he would model it on an Oxford oratory of which he was particularly fond. He did."

"It's ours," Rosa told him. "It's where they'll take Jack and me when we die, Mr Coad."

I'd never heard her say that before. She looked away, out of the window, because she hadn't meant to say it, not in front of me at any rate. Somehow I'd always had the idea that Rosa was going down with her father in the cathedral, that we'd all be somehow together in the end, as we once were, if not in the same then at least in adjacent pews. Two men in white coats and several guards stood outside the gates of Main. We swept in past the eagles and into Main's landscapes. It must have been a strange feeling for Jack. It seemed impossible at that moment, looking at him hunched and empty, that all this magnificence could once have been held at his command.

"Welcome home, Colonel," Dick said. "Welcome home to Main."

We rounded the final turn and were now purring uphill to a line of silver barriers placed midway across the drive. It looked less like the Main I knew than the outskirts of some race meeting: tens of people, hundreds of parked cars and clouds of dust. I could see guests who didn't want to walk the hill climbing into a maroon trap drawn by a cob.

"You know, war is a terrible thing," Jack said.

Rosa reached over and caught his hand and held it. The attendant drew back the barrier and we were gliding up the final rise, something I had done as often on bicycles as in cars.

"You see this, Madam Santry?"

Dick had lowered the glass partition and was handing Rosa back a slim, rectangular little telephone.

"Fifteen minutes before you think the Colonel wants to leave, just press this button here. I'll be at home standing by."

"Mr Coad, you've already gone to far too much trouble . . ."

"Madam, please, not a word. Not a syllable."

We crunched into the courtyard.

"Here goes," Jack said.

Beneath a canopy put up in case of rain but now, in the golden May evening gloriously unnecessary, stood guests in a line waiting to be received. I thought I saw Brigid Santry frown at us from the door. Dick leapt about, opening doors and fawning over Jack's emergence from the car; and then lost his hat which went skittering downhill, making poor Dick spring along after it like a crane chasing a coot. I heard the guests' laughter. More than any other moment, this one had worried me most. A correct bow to Brigid would be the best, I'd decided, a firm handshake for Kevin, and perhaps a muttered sentence containing the words "great day", which would render my sentiments suitably ambiguous while retaining a general air of dignity. The waiting line stood back. Rosa and Jack went first and I heard Kevin Santry's false laugh as he said to his mother, "Quite right, absolutely appropriate."

My grandfather had once made this journey in deep frost because he thought this man's grandfather had needed medical attention.

"Mr Church!"

Annabelle Santry Love stood there, dressed in cream, so glistening and perfect that she might just have stepped from wrapping. She kissed me, murmuring, "I'm so glad!"

She had me by the arm and was turning me.

"You come with me and don't worry about standing out here."

Before I knew it she had me sailing down the hall, past (to my eyes) the remarkably bright faces of her ancestors and into the (in my day) massive but little-used drawing room, whose press of people let off a solid, unremitting roar of sound.

"There. Have one of these," she smiled, taking a glass of champagne from a passing tray and putting it into my hand.

She was so like Jack had once been. Not just the fair hair and the blue eyes, nor just the way she stood straight like Jack once had, but the ever so faintly patronising attitude that made a Santry, however much they tried not to, look upon people from Monument not just as people but as a source of possible amusement.

"I remember you when I was a child. We used to live in the Kennel House then. I used to see you when I rode my pony up here."

"I remember you well," I said, the literal truth since I did recall a small shrieking child on a fat beast being led by a groom. But above all she recalled Jack's youth for me, which is to say, my own, and if you can ever

280

touch or hold your youth, or think you can, nothing in creation is more seductive. "You were very pretty," I said, "even then."

"You were up here a lot then," Annabelle said and I fancied her eyes were laughing. "We must have a chat some day."

"You know where I live."

I wondered how far her curiosity would take her. I wondered if she was the competitive type, which in her case might in reason mean at least equalling her grandmother's experiences, even if once.

"I'll say." She laughed. But she knew what I'd been thinking, and that to my mind, is always an essential pre-condition. "It wouldn't have been the same today without you," she was saying. "Are you going to be all right here?"

"Of course, thank you."

I watched her cream-chiffon-clad hips make their way back out through the crowd. I would lodge her, with ridiculous optimism, in my bank of hope, and then one day perhaps, before the great foreclosure, a single, even if only part-consummated but nonetheless real, transaction might take place in O'Gara Street, following which we would both continue our remaining, uneven journeys, one less question left to answer. Stranger things have happened. A girl in a pinafore gave me a fresh glass before I could tell her not to. Looking back for Rosa and Jack, all I could see were fresh people pressing into the room behind me, shuffling me ever deeper. Intense heat. In two swigs I emptied the glass and snatched another. The distinct impression that I was standing amid a throng from a taller race, as happened frequently on some television programmes, occurred to me. Now and then there appeared someone I thought I recognised, but I could not be sure, my eyes having become unreliable beyond six feet in such matters. Heat made me gulp. Against the wall stood a single, upright chair. I sat, just for a minute. Dredging for breath, all the back of my shirt sodden, I fought for my bearings. No feeling, all at once, no guts churning. A sensation of floating up from where I perched, cruising around the architraves, peering down at all the faces. Deaf too, all at once, if deafness was just a constant, seashore sound, a steady pitch the colour black in my dazed imagination; yet deafness was altogether fond and warm, too, womb-like in fact, although how I might have thought such a thing at my age I have no idea. This was some way-station, not Main. The number of rooms must have been infinite in number, all thronged like this one, or perhaps not, perhaps some of them were empty and cold and would rebound to my voice. In the small space of seconds, as images present and future fought within me for accommodation, I was gripped by loss for the past, something I had spent my whole life trying to come to terms with. Rosa and Jack would never find me here. They would go home and wait for years before trying again, and grow ever older, Rosa's hair turning and turning, Jack developing an even worse stoop, like all the Santrys, as the seasons played out their themes on the face of my lost town. It was not so bad, after all. After all the fuss. I had no wants except the company of friends, but that was the challenge. I saw Captain Ivory in front of me, his carroty mop bobbing at me, the right-hand sleeve of his tunic pinned emptily to the stump of his shoulder. Funny how he was the one who'd popped up.

"Give him air!"

That was the idea. I was watching television. An old man in a dinner jacket was being carried from a crowded room by a number of younger men. High drama, I loved it. Especially when they showed you the picture from the ceiling. How did they do that? How did they get the camera up so high and show all the people like ants? And Brigid Santry too! On television!

"Is he . . . dead?"

Time to turn in. My hand flapped around for the remote, but all I could feel was someone else, as if they'd jumped out from the television into the room.

"Oh my God, he's dead!"

Cut grass in heaven.

"Is he?"

Brigid Santry's voice outweighed the scents. Not heaven but somewhere else.

"He's all right, he just passed out with the heat in there. He's fine."

"Chud?"

Rosa and Jack. The bishop peering at me with vocational interest. Standing off, a little knot of people. We were out on the grass at the back of the courtyard. I could taste the sweet evening air.

"You passed out."

I sat up.

"I'll drive you home."

"No." I could see Brigid Santry's face thirty yards off. "No, I'll be grand. I'll stay."

Brigid walked in through the doors of the library, through the back hall, down the passage towards the kitchens whose efficient clatter were a testament to months of hard planning, and into a room marked "Private". Locking the door, she sank down on the toilet and, shaking, lit up.

Not just her hands but her entire body quivered. It was the disappointment, she admitted later, despite Kevin's attempts to silence her. She had been sure I was dead. My ashen face, the way I was being carried, the pandemonium – all the most wonderful vindications that Brigid could have wished. Then the cruel ebbing of the recent certainty, the sight of me sitting up, worse, the sound of my voice stating that I would stay. Brigid rose from the toilet in order to be sick.

It was the final matter to come between her and Kevin. Annabelle, Brigid believed, got all her Santry firmness and resolve not through Kevin but, as in the Old Testament, from the female side. It made sense. The Santrys had always renewed their bloodlines in order to sustain them-selves, but in Kevin the line was flawed by crucial weaknesses, never more obvious than where his mother was concerned. The concessions he had made regarding the party could not have been more significant. Into their midst he had invited on this greatest of days the creature of most evil. Only disaster could follow.

On the outside she and Kevin made a golden couple. The truth was, as usual, at variance with the appearance. In truth they had become a cold duo, rarely making love and then only in expensive, foreign locations, speaking to each other of nothing except matters of common, financial interest, or, in recent months, the party, pursuing separate lives and having only this great, uneconomical, and as far as Brigid was concerned, ugly old house in common. Yet Brigid at forty-two was an attractive woman. She had allowed herself to acquire a reputation as a flirt, and although she had begun the role with caution, as time wore on she had risked more until, only weeks earlier, she had allowed an aide to the reichs chancellor of Germany himself to slide his finger beneath the elastic of her knickers. In the aftermath, Brigid had dreamed of power and politics and a life free of Main.

Did she still love Kevin? She often asked herself. She often wondered how she had managed to become part of such an elaborate and futile structure. All she represented was a failed breeding enterprise, someone with no ultimate authority, not even a veto in the matter of who was invited into her house.

Brigid, calmer, sat and lit another cigarette. From her pearl-encrusted evening purse, a Santry heirloom, she took out various items of cosmetics and placed them on the window ledge. Between thumb and forefinger she lifted out the tiny derringer, her father's final bequest.

Whether or not she loved Kevin, Brigid was proud of what he personified. Nevertheless, since he had capitulated so appallingly over my invitation, Brigid had made a vow to herself. Whatever it took to preserve her own dignity, whatever that meant, she would not be found wanting. She would be the man Kevin had refused to be. In the great abyss of the lonely night Brigid made an oath.

She clasped the minute gun. Its twin chambers were full and although Brigid had no proof that the thing would work, instinctively she knew it would. Its grease had been applied by her own father. Even by her grandfather. He should have used it! Instead of creeping out of Monument, he should have fired his gun! The incident of ten minutes before had come as overwhelming justification of her righteousness to Brigid. Then the plunging proof of life still extant, her dash to the lavatory, her vomiting, subsequent weakness, reborn resolve and now, fervent prayer. Great God, Brigid begged, at whatever cost and soon let this much-overdue justice be done.

Great occasions had truly been understood by Ernesto Delamarre, he who had conceived the ballroom at Main. Now, whilst half the guests followed Kevin and Annabelle in a waltz and as the other half remained at their tables drinking champagne and eating slabs of fruity wedding cake, the room seemed at ease with its numbers.

My watch had just registered ten o'clock. As fingers of dusk began to creep into the courtyard outside the open window beside which I was seated, as the scents of dusk conjured from me feelings of great safety and contentment, I looked for Rosa and Jack out on the floor. They were by far the most elegant couple, although my eyes saw only one. I had all but forgotten the commotion I had created earlier. Odd but true. It was as if my crisis had purged the air. When Rosa and Jack swept into view again, I could do nothing but smile at the sight of her, her straight back, her fluid movements.

"Chud!" I looked up. Cyril Turner, big and damp as a whale stood over me. "You're still here! Some party! What did I tell you? This is some room. Some bloody house! God, I haven't danced like this for years. I suppose we'll see you out on the floor in a minute!" He winked at me, oafish. "Jesus, can you imagine what this is all costing? Can you even begin to imagine?"

"Excuse me."

I got up because the music had stopped and Rosa was walking back, glowing, on Jack's arm.

"My dance," I said and led her back onto the floor.

"You're trying to kill me."

"I'm escaping from that utter fool. You look so lovely."

"You're looking pretty good yourself."

284

"I feel twenty-five," I said as a brisk dance began. "From watching you."

The length of her fit me snugly as we set off. Not for years had she been in my arms in public like this. It was so important.

"I'm so happy, Chud."

"I've never in my life been happier than this moment."

As we clipped past the musicians and she pressed me, I felt my feet regain the old routines, skipping out of each other's way, my hips swinging. We passed Jack at the table and I spun Rosa once around, just for bravura, before we tripped away in lockstep. I could feel my breath coming cleaner than it had for years. The want of this that had blocked me up. Never again. From now on we were going to dance.

"Slow down a bit," Rosa said.

I laughed outright and she pinched me in the small of my back.

"Ah!"

"Slow down. You bastard."

We whirled and I led her faster still in a great cut through every other couple on the floor. She pinched me all across the shoulders and on my neck, causing even my toes to pucker.

"I love you."

"Chud."

What was all this fuss one heard about age? We had escaped, all three of us (including Jack), we would never fall into given categories, be subject to commonplace rules. Alive as never before, young inside, sovereign and free. I laughed.

"Dance!"

Rosa laughed.

My watch sounded.

I stopped dead and two other couples collided with us.

"What . . . ?"

"To hell with it! Come on!"

"No, Chud . . ."

"Come on!"

We resumed, although now in the shadow of this oriental wristpiece and its intrusive pulses. I would not be its marionette.

"You should . . ."

"No!"

As if to stamp out anything that dared undermine our evening, I hoofed us on with extra zeal, twirling Rosa by her fingertips, spinning us at fierce pace and cavorting the full length of the floor and back in half the time of any other couple. There was a handclap. We were the centre of a clapping, cheering circle, and the band responded by upping the rhythm, which meant I now had to keep going at that pace. Pride was my chief sensation. It was as if Rosa and I had won acceptance at last, that this was our victory dance.

In the corner of my jaw, deep within the soft secrets beneath my left ear, a vicious ache was born.

"Jesus."

I went to my pocket for the spray can, but even as I fastened on it I knew that to have to stop in front of several hundred people and squirt medication down my throat would ruin the performance. And so, as my chest began to clamp, I hurled Rosa for the doorway, out through the still clapping, cheering assembly and into the hall.

"Chud?"

"Just . . . a minute."

But some of the crowd, thinking that we were, perhaps, leading them on some jolly dance through Main, had followed us out, clapping along with the music, grinning in expectation.

Jaw was now joined to hip in spreading agony. I stumbled away from Rosa, into the library for refuge, meeting its door with my shoulder. From the library floor, where she had laid open an illustrated flowers book and from which she was tearing a watercolour, Cyril Turner's wife started in alarm. Where could I deal alone with my fallibility? Flinging myself on through the next door, into Jack's old study and through it and out into the back hall, scene of so many other moments of instant gratification, I prayed to God that the toilet would be empty. Its door gave way. I tore off the cap of the can and pumped its contents down my throat.

The aftermath, as always, was like waking early on a summer's morning and coming slowly to terms with the world outside the one you have just forsaken. A great tiredness, or sham peace, overcame me, for this was one war I could never win, just hold the line on, until the final skirmish, where only one outcome was possible. A strange, intermittent blueness beat against the mirror. Voices spoke close by, in my head, I thought, it being that sort of day. But then beyond the voices the evening bird chorus grew octave by octave in my hearing, unassailably real. The open toilet window, set in a discreet cleft of wall, was in the part of the courtyard nearest the entrance gate. Rinsing my hands, awarding myself a pass in a visual inspection, I began to search within me for the sense of elation which this interlude had robbed and to rehearse the steps needed to reattain with Rosa the position we had just relinquished.

"The best thing will be for me to go and bring him out so you can serve the warrant here."

"Very well, sir."

Kevin's Anglo-Irish voice, close as if he were with me in the toilet. And a different accent, but one that was, for reasons as yet unclear, familiar. I went nearer to the window. A blue lamp in the middle distance, revolving. The nearer, square shoulders of men, just around the recess in which the toilet window sat. Kevin's chin was unmistakable, although seen only in the instant that he walked away. Then, a warm flash of yellow, caused by what I had at first had no idea, but then as I stared and it swam into focus, made me clutch out for support and pitch once again into the unregulated struggle of my life. A yellow waistcoat. The angular, morose figure of Sergeant Fazakerley leaned, one elbow propped on the roof of a Garda patrol car the same way he had on my mantelpiece.

I could think only of Rosa. Of being taken without seeing her. Kevin, part of the conspiracy, was at that moment on his way to lure me out without fuss. I stepped into the small, back hall.

"Ahhh!"

Cyril Turner's wife cowered back, clutching her chest.

"Chud, please . . ." she began to plead, her face flushed and criminal.

For atoms of time I actually considered cashing in my advantage. Her face, now in consternation, and, for some reason, her open and it seemed, inviting mouth, still lit old fires; and then there was that whole, ancient business in her house, unconsummated lust for which she had seen fit to punish me over many years, outstanding business that could now, at last, be seen to. But the imperatives of my situation, although this thieving woman could never have known it, were far more overwhelming than hers; and although it would have been sweet revenge to have had her there and then as the last fuck of a man on his way to prison, I simply did not have the time, not to mention the ability, to enact any of these vindicating strategies.

I needed Rosa. Making my way back through the library, I spotted Kevin at the end of the main hall, where he had been buttonholed, probably by a client, since Kevin had on his dog-before-supper look. Dancing was still in full swing. I edged back in through the ballroom. Rosa and Jack were seated, laughing. I paused in the fringe, amid the dancers, where I could see but not be seen. I remembered with a rush other times, so far away as to be beyond memory, when I had so looked in from the outside at the people I had then, and still now, loved. All dead. Every one. What could I have done to change that? What could I do now to preserve the happiness I saw before my eyes? Jack leaned back in his chair and gazed out of the window. Rosa looked at her watch and said something. Jack smiled. I should have turned, slipped off. But then over my shoulder I saw Kevin's white, searching face approaching.

"Chud? You all right?"

Her concerned eyes.

"They're . . . here."

"Who are?"

"Those bastards from Manchester."

"Oh, God."

Kevin was marching towards us, up the middle of the ballroom, the set of a man about unsavoury business. Crisis is a chemical thing with its own textures and palpable compositions. Dancing had stopped. The musicians and the guests sat and stood in a variety of frozen poses.

"Mother, this has nothing to do with you," muttered Kevin in an opening attempt at firmness. "Chud, a word outside? In private?"

"Chud came with us, he's leaving with us," Rosa said.

"Mother, I just want to *talk* to him!" Kevin said. He turned to the band and made winding-up gestures with his arm. "For Christ's sake, don't spoil our party!"

"You're a liar," said Kevin's mother. "A Judas. You're bringing him out to be arrested. Why don't you say so?"

I saw Jack hunched forward, head between his knees, as if tying his shoelaces.

"Very well," heaved Kevin, trying as ever to break from the jungle of his youth, "yes, yes I am. And about time too, let it be said. Come on, then. Let's get it over with. Let's do what has to be done and allow the decent people here to enjoy themselves."

He caught me under the elbow.

"Take your hand off him!"

Rosa stood between Kevin and the rest of the room.

"Please get out of my way, Mother. You have no idea what is going on here."

"Take your hand off him!"

Kevin tried to walk me around Rosa; Rosa hit Kevin once across the face. As if the collective intake of breath had sucked him with it, Kevin took three rapid backward steps.

"Come along, Jack," Rosa said. "We're leaving."

Jack stood up and shook himself and handed Rosa her evening purse. We began the first of the many steps that leaving the ballroom would entail.

"*No!*"

At first I didn't see Brigid. She was rushing out at me from all the other people, one arm held straight from her body, for some reason.

"No, you don't go anywhere. Not you. Except the way you're meant to. In handcuffs."

"Mama . . ." Annabelle had stepped forward.

"Get back!" Brigid screamed and swung her arm. The crowd shrank in terror.

"She's got a gun!" someone said.

"Mama, please . . ."

"Murderer!" Brigid screamed. "Murderer!"

"Mama! This has gone too far!"

"He . . ." Brigid, shaking, ashen. "He. Killed. My. Uncle."

I said, "I did not."

"Brigid . . ." Kevin, parched of blood. "Darling, please give me . . ."

"Bruno," Brigid now wept, "Bruno Belli, my father's hero, the Great Tintini's oldest son. Bruno Belli."

A murmur gurgled through the crowd as the name expunged sixty years ago by these same people was now revived.

Rosa stepped forward. "Let me tell you, my dear, your uncle, if that's who he was, was a loathsome peeping Tom of the worst kind who fully deserved the end he came to."

I didn't want any more of this, really. If restoring sanity involved my surrendering at the hall door, then I would. I stepped out to Brigid.

"Listen . . ."

She shot me. I went back and down, conscious of widespread screaming, as thoughts in volume surged through me, foremost among them the realisation that no pain was involved, then, that this was the first time ever I had been shot, followed by the unavoidable irony for a D-Day survivor of being nailed by a crazy woman in a ballroom. With considerable detachment I watched Cyril Turner envelop Brigid with his arms, saw both of them totter backwards for the bandstand as Brigid's madness surged, registered little surprise at the second, loud report, knew as soon as I heard it the outcome.

"*Mama!*"

Annabelle Santry Love's awful shriek as she threw herself on Brigid Bell Santry's sprawled body. Then, past the unbelieving faces of, first, Monument, then those of the revarnished Santrys, I was transported without recourse to personal movement, along a passage that ran parallel with the main hall.

"Where . . . ?"

"It's all right, Chud."

Jack? God, give Jack a cause. Through kitchens, pantries, still rooms and sculleries, Rosa one side of me, Jack the other, we forged into a larder where a man in a chef's hat was astride a gasping waitress, then down the two outside steps at which point I fell from their grasp and into the back yard of Main.

For the second occasion in a very short time, a counterfeit peace prevailed.

I asked, "Where are we going?"

Rosa was helping me up.

"I rang Coad," Jack said. "I instructed him to rendezvous above Delaware."

From nearby shadows a horse's rubbery exhalation suggested a real world: horses and tackrooms and deep smells of leather, chamois and saddle soap.

"Hold this to your shoulder," Rosa said, folding her shawl. Pain, like something creeping from the shade. She pressed her cheek to mine. "You remember Delaware, Chud? We're going home."

The purple trim of the open carriage and the glow of the roan cob's coat in the light through the tackroom made me ache with loss. Rosa climbed up first. The pure, blue veins in the backs of her knees, details which I had always regarded as secrets, arose in me longings beyond sex, tendernesses blind to any danger. With one arm, Jack pushing behind, I dragged myself up after her. As my hand lay for a moment on her bare arm, she turned and kissed me before stooping down for Jack. In the driver's seat, Rosa unwound the reins from their handle and shook them down over the cob's back. We moved off. Each time the horse put its foot down on the cobbled yard, the echo rebounded from the stone surroundings like a rifle shot. Looking back over the yard wall, the sight of the ballroom made me pause in wonder. Light stretched outwards in great spars of premature triumph. The cob broke into a trot.

The urge to get back to our familiar habitat, to our own world that was ever reducing like ourselves, like the last light of the evening through which we whirled, like the dying days of this century, like . . . this urge overcame any logic at all, it was as if we were salmon that must come home from oceans to die. I heard Rosa click to the cob to stretch its stride. We left the reflected light from the house and moved evermore into the natural, the last shades of a thousand shadows. As the beeches came at us either side in exact, looming pairs like recurring Pillars of Hercules, as the wheel-spin of the cart made a crunching music, as we broke from trees and saw, I think with unified wonder, the cerise sky like a mourning shawl around the shoulders of Dollan, as we danced away and the evening air rushed at us with the warmth of memory and made our scalps tingle and eyes water, as these collective and cumulative happenings bombarded us in our transition, the direness of our situation was transcended by a welcome if unwise conviction that we had somehow succeeded in turning disaster into success.

We lurched right-handed off the back avenue and down the lesser track, the near wheel catching a rut for a perilous moment and canting Jack and myself together. The rim popped out again and we plunged downhill as if into a vat of ink. The cob, unsettled, began to shy and jink and after fifty, jerky yards stuck in its toes, pitching Rosa forward almost onto its trembling withers.

"Come on!" Rosa cried, fumbling the reins around the seat and groping her way back to us, for it was so dark down here beneath the rocks of Delaware that even our faces were invisible.

"I can't," I said, in pain with each further movement. "I can't climb that any more."

A thing of layers through which you could move, that darkness, deeper beneath the rock cliff but more manageable in the open space between the mountain and the pool as the moon sidled through thin cloud.

"You've climbed worse," said Jack, taking my weight on his arm as I dropped from the trap. "At least there aren't any Germans up here."

I could not go on like this. I cried out. Rosa was already climbing up the first and steepest part of the ascent, kicking back loose stones as she did so.

"Come on, Chud!"

Jack stood looking at me. He was an old man in a dinner jacket too big for him, in a shirt whose collar was too big for his neck, standing in intermittent light before a mountain that was too big for either of us to climb. And yet he was an essential part of all that remained to me, we had both, despite what either of us might have planned, shared our lives and for one or the other to strike out alone now would be unthinkable.

Rosa's face and outstretched hand were above me. Jack shoved, she caught me and pulled and I went up like a lift. Heather prickled at my unused hands, flinty earth made painful inroads beneath my fingernails. Hauling, one knee at a time as each cleft and loose stone left its penitential imprint on my kneecaps, I reached her, sitting in ferns and heather, looking out.

"It's so perfect," she said and put her arm through mine as Jack too arrived, all elbows.

The round face of Delaware shone with brilliance as if the moon was not somewhere miles overhead but was something integral to the water. Like a silver coin from which all wealth flows, Delaware lay surrounded by a world of shadow.

"How could we have done it any other way?" I asked.

"We couldn't," Jack said. "I always knew that. From the very first day we all swam here."

I felt the nearness of the old men-mountains, as if Tassy had long ago delivered me into their fostering and now at last I had come back to account for myself.

"Look!" cried Rosa.

Way above us the lights of a car were making their way at a steep angle down across the face of the mountain.

"That'll be our chap," Jack said, getting up.

As I climbed, throbbing, last of us, I prayed not that I wouldn't be led away in handcuffs, but that my heart would not give out. Pausing and looking back down at the ever perfect symbol of my life, I actually enjoyed a wheezing, recuperative moment in which to wonder what kind of a life it was that made a man prefer prison to death in such beautiful surroundings. As I saw the outline of the moon, a round within a round, pressed out on the armour-plated skin of the water, I thought of Ma Church dead and how her face skin had seemed so burnished. When I joined her I'd look at night for this beaming earth star pinned like a trophy to the skirts of Dollan.

As I resumed, in a beat briefer than creation, the whole night blossomed with sudden and awful iridescence. Winks of coloured light showed up Rosa's profile as she pivoted, Jack in mid-air, diving to earth, hands clapped on his head, and Dick Coad in his mad outfit including hat, a hundred yards above us, looking down for our little climbing knot as the hillside broke into opalescence.

"Colonel! Up here!" Dick yelled.

Rockets screamed and burst in the air over Main. Either side of the explosions the night stood in columns of tar, or in tar-black smoke palls far darker than the night itself.

"Jack!"

Rosa was shaking him, but Jack might have been dead, maybe was, back of his head only in view, now blue, now yellow, so that in the recesses of darkness you imagined he might be gone entirely by the time the next eruption of light took place. Forge-like fountains of yellow sparks poured from the sky. Each splash painted the face of the mountain in a different colour and showed Dick in a new position of descent, as if his progress towards us was being presented in a series of photographs. On the face of Delaware too each coloured spark was recorded in a miracle of reflection. A barrage hurtled up and lit the heavens like ack-ack fire. It was thrilling, not just for the moments that were so perfectly recalled, but for the newly minted taste of raw danger. The sky flushed white and I wondered how Dick had got down to us so quickly.

"They shall not pass, Colonel!"

Bizarre to my eyes was not the fact that Dick looked like some early nineteenth-century phantom on a midnight spree, nor the fact that I could see from his wild face in the blinking light that he must have passed the time since he had left us drinking; what struck me as most fantastic was that despite the place and circumstances, a lighted cigarette flourished in his mouth.

"We hold the ridge, sir!" he cried. "We still hold the ridge!"

His squinting face blooming orange, then blue, Dick caught up Jack under the armpits and began to drag him to the car. The bursts came every other second now as Kevin Santry's money ignited over Main. Taking Rosa's hand I tried to keep my eyes on the rising ground before me, for the glowing zigzags of the night, the inversion of the heavens, were making it difficult for me to keep my balance. Rosa was saying something, perhaps to herself, perhaps a repeated curse, over and over, or else it was the rasp of her breath that, like mine, was finding its passage difficult, its vigour sapped by the antics in the sky. I let go her hand and turned, as if to gaze back down but in reality because I didn't want to fall on my face like Jack and have to be carried the final stage. Up climbed a rocket, not too far from us given our height, and hung for a teasing blink of darkness, then bloomed in a great wheel of stars that in their fall turned blue as they disgorged over Delaware. I followed them down and saw, in their dying light, a bobbing yellow movement fifty yards further down the mountain. As the next flaring entertainment climbed and burst I stared again. In measured, climbing strides, Sergeant Fazakerley and Inspector Fish were closing on us.

Rosa heard me gasp.

"Come on!"

But if the wind in me had lacked before, now it had been taken altogether. Rosa was dragging my arm, but I couldn't even turn to address the final steps, I couldn't take my eyes off the two, gaining men nor rid myself of the sense of mystery that my misery was for them a matter of such pre-eminence.

"Has something happened to you, Chud?" We had reached level ground and Dick was pondering my shoulder.

"I've been shot."

Dick's head began to wobble and I realised that he knew nothing of the events we had left behind.

He took one, large breath. "Those bloody Frenchmen," he said gravely. "But we hold the ridge."

The ground was like a rainbow on water. At the car Jack was hunkered down beneath a largish stone.

I cried, "No, it's not worth . . ."

Jack's grunt of effort. The sound of shingle. The leaping heartbeats, ever more distanced and more faint, as the rock gathered pace. The entire night gave way to a red dawn in the shape of a brilliant heart.

"Watch out, sir!" came the cry from way below.

A tiny splash.

"Whenever you're ready, Colonel!"

We fell in a heap on the floor midway between the seats.

"May I remind you what the duke said at the Battle of Bussaco?" Dick asked.

We stared at him.

"'Upon my honour, Santry, I never witnessed a more gallant charge than just now made by your regiment.'"

"Drive us home, Dick."

Stones rattled against the underbody as Dick, unable to turn, rammed her back uphill in reverse, his foot to the floor. If I looked out of the car's windows I could see the entire valley bathed in greens and golds and triumphant, blinding whites.

Watching the fireworks for which he had written a cheque for twelve thousand pounds, from the back of the Garda patrol car as it tore down the avenue of Main, Kevin could only think, despite a thousand other competing images, of a summer's day in Main over forty years ago.

"I was five, hiding in a shrub," he said, his jaw atremble.

"What's that, Kevin?"

The superintendent of the guards owed a lot to Beagle & Co for the smooth working of his court days.

"Waiting for my mother to come and find me for tea," Kevin said. "Just a child."

"I know."

"It was a kind of game between us, I'd hide, she'd come out calling, pretending not to know where I was. The thrill of it."

The super made warm chuckles of unveering solidarity as the fields either side of them flashed alight beneath fresh sky bursts.

"I saw her open the doors of the library and, you know, I tucked myself up tight, closed my eyes. My whole skin was excited."

"Children."

"And then when I heard nothing, when she didn't come out and call me, I opened my eyes and looked for her."

The policeman grunted his friendly expectation.

"He was standing in the door kissing her."

"Pho-pho-pho-pho-pho," went the super.

"Running his hands all over her."

"Oh boy."

"My mother. Mine. He stole her, from me, from my fool of a father. I opened my mouth, but . . . I couldn't . . . nothing would . . ."

"Kevin."

A beech tree erupted biblically before them, its delicate green leaves shining like painted metal.

"Oh Jesus, I hate that bastard so fucking much. Poor Brigid did the right thing."

"Hmmm," said the super.

Kevin's mind would not be diverted from its fixation. "He's ruined the greatest day of my life. He's ruined my life."

"They have an extradition order. You'll never see him again. That's if he lives."

"I never thought I'd wish someone dead."

"He actually drowned an invalid. I wouldn't have believed it if I hadn't seen the file. He'll never walk out of gaol."

"I won't even begin to describe the other things I saw when I was growing up. The shame of it all. I'd come home from school at the end of term, hoping things had changed, but a few days later he'd be out here again. Any other man would have either thrown my mother out or shot the cuckolder, but not my father." Kevin gave a mighty sigh. "And I was foolish enough to think he was too old to cause trouble."

The Garda car had arrived at the main gates of Main, where two other cars from the Force with blue roof-lights snapping were drawn across the road. As Kevin stepped out the faces of the guards changed to orange as they all looked to the heavens.

"I don't want to risk injuring your parents," murmured the superintendent.

Kevin's face, as he turned to the man, was as empty as his soul.

In our gathering speed, the terrain either side of us belched brightly in stark reflections of light. We sat three in a row on the rear seat, rolling as one with the camber. I'd had enough, to be honest. Despite holding Rosa's shawl as best I could to my wound, every time a firework erupted the pain burst to a fresh peak. I was ready to give up, but Rosa saw the position differently. Her intensity on my behalf shocked me in a way, and if I say that up to this moment I had not fully realised how much I meant to her, you will no doubt scoff and understandably, but still, it's true. I'm talking about questions of degree. The heart is much bigger a vessel than is thought. You can never fill it so much with love that there isn't room for another drop.

Matters were also, to a large degree, beyond my control, Dick having taken the initiative. He had turned the car around in rough terrain and was now launched downhill for Monument, the belly of the long wheel-base scraping the flinty road at every provocation.

I've noticed the tendency of people in these situations to describe them as the opposite from reality. This or that was unreal. Or surreal. Their little worlds are so encapsuled that, for example, a headlong dash down the face of a night-time mountain beneath a barrage of fireworks, in a rented limousine driven by a deranged solicitor and with policemen waiting at the bottom: this has to be seen as divergent from real experience and labelled unreal. Dear, patient reader, I think we know each other well enough by now for me to speak frankly: that night for me was reality. Reality is feeling vital, is knowing at once all the compass points of your existence, is sorting your hands through the very gizzards of your own creation, is risking life itself for freedom in the company of the people you love. If you say that's unreal, I say, you haven't lived, my friend. I know, because I have. Once when I was too young to care about the difference between life and death, and once, that night, when I was old enough to savour it.

"Colonel!"

Dick's voice.

"There appear to be infantry below us!"

So many ways exist in which you can be damned. Rosa's lips were drawn back in a set snarl from her teeth. Jack's eyes were round and excited. Leaning forward I could see the flashing cluster of men and cars a hundred yards downhill of us. They'd brought barriers down from the parking field and had placed them across the road. I spoke into the tube on the bulkhead.

"Can you get through them?"

"I can try."

"Then do it. The colonel says, do it."

"Colonel?"

"Do it," Jack said.

"Lie down," I said. "Just in case."

We went down on our faces. Beneath us I could hear the ground gather speed.

"Bastards!" Jack muttered.

I braced my feet against the back seat, not as a strategy to avoid injury but in the hope that, if we did crash, my neck would be broken clean.

The comforts of a poor man. I heard a brief metallic impact, but no more than that. The floor of the car had been scoured that morning with a strong disinfectant.

"Chud!"

On my knees I could see that we were passing the golf course.

"What happened?"

"We went straight through everything, but now they're behind us," Dick said, but now doubtfully. "Is anything wrong?"

"Not a thing, Dick."

"Then they shall not pass."

Rosa was sitting on the floor, propped against the front seat, Jack's head in her lap.

"Jack."

"He's all right."

"I'm just very tired," Jack said.

So many times this homeward journey had been made and each time with its own little universe of life and death. It was hard to think that this was the last, for surely it was the last, surely we could not go on, as we had, as we were, expecting things ever to settle down, expecting the town to stay unchanged, just for us. Yet, even as the lights of Monument rose from the valley to meet us, I found myself arguing against the apparently terminal nature of our position, if only because the obvious is always the least likely, because in a two-horse race you always back the outsider, because I could not believe, given the relative buoyancy of my heart, that this day would end in the manner planned by other people.

A high-pitched whirring, like the mating call of a tropical bird, insisted.

"Rosa?"

Frowning, she opened her purse and took out Dick's telephone. "Yes? Yes, this is Mrs Santry." She looked at me. "They say we should turn on the television."

For a moment I feared some hitherto overlooked weapon, easily achieved in this age of technology where even the experts say they find it hard to keep abreast; but she found the catch on the walnut panel, slid the door over and switched on as she was told. A tiny, silent procession bathed in wavering light made its way down a twisting road. At the foremost end nosed a long, black and often gleaming shape, whilst behind it came smaller, white-coloured and blue-flashing units. Jack sat up and opened his eyes.

"What's on?"

"Just some programme," I said.

297

"Which one?"

"I don't know, Jack. Some old picture, I suppose."

I remembered out of nowhere how he and I had fought side by side for a day and a night once to take an apple orchard in Normandy. The Boche one side of those golden trees, us with our tin cans at the other. When at last we had won and counted out their dead, Jack lit a pipe and sat down against the warm, yellow-bricked wall upon which so much had been deemed to depend.

"Who's ever going to remember this bloody place?" he asked.

"Us," I replied.

Yet my words had taken more than fifty years to prove, because I can say honestly that I had never recalled that moment until then.

Jack and Rosa were engrossed with the happenings on the screen, absorbed in the vicarious relevance of their glaring images. I wondered for a moment if by turning the television off we might solve our problem, or instead, if by leaving it on and driving around Monument we might prolong indefinitely a resolution of the now universal dilemma in which we appeared embroiled. I looked out past Dick and saw the top of Long Quay in the distance. Dick was smoking one cigarette, but another lay curling bluely on the dashboard ashtray, a symbol of the chaotic nature of events, the amusing significance of which I had little time to indulge because a man in battledress was standing outside Samuel Love & Sons, pointing a submachine gun at our windscreen.

Two absurdities struck me as Dick swung us violently right into Ship Street: that I should be so determined to reach O'Gara Street and that they should be so determined to prevent me. The front of the car splintered through a wooden crash barrier and I heard Dick cry out.

"Chud." Rosa, kneeling beside me, had left Jack still watching television. "I'm afraid."

"No need to be. I promise."

She leaned her elbows on the ledge behind the glass partition and rested her chin on her hands. I slipped my arm around her waist. Passing the cathedral, the car seemed to take a deep breath ahead of Dudley's Hill. I drew Rosa closer. "When I was only a small boy I used to hang around on this hill so as to see you coming out from school."

Her profile in changing light, her lips. "Go on."

"I could pick you out from all the others at a hundred yards. The way you wore your hat. The way on a windy day you put your hand on your head to hold your hat. The driver used to stand with the back door open and you'd bend down as you got in and in that little second, as you bent, I'd be able to see your legs above your knees."

We passed the Esplanade, a public place set out on the plinth before the old Military Barracks. The car's general deportment was now the mechanical equivalent of a slouch.

"I came out here the day Tassy died. My grandmother brought me to lunch with you and your father."

"I know."

"But I'd loved you even before that day. I think I loved you before I was born."

Across the top of the Esplanade, a Garda car with strobe light in action, blocked the turn out of town to White City. Over the crown of Balaklava people had come out of their houses to watch our passage. Steam seeped from our bonnet. In the end our imperfection had survived intact, something no-one could have predicted. Even now, after seventy years, she and I would never analyse between us what we know to be the case: that we have loved one another not in spite of Jack, but because of him. That if Jack had died a hero in Riva Bouche I would never have married Rosa, or if I had succumbed to my wounds in Greenwich and been brought home and buried beside my mother in the cathedral, Jack and Rosa's marriage would scarcely have survived the mid-1950s. And what if Rosa had stayed in Leire, of which she might now be the beautiful, inaccessible abbess? I might still have married Joy, Jack would have found a girl from an English brewing or biscuit family and brought her home to Main, and one day in the first years of the 1960s he'd have been found stiff as a dog in his own tack room.

We slewed downhill to Buttermilk, patrol cars behind us and, now and then, on one or the other side. One of our wheels was making a grating, metal sound against the bodywork. I was taught to ride a bike here by Bruno. You could see the mountains from Buttermilk on a clear day and call their names. Ahead of us, in James Place, further white cars were drawn across the road.

Look, all I'm saying is, we got it right in our own, limping way. People would talk about us in terms of tragedy as if their own lives were models of prosperity. Look at them, they would say, on that day of days, having tried, as everyone would have it, to spoil the greatest party ever thrown in Main, hounded through the streets like criminals, loathed, ruined and best dead. Perhaps. But there has never been a tragedy in my life, and you know how many there have been, from which I did not emerge with hope in my heart. In the days after I buried Grace, in that seamless epilogue in which I am sure I died and only slowly resurrected, her dead spirit glowed like a night-light within me and over time – don't ask me to be specific – thawed me back into feeling flesh. Of course, they would then say, look at what his life in the end amounted to: pinned in a suffering, rented car with his whore and her cuckold, a scoundrel, an undischarged bankrupt (cruel, but true), a shameless philanderer with blood on his hands. Justify yourself! they would cry. Give us one reason why your life should not be committed to the limbo of the forgotten? I'm sorry, but these were not and are not matters I have ever been disposed to answer in the language of others. I never made any promises or spoke other than through my actions. I lived the truth of my life, which is the only thing I could vaguely think of as a matter of pride. But now, in the sudden confines of Skin Alley, we needed one more break.

Skin Alley, a long and narrow neck, ran from Binn's Street to the base of Cattleyard. They weren't going to let us come home. What were the moves that were left? There had to be moves. We could not run for ever. And even if all three of us were the suicidal type, which in essence we were not, it would in the circumstances be difficult to arrange. When you're young, death is a mystery, and then, with years it reveals itself ever more clearly until the point is reached when you realise that it is no more than just another accommodation. I wanted to think that in a hundred years' time, wherever we were, we three would be knocking our way through eternity, ever adjusting, readjusting, bound by the wayward chemicals that surely deserve the name of love. There might have been a time when Rosa would have told me, we'll wait for you, we'll still be here, but we were too old now for such words, no point existed in even speaking them. Time had run out. I never thought I'd see the day.

There had to be one more move, but all I could see was bright light ahead and behind, my ears crashing full of the dying car's torments, sirens and my own despairing heart. No reason or past experience existed for me to expect a sense of fair play from events, yet even as I plunged into a final shit-pool of despair, I still clung to the unrealistic expectation that lies in the heart of all gamblers, that we would be saved by a long shot, by the final move that would trump all the others and stand alone as a great victory of the heart.

"Colonel! We're going to have to stop!"

I looked out down Plunkett Hill. Thirty yards away stood what seemed like a battalion of infantry, men with guns and helmets. Behind us a squad car was jammed so tightly that reverse was impossible.

I got a fix on my bearings. Left stood the steep steps of Priests' Way, on which, tiered like a display of overweight gymnasts, were arrayed a selection of Monument's finest Gardai. Right, the door of the Friary. Shadows began closing in on us in grim phalanxes of blue and green, their armour bristling like hedgehogs'.

"Come on!" I shouted.

Jack was still staring at the screen, although without sound the milling street scene outside the distant church door can hardly have been worth watching. I turned it off, opened the door and got out.

"HALT!"

Even Jack heard that one as he emerged, turning his blinking head in the direction of the megaphone. But now was not the time, after a life of recklessness, to start complying with instructions. I saw Dick walking towards the guards and removing his tricorn the way emissaries do in costume dramas. I bore for the Friary door, Jack and Rosa after me as if on a string.

The bathing coolness was as distinct as the smell of a loved one. As if the great marble pillars with their painted stations of the cross, and the tiled floors, and the pews and kneelers gleaming from hundreds of years of constant union between personal cloth and wood, as if these otherwise inanimate objects breathed with one, cool collective breath, I paused for a moment, savouring the suspension of time, the quiet sigh of forgiveness and the carefree scent of peace.

"Chud?"

Outside I could hear shouts of tumult.

"Come on."

If pain made my chest burst open, I wondered as I struggled on, what would fall out? I could not straighten, so I grasped Rosa's hand and she led us up the nave, through the altar rail and one step at a time, upwards towards the sacristy. The church doors burst in behind us.

"Keep going."

We lurched inwards by sets of cruets, and candlesticks, and thuribles suspended by gold chains, and a great cross. Two hemp ropes, one thick, one half that size, fell through ceiling holes.

"We're trapped," Rosa said.

Kicking shut the door, I grabbed the rope with my good side. Wrapping it around me, I fell with it and then felt its pendulous action drag me up again onto my toes. And down again. With one eye locked on the door through which we'd come, with one ear dedicated to the shouts and voices outside, I rang the bell. I could feel its authority beat out all over Monument. I rang the bell. I knew it was being heard out along the distant bends of the river and that in people's back gardens dogs were creeping from their kennels and howling at the night. I rang. My breath left me in steady balloons and I cursed my wound that had now begun to bleed freely once more. Rosa came to the rope. Together we tugged down. The door held. My educated ear could discern the muffle of withdrawing footsteps, respectful, you might almost say.

This had been done before. As summer ebbed, autumn gave way to winter along the banks of the Lyle, as November edged in and cold fronts built up and people saw me as less than a sensation, life would go on. The cold when it came would not distract us from the beauty of winter. Ice-encrusted twigs would shine on white boughs like glass shards. Frozen shingle would make a muffled, underfoot crunch and bracken would stand in miniature forests on the slopes of the mountain down to Delaware.

"Come on, Jack," Rosa said. "Ring the bell."

I had to laugh when he got up, all elbows and knees. That was Jack. I left them at it for a bit. I didn't worry about time any more, because even in the coldest day of winter you keep in your memory the picture of early spring on the river here, the morning sunlight on the water at full tide, the way the water itself on days of south winds swells up in smooth cheeks to make the close flight of its river birds seem like endless undulations.

Rosa and Jack dipped and rose as one. Like a dance. He was nearly eighty then, you know. And Rosa? We never discussed her age, it was always something of a joke between us, because she was older than me, and I was already as old as a mountain.

I could have sat there and looked at them for ever.

Twenty-three

THERE'S TALK OF THE first cold front coming in tonight. I know the way it will strip the trees along the river, above all the ash, how more than any wind the frost will end their false glory and leave them stark and black and damned for what they are. And in those first few days of real cold the streets will all at once be empty as the old stagers like myself come to terms with the months that lie ahead and look to our hearths and woollens.

These nights I have a nice little fire on the go in the cast-iron, wood-burning stove that replaced my open fire, one of Rosa's last innovations. It was set yesterday with twigs by Mrs Tresadern when I told her that today she would not be needed. All it required was a match from me this morning, now it's busily acrackle and glowing red through its thick glass doors. In an hour you'll burn anything in there.

I finished today, you see. Something I'm a little proud of: twelve fat ring-binders, sitting here on the table in front of me, all pasted up, all done. My life. Or our lives, to be more accurate. They knew about it, Jack and Rosa, but they didn't worry. They knew their lives were in good hands.

When Rosa died – almost a year after the wedding – it was, Jack and I both agreed, a blessing. They had wanted to take out her lung, but she had said no – and you know Rosa once she had made up her mind. Of course, her son Kevin maintained that I had killed her, that the stress of all that went on out at Main that day, and my subsequent arrest – and release on bail awaiting trial, the current position – all exacerbated Rosa's condition. He even tried to exclude me from her funeral – the second time this has happened to me – but Jack was on my side. We must have made a funny old pair, walking arm in arm behind her coffin. Neither of us said much. We were both close enough to death – Rosa's and our own – not to fuss about it.

"We had a lot," I believe I said to Jack.

We were standing at the burial site that overlooks Dollan. I still remembered the general going down in ten degrees of frost here, although Rosa's funeral took place with swallows flitting high in the sun haze and butterflies purple and butter-coloured hovering over the very mouth of the grave. Jack looked over at me.

"Correct," he said.

It was as near as Jack would ever come to acknowledging how lucky we had been, although it had often not seemed like that.

A board upstairs creaks, and although it has been more than two years, a small pocket of belief within me, trapped like air in the quicksand of my mind, still holds that it's her up there and, cruelly, places her in whatever room and tries to say what she is doing.

I see Brigid Santry from time to time in the distance, not that I can make out people in the distance any more, but in her case she walks with a limp, a shame that in a woman of such natural athletic ability. The bullet hit a buckle or something and did a u-turn into her hip. Thank God they can't blame me for it, although Cyril Turner has not spoken to me since, a small mercy.

The news this summer was all of the heir to Main. Yes, sweet Annabelle produced a ten-pounder, God bless her, and so when an inch of mildew has long covered my headstone there'll be a John Love out in Main, who'll probably have done a tour of duty with the United Nations and will have come home with a mid-rank and a minor decoration. It won't matter that his name will be Love and not Santry. Although Kevin will not see it this way, a process of change was begun at Main by Jack, a shedding of traditions, one by one, not to any over-arching plan but because he followed his nature. Many people, including Kevin, always believed Jack to be weak; but I know, and you know by now, that it was the reverse, that nothing is stronger in the end than love. Jack's changes made it possible for Kevin to be the success he is (happiness is another thing) and, in turn, to hand down a re-invented Main to his grandson, Love, who will have the money and perhaps the ability to keep things intact for another century or so. And then, if Main has not been torn down by some impatient woman, or even if it has and its present appointments have been relocated to some villa of the modern age looking out on Dollan, some Santry–Love descendant will one night make his way to bed past Jack's doleful portrait and give an acknowledg;ing nod to the man who ultimately saved Main.

You might wonder, by the way, what they think of me in Monument, now that I'm alone. I wondered about that myself, the night that Annabelle's husband, Johnny, drove me back in from Main when we buried Jack. I wondered, now that Jack was gone, if people would see their opportunity to pay me back for all the notoriety I had brought upon Monument over the years. For just as certainly as Jack prolonged the Santry dynasty, so I ended the Church. Not that I care for dynasties, nor that the Churches went back much beyond either the turn of the century or the bend of the river; but I do sometimes wonder why some lines

304

endure and others wither, why out of all our teeming family, the many, many sons, the meals in St Melb's at which ten or twelve sat down, the bustling activity, the countless faces, the comings and goings, why I, arid and alone, remain; and why the Santrys, with never more than one child in a generation, persist. I ask myself that a lot, never more so than in the cemetery beside the cathedral, where are recorded the names of people who died before I even existed. Like the boy twins of Dr and Mrs Church, Darby and Matthew, who had taken the boat in 1914 to join an Irish regiment. I still have their photograph somewhere in my belongings: two handsome young men with pencil-line moustaches, their tam-o'-shanters on opposite sides of their heads making it seem as if one or the other is a mirror image. When they came home in identical coffins, it was the biggest funeral ever seen in Monument and my grandfather, with six years still left to him, spoke over their graves the lines that more than eighty years later I read on their headstone:

> Here dead we lie because we did not choose
> To live and shame the land from which we sprung.
> Life, to be sure, is nothing much to lose;
> But young men think it is, and we were young.

Dead in battle before I was born. And come home to lie for ever in Monument. I realised that I should never have worried about being alone here or that the town might take me to task or punish me for the lapses of the past. Monument, after all, is my home.

Kevin has been the problem. Surprise, you might say. Jack wasn't a month dead when letters came from Beagle & Co trying to increase my rent. They'll never give up, Kevin and Brigid, they'll only be happy when I'm in the County Home, the way I once remember Tassy. I wanted to have a word with Kevin himself, a difficult thing nowadays, since Kevin is so important that he doesn't see people like me. At any rate, they gave me a day and a time, but I told them, "Tell him I'll see him here, in his wife's house in O'Gara Street." And he came. Alone.

"What do you want all this for, Chud?" he asked with a pained expression. "All on your own? You'd be much better off where there are other people."

"This suits me," I said.

"No doubt," said Kevin, with a little twitch. "Listen, if for example you were, just for example, in the County Home, I don't think this wretched case against you would go ahead. I could put in a word. Of course, your own . . . solicitor would advise you on that – but that's my opinion."

"I have work to finish here," I said.

"Oh?"

"A memoir. The old days."

"I've heard something . . ."

"The war, all that. My life. Personal stuff."

"I . . . see." Kevin was blinking rapidly. "How personal?"

"My life? Very."

Kevin got up and blew air steadily for half a minute. Then without looking at me or saying another word, he walked out. That was five months ago and I've not, if you'll allow, been Beagle-ed since.

The fire is roaring now. It's ready. I go into my bedroom and from beneath my bed take out a small, cardboard suitcase. It is the one I was sent away with all those years ago to Father Tell's. I put it on the table beside the ring-binders and press the single catch.

What more is left to tell, you might ask? I lift out the loose sheaf of computer papers generated in Texas, the section that will never find its way onto my ring-binders. I'm never going to tell, that's the point. I love her so much, even dead, that it's time to destroy the only weapon I have left to defend myself with. Her reputation. I would never trade it anyway, although Kevin doesn't know that – he doesn't know anything – but even so, like the nuclear deterrent, its very existence is a risk. So I'm burning everything. The County Home can't take my memories. Dick Coad will be upset because he thinks my story has historical significance. Bad luck. I open the stove doors with a poker. First the uncollated sheets from the suitcase. My words. Distant yet adjacent. Look at them, one last time, warming in the glow.

I'd made sure to meet Bruno since coming upon him spying at Delaware.

"Not going on any expeditions, Bruno?"

In their garage on Half Loaf.

"Nah." Bruno filleted out a tube from a wheel and plunged it into a basin of water. "Too fuckin' hot."

"You could go swimming."

"In that fuckin' river?"

"There are clean pools in the mountains."

"Fuck-all good swimmin'll be to us if there's goin' to be a war," said Bruno, studying the unveering regularity of a front wheel.

"I know a pool in the mountains. Near Main."

"Wait till it's our turn, me papa says," and he ran the chain onto the teeth using the flat of his hand.

"You can swim in that pool with nobody watching. Bollock naked. Never know who you'd see up there."

"God help the people of Warsaw."

Bruno would not be drawn, nor was he going to utter. I should have told Rosa this. I should have said, do nothing; I didn't. I was afraid of seeming inadequate in her eyes.

The noon Angelus from the cathedral rolled over Monument as I stubbed my butt and set out for Main. Summer still clung stickily. This was the weather for Hitler to pounce, Mrs Finnerty said, and pounce soon he would, up the Lyle on a warship, strutting up and down the deck in his shining boots – and who was to say we would not be better off? I had heard her offer this point of view to Uncle Mary when they were on parcelling duty together. In Germany there were no longer any bosses, just workers, all equal, you could hear them singing their songs on the wireless, Mrs Finnerty said. You could hear how happy they were over there. What had we to sing about?

The plan was simple. Rosa, our cause, also became the key. She would speak to Bruno in the street, revealing her admiration. Bruno would respond warmly. She would suggest a meeting at the pool. It was so simple. She did, he did. She did.

I left the road and took the long track into the foothills that wound around the mountain and down to the boulder that stood above Delaware. My head was still mercifully free of any vista except that of a righteous world. The day in all its glory seemed to support this untroubled hypothesis, for where in a landscape of such beauty, beneath skies so benign, in an atmosphere so frankly munificent could there lurk a threat to our ambitions?

"The Earl of Monument himself!"

Desperately I flung myself sideways to fend off the attack and was swallowed in the consciousness of the mountain. I came to, curled spider-like on painful shingle.

"Say, 'Good morning, me lord!'"

If the butler, Fleming, has not been sufficiently described then time has almost run out in which to do so; because from the moment Fleming leapt into my path, his outstretched hands striking me off balance, his face contorted by the ferocity of his design, time began to run against us. He had a withered arm, of course, and his eyes and muzzle were distinctly canine, down to the pointed eye teeth that his curling lips revealed, and he could see simultaneously in front and to the side, and he wore a suit of soaring lapels and double breasts, no doubt once the property of General Santry; that was Fleming.

"Get away from me!"

He connected well with his toe to the small of my back.

"Little bastard of a tart's tart! I'll teach you to laugh at your betters!"

I tried to roll out of range, but Fleming was goose-stepping after me down the path, spittle flying from his mouth.

". . . give you something to laugh about!"

The kicks landed like rocks, for no doubt the shoes too shared a former wardrobe with the rest of Fleming's attire and had sprung, steel-capped, from the last of the best cobbler in London.

"Aagh! Please . . ."

"Beg, that's it! Beg, me lord!"

Rolling, I went too far into the gorge and grabbed out to save myself, catching Fleming by his trouser turn-up and yanking him off balance. Fleming sat down and in the process hiccuped a cloud of vaporised alcohol. I had two good arms and a bicycle. I got to my feet – which Fleming, heels now higher than his head and drunk, was incapable of – grabbed my machine and fled.

But how the day had changed! Far from being simple and uncluttered, now a witness to our planned lesson in manners had entered the settled universe, for butlers like Fleming did not spend their days off, however legless, lurking in furze bushes; no, he had been waiting.

I slewed downhill in reckless clouds of dust and showers of pebbles. Time, ever grudging, now devoured the remaining moments of sanity in voracious gulps. A gorge existed, creating a penultimate hill between me and Delaware. My encounter with Fleming had not only brought into flower all my instincts concerning the mechanics of melodrama but had, in addition, knocked out my inner clock, so that I had no idea how many minutes had been wasted. It thus seemed more important to inspect the scene as a prelude to further action, and consequently I abandoned the path, jumped from the bike and ran to the edge of the hill, scattering rabbits.

First there was no-one, either in the pool or on the hillside below me. Canticles of alarm died in my throat under the weight of relief and I went to my pocket for the full packet of Woodbines in which I had indulged myself, the decisive nature of the day seeming to require such a gesture. A small breeze blew smoke back into my face and made my eyes weep with gratitude. Then I saw Rosa.

Like an otter she was swimming cleanly inwards from the centre, where she had been hidden from my sight by the side of the mountain. Distance made her swimming silent. I stared as she glided to the base of our outcrop, then came up surrounded by many thousands of diamonds. Naked. Even though I stood more than a hundred yards away, as she climbed out like a crab each knob of her back from her neck to the cleft of her buttocks stood out to me cleanly. Then she straightened up and looked back out over the pool she had just left. Catching up her hair behind her neck in both hands she wrung water from it. The movement changed the entire configuration of her body, making her backbone disappear into the fold between the twin muscles of her back. Bum round and tight. I could discern the outlines of her breasts.

Then sudden movement below me dragged my reluctant eye and I remembered with a jolt what would happen next.

"Bruno?" I called. Then louder, "Bruno!"

The wind must have taken my voice, for Bruno Belli, hands and knees, wriggling out on the ledge I so well knew, gave no sign of having heard me. I allowed a moment of self-congratulation on behalf of the three of us, for we had guessed rightly that Bruno would like to peep rather than declare his presence, that he would favour the ledge over the pool; and then I remembered Fleming and what I had most urgently to prevent.

"Bruno!"

"Yaaaaahhhhhhhh!"

Two of us were meant to work the pole under the horse-like rock that had stood for all time beside the high path, but Jack had done the work of two.

"Yaaaaahhhhhhhh!"

"Bruno! Watch out!"

Bruno, beginning to register his shock – or rather his guilt, because he jerked around like a surprised thief, which in some ways he was – was too slow, just as I had been. Jack, the fool, was standing, arms in the air, the pole aloft. The rock was bounding downwards like a great, legless carnivore, with each stride gouging out mouthfuls of mountain. Bruno saw me. He saw the coming rock. Appeared to say something. Or at least opened his mouth as he turned his face again back to mine. His face. The expression of disappointment on his funny, twisted face. And in those fractions of seconds he lost the look of youth and took on all the years he would never know, and the ravages of old age. And disappeared.

Fleming was my principal concern. I jumped up, frantic, and began to scan the hillside behind me. And whereas he would be the one who found Bruno later that afternoon, and cycled incoherent back to Monument babbling murder and the fact that I alone had done it, now, as the sun shone and lambs bleated in the heather for their dams, Fleming was nowhere I could see.

It was for Rosa I began the downward scramble, not for Bruno. I thought of Rosa, naked and therefore vulnerable, and Bruno, perhaps dazed and certainly bruised and angry. Money would be needed to silence Bruno after this scrape, I reckoned.

Reaching the shelf on which Bruno had lain – stripped of heather, fresh gouged – I stared down. The big boulder now lay in the centre of Delaware. But Bruno had somehow been thrown clear and lay on his back, legs twisted under him, head hanging down from the very edge of the rock from which we always dived. His eyes were open. His fingers were feebly grasping for a hold on the smooth stone. And Rosa stood over him, a towel around her.

"Rosa!"

Jack's shout from the mountain. She looked up. Furtive. Something dark was licking from Bruno's mouth. Rosa dug her heel into his mid-section and put all her weight behind it. Bruno slipped, slowly at first but then unstoppably and with a great splash, headfirst into the water. Rosa stepped back, hands to her mouth.

"Rosa?"

Convulsions of air, each as big as a jellyfish, ruptured the surface.

"CHUD!"

Yes, Rosa was the one. She took it to her grave with her, as did Jack and as will I. I had to protect her. I did. I came back into Monument that evening and was hunted through the streets like a rat. Even Paddy Bensey came out to get me, I'll never forget him at the wheel of his Rolls, driving up Moneysack, guards hanging like bats from the car's woodwork.

But Rosa did it. She shouldn't have, but the fact that she did never made Jack nor me love her the less. You love someone for all their sins and imperfections, not despite them. And how do you weigh sins anyway? Mine sit on the scales in bindles. Rosa's was just one, dense and heavy as that stone.

The heat of the fire has flushed my face and is sending pleasant, small convulsions down my spine. I'm going to enjoy this, one sheet at a time. It will be like a ritual, burning the past, bringing it all with me, if you permit such a notion. My hand is shaking with the first leaf. Strange. A weight is rising in me, up one side. Oh. Rising right through me. Oh God. I turn, whirling, groping. My jaw. I know this, and yet, this time, it's all I know and more. A step. I must . . . I drop the paper. Oh, Rosa!

My watch chimes.